BEAUTIFUL
Little

Fool
A novel

Sarah Zane

To anyone who has ever felt
they needed to make themselves less to please others; you are
no one's beautiful little fool,
you are so much more than that.

A Note To My Readers:

This book means everything to me. I wrote it as a way to heal from things I didn't know were still causing me pain. I wrote it to explore and grow from my past. I wrote it to free the parts of me I kept trapped inside, the parts of me I kept closeted. I have poured a lot of myself into this book and love it with everything in me, but this book isn't for everyone. As a licensed therapist, I have done my best to ensure the following topics are handled sensitively, but everyone's experience is different and I would much rather risk giving spoilers than risk triggering someone.

The following are potential triggers in my book: emotional abuse, anxiety, depression, attempted sexual assault and misogyny.

If any of those themes are too much for you right now, you have my full support in putting this book down. Much of the themes come from my own experience, so if you have experienced anything similar know you aren't alone, and I wanted to share my coping mantra that got me through some of my darker days.

FADES

F: it wasn't your Fault

A: you are not Alone

D: you didn't Deserve it

E: Every pain fades with time

S: and you are Stronger than you think

On the days where just being you feels like too much, I want you to know you are not alone. Please reach out to someone, anyone. If it feels like no one understands, or could ever understand, please know there are people out there that will.

I want to believe things happen for a reason and if you're holding my book in your hands, and haven't skipped over the preface, I believe these are words you might need to hear. I want you to know, I hear you, I see you. You are no one's beautiful little fool, you are so much more than that.

With Love,

Sarah Zane

"I hope she'll be a fool—that's the best thing a girl can be in this world, a beautiful little fool."
The Great Gatsby by F. Scott Fitzgerald

Chapter One

Daisy

I was only eighteen when the army stole everything that mattered from me. In retrospect, I suppose the army wasn't to blame for everything that happened. Some of the choices were my own, and some were made by a certain lieutenant, but back then, I chose to blame the army.

It was the fall of 1917 when the lieutenant swept into town and took Louisville by storm. A month later, he was stolen away by the army, after having taken everything I had to give and more. I was as pure as could be until I met him.

Since I was a young girl, I had dreamt of being swept off my feet by the love of my life. I had dated a few boys, but nothing had felt right. I hadn't had that moment that young girls dream of where they know without a doubt they had found the one. There had been something wrong about every boy I had dated so far. Truth be told, I knew I was looking for excuses, looking for something wrong so I could write them off.

Deep down, I knew I had been jumping from boy to boy because I was scared to commit and let my guard down. I was scared at the prospect of a loveless marriage.

Society didn't care about how I felt, just demanded I find myself a man to wed. Society told me I was worthless unless I meant something to a man. I knew society couldn't be right, but the pressure was hard to ignore. Most of the society's pressure came in the form of my mother, who repetitively told me that I was only as valuable as men decided I was. She was resolved that I would marry rich and young while, in her words, I still had my beauty. She made it clear I was a burden and would remain so until I was married off. The older I became, the more eager she was to put me in the way of influential gentlemen.

She told me horrible story after story about the dangers of being an unmarried woman past a certain age. Her stories varied in their levels of horror, but had one common theme; after a certain age, it became unsafe for a woman to be unattached. After a certain age, a woman's father wasn't enough to protect her anymore. She cautioned that men would force themselves upon unattached young women with ease. While I hoped she was only trying to scare me, I wasn't naive enough to doubt the truth of her stories.

I knew the truth. It was dangerous for a woman to be unattached to any man. To be alone meant to be vulnerable and weak, but I resolved to be different. I would not find myself attached to someone I didn't love. Consequences be damned, I wouldn't settle for anything less than love.

But I was smart. I knew the societal pressure wouldn't lessen unless I appeared to be searching for a husband, so I chose carefully which men I spent my time with.

Thankfully, men were in no shortage. With Camp Taylor being nearby, there were always officers around. I liked the officers well enough, and most importantly, they posed no real danger since they would ship out soon. Even if they had less than virtuous intentions where I was concerned, they would be gone quickly. The other benefit of the officers was they were never around long enough for my mother to get ideas.

I was scared if I spent too much time with any one man, I might be pushed into marriage far sooner than I was ready for and with someone I didn't love. I kept waiting to feel that overwhelming love. I wanted to see someone and just know, somehow, that I was destined to be with them. I wanted to be swept off my feet. I kept my heart guarded, scared to let my guard down and get too close to any man … until him, that is.

Jay Gatsby is not a name I will soon forget. He swept into town that summer with the army, and was quick to seek out the daughters of the rich men of the town. I knew the type. This town had seen more than its fair share of penniless officers looking to make a name for themselves, looking to build status and wealth as quickly as possible, looking to marry rich. I knew his type and resolved to stay away from him. I didn't believe myself to be in any danger of falling for him, but knew it was best for my reputation to steer clear of him. It turns out I was more correct than I could have known about the latter and laughably wrong about the former.

I planned to avoid him, but fate had other plans. He had been going with a couple of other girls I knew from town, but I knew they couldn't be serious about him. They understood his type as well as I did and knew they were being used. I couldn't believe he wasn't even subtle enough to only give attention to one at a time. The others before him had taken the town one girl at a time, waiting until one proved to not be an option before moving on to the next. It said a lot about him and his ambitions that he was desperate enough to take the town two girls at a time. I had already built up an image of him in my mind, and I knew it wasn't to my liking. I thought with some amusement about how I would turn him down when he eventually made his way through the other rich girls and came knocking at my door. That fantasy was shattered when I met him.

He said he was swept away by my beauty, but I was the one who was truly swept away. The moment I saw him, I knew. I felt the overwhelming passion I had been looking for. He was the man I was going to marry. He was tall, tan, and fit, but what I noticed most was his smile. He had a smile that made you want to know more about him.

The longer I spent with him, the more I felt myself falling. His smile drew me in. His smile made you want to smile, too, made you want to please him. It made you want to do whatever you could to see that smile again. There was something special about him. Jordan told me later that his affliction was ambition mixed with incurable optimism, but I called it hope.

His hope married with his ambition made him an unstoppable force. He was a whirlwind that wrapped people up in his ideas and beliefs until they couldn't help but believe what he said. I was by no means immune to that. There was only one thing he told me that I never believed. He said he came from money, but even then, as naive as I was, I knew that was a lie. He was too ambitious to have been born into wealth, but I didn't doubt he would make something of himself one day or die trying.

It was the dying I worried most about. I had sworn to not become attached. I knew the risks as well as everyone. I had heard the horror stories about the war. Some people were lucky and made it back with their lives, but I doubted he would be one of the lucky ones. He was too ambitious and too desperate to make a name for himself. It was the worst possible combination in a soldier. It would make him reckless. I knew without a doubt his heroics and need for notoriety would get him killed. The moment he shipped out he was likely as good as dead.

I knew better than to get attached to this living ghost of a lieutenant. I saw the writing on the wall and knew I should stay away, but I couldn't help it with him. He broke down my walls and forced his way into my heart. One by one, my reasons to stay away stopped mattering. I had worried he was only interested in me for my money, but after spending more time with him, I knew that couldn't be the case. There was no way he could be faking the feelings he had. When I looked into his eyes, I knew he felt the same as I did. He told me he stopped dating any other women the moment he met me. He told me that once he saw me, he knew no one else could possibly compare. He told me he wanted the best and that he couldn't possibly go back to any other woman after having witnessed my beauty. He was smooth with the compliments, but looking in his eyes, I could tell he meant them. I stopped caring about the obstacles.

As his departure date crept closer, I became more and more desperate. I felt him slipping from my fingertips. The love I had been waiting for was going to be ripped away from me. I had no doubt in my mind that he wouldn't survive the war. I couldn't bear the thought of losing him.

I didn't want to burden him with my worries. I wasn't supposed to have fallen for him, we weren't supposed to be serious. But I couldn't bear the thought of losing him. I finally broke down to him.

"Jay, I can't lose you."

He looked at me with surprise, "Of course you won't lose me, love. I'm right here and I can assure you nothing could tear me away from you, especially with how beautiful you look tonight."

I smiled at that, but I had to make him understand how I was feeling. "That's not what I mean. You're here now, but what about a couple weeks from now?" I caressed his face with my hand. "I can't bear the thought of losing you."

He sighed. "My love, it won't help to dwell on such negative thoughts. Yes, I'll be gone a while, but after the war I'll rush back to you straight away. I'll be on the first ship back. Nothing could stop me from getting home to you."

I felt tears starting to form, and tried to hold them back. I was trying not to picture him on the battlefield, but all I could see was the handsome lieutenant that I loved bleeding out on the battlefield. I could picture the life draining from his eyes as he realized this was the end and that he would never make it home. I pictured his body going cold and being left on the battlefield, alone. I couldn't bear it. "You don't have to leave." I blurted out.

He chuckled humorlessly and said "Of course I do. I'm a part of the army, love. The country needs me. I'll come back a hero. You'll see, it'll all be worth it, I promise."

"The country needs you? Damn the country, I need you Jay! The country can do without another soldier, but I can't do without you. I love you."

He seemed startled by my outburst. "I love you too, more than all the money in the world, but you don't get it. I have to do this."

"Enlighten me then, what is it about the war that's so much more important than staying here with me?"

"I'll be a hero. I'll make a name for myself. I need to."

"You don't need to, you could stay here with me."

He let out a short breath. I could see from how his jaw was clenched that he was starting to get annoyed, but so was I. He was being so stubborn and careless with his own life and future. The last thing I wanted was to argue with him, but I knew this was a battle worth fighting.

"You're quite young and still a bit naïve to the world, but when a man gives his word, it's something he must stand by. I can't desert the army. I would be branded a coward and a traitor. I can't imagine a worse fate."

"Can't imagine a worse fate? You lying dead somewhere in Europe is a much worse fate!"

"You're being ridiculous. I'll be fine. I'm quite capable."

"And if you're not fine? Would you really rather die for your principles than stay here with me?"

"You don't understand! I can't abandon the army! They don't just let you leave, Daisy!"

"So, we run! They won't even notice you're missing. You're just another number to them, but you're everything to me."

I could tell he was getting more and more frustrated with me by the minute, but I couldn't stop myself. Now that the words were coming out, I couldn't stop them. "Marry me!"

His eyes widened and his mouth fell open. Whatever he planned to say died on his lips. He only uttered, "What?"

I couldn't believe I had said it, but now that I had, I couldn't believe I hadn't thought of it sooner! It was the perfect solution. Of course it was! "Marry me, Jay. You'll have your treasured important name, and my father could pay your way out of the army. Your precious reputation would stay intact and you would have me."

"No. You don't understand. How could you? You're just a woman; you couldn't possibly understand the struggles a man goes through. How important it is for a man to make his own way in the world. In marriage, you would take my name and reputation. The reputation you're so carelessly trying to destroy! It's so easy for you women! All you have to do is marry well! I don't have that option!"

"Of course you do, Jay! Marry me! Stay here with me!"

He laughed in my face; a cold, cruel laugh. "And be just the husband of Daisy Fay? I could never. Everyone would know I took the easy way out, that I ran from my troubles when things got tough into the arms of a woman. I would be a laughing stock. I won't marry you like that."

I was shocked. "Don't you want to spend your life with me? Marry me and everything that I have will be yours, I promise."

"You don't have anything! Everything you 'own' is your father's! You don't have a dime to your name! I knew you were young, but I thought the innocence and stupidity was an act. Maybe you are just a beautiful little fool after all."

I couldn't believe him. The tears stung my eyes, threatening to fall, but I wouldn't let them. I couldn't. "Me, the fool? I'm not the one throwing my life away to play the hero. What good are your precious principles and reputation if you're dead?"

He took my hands, and I could see some of his anger had faded, but mine was still alive and well. "Love, you're being dramatic. I'll make a hero of myself. I'll make a name for myself in the army. Gatsby will be a household name. All the girls will want to marry a man like me and all the boys will want to be me. Then and only then will I come back and sweep you off your feet. Once I've made more of a name for myself and have more to offer you, I'll come back for you and we'll get our happy ending."

"And how long might that be?"

"However long it takes."

"I won't wait forever, Jay. I asked you to choose me and you laughed in my face. If your precious reputation is more important than our future and our happiness, then so be it, but don't expect me to wait around forever."

"It won't be forever. The minute the war is done, I'll come home to you a hero. You'll see. We can even get married before I leave, that way you'll know I'm coming back for you."

It was tempting. I loved him with every fiber of my being and wanted to be his, but not that way. I shook my head. "I can't, Jay. I won't marry a ghost. Either we marry and you stay here with me, or we don't marry."

His face blanched. "You can't mean that! We can get married in New York before I leave. The moment I get to New York, I can send word of where I am so you'll know where to meet me. My buddies know a place where we can get married quick there, without any of the paperwork. Without your parents' approval." His eyes shone with hope. "Say you will."

"I won't. I love you, but you can't ask that of me."

His face fell. "And you can't ask me to leave the army."

I wanted to curl up into a ball and cry. I was so frustrated I wanted to yell and hit something. I didn't know what to do with all my feelings. I didn't think it was possible for one person to feel so much at the same time.

"You'll change your mind. I know you will, love. I'll send word of where you should meet me."

"I won't change my mind. I won't marry you until you either leave the army or make it home safe."

He chuckled. "That's what you think now, but I know the moment I leave you'll be rushing to follow me to New York. Just you wait. I know it! I'll make the arrangements for the wedding there."

"I'm not coming, Jay."

"Sure you aren't." He laughed again and winked at me. "But I'll make the preparations for when you change your mind."

I wondered if he was right. I knew the moment he left, everything in me would be screaming at me to follow him. *Marry him! Don't let him get away! You love him; you have to fight for him!* But I knew I couldn't let myself. I wouldn't chase him, and I wouldn't marry a ghost. He was as good as dead the moment he stepped on that boat.

He thought he would be one of the lucky ones, and with every fiber of my being, I hoped he was right, but I wasn't gifted with his optimism. I had offered him everything I had, all my money and influence, if he would just leave the army and stay with me, but he refused. I wasn't enough.

Chapter Two

At eighteen, I was more sure of my love for him than of anything else in my life. I felt sure that some divine intervention would stop him from going. I felt the universe couldn't be cruel enough to tear us apart after we had essentially just met.

Against my hopes and wishes, the days passed by until only one night stood between us and what I knew would be a permanent separation.

I still remember that last night like it was yesterday. We were sitting in my car talking softly about life and our dreams and hopes for the future as we looked at the stars. My head was resting on his shoulder. He was holding me close, like he couldn't bear for there to be any space between us. I was trying to hold off the emotions that had been threatening to overwhelm me all night. I was worried about him going off to war, and scared to be alone again. I had just found him. The universe was a cruel, cruel place to let me find love just to snatch it away. In the depths of my heart, I knew this would likely be the last time I saw him. I couldn't help a tear sliding down my face as I tried to keep the thoughts away.

Jay wiped away my tear and looked into my eyes, asking what was the matter.

"You already know what's on my mind."

"I know this uniform makes me look so devilishly handsome, but it's okay, my love, you don't need to cry over it."

I couldn't help but laugh. He always had a way of making me smile when it felt like there was nothing to smile about. I humored him and let my eyes roam over his body appreciatively. He was right about one thing. The uniform clung tightly to his muscles, not that he needed the help. Standing at around six feet tall with his dazzling smile and eyes sparkling with hope, he was easily one of the most attractive men I had ever seen. I still couldn't believe this twenty-seven-year-old Adonis wanted to be with me.

"Be careful, officer. If you keep it up, I might just have to take it off of you. Such a lovely uniform, but what a tragic crime to cover up such a body."

I am sure I heard his heart skip a beat and saw his eyes bulge out of their sockets. I was a little shocked, too. I wasn't normally so bold. But there was something about him that brought out the best, and worst, in me.

"Woah there, Daisy, my love. I think you're forgetting who's in charge. I *am* the highest-ranking officer here."

"And thank goodness for that. What would I do without my big, strong officer? Heaven knows how I need direction to stay out of trouble."

"My love, you *are* trouble."

"You certainly aren't the first to think so."

"But I know I'll be the last."

"I wouldn't be so sure you can handle me all by yourself, officer. After all, I am quite the handful."

"Oh, I think I know just how to handle you."

"Oh, you do, do you?"

"I think so."

"Well then, I'd like to see you-"

I didn't get to finish saying "try" before his lips were on mine. As we battled for dominance, I felt him pull me closer, dangerously close. I was on top of him now. I could feel his eagerness pressed against me. That was a wake-up call. Things were getting too intense. I tried to pull back, but he held tighter. He must have thought I was trying to play hard to get. I tried to relax myself back into his arms, but I couldn't shake my fears. What was I doing? I knew there couldn't be a future with him. As much as I loved him, I knew this was wrong.

How, though, could it be wrong if it felt so right? It was hard to focus with his lips on mine. I tried to clear my thoughts. *No. I have to stop this. I can't let this continue.* I pushed back against him harder this time. That caught his attention.

He pulled away enough for me to see the wicked gleam in his eye as he said, "Oh, you like it rough, do you?"

Before I could say anything, he slammed us against the passenger side door. The door handle dug into my back as he planted his lips all over my neck. "Jay"

"I know, baby..." He kept going.

"Jay," I said louder, trying to get his attention. It didn't work. "JAY!"

This time, he looked up and finally noticed the expression on my face. He pulled back a little. His hands were still wrapped around me, but he added enough distance to see my face and said, "What is it, my love?"

"I'm so sorry, Jay. I don't think I can do this.""

"Of course you can, my love. You're doing great. Magnificent. You're the loveliest woman I've ever laid eyes on, and everything you do is perfect. I know how perfect you'll make this." His fingers travelled up and down my arms, giving me goosebumps.

"No, Jay. I really don't think we should do this. You know it isn't right. We're not married. I don't think I can do this."

He leaned forward again and whispered in my ear, "But, my love, that's just a formality. We'll be married tomorrow if I have anything to say about it." He suddenly pulled back again, and I could see the excitement in his eyes. "Say yes, my love."

"You know my parents would never allow it."

"We'll run away if we must." He leaned back in and started to nibble on my ear in a way that made me shiver and almost lose my reason.

"But you're leaving. I won't marry you with you leaving, not with you going to fight in the war…"

"I'll be back before you know it."

"Jay, I'm serious. I can't do this."

He kept planting kisses up and down my neck.

"Why, of course you can, my love. Don't you want to give me something to remember you by? To get me through those long, lonely nights without you?"

Something about the reminder of his leaving made my heart break all over again. I didn't know what to say. All that came out was, "I can't bear to think about you leaving."

"So don't think. I can help with that." I gasped as he bit down on my neck. "A little something for you to remember me by. "

"Jay, you have to stop! Someone will see that!"

He bit down once more, harder this time.

"I know. Now everyone will know you're mine." He went back to kisses and slid his hand up my arm. He grasped the strap of my dress and pushed it off my shoulder. I had to grab hold of my dress to keep it from falling.

"Jay, I really can't do this."

He lightly stroked my collarbone with his fingers, eliciting a moan I couldn't help.

"I never took you as a good girl, my love."

"I'm not. This just isn't right. You know it isn't."

"Of course it's right. You love me, don't you?" He pulled away again to look me in the eye.

"You know I do, Jay."

He looked away despondently before saying, "I'm not so sure."

My throat tightened and I felt nauseous. I couldn't decide if I was more surprised or hurt. Through the tightness in my throat, I managed to whisper, "You're not sure how you feel about me…?"

He looked back quickly and shook his head. "Of course not, my love. I know the depths of my feelings for you. I know how much I love you. It's your feelings I'm not sure about." He moved his hands from my back and pulled away further.

I leaned back into him and tried to put his arms back around me, but he wouldn't budge. I tried to get him to look at me, but he wouldn't meet my gaze.

"Jay, I swear you're the only man for me."

He still wouldn't look at me.

"I'm not so sure. I know how much I'll miss you while I'm gone, but it sounds like you'll just find someone new when I'm gone. The man you're saving yourself for in marriage."

I was close to tears and didn't know how to make things right. I needed him to know how much I cared. I couldn't let him leave like this. I needed him to believe me. "How could you say that?"

He looked up, and I leaned in and pressed my lips to his, but his lips didn't move against mine. He pulled back again and said, "You said yourself you're saving yourself for marriage, for another man. How much could you really care for me if you're not willing to be mine?"

I grabbed his hand and squeezed tight. "Of course I want to be yours, Jay."

"I don't know, Daisy. It seems like one of us here cares too much and the other won't bat an eye when he leaves."

I could feel my heart breaking all over again. As more tears began to fall, I pushed him into the driver's side door and moved my body on top of his. "I can't bear the thought of you leaving without you knowing how much you mean to me. I love you, Jay Gatsby." I leaned in and pressed my lips against his hard. He kissed back harder.

I felt his lips curve into a smile beneath mine and he whispered to me, "I knew you felt the same. I love you, Daisy. It has always been you and will always be you." With that, the last part of my resistance melted…

Chapter Three

When I woke the next morning, I was in my bed, alone. After a moment, the night started to come back to me. What Jay and I did in my car. The last thing I remember was being in the car. I must have dozed off, so how did I get here? I smiled to myself. Jay must have carried me.

I glanced around the room, looking for him, but he wasn't there. Maybe he had left a note? But I didn't see a note or anything out of place. I got up from the bed, noticing as I did that I was still wearing my dress from last night and that I had not managed to fully re-lace it. I giggled a little, thinking about how scandalous it would be if someone were to have seen me, but I knew Jay must have been careful. I knew he would protect my honor, just as I knew he must be coming back later that day, for I knew without a doubt he wouldn't leave without saying goodbye, especially not after what we had done last night.

I couldn't believe I had taken things that far, but I couldn't bring myself to regret it. I loved him. I was his in all but name now. I didn't know what the future would hold for us, but I knew the universe wouldn't be cruel enough to bring him to my doorstep and let me fall for him just for him to be killed in the war. He would survive the war; he had something to live for now. He had me to come home to. I hoped that would be enough.

I shook my head. I couldn't let myself think it might not be enough. It would be enough. He would return and we would marry and spend the rest of our days together in marital bliss. I even thought maybe we might marry before he went. Now that we had done what we did, my doubts had gone away. I was his, and wanted the world to know it. Well, to know we were to be married, anyway. I had no desire for anyone except the two of us to know what happened last night.

A wave of anxiety passed over me at the thought. I hoped our entrance last night had been discreet enough to not have alerted anyone. I quickly dismissed my worries. I knew Jay would have been careful. I needed to be just as careful. I needed to keep up the pretense that I had been here alone all night, so I changed into my nightclothes and descended in search of breakfast. It wasn't until I made it to the main floor that I realized how quiet it was in the house.

Normally, there were people bustling about cleaning and organizing and preparing for company, but it was eerily quiet. I tried to find anyone to bring my breakfast order to our cook, but the house was inexplicably empty. Having looked everywhere else, I saw no choice but to seek out my father. I knew he would be in his library and, under normal circumstances, would never dare to intrude, but something felt wrong and I didn't know what else to do.

I hastened through the corridors to his library, my anxiety building with each echo of my steps through the deserted halls. As I got closer to the library door, I heard a raised voice. Instinctively, I quieted my steps as I approached. When I got a little closer, I was able to identify two voices; my mother and father. My mother never entered my father's study either. This must be worse than I thought. Something was dreadfully wrong. Unsure whether or not they were likely to tell me the truth of what was going on, I tiptoed to the door to see what I could find out for myself.

I only heard bits and pieces of their conversation.

"A disgrace...laughing stock of the town."

Now I was sure that was definitely my mother's voice, but what could she possibly be so distraught about?

Luckily for me, my father's deep voice carried further than my mother's. "My dear, it will be okay. We'll make things right. I dismissed everyone. After all, what choice did I have? But we will figure this out together."

Dismissed everyone? I could hardly believe my ears. No wonder the house was so quiet without the hustle and bustle of the staff. My anxiety spiked higher than I thought possible. I wondered what could have possibly prompted such a drastic move. For as long as I could remember, there had never been a time when it was just me and my parents in the house.

Lost in thought, I must have leaned a little too hard on the door. It swung open. I tumbled in with it and toppled onto the floor. My mother yelped in surprise. My father, after seeing it was me, said nothing. There was a long pause, too long for comfort. I finally blurted out, "What's wrong? You dismissed everyone?" I figured I couldn't possibly make things worse. After all, they had already caught me eavesdropping. Wow, was I wrong. I looked up to see both my parents glaring at me.

My father had always been more sympathetic, so I looked to him, but his face was so red I could almost see steam coming off him. "I know I shouldn't have listened without your permission. I truly am sorry. But when I woke up, the house was so quiet. I got worried sand I looked everywhere for anyone, but couldn't find anyone, so I came here."

My father banged his hand on his desk and said, "Daisy, are you daft? You think we're upset about the eavesdropping?"

My mother was glaring daggers at me. I decided it would be best to look back at my father.

"I mean, I know that isn't the only reason you're upset. There must be something really serious going on if you had to dismiss the staff."

My father sat down and put his head in his hands. After a few moments, he picked his head up and stared at me before turning to my mother and saying, "She must really be daft."

"We knew she had to be stupider than we thought to put us in this situation in the first place."

"Me? How did I put you guys in any situation? I just woke up. There's no way I have any blame for whatever happened."

My father was still looking at my mother. "She really doesn't know?"

"She really must think we are too stupid to know."

"Know what?" I blurted out. "I must be the stupid one, since I'm the only one in the dark."

My father looked at me. "Daisy, we know what you did last night."

I started to sweat, but I knew I had to keep my cool. There was no way they knew. They must be talking about something else. "What do you mean, Father? I didn't do anything out of the ordinary last night."

My mother rolled her eyes and turned her back on me. She crossed the room to stand behind my father and whispered in his ear. I couldn't hear what she said, but from the change on my father's face I know it wasn't good. His nostrils flared and the vein on his forehead had begun to pulse. I gulped.

"Nothing out of the ordinary? Young lady, you have no idea how much trouble you have caused us and now you have the audacity to lie to my face, saying you did nothing out of the ordinary."

I didn't know what to say. By the time I had gathered what I could of my thoughts and started to speak, my mother beat me to it. She still wouldn't look at me. Instead, to my father, she said, "Well, we really don't know if it's a lie or not-" *Thank goodness my mother is on my side*. The thought formed a minute too soon, for it seemed she was not quite done. "Maybe we did raise enough of a floozy that last night really wasn't out of the ordinary."

My jaw dropped. While I had never had the best relationship with my mother, she certainly had never said anything so hurtful or been so cruel. I was simultaneously speechless and on the verge of tears.

My father sighed and looked at my mother and then at me. "Daisy, dear, you've really done it this time."

"Will somebody please tell me what it is I'm supposed to have done?" I was praying harder than I ever had that they didn't know.

I held my breath but wasn't kept in suspense long. My mother didn't hesitate before jumping at the chance to say, "It's not a what, daughter dearest, it's a *who* you're supposed to have done."

I felt like sinking through the floor from sheer embarrassment. I knew my red face was too much of a confession to give any weight to an objection, but I knew I had to try.

"Mama, Papa, I really don't understand what it is you're talking about."

My mother rolled her eyes. I begrudgingly understood. I was laying it on a bit thick. It had been years since I had last called them Mama and Papa.

"What are we going to do with you?" my father said.

"If only the innocence wasn't an act. I don't know who will possibly want you now that you have nothing of value left to give."

I clenched my fists and tried to fight through the pounding in my ears. I was outraged. No one had ever spoken to me in that way. I wouldn't stand for it. I stood up and made for the door.

"I'll have you know I'm a grown woman. I make my own choices and I choose to not be spoken to in such a manner." I turned to my mother. "What have I ever done to you?"

She had the audacity to look the victim. "What have you done to me? Why me and your poor father had to dismiss the entirety of our staff, so word of our floozy daughter wouldn't make it all over town. Could you imagine what the neighbors would say? What the town would say? Of course, your dear father and I are the ones to suffer when you get to go around having a grand old time."

I couldn't believe my ears. "Mother, what has gotten into you?"

"What's gotten into me? I am afflicted with a daughter so loose in her morals that she can't keep her legs closed and insists on sleeping with half the army."

I was so shocked and upset I stuttered over my next words, "Ha-half the army? It was one man. His name is Jay Gatsby. He's not just some officer; he's a lieutenant. And Mama, Papa, I love him."

My mother laughed. "Love? What does that matter?"

"Of course it matters. Love is the only thing that matters. I love him and know he's the one for me." I knew as I said it that it was the truth. The small amount of doubt I had been clinging to about our future vanished. I knew what I wanted, and it was Jay. It no longer mattered to me that he was in the army or that he was in danger. I knew how strongly he felt about me and that he wouldn't let anything, even war and possible death, separate us. He would find his way back to me. He believed so strongly in us that I knew he would. I couldn't believe I hadn't seen it sooner. I couldn't believe I had ever doubted him. He was the only thing I needed. "I'm going to marry him."

At the silence and shocked looks directed my way, I realized my last thought must have been out loud. It didn't matter. I would have said it sooner or later. If they hadn't been taking me seriously before, they certainly were now. I had their full attention. Both were speechless and my mother swayed a little on her feet. She recovered her speech first. Looking at my father she said, "Dear Lord, where she gets these crazy ideas I'll never know."

"It's not crazy! Mama, Papa, I know you both would like him if you would just give him a chance."

This time, my father beat my mother to reply, "A chance? After what he took from us? How could I?"

"What do you mean 'what he took'? What did he take? I promise he would never intentionally hurt anyone."

My mother would not stay silent for long. "He wouldn't hurt a fly? Then tell me what he meant by this."

"Meant by what?"

"He stole your virtue, daughter dearest. He stripped you of any value you had and ensured you would continue to be a burden on your family. No one will marry the floozy of Louisville. You can bet on that."

I wouldn't give her the satisfaction of tears. It would take all the strength I had, but I would not break. I had to get to the safety of my room before the tears overtook me. I looked to my father for some, any, support he might offer.

"Papa, you really would like him if you just gave him a chance. You don't even know him."

"I know enough. He has no money, no family name, has made no name for himself, and yet is arrogant enough to believe he is entitled to my daughter. It's a crime I won't stand for. The man better count his lucky stars that I don't press charges."

"Charges? But, Papa, you wouldn't!"

"You're right. I wouldn't want to bring that sort of negative attention to this family. You've brought us enough shame as it is."

"Papa, you don't get it! He didn't do anything wrong. I love him, and he promised to marry me."

My mother burst out in cruel laughter. "Of course he did! Men always say that. Tell me, if he loves you so much, where is he now?"

I faltered a little. I hadn't seen him since last night, but I wouldn't let her shake me. I knew he would come back. He had to. I knew he wouldn't leave without a goodbye. "He leaves for the army today-"

"How convenient," butted in my mother.

"You didn't let me finish. I know he'll be back to say goodbye. He truly is a good man, and he really loves me. I know it."

"Love or not, he won't be my son."

"Papa, you can't mean that. You must want me to be happy. Jay makes me happy."

"Ha," scoffed my mother. "What do you know of happiness? You're only eighteen. This officer might make you happy today, but next month? You would still be wed to a no-name officer and penniless. You would really throw away your only chance at greatness to marry for something as silly as love?"

I was again speechless. I couldn't believe she would tell me that marrying for love was silly. Didn't she love my father? I looked at his face but saw no surprise or hurt there. I should have known. I knew my mother had a tough past. My father always told me to not trouble her as much as I did because she had had things so tough. I had thought it was lucky she found him. I knew he cared for her and assumed she felt the same, but I should have known I was wrong. I didn't know what to say, but she didn't give me a chance.

She continued to rant, "What do you think your happiness is worth to us after you have hurt us so? If we can't be happy, why should you? You have brought ruin and dishonor to your family."

"I wasn't thinking. I know I didn't make the best decision, but we can fix it. We can go get married and then no one will have to know. We'll fix this, make things right. I know he will. He'll make me the happiest woman in the world."

"There you go again about your happiness, as if I care a wit. You know what would make me happy? Having a daughter successfully marry rich. I will not have you marry below your station and further bring shame to our household."

I knew my mother was a lost cause, so I turned my pleas to my father. "Papa, I don't want a rich man. I want *him*."

"Well, my darling, unfortunately, we don't always get what we want in life."

My mother added, "Besides, what makes you so sure he would have you? After all, he's taken your virtue and left you worthless."

"It's not like that, Mama, I swear! He was sweet and romantic, and he loves me."

"They're all like that, darling."

"Papa was never like that. Were you, Papa?"

He looked awkwardly between us before shrugging apologetically and saying, "Men will be men. What can I say?"

I gagged a little at the thought. That had certainly backfired.

"Well, you're both wrong. Jay isn't like that! You'll see! He'll be back today to ask for my hand. I just know it!"

They shared an incredulous look. My father said, "Well, if that happens, I will consider taking the man seriously."

"Oh, Papa, thank you!" I flung myself around as much of his shoulders as I could, pulling him into a hug. "Thank you! Thank you! Thank you! I know you won't regret this!"

"Daisy dear, when he doesn't come, you will have to entertain more suitable options."

"Oh, Papa, I know he'll come!"

"I wouldn't hold your breath, dear," chimed in my mother. She added with a shrug, "Or do. It makes no difference to me."

I held my tongue. Arguing with my mother wasn't worth the risk of angering my father. I was too worried he might change his mind. Not wanting to stick around long enough to risk that, I ran off to my room to make myself presentable for when Jay showed up. It was harder than usual without the assistance I was used to from our staff, but I knew it wouldn't matter to Jay. He would come, sweep me off my feet, win over my parents, and take my hand in marriage. I had always dreamed of the perfect wedding with everyone I loved there to worship me in white, but with Jay, that hardly mattered. I would marry him this afternoon if it meant I got to spend my life with him.

I put on my best dress and stationed myself by the door. I wanted to be sure to meet him right away when he arrived. I didn't want to risk either of my parents scaring him off or him thinking no one was home because none of the staff was there to answer the door.

I waited... and waited. The minutes ticked by, but my faith did not shake. I knew he would come. As the minutes passed, I started to pace. It was getting later. I didn't think he would make me wait this long, but still I knew he was coming. I would make sure he knew I didn't like to be kept waiting. I giggled at the thought of how I would tease him and make him work for my forgiveness.

As the minutes turned to hours, I started to worry. But I knew nothing short of death would keep him away. I knew he would show up. I just knew it. He had to. I couldn't let myself think of what it would mean if he didn't, both for himself and for me. The hours crept past and the sun went down, but I still didn't move. He had to come; I knew he would.

Chapter Four

The rest of the night was a bit of a blur. I will spare you the agony of recounting the long moments that made up the rest of the night and instead skip to their conclusion.

He did not come.

The realization that he hadn't come and the consequences of his absence only hit me the next morning when I woke up crammed in a chair in the front hall. The emotions swept over me. I was confused, upset, worried, and humiliated all at the same time.

I stayed in my room for the next few days, refusing to leave or to admit anyone. My parents tried to talk to me a few times, but the bitter taste from our last conversation had not left my mouth enough for me to be willing to further talk to them.

I went through a wide range of emotions. The sadness hit first. I missed him already and couldn't believe he hadn't come to say goodbye. I must not have meant as much to him as he did to me. Then denial crept in. There was no possible way he would have left without saying goodbye. I reasoned maybe his departure was delayed. Maybe he wasn't allowed away from camp all day yesterday. Maybe he would still come to say goodbye. I hoped my father would stay true to his promise to let me marry him. I hoped it wasn't too late.

Again, I dressed up and waited. Not quite as optimistic this time, I didn't venture downstairs. If I'm being honest, I think even then I knew he wasn't coming. I think if I truly thought there was still a chance, I would have waited in the front hall, but I didn't leave my room.

I held on to my delusional beliefs for most of the day, but when the day came and passed without any appearance, even I had to admit it was unlikely he was coming at all. Then came the worry. He wouldn't have just left without saying goodbye. Something must have happened to him. I prayed to the universe that he was okay. I wondered what could have possibly happened between him leaving late that night and the next day that kept him away. And why didn't he wake me when he left? If he had just woken me, I wouldn't be plagued by the worries and doubts that I had now. A simple goodbye was all I would have needed. He didn't even give me that.

I couldn't believe how far I had fallen for him. I knew we had no future, but here I was crying over a man who didn't even bother to say goodbye. I had thought leaving would be as hard for him as it was for me to see him go. Apparently not. Maybe my parents were right. Maybe he had everything he wanted from me now. I had given him everything. He took everything I had to give and left me without even a goodbye.

How could I have let myself be so foolish? I had believed in him. I hadn't had a doubt in my mind that he would be back. I had waited and waited. If he truly cared for me, how could he have possibly embarrassed me like that? To think he had talked of running away together, of secretly marrying in New York. I had fallen for it. I had truly believed he wanted a future with me, and now here I was alone again.

I thought I knew his type. I thought he might be using me for my money, but I never imagined he would use me far worse. He used me for my body and then left me broken-hearted without a word of explanation or a goodbye. I couldn't believe this was the same man who had talked endlessly of marriage. I knew he needed the money, but even then I hadn't doubted his intentions. I wondered what could have possibly made him disappear without solidifying a commitment from me. My parents were rich enough, and I thought he loved me. It would have been the ideal match for him, but maybe he found a better offer, or maybe it was never actually about that. Maybe he never really wanted my money or my hand in marriage. Maybe he was always just after my body.

I tried to stop the thoughts, but they just kept coming. I struggled to believe Jay was that much of a monster, but the evidence was insurmountable. He had left.

I felt certain I would not be leaving my room anytime soon. The idea of seeing the 'I told you so' smirk on my mother's face or hearing anything she or my father had to say about the situation or about entertaining more suitable options was enough to make a permanent stay in my bedroom seem unavoidable.

I don't know how long I was in there, but it couldn't have been more than a few days when I heard a knock on the door.

It wasn't the clear rapping of my father or the assertive knock of my mother. There was a bang on the door followed by two short, more hesitant knocks. My curiosity insisted I open the door. I thought maybe my parents had quit their ridiculous antics and hired back our staff.

That wasn't the case. When I opened the door, my surprise intensified. It was little Jordan Baker from down the street. Well, little might not be an apt description. She was certainly coming into her own. We had known one another for a while now, having both grown up in the same part of town, and passed most of our childhood together. I was two years her senior, but we were on friendly terms.

I wouldn't say Jordan was part of my group of friends. Since she was younger, my friends didn't give her the time of day. My friends never understood it, but I had a bit of a soft spot for Jordan. She was always so sweet to me and seemed to look up to me. On the occasions that I invited her to spend time with my friends, they had never been as nice to her as they should have been.

I wondered what my friends were up to now. Things had been rocky between us lately. They had been giving me the cold shoulder, which I can't say I didn't understand. I had been neglecting them in favor of the company of a certain lieutenant. I thought they would understand, but it seems I was wrong.

I wondered both at why my friends had not come and why Jordan had. The first mystery required little thought. They likely hadn't noticed my absence, or if they had, thought I was continuing to neglect them to keep the company of officers. Little Jordan being here was more of a mystery. We were friendly, but a house call was out of the ordinary. She was about the last person I expected to knock on my bedroom door. I looked behind her to see if anyone was with her, but she was alone.

I grabbed her arm and pulled her into my room before quickly shutting and re-latching the door. I wouldn't give my parents the satisfaction of seeing me outside of my room. I couldn't face them and their judgment just yet. After re-securing the latch, I turned to face Jordan. I took a good look at her and noticed with surprise that she had grown a lot taller in this last year. She stood just a hair shorter than me. If she kept going at this rate, she would tower over me before I knew it.

The shock of seeing her was wearing off, so I asked what she was doing here.

She looked me up and down and seemed surprised at the state I was in. I was sure I didn't look half as presentable as usual, considering I didn't have the assistance I normally did or the will to make myself look presentable. After all, I hadn't left my room in days and now that Jay was gone, I had no one I desired to impress. Out of curiosity, I made my way to the mirror and was a little taken-aback at what I saw; I had expected worse.

I felt the worst I ever had. My heart was broken, and I was dying inside. However, on the outside, aside from my ruined makeup and undone hair, I didn't look nearly as bad as I felt. I resolved to fix that after Jordan left. After all, I had not forgotten my parents saying I would need to entertain more suitable gentlemen. I wouldn't allow myself to be married off to whatever rich man they decided was preferable to Jay. I resolved to make myself look even less presentable in the future. Let them try to marry me off when no gentlemen will want to look my way.

Jordan took my hands in hers and asked, "Daisy, what happened to you?"

She looked to be holding back tears, which instantly made me feel more deeply for my young friend. I knew she was a caring person, but her level of concern for me surprised me. I was at a loss for words. She pulled me into a hug and my armor melted. The tears I didn't know I was holding came. She stroked my hair and told me it was going to be okay and that I wasn't alone. I didn't know until then just how badly I needed to hear that. Since Jay left, I had felt so alone. I had felt there wasn't a soul in the world who cared. I couldn't believe dear little Jordan was proving to be my only true friend.

She had nothing to gain by coming to see me, but still she had come. She had come when none of my other so-called friends could be bothered, and she didn't ask me for anything. She didn't need to be here and yet she came anyway with no other motive than to make sure I was okay. She continued to hold me until my racing heart and tears both slowed. Feeling a little calmer, I pulled away.

She seemed to sense I was in a better place to talk, which she looked grateful for. Judging by the speed at which the questions raced out of her mouth, I don't know how she found the restraint to not ask before.

"What happened? The whole town is a whirl with rumors of Louisville's sweetheart. You should really hear those heartless gossipmongers. They do love a good scandal. One day, you had run off to be married to an officer. The next you were ill-used and abandoned by the same officer you were supposed to have run off with." My heart dropped. How was it possible that anyone had found out? Seeing the anguish on my face and misinterpreting the cause, Jordan raced on to say, "Worry not, though. The very next day, you were returned to glory and had been married off to someone's rich cousin. Today, it seems your fate has taken a turn for the worse again, though. I'm afraid today your family is penniless, leaving Louisville's sweetheart destitute and prospectless."

What an unpleasant surprise. I didn't think my absence would be noticed so soon. I had also hoped the absence of our staff would escape notice for longer than it had. I should have known that hope was foolish. With the elite of Louisville, nothing goes unnoticed for long, especially negative news. Jordan was looking at me with such concern that my resolve to stay silent melted away. I felt indebted to her for her visit, her kindness, and her concern. The least I could do was satisfy her curiosity by explaining. Besides, I knew she was trustworthy.

She had done more for me in a single afternoon than my parents or friends had throughout most of my life. Besides, I felt comfortable with her. I felt she shared in my misery in a way I couldn't explain. I felt like telling her would help relieve some of my feelings. I had been bottling them up with no one to talk to. I could really use a friend and was more grateful than I could express that she had come. I didn't know where to start.

With a small smile of gratitude for her presence, I replied, "Well, it seems those wild gossipmongers finally hit on part of the truth."

She gasped and said, "You can't mean your family is really penniless? I mean, I did notice it seems much quieter than it should for such a large home, but you can't actually mean that."

"Normally, there would be much more noise, but my father dismissed all our staff." As easy as it would be to not correct her erroneous conclusion, I felt I owed her more honesty than that. I knew she, at sixteen, might not understand what I had done, but I felt I owed her the truth.

She didn't wait for my further explanation and rushed to comfort me. "Oh, dear sweet Daisy, that is truly terrible. I'm so sorry, but I'm sure we'll find a way out of this."

I was a little glad I hadn't interrupted her, if only to be able to continue to witness just how kindhearted she was. I was floored that she, thinking I was destitute and unable to give her anything, was not only still here but was including herself in my troubles, saying we would get through them together. In that brief time, she had gained more of my trust and respect than all my other friends combined.

"You truly are such a wonderful friend. I really appreciate that more than you know, but unfortunately, the truth is a bit better and a bit worse."

I didn't get to finish explaining before she exclaimed, "How could things possibly be worse?"

I paused, not really knowing how to say what I needed to, but I knew I needed to get it over with. I took a deep breath and said, "Well, it turns out the officer ran off without me."

She paused for a minute before letting out a laugh. "I nearly believed you for a moment there. But you can trust me. What actually happened?" I stayed silent, willing her to understand. It took a minute for the comprehension to dawn on her face. "Oh, Daisy..." The sadness on her face seemed only to be surpassed by my own. "What happened?"

I told her all that I had to tell. How the events unfolded that night and the following one; how happy I was one day and how devastated the next.

She listened intently, her attention focused on me through my long winded rambling. Her attentiveness only further endeared her to me. She let me finish without interruption, somehow knowing that was just what I needed. She was silent, but her face betrayed the turbulence of emotions she went through with me. Her face plainly expressed how deeply she felt my happiness and how much deeper still she felt my pain.

When I finished my story, she pulled me back into her arms and held me through the tears that had started somewhere near the end of my tale; I can't say when. I had been crying so frequently as of late that I hardly noticed the tears anymore. By the time she let go of me, I was feeling lighter in spirits. I gave her a small smile. I could tell she had been holding back and giving me space to feel how I was feeling. How she managed to hold back, I do not know. However, now that she determined I had released everything inside of me, she took leave to speak again.

"My dear sweet Daisy, you must not listen to anyone who tells you that you're worth any less than you are. You must know you're worth more than all the money in the world. You're truly such a wonderful, caring woman and you deserve the world. I will not deign to give that man the energy to utter how I loathe him for how he has made you feel, but I will say that you truly deserve so much better. Do not ever let yourself settle for less."

"You're too kind. I don't know how you swear of my sainthood when you've just heard how far I've fallen."

"I simply won't hear a word against you, even if you are the culprit. No matter what you have done, I swear you will always be an angel to me. I know your heart is purer than you give yourself credit for."

"And now you talk of my purity when it has never had more reason to be in question. But you must know this changes things! I thought I was to be married... I thought he loved me. I thought the worst thing that could happen would be him leaving for war. I never imagined it was possible for anything worse than that to happen. I can't believe how naive I was. Now who will have me?"

"You are still as pure-hearted as you were, and any person worth your while will know just how lucky they are to be with you. This doesn't change a thing, and anyone worthwhile won't care."

"If only that were true. You're still young and still a bit naive to the minds of men, but I promise you, it matters. No one will want me now. And my parents have made it clear they mean to find me a more suitable option, whatever that means. It seems I'm destined for a life of suffering and misery with the first man my parents find who is willing to look past my indiscretion."

She shocked me by rolling her eyes at me. "Well, that's a bit dramatic, don't you think?"

I couldn't help but giggle. Yes, my situation was bad, but I was definitely getting ahead of myself. I would come up with a way to gain some control over my future. I smiled. "You really are an angel. Here I was lamenting how ill-used I have been and how miserable I will be for the rest of my days. And then in the matter of a few hours, you come along and make me feel foolish for doing so."

She paled and blurted out, "I really never meant to make you feel foolish."

"Oh no matter, don't you see? It's a good thing. It's just what I needed."

"I'm glad to hear it, but pray, do enlighten me as to why it's good to feel foolish?"

My smile widened. "Now that I see how foolish my wallowing is, I can wash my hands of it and move on to plotting and planning."

"I'm behind anything that puts a smile back on your face, but that mischievous glint in your eye rightfully would make anyone nervous."

I laughed at that. She was right. I would find a way to take back my power and my future. I just wasn't sure how yet. Jordan, relieved to see me in better spirits, remained by my side for the rest of the day and well into the night, helping me to plot and scheme my way into a happy future.

She seemed more determined than I that I should be happy and not forced to settle. Until then, I hadn't realized what an amazing person she was and just how lucky I was to have her in my life. Until that day, and until my indiscretion, I had taken a lot for granted. I had assumed I would be happily married to whomever I chose and that everyone who knew me would love me. After all, as the widely known sweetheart of

Louisville, it was what I came to expect. I had taken my friendships for granted, too. Yes, my friends had also taken me for granted, but sweet little Jordan never did. She had always been there and refused to see any bad in me despite how I had taken her for granted and only given her the time of day when I was in the mood. I knew now that it had been a mistake to lump her in with my other fair-weather friends. After all, Jordan was the only visitor I received out of all my numerous so-called friends.

In fact, even after the end of my self-imposed isolation, I found what I might have expected. My friends were nowhere to be found. Sure, I would see them around town, but they would do everything they could to avoid interaction. When interaction could not be avoided, there would be the false pleasantries asking how I was doing and expressing what I knew to be a false desire to spend time together soon.

Those were the kinder of the interactions. Others would ask how I am doing and say I looked well despite my condition. I knew not then, nor now, whether the condition they were referring to was the true nature of my indiscretion or the assumed nature of my poverty, but it didn't matter. Regardless of the words they spoke or how they acted, the bottom line was the same. They weren't interested in being around me now that I had fallen from grace. They cared only for Louisville's sweetheart, not Daisy Fay.

I mention my so-called friends' reactions because I was most surprised by their swift and full abandonment, but their reactions were tame compared to the rest of the town. Those women who had always envied me and vied for my attention and friendship reveled in my fall from grace. They would walk by, whispering and giggling to each other. It might be thought that I was overly sensitive, and it was mere coincidence, if not for the frequent looks in my direction that resulted in more giggling.

After the first few of those encounters, I would have resolved to resume my isolation if not for the dedicated efforts of Jordan to keep me in good spirits and my own determination to take back control of my future. I knew my parents would have preferred my continued isolation, but I no longer cared. Knowing they wanted me inside where I couldn't cause further harm to the family name was a large reason I was so determined to not let anything keep me inside. Jordan was truly my rock. She was as much, if not more, stubborn than I was, and refused to let me falter during my moments of doubt.

She saw me through all my moods and helped with my plans, whether she agreed with them or not. She supported my attempting to ruin my parents' plans for me, but she thought my ideas were less than ideal. I knew my parents well enough to know that they would not wait long before looking for more suitable options for marriage. It was possible, more than likely actually, that they already had some in mind. I knew their choices would be rich and ready to marry.

While I do not pretend that the money would not be a plus, I knew I wasn't ready for marriage and knew I couldn't be happy in a marriage so soon after the devastating heartbreak I had suffered. I took to going out on the town with whomever struck my fancy that day. I hoped that would delay the inevitability of my parents finding an eligible gentleman who would have me. I hoped to dissuade potential suitors by always being seen with different men.

My plan worked better than I could ever have hoped. I was a bit taken back by just how well it worked. Soon, the town was abuzz with how much of a floozy the former sweetheart of Louisville had become. While I was happy the rumors served to drive off offers of marriage, I was surprised at how negatively my behavior was being talked about. I was doing the same things I used to, but they used to say I was young, beautiful, popular, and in high demand. Now that I had fallen from grace, I was being called a floozy, a whore, and it was being said I had slept with the whole of the town. It seems when you are favored, any manner of behavior is looked upon favorably. With a now ruined reputation, instead of being unable to do any wrong, now I was unable to do anything right. I had imagined it would be far more difficult than it had proved to further tarnish my reputation.

After I kept on with this behavior for a few weeks, my reputation seemed irredeemable. With how disliked I was throughout town, it would have taken more money than my parents had to bribe me into a favorable marriage. Things were going wonderfully, and I felt secure in my triumph.

My parents continually expressed their anger and disapproval at my spending time with so many men, to which I, as innocently as I could muster, reminded them they had tasked me with finding a more suitable husband. My mother nearly suffered an aneurysm upon hearing that. I fled to my bedroom to escape her wrath, but her volume was not sufficiently stifled by the distance and the closed door I had put between us.

Chapter Five

After that, they gave up on attempting to control my behavior. Instead, they pushed for me to use more discretion in my dalliances. As a consequence, I made sure to make more of a scene than I had been. I would have carried on like this for who knows how long, but things came to a crashing halt with a casual remark from an officer.

I had been going about with officers as usual and had been content enough. I hadn't had any trouble with the officers, but knew from the start there was something dangerous about this one. There was something about this particular officer that I quite liked. That scared me. I only agreed to spend the afternoon with him because I knew he was shipping out soon. Looking back, I am sure my soft spot for him came from his straw-blond hair that reminded me of a certain someone. I knew better than to spend time with him. My gut had been screaming it was a bad idea, but I ignored it. That proved to be a mistake.

He was a perfect gentleman, and the afternoon passed pleasantly enough until he mentioned his company was headed to New York. He talked of their joining another company there before shipping overseas. My heart dropped at the mere mention of New York. The thoughts I had been blocking out all came rushing back and I couldn't help but think of Jay, of our last night together, and our plans.

Unless things had changed, he was shipping out soon. Maybe he was even a part of the company this officer was meeting up with. I felt the breath go from my lungs. Jay was leaving. He was leaving, and he may or may not be waiting for me in New York.

I had tried to convince myself otherwise, to drop my foolish fantasies, and I had succeeded, for a while at least. Now, I was right back where I was when he left. My mind was plagued with what ifs.

What if he was still waiting for me? What if he truly intended for us to be wed in New York? What if I went to New York? What if I was wrong again and he didn't want to see me? What if he had just been using me all along? What if I never found out either way what happened? Could I be okay without ever having any closure?

It was with these thoughts rushing through my head that I went straight home and, before I knew what I was doing, I was packing. I truly don't know what I would have done next. I had resolved to go when I heard a bang followed by two short hesitant knocks on my door. I realized immediately what that meant and looked down at what I was doing.

I had packed up about half my wardrobe and meaningful possessions by that point. I must have been mad. There was no other explanation. Was I really packing to go halfway across the country to see the man who had left me without so much as a goodbye? How could I possibly explain that to Jordan? I didn't have long to think. A moment later, Jordan, who had become much more comfortable invading my space, entered without waiting for a response.

Jordan was the most loyal person in my life. She had been by my side whether or not she agreed with my actions. As it so happened, she was strongly opposed to this particular action. The disapproval was etched on her face before her lips had uttered a word.

While I anxiously awaited some speech from her, I wondered how she knew I needed her now. At the time, I felt she must be a mind reader. It wasn't until later that she explained she had been keeping more of a watch on me lately since she knew from what I had told her that he was leaving soon.

She guessed something like this might happen. I didn't have the nerve to face her yet, so I turned back to look at the results of my packing. Anything to avoid seeing the disapproval on her face. I heard her sigh and then ask, "Daisy dear, what are you doing?"

I had been asking myself the same thing. I took a deep breath and, after a moment, slowly exhaled and turned around to face her.

"I don't know. I truly don't," was all I could say in explanation.

"I worried this might happen. You know this is crazy, right?"

I did know it now, but before she had entered, I had pushed the concerns out of my mind. I had convinced myself that he might still be waiting for me or that I could get the closure I needed. Even if he didn't want me, at least I would have the closure of knowing.

I had convinced myself I would travel halfway across the country chasing that man just to find out what he was thinking and why he didn't say goodbye. I had convinced myself that it would be worth it, whatever the outcome, but seeing Jordan brought back all my doubts. I didn't know what to say, but Jordan didn't wait for me to say anything. She crossed the room and wrapped her arms around me.

After a few minutes, she pulled back and looked into my eyes. The disapproval had been replaced with an overwhelming amount of concern. I had been prepared for disapproval; the concern was too much to handle. My tears started before I could stop them. She went to wrap her arms back around me, but I pulled away. I needed to be in motion; I needed to be doing something.

I had half a mind to go back to packing just for something to be doing with my hands, but thought better of it. I settled for pacing the length of my room. Half to myself and half to her, I said, "I know it seems crazy, but what if he is waiting for me? What if he truly expected us to be wed in New York and I don't show up? He must mean to be married. If he hadn't meant it before our last night together, he must mean it now. He must."

As I spoke, even *I* realized how crazy I sounded, crazy and desperate. I collapsed in front of the vanity and saw myself reflected back in the mirror. My face was red and splotchy. The bodice of my dress was damp from my tears. My eyes betrayed such anguish that even I was startled by the sight. As bad as I looked, it still came nowhere close to how distressed I felt.

Over my shoulder, I saw Jordan move closer to me. She advanced slowly, like she was unsure of how I would react. She gave me the caution one would give a caged wild animal, proceeding slowly but deliberately toward me as if afraid of spooking me. My attention was captured by watching her graceful advance in the mirror toward me. When she reached me, she tried to meet my eye, but I didn't turn toward her. She settled for meeting my eye in the mirror.

I watched her pick up my brush from the counter and start to brush my hair. It was comforting to have someone care for me in that way. No one had ever taken care of me like that, except for the staff my parents employed. My parents had done a good job of making sure my needs were met, but I hadn't felt cared for by them as a child should. I had always felt I was someone's obligation, whether it was the staff being paid and obligated to care for me or my parents, who made me feel a burden to them. I had always felt I was someone's burden.

I had thought that Jay cared about me, not my money, not my beauty, not my purity, but just me, Daisy; not Daisy Fay, Louisville's sweetheart. Now that I was without my perfect reputation, would he even want me? I had given him everything... He had taken everything. He didn't even come to say goodbye. I must have truly been crazy to think he would keep his promise to marry me when he hadn't even come to say goodbye.

Still, after everything, I needed him to be true to his word; I needed him to still want me after what we had done together. "He was my everything… I gave him everything…" The tears kept falling. My head fell into my arms as the truth washed over me. It came out as a whisper when I finally said, "He took everything from me."

There it was; the truth of the matter. He took everything I had to give and gave nothing in return. He told me he loved me, and maybe he did, but he left without so much as a goodbye. I thought I would feel more as the realization hit me at last, but I felt nothing. The numbness was new to me. These long weeks I had been in the depths of despair and grief. When I should now have been feeling my lowest, I felt nothing.

I suspect my mind couldn't comprehend or cope with the realization that he had knowingly ruined my reputation and left me without so much as a farewell. He couldn't be the man I thought he was. I had never dreamed he would hurt me like this. I took my thoughts in stride, thankful for the numbness allowing me distance from my feelings and enabling me to think more clearly.

After a moment of silence, Jordan spoke up. "My dear, you're still the same strong, loving, wonderful woman you were. With or without him, you're not anything less. Don't let yourself believe less of yourself. If you insist on going on this— pardon my frankness, but I must say it—this fool's errand to see him again, I can go pack and we can leave in an hour."

I couldn't believe her. She didn't believe for one moment that this was a trip worth taking, and yet she was willing to go for me. I couldn't make her do that. If I had still been on the fence, I knew now I wasn't going. She continued, "I truly do hope I'm wrong, but I won't lie and tell you I believe it likely. I would never try to stop you from something I believed would make you happy, but dear, I really don't think any good will come from this. I mean, honestly, even if he is waiting there for you as you hope, what then? Would you marry before he leaves for the war? You have no way of knowing how long he'll be gone or what he'll be like when he returns. The stories we've heard are chilling. He might not be the same man he was when he returns, if he returns."

It hadn't occurred to me just how little I had thought things through and how little I truly knew of him. I'd known him for a few short months. Did I really know him well enough to attach myself to him for the rest of my life? It was funny that I was the older one when Jordan often seemed wiser.

I looked around at the chaos that was now my room. I had a suitcase open on my bed that was haphazardly stuffed with whatever clothes I had laid my hands on in my frenzied hurry to leave. I had nearly stuffed the suitcase to the brim and clothing was overflowing onto the bed. As I surveyed the mess I had made, I realized I had packed my summer things instead of the warmer clothing I would have needed for the New York winter.

And there was something off about my heels. I bent over to get a closer look. I had been trying to pack my black heels. I had quite a few pairs, but I wanted to pack my favorite. On closer inspection, I realized what was wrong. They were both black heels, but the two shoes I had managed to pack were not from the same pair. Worse still, they were both left shoes.

The image came to mind of me wandering around New York nearly freezing to death in a summer dress, limping with only one heel on my feet. It was such a funny thought I couldn't help laughing. Jordan looked at me inquisitively, quirked her eyebrow at me, and followed my gaze. Her eyes roamed over my strewn about clothing and landed on the shoes. She leaned in closer, reaching for both shoes.

When she saw what I had, she chuckled. "Just how far were you planning to get in these?"

I moved to take them back, but she held them away from me. "Hey!" I said in mock indignation. "They're perfectly nice shoes!"

She laughed harder. "Well, one of them is, unless you're finally admitting to having two left feet?"

"Hey! I'll have you know I've been said to be quite graceful."

"And just how enamored with you was the man who told you that whopper of a lie?"

Neither of us could contain our laughter or gain enough composure to speak for quite some time. When I felt calmer, all it took was one look from Jordan to get me laughing again. It is likely we would have kept relapsing into fits of laughter if not for the curt knock on my door serving to sober us up. Without waiting for a response, in came my mother. I don't know what it was originally that she wanted, but I saw her shock when she took in the scene before her. Jordan and I were sprawled out on my clothes on my bed in the middle of the chaos that was now my room. I knew whatever she was coming in for originally had now fled her mind. The look on her face told me I was in for it.

I started to say, "Mama, I know what this looks like-" but that was as far as I got before I saw her see the suitcase. The look on her face stalled my explanation right in its tracks.

"And just where do you think you might be going, young lady?" she asked in a sickeningly calm voice.

I knew there was no right answer and could think of no better answer than the truth, so I admitted, "I was going to meet Jay, the lieutenant. He had talked of us marrying in New York before he shipped out, and I had hoped to see if he was still true to his word." Seizing the opportunity to endear Jordan to my family and to facilitate her escape from the situation that I knew would only get worse, I quickly added, "But Jordan convinced me I was being foolish. Jordan, you are truly such a blessing and I know you would love to stay longer, but I know your family is waiting for you and I would be a terrible host to keep them waiting on my account."

I glanced over at Jordan, pleading with her to understand my meaning and go along with my hastily made excuse.

The concern showed on her face as she replied with meaning, "I think I can be spared there. I'm not sure about here." She paused, making sure I caught her true meaning before adding, "After all, there's quite a mess here. I can't imagine you wish to pick this all up yourself."

I was incredibly touched. Of course she wanted to stay and protect me, and as much as I still wanted her around, I knew the scene my mother was about to make wasn't one I wanted her to have to witness. I shot her what I hoped was a convincing look that said I would be fine, but I can't be sure the look conveyed the feeling I knew I didn't feel.

Jordan didn't look convinced. "Jordan, what kind of friend would I be if I kept you from your family? I will be just fine. After all," I shot a contrite look toward my mother while saying, "I made this mess and I need to be prepared to clean it up myself."

Jordan caught my double meaning and nodded. "Alright, but don't hesitate to change your mind if you need me. I'm only a short distance away. I'll stop by tomorrow like usual." She turned to my mother. "As always, Mrs. Fay, it was lovely seeing you." It took a miraculous effort on my part not to laugh at that. I have no idea how she maintained her composure while saying it.

On her way out, Jordan left my door open, which I'm sure she did to keep my mother on her best behavior. It seemed to work, since she didn't start yelling immediately, but turned her back to me to continue looking around the room.

Almost to herself, she said quietly, "To think my only daughter…" Her volume rose. "…the ungrateful daughter who has so wholly ruined the reputation of her entire family…" She turned to look at me and I saw the anger in her eyes. "After dragging the Fay name through the dirt and forcing your poor father and me to suffer with you, you were just going to abandon us?!"

"Mama, it wasn't like that, I swear. Don't you see? If I went to New York, Jay and I would be married. Things would be fixed. We wouldn't be disgraced anymore."

She let out a humorless laugh as she glared at me.

"How would you marrying that poor nobody possibly fix all the trouble you have caused? We have plans for you, plans you almost ruined. If we weren't so rich and I wasn't so clever, I'm sure you would have kept us in ruin with your whoring about."

Ignoring the whore comment that I sadly had become used to lately, I asked, "What plans, Mama?" Although, to be truthful, I was pretty sure I already knew what she was going to say.

"Don't be daft, Daisy. You're already a whore; don't be a dumb one. You know your father and I have been talking to our friends and connections … what is left of them anyway, after your little stunt. We have a few gentlemen picked out who might still be foolish enough to want you. The moment you stop whoring yourself around with anyone who looks your way, we could have you married and no longer a burden on this family.

"But, Mama-"

"I won't hear arguments. You tried your best to put this family in ruin and I won't continue to stand for it! You'll stop going about with officers at once! I don't want to hear another word about it!"

With that, she stormed out of my room, slamming the door behind her. While her words were most definitely unkind, she had let me off easier than I had dared to dream.

Normally, the only thing that stopped my mother when she was wound up like that was my father. I was grateful that proved untrue this time because my father seemed to be nowhere to be found until much later that evening. Feeling a bit better thanks to Jordan's intervention, I went about righting my things and unpacking. As I did, I let my mind wander and daydream about what my future might be like. However, I couldn't shake my mother's words.

I pictured myself unhappy in a loveless marriage to a rich man who couldn't care less about me. I pictured myself being ordered around by a man who thought he owned me and thought his money could, or did, buy me. As my mind came up with one unhappy future after another, my resolve hardened. They would not force me into a marriage that my heart wasn't in. My mother could force me to do a lot of things by wielding her power over me, but she held no power over my heart. I agreed with her on one point, though; after that day, I resolved to be done playing with officers.

Chapter Six

I stayed true to my resolution to steer clear of officers and only went around town with the men the war left behind. Jordan was ever faithful to me and supported my rebellion, although she told me numerous times she couldn't understand why I would bother running around with men at all. Regardless of her feelings about my behavior, she never failed to be there for me when I needed her most, often at the expense of her own goals. It was likely her dedication to me that prevented her golf career from taking off earlier than it did, but her talent wouldn't be stifled for long. She had a natural talent that any man would have killed for.

Over the next year, she started playing in tournaments, and her talent was noticed. Now she was the one people noticed and paid attention to. I hadn't noticed until then, but Jordan had essentially been living in my shadow for the entirety of our friendship. It seemed my shadow had been broader than I noticed, since most of my friends had lived there. But Jordan was the only one left who still stood by me and who had remained my friend all those years in my shadow. When her career took off, I was her biggest fan. I knew no one more deserving of success than my dear Jordan.

It was a surprising consequence that men started to take notice of her. Many were jealous of her talent. They couldn't handle losing to a woman, but those with less fragile egos took a liking to her. Prior to then, Jordan had been very much unattached to anyone, being of a fiercely independent nature and still young; it was hardly surprising.

Nor was it surprising that men took to notice her, especially since she had grown more into her figure. What was surprising was that she returned their notice.

I couldn't quite pinpoint why this surprised me. As a seventeen-year-old woman, it was hardly surprising she should be dating, so I couldn't understand my own feelings of confusion. Nevertheless, I was taken aback by her taking interest. I tried to be happy for her, but it was hard to cope with the loss I felt, the loss of her time.

With golf, she still put me first but I discovered quickly that when it came to her boyfriends, things were different. I began to see less and less of her. By the time Autumn came back around, I was relieved for the change of pace that I was anticipating. Jordan and I would make more time for each other again. She just had one last tournament lined up for the season and then we would have more time together again.

Unfortunately for me, Jordan was extremely talented. The one more tournament turned into another and another. I understood she was busy, but it was hard to be away from her for so long, especially with her being my only friend. I missed her terribly. Not that she didn't make time for me, because she did her best to be around, but I wasn't her top priority anymore. I don't mean to sound vain; I was truly happy she was putting herself first. If anyone deserves the recognition she received, it was her. I just wasn't used to having to share her, especially not with men.

Her latest boyfriend, James, was no friend of mine. I had tried to be kind to this one, since she seemed to have had a stronger attachment to him than most, but he seemed to go out of his way to be oppositional to me. I wasn't used to this type of treatment from men. I had been largely used to more favorable attention. Not that I wanted that kind of attention from him, but I did want to be respected and have attempts made to win me over as Jordan's best friend.

However, it seemed he thought our friendship was a little strange, and that we were too close. I had even heard him ask Jordan when her shadow would be leaving. Hearing myself referred to as her shadow was jarring, but I hardly minded being in her shadow as long as I could be around her. It was his implication that I was always around that I took issue with. However he felt about me, he was wrong about me taking up Jordan's time.

I felt like since they had become more serious, I had hardly seen her. I most definitely hadn't spent time alone with her like we used to. He continued to complain to her that she spent too much time with me. I knew how difficult it must have been for Jordan to have her best friend and her beau not get along. She didn't deserve to be unhappy on my account, so I tried to hide my feelings. I tried as best as I could to ignore the way he acted toward me, but he seemed determined to push me away from him and by extent, push me further from Jordan. For Jordan's sake, I was resolved that his attempts would not work. For Jordan, my dear sweet Jordan who had never asked me for anything, I resolved to ignore his shortcomings and do my best to make him warm to me.

Jordan continued to invite me to spend time with them. I knew she missed me and was trying to make sure I felt included and didn't feel discarded by her. As much as I treasured any time with her, I knew James wasn't happy that she always invited me to tag along. I bowed out of many of Jordan's invitations in order to give them time alone. Although sometimes my motives were less altruistic, sometimes I only bowed out because I couldn't stand the thought of spending more time with him. However, when I didn't see her *with* him, I didn't see her. I wasn't willing to surrender spending time with her to please her latest boyfriend, so I came up with what I thought was a suitable compromise. I started bringing along whomever I was seeing that day in order to not show up alone and to allow Jordan and James to feel less intruded upon.

I hoped this would improve things with him while still letting me spend the time I craved with Jordan. However, he continued to make his comments about me. He continued to bemoan how much time she spent with me. He told her I was a bad influence on her.

She shut his critiques down almost as soon as he voiced them, but that didn't stop him. He started saying things to the men I was with while Jordan was out of earshot. To most, he would comment on how it seemed I was quite popular with the men of the town. On the occasions where I truly liked the gentleman I was with and was enjoying myself, he would say to me in a loud whisper, that he was certain would be audible to the gentleman, that I looked quite miserable compared to how I looked yesterday with another gentleman. While this was a blatant falsehood, it served his purpose by disrupting the pleasant time I was having and usually ended the date abruptly, since nothing I did or said would wipe the thought from the man's mind that I was miserable in his company and was better entertained by another man.

After one too many of those such dates, I stopped caring about making him like me. I now knew that to be quite an impossible feat. Knowing the futility of my efforts, I went back to spending every possible moment I could with her.

Unsurprisingly, the rift between James and me intensified, making me feel even further disconnected from Jordan. I saw how her and him interacted and seemed to grow closer each time I saw them. I was already severely feeling the loss of my time with Jordan, but seeing how she interacted with him, I felt a spark of jealousy. I hadn't felt connected to anyone except Jordan lately. As much as I didn't want to share her, I knew her happiness was more important. James made her happy, so I tried to be happy for her. Although I couldn't understand what she saw in him, it was clear she saw something special. I also couldn't begrudge the way he treated her. He truly seemed to care for her and treat her well.

I envied what they had. While I was by no means without the company of men, I had been careful not to let things get serious. I had resolved that I had loved once and been burned and wouldn't allow it to happen again. While I was still entertaining different suitors and actually enjoyed my time with a few of them, I had closed myself off to the possibility of any emotional connection. Having done so in order to protect my heart and happiness, I had thought I would be feeling happier.

All I felt was alone. Spending time day after day with different men having to start all over every day and pretend to be interested in their lives; it was exhausting and depressing. I had been feeling discontent with my chosen way of life for a while now, but seeing Jordan with James really highlighted what it was I felt I was missing. I had given myself ample time to grieve Jay and the future I had imagined for us; now I just felt alone.

Chapter Seven

I hoped with time I would start to feel in better spirits again, but much to my dismay, after a few days' time, I still felt no relief to my feelings. Truth be told, I felt worse than I had a few short days ago.

I knew there was an easy option, but until now I had scorned it as non-optional. I asked myself many times over the past few days if it had really come to this, if I had really become this desperate. It appears I had, for I had no solution of my own.

The next day, I sucked up my pride and went to see my father. As my footsteps echoed back at me on my trek to his library, I couldn't help but remember the last time I had made this journey. I could still hear their words echoing back at me. I almost turned around, but I knew that would just be delaying the inevitable. With how I was feeling, I knew even if I turned around then, I would be back soon. I pressed onward.

As I continued down the hallway, I thought about what this choice would mean for my future. Ever since Jay left, I had had trouble picturing a happy future for myself. Now I felt the first stirrings of hope. I dared to hope that I might have a chance at happiness. My dreams for the future were fuzzy at best but for the first time since he left, I had regained some hope. When

I saw the door to Father's library, I hesitated, sensing the gravity of this action and the finality of my decision once I knocked. I swallowed my nerves and my pride and knocked softly on the door.

"Come in."

I gulped and let myself in before I could change my mind. He looked up from his desk, surprised to see me. I wondered who he might have been expecting. I was nervous and didn't know how to start, but I knew I had to start somewhere so I blurted out, "I'm ready."

"Ready for what?"

I sighed. I couldn't decide if he didn't understand my meaning or if he wished to embarrass me by making me say it. Either way, it looked like I would have to say more.

"Ready to admit I need help."

He threw up his hands in the air and exclaimed, "How can I help if you don't tell me what I'm supposed to help with? I'll help if it gets me back to my affairs sooner rather than later." He gestured to the piles of paper on his desk.

I knew I would have to be quick if I had any hope of keeping his interest and it was imperative that I did since I wasn't ready to have this conversation with my mother. I rushed to say, "I'm not happy. Nothing I've done is working, and clearly Mama is dying to set me up with a husband. I'm feeling more alone than ever. Maybe she's not wrong."

His eyes widened, his eyebrows raising almost to his hairline. Before he could say anything, I rushed to add, "I mean, I still won't settle. I won't marry for anything less than love, but I don't think meeting some eligible gentlemen would be the worst thing in the world."

He laughed at that. Just then, I heard a voice behind me ask what was so funny. Too late, I realized my mistake. I had left the door open. In came my mother, shooting me her usual glare before turning to my father and asking again, "Just what's so funny?"

He smiled at her, which confused her. I had hoped to have been long gone when he filled her in, so I didn't have to see her gloat, but now I was trapped.

"It seems our daughter is finally willing to admit she was wrong. She wants my help finding herself a husband."

My mother's jaw hit the floor. "Your help?" She turned to me, outraged. "What does your father know about eligible men?"

I glared at him, causing him to laugh more. It seemed he was in a teasing mood and if anyone knew how to get my mother more riled up than I could, it was my father. I quickly told her, "Papa's teasing! Of course I was asking for both your help."

She looked placated and said, "I'm glad you haven't lost all sense." She considered for a moment, and her face lit up. "We'll start planning at once."

I was confused and worried. "Planning? Planning what?"

She looked at me as if I were stupid. "Planning what?" she repeated. "Why, your debut, of course!"

My heart dropped at that. I had meant to meet a few of the men she had deemed eligible. I hadn't in my wildest dreams thought about ever having a debut. "A debut? You can't be serious."

"Of course I'm serious! It's been a tradition in our family for years. My grandmother had one, my mother had one, I had one, and now you will have one! It'll be just what this family needs to get our lives and reputations back. What better way to announce to the world that we're still to be respected than to debut you respectably to society?" She suddenly looked at my father. "You'll have to hire the staff back at once! What a foolish idea of yours to let them go!"

I couldn't believe her. It was just like her to blame my father for letting the staff go when it must have been her decision. There was no way my father would have made such a hasty, drastic decision like that without a push from her. I couldn't believe how quickly things were getting out of hand. I didn't want any of this—well, maybe the dress wouldn't be half bad—but the rest of it was overkill. I didn't want to be paraded around in front of everyone as if I were for sale to the highest bidder.

I would have walked out right then, if not for my mother's words echoing in my head, "What better way to announce to the world that we are still to be respected?" After all the trouble I had caused them, what kind of daughter would I be to not agree to the one thing that might help? I saw the hope and excitement on both their faces and couldn't walk out. I knew I had to make this small sacrifice for the family. Plus, if this would help my reputation, that wouldn't be the worst thing in the world.

I had grown tired of being the talk of the town. Maybe this wouldn't be so bad after all. I had wanted to meet some new eligible men. This would allow me to meet quite a few at the same time. It's not like I was stuck with anyone I didn't like, and this would surely bring in some fresh faces that hadn't heard as much about me already. Maybe I could find someone who would like me for me, maybe I could have happiness after all.

Now that my parents and I were on the same page, everything was settled except for the small matter of picking a date. My father urged for speed, likely thinking I would change my mind. My mother was of a different mind. She was in quite a panic about the details. She said more than once that "It simply must be the event of the season." When my father asked why it had to be so grand, she shot him a look that would have withered even the most hardened soldier. My father, who knew my mother well enough to know he had already lost, didn't push the issue.

Although she no longer needed to, she graced him with her explanation. She explained that my debut must be the event of the season to show any and all eligible bachelors how desirable I still was, despite my indiscretion. She was determined that a show of wealth and the perfect dress would raise me back into my former virtue and my former popularity in town. As we were getting along for the first time in a long time, I didn't argue.

It had been a long while since my mother had been this worked up about something positive, so my father and I stepped back and let her take charge. What mattered most to me—well besides the dress, of course—was that I would be putting myself back out there in a way that I hadn't dared to since Jay left. I would stop playing games with boys and find a man that I could spend my life with. I saw this as the first step on the road to happiness and to a positive future.

It also didn't hurt that I was getting along with my parents again. They seemed to tiptoe around me, which was a first. It seemed they were both worried I might change my mind. My mother didn't nag nearly as much as usual; in fact, she was so busy with preparations that I barely saw her. There was still the small matter of picking a date that she had yet to attend to, but as it turns out, luck was on her side, for just when she had finished preparations and was getting ready to pick and announce a date, word of the armistice reached Louisville.

The Great War that took so many lives and ripped so many families apart was finally over. For a long time, we thought it would never end, but the nightmare had finally come to an end. To most, the end of the war meant relief that their men would be returning and that their boys wouldn't be stolen away by the war that claimed so many. To my mother, it meant she was already prepared, a step ahead of the other women of the town, to throw the event of the year. She told me multiple times that she would be damned if she let another of the town's women throw the first event after the Armistice.

She told anyone who would listen about how fitting it was that just when we had won our battle overseas, the family was finally ready to thrust their beautiful daughter into the waiting arms of society. Never mind that I had already been dating for years and society did not seem to want me; my mother would hear none of it, but her optimism and excitement were contagious. I felt better about my future prospects than I ever had. The date for my debut was set for a few weeks' time. Now the only thing left was to deliver the invitations. I chose to hand deliver Jordan's invitation. I hadn't seen much of her since making the arrangements with my parents and wanted to make sure she heard about it from me. I was worried about her reaction and I needed her to understand and support me. Not to mention I needed her there.

Without her by my side, I shuddered to think of how I would make it through the night. I needed her cool, level head to help me pick out worthy potential husbands. As questionable as her current choice was to me, she knew me better than anyone, and if there was anyone I trusted to help me find future happiness, it was Jordan. I didn't even trust my own judgement, since I had erred so in the past, but I trusted hers.

I worried the entire way that she would think me foolish for going along with what I knew she considered to be a sexist and outdated tradition. When I made it to her home, she wasn't there. Not wanting to wait alone in her home, I paced back and forth outside. I hoped she might return soon, but I knew it didn't matter how long she was out. I would wait. I needed to get this over with.

When she did arrive back home, she wasn't alone. I shouldn't have been surprised that he was with her, but I had been hoping to catch her alone. I didn't really want an audience. I sighed inwardly but pasted on what I hoped looked to be a real smile and approached them.

"Jordan, it's so good to see you!" I glanced at him. I didn't relish lying and always tried to abstain unless absolutely necessary. In this case, society dictated I must. "And how wonderful to see you, too."

I noticed his barely contained eye roll, but I didn't think Jordan did. "Why yes, what a surprise it is to see Jordan... outside her home... where you were waiting for her. What a surprise it is that you once again intrude on our time. How lovely."

Jordan laughed and playfully smacked him lightly on the shoulder. How she could think him kidding when his voice dripped venom, I didn't know. To him, she said, "Darling, play nice. You know as well as I do that it's always a delight to see my dear Daisy." She turned to me and smiled. "Love, don't listen to him. You're always welcome wherever I am."

That didn't help his mood. "I'm sure she knows it. She turns up wherever we go."

"Oh darling, it can hardly be considered turning up when I always invite her." She turned back to me and asked, "Not that I'm complaining, but what brings you here? I didn't expect to see you. You've seemed so busy lately, I feel like I've hardly seen you!"

Not one to stay silent, James added, "I'm definitely not complaining."

Jordan laughed again before saying, "Oh shush. Stop messing with her. Really, though, I do hope everything is alright?"

I couldn't help but smile at her concern. How such a caring, selfless person could be with that selfish brute of a man I couldn't understand. I doubted I would ever understand. But she seemed happy. If it meant her happiness, I would spend every day for the rest of my life with that brute of a man. Well, maybe not every day, but for her happiness I would have suffered his company as much as I could bear. For her smile, it was a small price to ask.

"No need for concern, love. Things are just fine." The look on her face rather than her words asked if I was quite sure. "I swear I'm doing well. There was a matter of slight import that I wanted to discuss with you later, though..." I had been trying to convey to her I wanted to talk to her about it alone, but she didn't seem to understand. She looked to be waiting for me to continue or to explain the need to be secret.

It seemed this caught James's attention and intrigue. He looked more appraisingly at me. My cheeks tinged pink ever so slightly. I hoped he wouldn't notice, but he did. I was usually so careful not to show weakness in his presence, and I knew I would soon regret my lapse. Sensing I wasn't myself, he pressed, "You aren't usually so withholding." He looked at Jordan. "Is she, my dear?" Jordan's face was a cross between confusion, curiosity, and concern. It seemed she was at a loss for words; a most rare occasion for her.

She didn't break eye contact with me and simply shook her head. I was too busy trying to both reassure Jordan and convey to her that I wished to speak to her in private, a feat that was near impossible with only my eyes and expression, to take advantage of his pause. Had I been more myself, I would have likely changed the subject. Emboldened by the lack of interruption, he continued, "Normally, there's no end to the chatter between you and Jordan. I do wonder what it is that has you so quiet all of a sudden." I shot a thinly veiled glare in his direction that I hoped Jordan missed. I had hoped to silence him, but he added, "Please do tell us. Don't you see how worried you're making my dear Jordan?"

I didn't need to look in Jordan's direction to know the truth of his words. She always worried too much about me. In this instance, it was unwarranted, but she didn't yet know that. I held his gaze, both to avoid looking at Jordan because I already knew the worry I would see on her face, and to make sure he knew he didn't intimidate me. I had hoped to wipe the smirk off his face, but he knew he had the upper hand.

He pulled Jordan in front of him, pressing her body against his while snaking his arms around her waist. To see her manhandled like that by such a brute was nearly too much for me to hold my composure. Jordan seemed a little startled but didn't protest. I had never felt more distant from her throughout the entirety of our friendship than I did now, with her standing less than a foot away. My Jordan, my fiercely strong, independent Jordan, wouldn't have let a man move her without her permission. It seemed she had softened as they had grown closer.

Having placed her in front of him, it was impossible to avoid looking at her. Her expression radiated concern and her eyes pleaded to know that I was okay. He knew I would cave, but it seemed he was in the mood to twist the knife by saying, "You can't mean to be cruel enough to prolong her suffering."

I knew I had lost. I wouldn't make her wait. I knew I would cave and tell the both of them to alleviate the concern I was causing her, but I still held back a few moments.

I knew I would be inviting his scorn and mocking, which I had hoped to avoid, and I was nervous about Jordan's reaction. I worried my fiercely independent best friend might think I was signing myself up to be auctioned off to the highest bidder. I worried she would think it unwise of me to go along with my parents' wishes. I worried she would think I was settling when I didn't need to.

They both continued to stare at me, Jordan with an anxious gaze and him with a look of anticipation. "Please do tell us. You know you can confide in me and Jordan." He had the audacity to wink after saying that. We both knew the truth. He was as trustworthy as a crook; he would surely do anything he could to steal my happiness.

But I saw no way out of telling them both, so I turned my attention back to Jordan. "My dear, I wanted to be the first to tell you the news…" I paused for a moment too long, and he seized the opportunity.

"You're pregnant! I knew it!"

My jaw dropped. I glared daggers at him. Jordan moved away from him and gave him a warning look. "Darling, we talked about this! Do be polite. Of course she's not pregnant." She looked at me and took a step closer to me and reached for my hands. "Sweetie, I swear he's joking." She looked at him and rolled her eyes. "We've been over how Daisy doesn't get your jokes. You really must stop. I really want you two to get along."

She turned back to me and gave me a pleading look, asking me to ignore him. For her, I knew I would. She had proven to be such a loyal friend that there was not much I wouldn't do for her if she asked. I took her proffered hands in mine and gave her a small smile. Her grateful smile back was more than reward enough to compensate me for ignoring him. "Darling, please forgive his interruption." She shot him another warning look and then turned her attention back to me and continued. "Please, tell us your news. I'm anxious to hear what's going on."

"It's good news, I think. I feel good about it, but I'm worried you might not agree."

"If it's something you feel good about, I'm sure I'll be positively joyful for you."

"It's so wonderful to hear you say so. I hope it'll prove to be true."

"I swear, darling, if it's something good for you, I will be positively brimming with happiness. Your delight is my own."

"Well then, I would be honored if you would do me the honor of attending my debut." There was a moment of silence in which I glanced at both of them and saw surprise on both their faces. I turned my attention fully to Jordan, who, after a moment, grinned and hugged me. "Darling, that's wonderful! Of course we'll be there! I wouldn't miss it for the world! Did you really worry about my reaction?"

"Of course I did! You always tell me the old traditions are outdated and serve primarily to objectify women. I was worried you would think I was making a mistake."

"I won't lie to you. It isn't a choice I would make for myself. I don't pretend to like the old traditions, but this isn't about me. It's been a while since I've seen you this excited about anything, so of course I'm as excited as can be for you!"

I smiled at her. I was truly grateful she understood me so well. Having stayed silent for a remarkable amount of time, James chimed in. "I pity the man who gets saddled with you, but I do hope you find him soon so he can take you off our hands more often."

Jordan rushed to add, "And so you'll be just as happy as we are, of course! But, darling, we have so much to discuss!" She looked at him and added, "I can't imagine you would be interested in planning her debut, but you can stay if you would like." I grimaced at the thought, but she turned to me and gave me a subtle wink. She quickly turned back to him. I looked at him, too. I could see he was torn. I was sure he didn't actually want to stay, but he also knew I didn't want him to stay, which I was sure made him actually consider staying.

After a moment, his own desires won out and he told Jordan he would leave and see her again tomorrow. I excused myself and went inside to give them a bit of privacy. I didn't want to see any sort of intimacy between them. The thought of him touching her, and the memory of him pulling her against his body earlier, was repulsive enough. Why she let that brute of a man touch her, I couldn't understand.

I was pleasantly surprised that she didn't leave me waiting for long. After a few moments, she came inside. She crossed the room and took a seat beside me on the sofa. She took my hands in hers. "I'm so sorry for the way he acted. I swear I've talked to him about it many times. He just doesn't know when to stop, and doesn't get that others sometimes don't understand his jokes."

"Jord, I really don't think he likes me very much."

"Oh shush. Of course he does! He knows how important you are to me and how much joy you bring me. Of course he likes you!"

"He has a unique way of showing it."

"I know, darling, I know. I'll talk to him again. I really am sorry he can be so thickheaded sometimes." She rolled her eyes and then went back to smiling at me. "But let's not talk about him. I want to talk about you! I'm so happy for you. I can't believe this is the first I'm hearing about this, though! What changed your mind all of a sudden?"

I wasn't quite sure what to tell her. I was still worried she would think my change of heart was too sudden or too irrational, but without any other ideas of how to explain myself, I opted for the truth. "Honestly, you happened … well, you and James. Seeing how you guys are together and how happy you are with him, it really made me think about what I truly want out of life. It's no secret that I haven't been happy for a long time. I let myself mourn my lost love and my hopes for the future. I kept pushing people away because I was so afraid, afraid of getting hurt like that again. I thought it was us against the world, but seeing you open up your heart and mind to James and seeing you happy made me want to take that risk again."

Jordan's smile widened as she pulled me in for another hug. "Sweetie, that's so wonderful! I'm so happy for you! It might be hard to find someone worthy of you, but I'm sure there will be many willing to try to be worthy." She pulled back, her eyes having a more serious note in them, her face displaying concern. "But are you quite sure this is what you want? You know there really isn't any rush. You're still quite young."

I sighed and broke eye contact, looking down at my feet. I knew she would think it a rash decision. I hoped I was wrong, but of course she thought it was too soon. "I feel like this will be good for me. I really hoped you would feel the same."

"I am so sorry, sweetie. Of course I do! I'm truly happy for you. It was just a sudden change of heart, so I was a little worried you might be acting a bit rashly. But you must know I support you and will do everything in my power to make sure things go how you want them to."

I looked back up at her and gave her a grateful smile. I couldn't explain how badly I had needed to hear that. I was relieved knowing I had her support. "I'm so glad to hear you say that and I truly appreciate your concern, but I know I'm ready. I know there isn't a rush, but I'm done with being alone and feeling alone. I want to find someone I can connect with, someone who cares about me and my happiness and who wants to spend all their time with me. I want someone to make me a priority, someone that will love me for me, not for my looks or for my money, but for me. I'm sick and tired of being alone. I'm ready to put myself back out there again."

"I'm so happy to hear you say that! You truly don't know how much I worried about you. It was hard to see you so unhappy, but I knew you would come around. I didn't want to push you, though. I hoped you would come to that conclusion on your own. But enough about that. Are you really throwing an actual debut?" Her voice had risen with a mix of excitement and disbelief. "When is it? How long do we have to work out the details? Are you sure you want such a big event?"

I couldn't help but laugh at her rushed questions.

"Slow down, Jord! How can one person be expected to answer that many questions all at once?"

She laughed and added with an apologetic grin, "I guess I got a little carried away, but it's not every day your best friend announces her eligibility for marriage to the world!"

I laughed at that and rolled my eyes at her exaggeration. "It's hardly the world, but point taken."

She grinned back at me and said, "Well, if your mother has caught wind of this, it might actually be the world."

I blanched. I hadn't thought there was any reason to attempt to keep my mother in check. I had been content to leave the details to her and was happy to not have to bother with them myself. I hadn't thought there might be consequences to that decision.

Seeing the change in my mood, the worry returned to her face. She knew me well enough to correctly interpret the cause of my anxiety. "You didn't…?"

I slowly nodded. "I didn't even think that it might not be the right thing to do. I mean, of course, she wasn't the first person I spoke to. I told my father first. I knew I should have told you sooner! I was too nervous, but I really should have. I didn't even think there might be a reason to monitor her involvement."

"Yes! You absolutely should have!" She looked at me with a mixture of awe, pity, and concern. "How long has she known? How bad is it?"

"It's been a few weeks, but it can't be that bad, can it? How much could she have possibly done in that small amount of time?"

She gasped and pulled away from me. "Daisy Fay, you mean to tell me you've been keeping this from me for a few weeks?!" I'm sure the guilt and anxiety showed on my face. I hadn't meant to keep things from her. I just hadn't had time to talk to her about it. If I was being honest with myself, I had been putting off telling her. I was too nervous she wouldn't approve and wasn't ready to have her doubts added to my own. She stayed silent for a moment, watching the emotions play across my face. Evidently, she decided I had suffered enough and ended my misery by smirking at me before she continued. She put her hand over her heart. "I truly thought we were closer than that."

I rolled my eyes at her and playfully shoved her. "You truly have a flair for the dramatic. You had me worried you actually felt ill-used."

She laughed and said, "And just where do you imagine I picked up the dramatics?"

I stifled a laugh, donning my most serious face. "Whatever do you mean?" Try as I might, when I met her eye, I could not keep a straight face. We both fell into a fit of laughter. When I caught my breath, I agreed, "Okay, okay, I give. Maybe I'm to blame for part of your dramatics."

"Daisy Fay, you are the most irksome, dramatic, and downright loveable person I know."

"And you're the only person I know who can so flawlessly pull off simultaneously insulting and praising someone."

"Well, would it really be genuine without some form of critique? You know me too well to think I would seek to flatter anyone. I only speak the truth. But you distract me way too easily. I was asking what the plans are."

I sighed, but knew it was best to get the inevitable out of the way. "To be honest, I haven't really been involved in the planning."

Her jaw nearly hit the floor. "You truly mean to say you left your mother, the queen of all things over the top, the woman capable of making a big deal of the most mundane of things, the woman who insists you can do nothing right... you truly mean to say you left her in charge of your debut?"

I shrugged. "It seemed like a good idea at the time. I didn't really want to worry about the details. I'm sure you can imagine how frantic she's been the past few weeks about planning. I was counting myself lucky that it gave me a break from her scrutiny."

"And not once did you think you should have intervened or found out what she has in store for you?"

"It honestly never occurred to me."

"Well, there's no use dwelling on it now." She waved her hand dismissively, as if banishing the thought. "The past is the past. I am sure whatever she has planned will be lovely.

Probably a bit too extravagant for my taste, but maybe that isn't a bad thing. It could be good to kick off your debut in style."

"Maybe you're right. Yes, she absolutely will have planned something over the top, but that might not be a bad thing. I know I'll look stunning in the dress I picked out, so why shouldn't I want people to see it? Plus, you wouldn't believe me when I tell you how happy she's been planning my debut. On the rare occasions I've seen her lately, she's been downright pleasant. I don't think it would be an exaggeration to say she's been kind to me."

The look of disbelief on Jordan's face made me burst into laughter. She quickly fell victim to a fit of laughter as well. Per usual, I was glad to have Jordan around. She never had been one to dwell on things. Positive or negative, she took all things in stride. We talked well into the night like we used to before James came into the picture. The pleasure it gave me to pass the time with her like we had before was indescribable. While I still had some anxiety about my mother's plans, it was far less now that Jordan was by my side to support me.

Chapter Eight

    I had thought the weeks would drag on as I waited in anticipation for the day to come. It turns out I was so nervous that the days quickly dwindled down until, before I knew it, my debut was only a couple days away. I had spent most of my time since finding out about the debut wondering what my future would be like. I had daydreamed countless versions of what my future might look like.

    I had envisioned myself swept off my feet at my debut by a handsome rich stranger. I had imagined numerous men swooning over me at the debut and falling all over themselves to ask me to dance. I had imagined how wonderful I would look in my dress and had envisioned myself dancing the night away. I thought that any man would be lucky if I danced with him more than once. I knew my fantasies to be just that, fantasies, but I thought there was no harm in letting myself dream big. I knew how unlikely it was that I would meet my future husband at my debut, but a girl could dream.

When I told Jordan about my daydreams, she smiled and told me indulgently that anything was possible and she truly hoped I did find the one there. I had expected her to tell me the odds of finding him there were incredibly low or that I had plenty of time to continue enjoying being young before finding the one and settling down, but she didn't. I think she knew even better than I did how much I needed her support and needed her to be in my corner for this. She did everything she could to make me feel less anxious. She even let me pick out her dress.

I felt sure she would've changed her mind when she saw the dress I picked out for her, but she stayed true to her word. There wasn't anything wrong with the dress I picked for her, but I knew it was out of her comfort zone. She wore her dresses loose and flowy. She didn't like to have her movements restricted. This dress hugged her in all the places a woman liked to be hugged. It would have been rather scandalous on another woman, but the composure and grace that Jordan carried herself with would allow her to pull off the dress in a way most others couldn't have.

It was a deep plum colored dress that dropped into a square neckline and hugged her chest and hips, accentuating her curves. The hem of the dress ended just above her knee before flaring out. The outward flare at the bottom served to both make the dress longer and to draw the eye back up. It was a dress that Jordan would normally not have been caught dead in, so I felt distinctly how much she cared about me when she stayed true to her word. I knew the dress would look amazing on her.

Had I been second guessing the decision about her dress, my mother's reaction to it would have reassured me it was the right choice. She didn't hold back from telling me how inappropriate the dress was and how I would need to make Jordan find another. She told me that Jordan was a terrible friend for wanting to take the attention from me on such an important day. When I told her I was the one who had picked out the dress for Jordan, her jaw dropped to the floor. She told me I needed to change my mind and find her a new dress immediately. I declined as politely as I could, but I stuck to my decision. As much as she pressed, pleaded, and tormented, I didn't cave. I knew the dress would make Jordan shine, and it didn't hurt how well it complimented my own dress. My mother's notion that Jordan would steal the spotlight from me was utterly ridiculous. Jordan didn't even like being the center of attention. Even if she had wanted the spotlight, she couldn't have stolen it from me. I would have willingly given it to her. She had done so much for me and had always been there for me. I would have given her anything she asked.

However, as things were, the only place she liked the spotlight was on the golf course. She was less than thrilled with my choice for her dress, but reluctantly agreed to it when she saw my own dress. She must have harbored some of the same concerns as my mother that she would somehow upstage me, since she relaxed a little when she saw my dress next to hers. They complimented each other so well. Jordan was privileged to be the only one allowed a sneak peek at my dress. I hadn't even allowed my mother to see it. It was possible she had ignored my request and seen it anyway, but I highly doubted that.

I'm sure she wouldn't have been able to hold back her critique, shock, and anger. She expected, as everyone else would, that my dress would be a traditional white, but as my dress was the only thing I was in control of and everything else would be according to her precious tradition, I had gone in a different direction with my dress.

When the seamstress found out the dress was for my debut, she tried to talk me out of it. She said we should change the design, or at very least the color, but I didn't budge. I knew the dress would be a little over-the-top and not at all in line with the traditions of the day, but I wasn't the most traditional anyway. I knew my mother felt strongly that I should wear white, but I didn't feel it suited me. The color itself didn't particularly do me any favors, but that wasn't my largest objection. My biggest problem with the color was the pretense of it.

White was the only color worn at a woman's debut because it signified her purity. It signified she was saving herself for her husband. While I had made strides in overcoming my heartbreak and forgiving myself for my indiscretion, I still didn't want to wear white. I refused to make any false pretenses about myself. Even if I had desired to, the way news travels around the town, it would have been a fool's wish. The entire town, more or less, knew of my past. Whether it was the truth of the matter or the false rumors they had heard, no one in town believed my purity still existed. I felt they would subject me to ridicule enough as it was throwing a debut for myself when everyone knew my indiscretion and that any future husband would not be my first. I refused to open myself to further ridicule by adopting any pretense.

If I had learned one thing from being an outcast, it was that the harder you tried to hide and blend in, the more you were ridiculed. If I was going to be the object of their talk anyway, I resolved I would give them something to talk about.

Chapter Nine

Before I knew it, the day had arrived, and my anxiety intensified. I had heard about women having nerves and cold feet before their wedding day and had never understood until now. I was full of anxiety and had a few crazy thoughts of running away before the debut that night. I knew they were crazy. I knew this was the right thing to do, knew it was what I wanted, so why did I feel so nervous? I had a frantic thought that I needed to take a walk. I didn't give it a second thought as I fled from my bedroom, feeling like the room was too small to contain my feelings and give me any space to breathe.

I didn't have long to wait until Jordan would be there. She would know how to help calm me down. She originally wasn't coming until this afternoon, but now I felt keenly how lucky I was that she had arranged to come over early and get ready with me. James would meet her tonight instead of arriving with her like he had wanted. I had worried she would cave and come later with him, but she ignored his requests and was coming early anyway.

I had hoped a walk about the house would help calm me, but I couldn't think straight with all the hustle and bustle going on in preparation for tonight. The staff were in a frenzy of activity and there wasn't a single place throughout the house that was untouched by the frenzy. I sought to sneak out to the gardens to get some fresh air, but upon looking out the window, I noticed the gardens were not spared either. There were staff pruning trees and sweeping the paths clean.

As I watched in awe, I noticed they were hanging garlands on the hedges. I couldn't believe it, only my mother would decorate greenery with even more greenery. I couldn't deny it looked extravagant, but it was ridiculously over the top. With my mother, the event being over the top shouldn't have surprised me, but I was caught off guard nevertheless. Seeing the spectacle that was being made increased my nerves. I needed fresh air and had now seen I wouldn't obtain it in the gardens. Knowing I would need to venture out of the house to find some sense of peace, I headed back to my room to change into more suitable clothing since I hadn't yet changed to face the day.

However, when I reached my hallway, I heard my mother's loud inquiries to the staff about my whereabouts. I knew I would have to submit myself to her whims soon, but I wasn't ready to start the whirlwind I knew the morning would be quite yet. I looked down at my nightdress and weighed my options. It would be downright scandalous to be caught outside our home in this, but I hardly had another choice. Without giving it a second thought, I turned around and hurried away before my mother could see me or my sense of propriety stopped me.

I headed in the direction of the staffing quarters toward one of the many back entrances. I hoped to escape attention, but I stuck out like a sore thumb and several members of the staff, who bid me a confused, "Good morning, Miss," as I passed, had begun to whisper. I was too conspicuous. I was struck with an idea. I went to what I knew to be the most frequented back entrance and looked into what served as a coatroom. There were dozens of coats lining the walls.

As I eyed them, I picked a long tan coat that came just above my ankles. I fastened the coat and straightened my hair the best I could with my fingers. I hoped this would allow me outside without drawing too much attention. I surveyed my work and was nearly satisfied. The coat served its purpose in covering my nightclothes, but I would still likely be spotted by quite a few people. I almost abandoned my venture when my eyes landed on a hat that had been casually hung up with the coats. It was big enough to hide most of my hair and some of my face, but not too large as to be too conspicuous.

I took this as a sign from the universe that I should continue. With an inward sigh of relief, I grabbed the hat and pulled it down over my hair and as much of my face as I could. When I had adjusted the hat and coat to look as casual as possible, I stepped out the back door. I didn't know where I was headed, but I knew I didn't have long. The destination itself was inconsequential, considering my only aim was to get some fresh air. Knowing I wanted to get beyond the gates, I doubled back around the house and out the side entrance.

Seeing people scattered about the road all heading toward town, I headed in that direction myself. As I came around the front of the house, I tried to steer as clear of the fence and gate as possible. I had made it out; I didn't want to be seen now. I crossed to the far side of the road and resolved to pass hurriedly by, but curiosity delayed me. There were a few large parties gathered outside the gate.

I slowed to look at the parties and see if any of the people were known to me. I couldn't understand why they were all gathered outside my home. Upon closer inspection, one party was known to me. It was made up of a few women from town and a couple of my old friends with whom I was no longer on speaking terms. I strained my ears to hear what brought them here. I was only able to hear small snippets of their conversation, but what I did hear was enough to know their opinions of me had not changed.

Not interested in listening to them continue to prattle on about me, I focused my attention on the other group. They didn't look familiar to me, so I took them to be from out of town, from where I didn't know. I heard bits of their conversation. "…felt like we were travelling for days… must be a beauty… all that money." I felt the hairs on the back of my neck stand up as I realized there was a chance they were attending my debut.

I took a renewed interest in the group. As I strained to hear more, I more carefully observed. There were a few men and a couple of women among them, but one man in particular captured my attention. He was standing a little ways apart from the group and was looking with keen interest at my home. He was taller than his companions and had broad shoulders and dark hair. I blushed at the thought that he might be here to meet me. My daydreams about the tall, dark stranger came to mind. My blush deepened as I tried to clear my thoughts. Not wanting to be noticed by the new group, or recognized by the women I knew, I quickened my pace. However, it seemed my earlier luck had run out.

As I was passing the group of strangers, one of them called out, "Hey, you there!" I prayed it wasn't me they were referring to and kept moving. However, the voice called out again. "You there, girl! Stop this instant!"

Surprised at being spoken to in that manner, I stopped. I wasn't used to being spoken to so rudely. While my family money offered me up to higher scrutiny from the town, it protected me from being spoken to harshly or having the cruel things said about me said directly to me. Confused and curious, dreading what might happen, I slowly turned around. When I turned, I realized it had been my tall, dark stranger who had spoken.

Seeing he had my attention, he smirked and said to his companions, "Aha, she does listen."

They snickered at his comment. The couple women both looked me up and down before one turned and whispered to the other. The other outright laughed. I didn't need context to know I disliked them. I gave them my most intimidating glare. The same glare had stopped the staff in their tracks and immediately stolen the voices of gossiping women. However, it had less than the desired effect. The group all started laughing in response.

I was astounded. Never in my life had I been so disrespected by mere strangers. I wanted to give them a piece of my mind, but the worry that the other group of women would recognize me if I made a scene stilled my tongue. The last thing I needed was to be seen appearing to be sneaking back into my own home in my nightclothes.

I turned my glare to the tall, dark stranger, daring him to speak to me like that again. His grin widened when he saw how I was looking at him, evidently delighted to be the object of my scorn. He seemed to reevaluate me, looking me up and down appraisingly. As his eyes raked over my body, he licked his lips. I shuddered at the look in his eye but couldn't help it as my gaze dropped to his lips, tracking the movement of his tongue across his lush, alluring lips.

He cleared his throat, startling me out of my thoughts. I quickly rose my eyes back to meet his, hoping my distraction had escaped his notice. From the smirk on his face, it seems today was not my lucky day. I internally grimaced at my lack of self-control. I knew I would die of embarrassment later while replaying that moment. However, I refused to show weakness in front of these people who had already made me the butt of their jokes.

I squared my shoulders back, assumed a haughty look of bored arrogance, cocked my head to the side, and asked, "Well?"

He grinned wider at my tone. Again, that wasn't the desired effect. I couldn't fail to notice how his eyes lit up when he grinned. I'm sure that grin would have been enough to make most women swoon, but I wasn't so easily tamed after being mistreated.

Without taking his eyes from me, he addressed his companions again. "It seems this bitch has a bark."

How dare he! I had never been spoken to in such a manner in my life! I couldn't find the words to express my anger.

One woman was quick to add, "And far too much pride, considering her sense of fashion."

I had been so indignant and angered by their remarks, I had forgotten how I was dressed. They must have believed me to not be anyone of importance. I wondered if I should bother introducing myself if only to see the startled, guilty, horrified looks that would be sure to cross their faces when they learned who they were disrespecting. I had half a mind to do so, consequences be damned, but before I could make up my mind, one of the other men spoke.

"It seems in Louisville they give their servants a good deal more liberty than would be considered proper in New Orleans."

The tall, dark stranger hadn't taken his eyes from me. "If we were staying longer, I should have rather liked to teach this one some manners. It's a pity we don't have the time, but no matter, I am sure Louisville's sweetheart will keep me well entertained while I'm here."

My eyes widened in surprise at his mention of my former nickname and at the arrogance in his claim. I wondered if he could really be talking about me, if he really thought that Daisy Fay of the Louisville Fays would be so easily won.

He noticed my look of surprise and said, "Before you so rudely disrespected your betters..." He paused a long moment, looking at me challengingly.

I glanced past him to see if the other group of women were still there. I hoped they had wandered off so I could give him a piece of my mind without consequence. I deflated when I saw they were still there. I resigned myself to stay silent and ignore his slight. I internally bristled at the notion that he would ever be referred to as my better, but I held back. The consequences of an outburst far outweighed my indignation.

His smile widened as he continued, "That's a good girl." To his companions, without looking away from me, he added, "Learning her place already... What a smart girl." I heard the snickering of his companions but refused to break eye contact with him to see their faces. "As I was saying, I called you over here to hear about my future wife, the sweetheart of Louisville."

It was a strange experience hearing myself talked about in such a manner. I should have known they were in town for my debut. I wasn't surprised that my mother had extended invitations as far and wide as she could, but it surprised me they made the trip all the way from New Orleans. It occurred to me to be concerned about just how many people would turn up, how many invitations my mother might have sent, and what was being said about me both around town and apparently around the country. What could this man have possibly heard to make it worth his while to travel all the way to Louisville from New Orleans to meet me?

Furthermore, he was arrogantly proclaiming he would marry me before ever having laid eyes on me. I couldn't believe he had arrived already planning to marry me. My blood ran cold as it occurred to me that it was quite possible many of the other men coming would have the same notions in their head. I would have to turn down so many. In my experience, men didn't take kindly to being rejected. Would any of them take the rejection well? I realized then just how much more I had agreed to than I had previously thought.

I realized I had been silent for a bit too long, when I noticed them all staring at me. I took a breath and considered maybe it wasn't me he was talking about. After all, it had been a long while since anyone had called me the sweetheart of Louisville. I decided to play dumb and asked, "Who?"

He rolled his eyes in annoyance at me and, turning to his entourage, said, "She must be more daft than I thought. Does she need it spelled out for her?" He turned back to me and slowly pointed at my home and drawled, "Louis...ville's sweet...heart. She lives in that big house behind us, the one you were walking away from."

The evidence seemed undeniable he meant me, but for lack of anything better to say, I asked, "You mean Daisy Fay?"

"Is that her name? Daisy? I thought it was Rose." He shrugged. "One flower or another, it hardly matters-"

Unable to stop myself, I blurted out, "I think it would matter very much to the lady in question."

He looked curiously at me and smiled. "You aren't wrong. I'll remember that. Tell me, what type of lady is she?"

I pondered over what to say. I settled on, "She's a kind, loving person who-"

He cut me off, shaking his head in disgust. "No, no, no. I asked what she looked like. Is she as beautiful as they say? Is she worthy of being my wife?"

I rolled my eyes. "You did not! You asked what type of lady she is." I couldn't hold back, despite knowing I was likely saying too much. I added, "And I can assure you I know her to be a lady who wants to be admired for more than her looks."

He chuckled. "Saucy little thing, aren't we? How anyone of importance puts up with your impertinence, I don't know. But you told me what I needed to know. Her looks are to be admired. I had heard as much and hoped to see for myself. Maybe this is her now." He looked over my shoulder at what I can only assume was an approaching woman. I didn't break eye contact with him. "A pretty face, and those legs go for miles." I saw his eyes move up and down, roaming over the woman's body, likely making the poor girl feel as violated as I had.

I knew if I turned, he would think me either weak for looking away from him or jealous now that I was not the object of his attention. More than likely, he would think I needed to see who it was that stole his attention from me. That his attention on me was unwanted wouldn't have entered his mind. This man who seemed to believe himself to be God's gift to women, able to make a wife of whoever he pleased, would not have imagined that the servant girl he thought was in front of him didn't like his attention. I refused to give him further satisfaction and kept my eyes trained on his face.

He looked a bit longer before his smile turned a bit sour. "Her curves leave much to be desired. Oh well, you can't be greedy about these things. A pretty face, long legs, and, most importantly, rich. She'll make a good wife." Curiosity got the best of me since I knew he wasn't talking about me, who he had already referred to as his future wife. I turned around and what I saw simultaneously drained the color from my face and made my blood boil.

The woman who he had so wantonly judged and violated right in front of me was the one and only, my dear

Jordan. Had I not been so worried she would accidentally reveal me to the strangers, I wouldn't have been able to hold my tongue from giving this man a piece of my mind. Just who did he think he was to so crudely and harshly judge my precious Jordan?

At a loss for what to do, I stood frozen in place. As she approached, she looked past the group, saying, "Excuse me, beg your pardon, but I am wanted inside." It was just like Jordan to be earlier than planned. She knew I would need her today, but she couldn't have imagined how badly. Nor could she have known how bad her timing was at this moment. She went to move past the strangers and pass through the gate.

The entire party turned to watch her enter, their curiosity peaked. With them turned, I was directly in her line of sight. I feared she would see me and accidentally give me away, but she wasn't looking my way. She continued to move past, but as she did, the tall stranger stepped toward her and bowed. She looked startled, and I saw the barely contained laughter in her eye. As she looked on in amusement, she saw me.

She gasped in surprise, looking at me. She must have seen the color drain from my face. As subtly as I could, I shook my head, signaling to her not to say anything. The stranger must have mistaken her reaction to me as a compliment to himself. I was sure he believed his appearance was enough to take a woman's breath away.

He straightened himself and said, "Marcos Hortense the Third. Charmed, I'm sure." He reached for her hand that she hadn't moved from her side. He took her hand and put his lips to it. His attention was so focused on her, he failed to notice he didn't have her attention.

She was focused on me, with a look on her face that was a cross between confusion and amusement. She cocked her head at me and indicated him with her eyes. I knew as surely as if she had spoken that she was asking, "Is this man for real?" I don't know how she held in her laughter. Jordan didn't think highly of the old traditions, and I knew her to think his manner was much too over the top.

He missed the entirety of our interaction and added, "Pleased to meet you, Daisy, and may I say you look even more radiant than they described."

Her confusion multiplied, and she turned to me. "I'm sorry. I think there must be some confusion. I'm not Daisy. Daisy-"

Unsure about what she planned to say, I cut her off. "Daisy lives right here and is probably expecting you any minute, Miss."

Marcos looked flustered for the first time. "I am so sorry. It was an honest mistake. I had heard tales of Daisy's beauty and when I saw you, I couldn't help but think you must be her."

Jordan, who had still been looking at me, glanced at him and told him it was quite alright. She looked back to me for direction. This time the group noticed and looked on with confusion and intrigue. Marcos looked at me with renewed interest.

Jordan must have sensed my distress because she stepped closer to me. "Now what in the Heavens are you doing out here? I'm sure you're needed inside, too."

I felt some relief that she hadn't used my name, but I needed to make sure she understood. "Of course! I know Daisy must require more help inside."

She shot me a curious look, but, thankfully, played along. "Of course! Daisy couldn't possibly get ready without her..." She paused at a loss for words

"Maid!" I supplied.

She picked up where she left off. "Of course! Daisy couldn't possibly hope to get ready without her maid, her dear-" She trailed off again.

"Pam," I blurted out.

She grinned. "Of course, Pam, you really must come with me at once. We don't have a minute to lose! There is so much to be done! You'll have to excuse us both."

Marcos, clearly the ringleader of his group, spoke up for them, saying, "Of course. I wouldn't dream of keeping you away from Daisy for another moment. I hope to have the pleasure of her company soon and would not dream of prolonging my wait any longer. I do hope I might have the pleasure of meeting with you again?" He looked to Jordan, who replied that she would be at the debut. He looked at me and said, "Farewell, Pam. It was nice meeting you."

Jordan turned and walked away, motioning for me to follow her. I started to go but was stopped for a moment when Marcos grabbed my arm and pulled me back toward him. I was caught off guard for a moment, which was all he needed to whisper in my ear, "Until next time. If we meet again, I'll be sure to teach you some manners." I pulled back but he held tight. He leered at me, looking me up and down again, making me shudder. My eyes were again drawn to his lips as his tongue swept across them. "And I can assure you I won't give you the luxury of hiding such a body from me."

I shuddered and yanked my arm out of his grip.

Jordan, having noticed I wasn't behind her, stopped. She saw me hurrying after her now and shot me a questioning look. "Later," was all I could say. It was both a request and promise.

She nodded but as we hurried up the stairs, I felt her eyes on me, asking all the questions she had not yet said out loud. But I was far too anxious and out of breath to explain. I knew she was dying of curiosity, which was understandable for what she witnessed. I would have had questions too had the roles been reversed. However, as we hurried through the corridors, avoiding the staff when possible, she did me the courtesy of not asking.

After she realized we were heading away from my room, she looked back and forth, checking the coast was clear, before pulling me into an alcove off the hallway. She looked panicked and asked, "Are you okay? I know there isn't time now. I just need to know if you're okay?"

I nodded, not trusting my voice but needing her to believe me. I was okay. I really was just overwhelmed. Part of that would be fixed when these clothes were returned and I was safely back in my room getting ready.

I hadn't had time to process the interaction with Marcos, and didn't even want to think about how many prospective suitors like him might turn up tonight. I took a deep breath and told her, "Truly I'm okay. Please don't worry. I'm just really overwhelmed about tonight. I needed some fresh air, but my mother was already on the hunt for me."

"Ah yes, that explains the disguise."

I laughed despite myself. "I think it's some of my best work, don't you?" I twirled in front of her while laughing. She smiled widely, rolling her eyes at me in mock annoyance. Her smile helped restore some of my sense of calm. "I think I should scrap the dress and wear this instead, don't you?" I twirled once more before stopping to face her. At the look on her face, I burst out laughing, and she quickly fell victim, too.

After a moment, Jordan regained her composure and took control, asking, "Where is it we're going, anyway?"

"I have to return these," I said, gesturing to my outfit, "before they are missed and before I make more of a scene."

She laughed. "My dear, if you discard all your clothes, you will make much more of a scene than you have already."

I laughed and playfully pushed her. "You know I meant just the coat and hat."

"Of course, but what a sight that would be. Where did you find those, anyway?"

"The staff coatroom. I really hope they haven't been missed. I have to return them as soon as possible and get back to my room. By now, it's entirely likely my mother has everyone in town, including the police, on the lookout for me." I had said that in what I meant to be a joking tone, but Jordan saw through my attempt at being lighthearted and told me to take a deep breath. I did. She was right, it helped a little.

She smiled at me and brushed a stray hair off my face before stepping back and taking a look at me. "That won't do."

She took the hat off my head and ran her fingers through my hair, messing it up more than it already was. She gestured for my coat. I went to unbutton it, but my fingers were still trembling. She waved my hands away and put her fingers to work on my buttons. She expertly finessed the buttons and pulled the coat off my left shoulder and then more slowly off my right. She looked at me curiously in my nightclothes. I blushed, feeling her eyes on me. My nightclothes were a bit tighter than I normally would wear, showing more of my body than I would normally be comfortable with in public. Knowing Jordan's style to be more modest, I knew it was something she would not be caught dead in, never mind seen in public in.

I waited for her to say something to that effect since she rarely held her tongue, but as her eyes took in the entirety of my body in my nightgown, she stayed quiet. The only sound was her pulling in a quick breath. She leaned closer, staring into my eyes and, after a moment, tenderly brushed another strand of hair from my face with her fingertips. She looked into my eyes for another long moment . When she pulled away, she took the coat with her. I felt out of breath and confused. My stomach was doing flips. *I must be more nervous than I thought about tonight.*

She looked me up and down once more, much more quickly this time, and said with a smirk, "You're so lucky no one outside saw under that coat. You would have had to beat off the men with a stick to get back home." I laughed a little, but her comment reminded me of the men I would have to meet and disappoint tonight, making me nervous all over again. She saw the look on my face and quickly added, "Don't worry, you know I have your back and as your self-appointed bodyguard," she winked at me, making me laugh, "I won't let anything happen to you. I will single-handedly beat away all the men chasing you if you want. But we've been here for too long. Hurry to your room before your mother finds you outside of your rooms in only your dressing gown."

I blanched at the thought and turned to go. At the last moment, I remembered the coat and hat, but when I turned back, Jordan was already rushing down the hallway with them in the direction of the coatroom. Not for the first time that day, I couldn't help but think how lucky I was to have Jordan by my side.

Chapter Ten

Jordan

As I rushed the hat and coat back to the coatroom, I couldn't help but appreciate the hilarity of the situation. I doubted whether I would ever forget the image of her disguised in that ridiculously large hat and giant coat outside her own gate. I was barely able to hold in my laughter until I noticed the look on her face.

Something had upset her, or, more likely, someone. Personally, I thought he seemed harmless enough, but Daisy was never one to jump to judgments, so I was inclined to believe her. She always gave everyone too many chances and the benefit of the doubt, so if *she* didn't like him, that spoke volumes.

My own judgments were always more decisive and harsh in nature than hers. She was too kindhearted of a person to see the world for what it was. She always looked for and found the best in people. If she, of all people, had taken a disliking to him, then I would have to keep a close eye on him.

Well, him and every other man in the place. The more I thought about tonight, the more I didn't like it. I would have to be everywhere at once, but I would be sure she was happy and safe. She would need it. She was sweet and caring, but too naive. A person with a heart as big as hers needed someone to protect them from the world.

I had learned quickly that in our friendship, I was going to have to be her protector, otherwise I was sure the world would take advantage of her.

When I was younger, I had always looked up to her, thinking how lucky I was that such an older, wiser, beautiful, popular girl was willing to spend time with me. I would have done anything to be her friend, to spend more time with her.

She had occasionally invited me to spend time with her and her friends, but I never liked her friends. I could see all too clearly that they were only around her for her popularity and her money. I hoped they might disprove my theory, but my judgments were seldom wrong. I wondered what it was she saw in them. I wondered why she let them so obviously use her. I couldn't make sense of it. Then everything changed.

Her whole life, and mine as well, changed when her lieutenant left.

When I heard the rumors around town about how she had run away with an officer, I couldn't explain the deep sense of loss I felt at hearing she might be gone. I worried about her and hoped she would be okay. I hoped she was happy.

A couple days passed, and I heard more rumors that the Fays were broke, that she was left behind and ill-used by an officer. I couldn't shake my worry for her and the feeling that she might need a friend.

I had no delusions about our friendship. I knew it was one sided and that I cared way more for her than she did for me, but if she needed someone, I would be there. I doubted very much that her 'friends' would do the same.

When I entered the Fays' mansion, the halls were empty and the house was quiet. Much quieter than a large house should be. I had wandered the halls, guessing at the directions to turn. After only a few wrong guesses, the door I had knocked on swung open. *She's here!* I remember thinking. I was shocked at how distraught she had looked. It killed me to see her like that. I couldn't put into words how worried I was about her. I couldn't even explain why I was there.

I knew she was surprised to see me, and that was fair. I was probably the last person she expected to come knocking, but I had a feeling she had needed a friend, and I wouldn't leave her alone in her time of need. Eventually, I did all I could think to do. I took her hands in my own, and looked into her eyes, letting her see the whole of my concern for her and asked, "Daisy, what happened to you?"

From that day on, we were inseparable. Seeing how broken she was that day, I vowed I would do everything in my power to make sure she never felt like that again. I wouldn't let anyone hurt her like that again. God help anyone who did. They would have to deal with me.

Lately, it seemed like my own skepticism about the world was starting to rub off on her. I had mixed feelings about that. I worried about her and wanted her to be wiser to the ways of the world so she could protect herself, but I couldn't imagine losing the ray of hope she brought to the world.

She was usually so determined to see the best in everyone. I couldn't imagine what made this Marcos different. I had tried to ask her, but she hadn't wanted to discuss it yet. I might've pressed her more, but I had to admit I was distracted by being so close to her. I was sure I would be thinking about that for a long while.

There was something about her body being inches from mine that made it hard to think. I had had to fight to keep my fingers steady as I worked the buttons to remove the coat from her body. I had slipped the jacket from her left shoulder and then started to take it off her right but was in shock when I saw what she was wearing, or rather, how little she was wearing.

I couldn't control my thoughts. I pictured myself undressing her further, running my hands over her body, kissing her neck. Kissing her. I pulled in a quick breath and leaned in closer. A moment later, I caught myself. *What was I doing?* This was Daisy we were talking about. My sweet, innocent Daisy. I couldn't believe my thoughts, and was appalled at my own actions as she looked up at me wide-eyed with a questioning look on her face. I couldn't believe the line I had almost crossed.

I was so distracted with my thoughts that I walked by the coatroom. I only noticed when I was already halfway down the hallway. I quickly turned back and slipped the hat and coat back where they belonged. Thankfully, I wasn't noticed. I wouldn't have been able to answer any questions and didn't really have the time for delay. I had to make it back to Daisy quickly. She needed me. Her mother was difficult on the best of days. Today, I knew her mother would be unbearable, and I knew how nervous Daisy was. She needed her best friend.

I still couldn't believe how close I had come to crossing a line that couldn't be uncrossed. She was my best friend. She trusted me! I couldn't do anything that might jeopardize that. Besides, I knew Daisy was as straight as they came. And I was dating James.

James! How could I have forgotten about him!

Things had been a little weird between us lately. He had been pushing me to stop spending as much time with Daisy. I loved spending time with James, and I really cared about him, but I couldn't believe he would ask that of me. I wouldn't abandon her like everyone else in her life had. As long as she needed me, I would always be there for her. He kept saying our friendship was unnatural, that I cared about her more than him. He seemed to be pushing me to choose between them. I'd told him I wouldn't do that and that they'd have to get along. I hoped I wouldn't have to make that choice. I hoped he wouldn't push me, because in my heart I already knew. If I did have to choose, he wouldn't be my choice.

I cared about James and liked how things were going with him. I was more attracted to him than I had ever been to any man, and we got along great together ... when Daisy wasn't around anyway. He always insisted on tormenting her. I wondered now if he might've suspected the truth, that I was far more interested in women than I was in men, but until that day, I hadn't let myself think about Daisy in that way. Yes, there were times when those thoughts had entered my mind, but I had always immediately shut them down. I never indulged them, until that day. But I knew I couldn't let myself.

She was different. She was my best friend, and I knew she wouldn't feel the same. She was incurably straight and incredibly innocent. She trusted me, and she needed my protection. I wouldn't break her trust in me for the world. Besides, she needed someone who could guarantee her a comfortable future that she was accustomed to. With her reputation in tatters already, she needed a man who could provide for her and restore her into society's good graces. I can't say I understood why she cared about being in society's good graces, and she would have never admitted it, but it was easy to see how it pained her to no longer be loved by Louisville. I hoped tonight would help fix that and bring her all the happiness she deserved.

Chapter Eleven

Daisy

I made it back to my room without incident and had a few moments peace before my mother came bursting in, dragging a few maids behind her. "There you are!" she cried. "I've been looking all over for you! No matter; no time to spare." She turned to the maids and directed one to draw me a bath, one to fix up my room, and one to prepare my jewelry and dress. She turned back to me. "I don't expect to see you again until you're ready, and don't you dare dream of leaving this room again until you are." Not wanting to push my luck any further than I already had, I simply nodded. This must have satisfied her, since, after sending me a look that said she meant business, she turned on her heel and swept out of the room.

I exhaled a breath I didn't know I was holding and flopped on my bed. I laid there for a few moments before hearing a high-pitched little cough. I looked up to see the maids all looking worriedly at me. It seemed my mother's anxiety had infected the staff. I sighed and followed the maid to the bath she had drawn.

Jordan

I quietly entered Daisy's room, not wanting to disturb her, but it turns out I needn't have worried since the maids were already there hustling about.

I sat down on her bed and settled in to wait. I figured she might be a while. After all, a girl only debuts once. I chuckled to myself. This whole thing seemed pretty ridiculous and outdated to me, but I approved of anything that made Daisy happy. I couldn't believe she'd been so worried about telling me. She had to have known I would be happy for her. I had been so worried about her lately. It hadn't escaped my notice how sad she'd been. I highly doubted any of her dates noticed, but there was a somber note to her smile that broke my heart every time I saw it.

I heard the inner door open and looked up, smiling at her. A moment later, I noticed what she was wearing.

I couldn't stop my eyes from trailing down her body. Her dressing gown clung to her damp body, leaving nothing to the imagination. She continued to stand there, making no move to cover up more. I couldn't stop my eyes from lingering.

What was with her today? Throughout the entirety of our friendship, I hadn't seen nearly as much of her as I was today. A tiny piece of my mind wondered if she might be doing this on purpose. But I knew that wasn't the case.

Daisy would never be able to guess I might appreciate her body as much as any man would. I forced my eyes up to her face. When I saw her staring at me wide-eyed and questioning,

I blushed. She looked confused, but excused herself, presumably to go cover up more.

A million thoughts raced through my head. How could I possibly explain my reaction to her? She was being more than kind about how weird I was being, but I was sure she must be confused. What would I say to her? I needed to pull myself together. I took a few deep breaths and tried to calm my racing heart. This was Daisy. I couldn't be thinking these things about my best friend. I had to get ahold of myself. I would pull myself together by the time she returned. I had to.

Daisy

It felt like I was only in the water for a few minutes before it turned cold, but it must have been longer because by the time I got out, dried off, and made it back into the main bedchamber, Jordan had returned.

I saw her smile as I walked in, then she took in my clothing, or lack-there-of. I hadn't expected her so soon, so I had simply thrown on and loosely tied my dressing gown. The gown was shorter than my nightgown she had seen me in earlier, and the dampness of my skin made the gown cling to my curves. Had I known she was coming so soon, I would have made more of an attempt for modesty, not that I minded. It was just Jordan, but since she always dressed so modestly, I felt self-conscious. I watched her eyes trail down my body and expected her to make another joke about how she would have to chase men away from me tonight, but she didn't say anything. There was what I could only describe as an odd look in her eye and a tension I couldn't quite identify.

As her eyes made their way back up to my face, she must have seen my confusion. She broke out in a blush and averted her eyes from me. I didn't know what to make of that. Throughout the entirety of our friendship, I couldn't recall ever seeing Jordan blush. I felt that she must have been embarrassed by my lack of modesty, so I smiled gently at her and told her I would be right back. I went back into the bathing chamber and dried off more and donned a more modest and form-covering dressing gown before re-entering. When I returned, the blush was gone from her face and so was the odd look from her eyes. She seemed back to her old self.

The next few hours flew by as we surrendered ourselves into the capable hands of my maids. We talked and laughed and wondered about what the night would bring. I could tell from the look she gave me that she wanted to ask about this morning, but she knew it wasn't a conversation to be had in front of the maids, so it would have to wait. I was grateful once again for her discretion and her uncanny ability to know what I was thinking at all times.

Luckily, we had plenty to discuss with tonight looming over my head. I was beyond nervous, and Jordan, wanting to ease my anxiety, promised me she would keep a close eye on me tonight and intervene with unwanted suitors if necessary. I thanked her profusely. Hearing that she would be by my side eased much of my anxiety.

Before we knew it, my mother was back. I didn't know the time, but looking outside, I guessed it was midafternoon. It was later than I had thought. She took one look at me, still in my dressing gown, and demanded we hurry and stop fooling around. I was sitting in front of my vanity with one of my maids working on my hair and the other on my face. I looked at my mother questioningly through the mirror, wondering what more she wished me to be doing, but I was smarter than to ask. I said we would hurry.

She hurried back out of the room, no doubt to go make sure everything else was in order. As she left, she muttered something about incompetence. I wasn't sure whether it was myself or the maids who she supposed incompetent, but it hardly mattered. We could go no faster if we tried.

I wanted my hair loosely hanging around my shoulders in curls. My hair had grown long and fell halfway down my back. I knew leaving it long with curls would look stunning, but, traditionally, a debutant would wear her hair in an updo. There were some that didn't, but my mother said it was classless of them to wear their hair loose to their own debut. My mother had instructed the maids to do an updo. I wasted half my time getting ready pleading with them to let me leave my hair down how I liked it.

After much prodding, begging, and pleading, the maids and I agreed on a compromise. They would pull about half of my hair away from my face to the back of my head and twist that together in a braided updo, leaving the other half of my hair in loose curls down my back. I was thrilled with how well it turned out. The maids wanted to put jewels in my hair, but I thought that was sure to be too much with the dress. I decided, against their wishes, also known as my mother's wishes since she had given them strict orders ahead of time, to forgo any adornments in my hair. I didn't want to take attention away from what I considered to be a masterpiece of a dress.

To my maids' relief, I was amendable to pairing a necklace with the dress. I hadn't originally wanted jewelry since I thought it too might take away from the dress, but I knew my mother would truly throw a fit if I didn't have any jewelry on. As she had told me a few times already today, "Today is about showing off your best assets, my dear, not the least of which is our money." To her, the idea that I would choose to forgo wearing any of our best jewels was abhorrent.

I already knew how upset she was going to be when she saw my dress for the first time, so I decided to take a look at the jewelry. I doubted anything would work with the dress, but I tried to keep an open mind as the maids brought in the jewels and laid them out on my vanity. As my eyes passed over the array of rubies, garnet, topaz, amethyst, and diamonds, I ruled each one out in turn.

The rubies and garnet I ruled out immediately, as they would clash with my dress. I ruled out the topaz, since I wasn't a fan of its brownish hue. I gave some consideration to the amethyst but ultimately decided the combination of the purple with my dress would be too much for the eye. The diamonds didn't seem right either. They were beautiful, of course, but I felt they were too classic. Everyone who owned them would be wearing diamonds tonight.

I frowned at the selection and asked if there were any other options. The maids all rushed away to look while Jordan and I took another look at the jewels on the table. I picked up the diamonds and held them up to my neck. I cocked my head to the side, considering. After a moment, I decided my first instinct was right. They wouldn't do. Just as I felt it was hopeless and I would have to deal with yet another instance of my mother's wrath, the maids returned. Two of them were holding wrapped packages, but only one approached me.

She unwrapped the package, which was holding the finest strings of pearls we owned. Pearls were a favorite of mine. I never left the house without some sort of pearls adorning my person. I considered the pearls. It was possible they might work. I took my favorite strand of the options and held it to my neck to envision how they would fall with the dress. I turned from side to side to see how they would move with me and catch the light.

After a few moments of careful consideration, during which the maids held their breaths, I put down the pearls. I had the same objection to pearls as I did to the diamonds. They would be everywhere tonight. On a night where I wanted to stand out more than usual, I didn't think the pearls would add anything to the look I had already crafted with my dress. I would wear my pearl earrings, but that was a given, as I rarely took them off.

I turned to the maids and shook my head. "None of these are quite right. I don't think I'll be wearing any jewels tonight."

The maids sighed and exchanged a look of uncertainty. I took that to be their concern over how my mother would take the news. I knew it wouldn't be well. However, that wasn't the case. The maid with the other package looked reluctant but stepped forward. "Miss Daisy, we know your mother wouldn't approve of how bold this piece is and were hoping you would like one of the others, but since you didn't, we thought maybe this piece might be more what you were looking for."

I was incredibly touched they cared enough to present me with an option they knew my mother wouldn't be pleased by. She stepped closer and held out the package in the palms of her hands, gesturing for me to do the honors of unwrapping it. The maids had all seen my dress, so I hoped this piece would at least not clash with the dress. I resolved to more highly consider the piece simply because the maids had put their necks on the line by showing it to me. Their dedication to me was touching. I slowly unwrapped the piece, praying it would be something I would, at the very least, like.

When I uncovered the necklace, I was in awe. The light coming in through the window hit the necklace, making the room awash in dancing color. The blue from the sapphires and the green from the emeralds chased each other around the room in an enthralling dance that was enchanting to watch, but the real enchantment was the necklace itself. The necklace took my breath away. It was truly a statement piece that would not only compliment my dress and enchant anyone who saw it, but it would also serve my mother's purpose of flaunting our money.

I moved my loose curls and had another of the maids fasten the necklace around my neck so I could see myself in the mirror. When I looked in the mirror, I knew it was perfect. Sapphires and emeralds of different sizes and shapes were interspersed in two rows. The larger gems were teardrop shaped, and the smaller were round. The intertwined sapphires and emeralds chased each other to a deep point that would fall right above the neckline of my dress. At the center point, where all the gems converged, were two large teardrop gems, one emerald and the other sapphire. They were completely surrounded by small, circular gems. The necklace on its own was breathtaking, but together with my dress, the effect would be indescribable. I would be the envy of every woman in the room and the object of desire to any man who saw me. There would be love songs written about me tonight thanks to this necklace and my dress.

I turned to face Jordan and was rewarded with the awed look on her face. "What do you think?" It wasn't often that Jordan was found at a loss for words as she was now.

She took her time tearing her eyes away from the necklace to look back up at me. When she met my eyes, she said breathlessly, with wonder in her eyes, "It's perfect."

A moment later, a maid rushed into the room. She frantically asked how much longer we would need to be ready. My mother must have sent her. I was grateful to be spared my mother's wrath, which I knew would have been provoked by the fact that neither Jordan nor I were in our dresses yet. I gulped and looked at Jordan, calculating roughly how long we would need, and told the maid an hour. The panicked look on her face told me we didn't have an hour, so I asked hesitantly, "A half hour?" From the relief on her face, this seemed to be the right answer. She urged for haste and rushed back out of the room.

The moment she was gone, the other maids sprung into action. They wanted to start with me, but I insisted Jordan needed to be helped first. She still needed to go find James and make it to the ballroom in time for my entrance. I had a bit more time. Plus, I was dying to see how her dress looked on her. I had been praying she wouldn't hate the dress. I knew it would look amazing on her, but I hoped she agreed.

The maids reluctantly agreed and brought out her dress. In record time, they had her all dressed and ready to go. The moment I saw the plum against Jordan's complexion, I knew I had made the right choice. The deep plum contrasted beautifully with her tan skin and made her blonde hair look lighter in comparison. My eyes moved down appraisingly to take in the rest of the dress. It looked even more stunning on her than I had imagined. The dress hugged her in all the right places, accentuating her usually less pronounced curves. The flare at the bottom served its purpose perfectly in drawing the eye back to her curves. My eyes passed over her once more before heading back to meet her eye.

It was nearly perfect, but there was something missing. I couldn't quite put my finger on what it was. My eyes stopped at the neckline. Her neck was bare. I looked back at the pile of jewels on the vanity. I quickly dismissed most of them, knowing she wouldn't want to wear what she considered flashy jewelry. I wasn't sure what she needed until my eyes fell on my favorite strand of pearls. They were perfect. Normally, I wouldn't dream of parting with them, but they would be as safe with Jordan as they would have been with me; maybe safer because she knew how precious they were to me. I hoped she wouldn't protest too strongly about borrowing them. It was just what the dress needed. Tearing my eyes away from her neckline and back up to her face, I saw a poorly suppressed smile on her lips.

"You love it, you know you do."

She rolled her eyes and put more effort into suppressing her smile. "I told you before, it isn't my style and the color is flashy."

"That may be true, but the truth remains, you love it."

"Okay, maybe I like it a bit more than I thought I would."

"You might not be ready to admit you love it yet, but I have just the thing for you."

Her eyebrows rose as she asked, "And just what would that be? What else would you see done to me tonight?"

I just giggled and told her to close her eyes. She rolled her eyes again but was indulgent and slowly closed her eyes. I moved her to the vanity and took the strand of pearls in my hand. They felt cool to the touch. I always loved how they felt against my skin and wondered if she would like them as much as I did. I moved behind her and pushed her hair away from her neck. I softly snaked the pearls around her neck. She gasped in surprise, adopting an exaggerated pout.

"You didn't warn me it would be cold. Are you quite finished yet? I would like my sight back."

I couldn't help the soft laugh that escaped my lips. I turned my attention to the clasp. She was always quite impatient. "It's hardly been a minute…"

Thinking she was truly the most impatient person I had ever met, I redoubled my efforts to secure the clasp. After a moment, I secured it. I took a small step back to see the effect for myself. It was a breathtaking combination. I smiled widely. She would love it.

"Okay now, open." She smiled indulgently before slowly, dramatically opening her eyes. I watched her eyes light up as she took in the sight in the mirror. She met my eyes in the mirror with a look of surprise.

"Wow," she said under her breath.

"You really are a vision in that dress. I knew it was perfect." I noticed the clasp had moved a little to the front, so I lightly moved the clasp back into place. "It just needed a little something, but now it's-"

"Perfect," she uttered in the same breathless tone of wonder.

My smile stretched so wide I thought my face would likely be sore later. I was so happy she loved it. She must have really loved it, since she seldom ever admitted she was wrong. She really didn't like to be wrong or to admit her feelings, so her admitting she loved it brought me a tremendous amount of joy. I couldn't take my eyes off her. She looked incredible, but neither I, nor the dress and pearls, could take all the credit for that. The smile on her face was what really made her shine. I kept looking at her, basking in the glow of her happiness and likely would have continued to do so for who knows how long if one of the maids hadn't cleared her throat.

The spell was broken. I tore my eyes away from Jordan and looked to the maid. She looked apologetically at me, saying, "I'm sorry, Miss Daisy, but we must finish getting you ready at once. There isn't time to spare."

I sighed, but I knew they were right. I turned back to Jordan. "You should probably get a head start so you can find James." I really wished she didn't have to go, but I knew she did.

She made to move for the door but hung back a moment, hesitating. "Are you sure you don't need me?" She had a look on her face that told me she felt guilty about leaving me. I didn't want her to leave, but knew she wanted to go find James. I had already held her back longer than we had planned.

I smiled at her. "Dear, I will always need you, but right now I'm in good hands. I know you must be dying to see James, and it would be a crime to deprive him another moment of the privilege of seeing you in that dress."

She laughed at that but met my eyes again, looking for any sign that I wasn't okay with her leaving. As much as I wanted her all to myself the entire night, that wouldn't be fair to her, and as much as I disliked James, I knew it wouldn't be fair to him, either. Despite my own feelings, I often had to remind myself that Jordan truly cared for him.

With this in mind, I added, "I promise I'll be fine. I'll be right along soon. You won't be able to miss me. I'll be the one making the grand entrance."

We both laughed at that, and she rushed back and wrapped me in a hug. After what felt like far too soon, she pulled back. "I'll see you soon. You're going to be great out there, and I can't wait to see you in that dress. You're going to look incredible. Hearts will shatter tonight." I was spared trying to find words for my gratitude when not a moment later, she turned and rushed out of the room. I turned back to the maids and once again surrendered myself into their waiting hands.

Chapter Twelve

Jordan

I didn't like leaving her, but it was already later than planned and I guessed James probably wasn't happy. It was getting harder and harder to deal with his moods lately. It seemed anytime I brought up Daisy or Daisy came with us anywhere, he was in a foul mood. I knew he wasn't crazy about her, but he was really taking things too far. If he couldn't at least pretend to get along with her and be civil toward her, I really didn't know how much longer I could keep this up.

I was worried about what would happen if I ended things, though. The rumors about me had started at an early age. I was too much of a tomboy. I was too loud and proud. I was too manly. I was too much, and especially in a place like Louisville, people talked. But James coming around put a stop to that. I could tell most of the town was surprised that anyone would be interested in me, never mind someone as handsome as him.

I couldn't understand it myself.

When I first met him, I thought for sure he was approaching me to ask about Daisy, but for some reason, he was interested in me. It was nice to have that sort of attention. To be told you're someone's first choice when all you've ever felt like is second best. I didn't mind being second best to Daisy, though. When you're around Daisy as much as I was, I knew there was no comparison.

But for some reason James was interested in me. I was flattered, and before long, he won me over. The more time I spent with him, the more I liked him. It took a secure gentleman to be supportive of my career, but he always was. I could find no fault in him, until I started bringing him around Daisy.

It didn't happen all at once, but after the first couple times of him seeing us together, I could tell something had changed. It wasn't long before he started making comments about her and about my friendship with her. I tried to explain to him just how important she was to me and how much she meant to me, but it didn't seem to matter. He decided he didn't like her and refused to give her more of a chance.

I had to wonder if he saw something more in our friendship than was actually there. I had suppressed any thoughts about her like that, but I couldn't control the way I looked at her or the way I felt about her.

I couldn't help it sometimes. She'd smile and my heart would soar. Seeing her upset caused me physical pain. Being around her was the easiest and hardest thing in the world. I had to hide my thoughts about her and my feelings for her, but that was a small price to pay for the privilege of being around her. I was happy to be her friend if that meant being in her life. I was happy to be with her in any capacity she would have me.

James didn't understand and I couldn't really blame him, but I didn't know what to do about it. But if he continued to push me to choose, I think he knew he wouldn't like my choice.

I made it to the ballroom and was in awe of just how many people had turned up. I couldn't believe how many men Daisy's mother had invited, or, more accurately, I couldn't believe how many had turned up.

I couldn't help but worry about Daisy. I knew she wanted to find love and find someone she could happily spend her life with, but this couldn't be the way. How would she ever get to know anyone with all these people here?

The crowd was so big, I was having trouble finding James. When I finally found him, he was as far from the main entrance as possible. I couldn't help rolling my eyes at that. He knew he was supposed to be waiting by the stairs so I could easily find him and so Daisy could easily find us. I was ready to go give him a piece of my mind when I saw him notice me. His surprise quickly turned to thinly veiled lust. Well, at least someone appreciated the dress.

"Wow!"

I laughed. "Get a good look. I certainly won't be wearing this again."

"What a crime." He looked me up and down before adding, "On second thought, we should get you out of that as soon as humanly possible."

I couldn't help but laugh. He was so predictable, but it was nice to be appreciated. And he wasn't wrong. I hadn't liked the dress from the first moment Daisy showed me. It was way too form fitting, but I knew how important it was to her, so I humored her. When her mother threw a tantrum about the dress, I thought that would be the end of it. I hadn't counted on Daisy actually standing up to her mother. I was so proud of her and couldn't help but think maybe I was rubbing off on her.

After that, I resigned myself to wearing the dress and pretending to like it. I was shocked when instead of pretending to like it, I had to pretend I didn't. There wasn't anything I hated more than being wrong, and I wasn't often wrong. But in this case, she was right. The dress was perfect. It was even more perfect how well the jeweled tones of our dresses went together. You could almost look at the two of us and know we belonged together, that we were two halves of a whole. How could I possibly hate it?

He saw I was lost in thought and moved forward, brushing a stray hair from my forehead. He looked into my eyes. "Darling, what's on your mind? You look a million miles away."

I blushed. I couldn't tell him Daisy was on my mind. I needed to get a grip on my feelings. He didn't wait for a response. He chuckled. "Ohhhh. I like the way you think."

I laughed and rolled my eyes. Of course that's what he would think I was thinking. "Of course you do. Speaking of a million miles away, we have to go closer. I told Daisy we'd be waiting for her right when she walked in."

It was his turn to roll his eyes. "Of course you did. Well, lead the way. I'd follow you anywhere in that dress."

I couldn't help but laugh as I pulled him through the crowd. I stopped when we reached the bottom of the stairs. We stood and waited with the rest of the crowd for Daisy. People were starting to get restless, but unlike the rest of the crowd, I would wait however long I needed to for her. She was well worth the wait.

Daisy

Before I knew it, they had me ready to go. I was overflowing with nerves and excitement. I went to turn to the mirror to see how I looked, but it must have been later than I thought because at that moment, my mother's maid came rushing in, asking if I was ready. I turned from the mirror to face her. I trusted my vision had come together. I would have liked to have seen it for myself, but it seemed there wasn't time. However, from my mother's maid's horrified look, I gathered I looked stunning. I would need to brace myself for my mother's reaction to my dress, which I assumed would be worse and louder than her maid's, but it was well worth it. I felt powerful in this dress. I was stepping into my own future and I would be the one calling the shots. This was truly a life-changing dress.

I heard my mother's maid mutter under her breath something about how, "Mrs. Fay will have our necks for this." I worried for a moment that my mother might put some of the blame on our staff for what had been solely my own actions. After a moment, I dismissed the concern. She knew me well enough to know this was my decision and mine alone. I would be sure no one lost their jobs over this, but I knew as long as I charmed some wealthy men, she would likely ignore my clothing choice.

My mother and I had very different goals for me tonight. I would be as charming as possible to everyone in attendance, but I hoped to find someone who would capture my heart. She hoped I would capture the heart of whomever had the deepest pockets. While it would be nice to be swept off my feet by a rich man, I didn't want just any rich man. I wanted to find true love. I wanted something that felt even better than I had with Jay. I refused to settle for anything less.

Feeling like a warrior headed to battle, I gathered my courage and swept out of the room. The train of my dress followed me through the empty halls, making an eerie swishing noise. The closer I got to the ballroom, the more nervous I got. I could hear the noise of what sounded like thousands laughing and talking. I really hoped this would go well, and hoped it was a manageable crowd, especially since I was expected to make myself acquainted with and ingratiate myself with everyone there. I hurried to where some of the staff were waiting at the entrance to the ballroom. One butler quickly opened the door and slipped into the ballroom to prepare the musicians for my entrance. He closed the door behind him too quickly for me to catch a glimpse inside.

I was the only one using this entrance tonight. I knew from her plans that my mother had had everyone else enter through the gardens into the ballroom. She wanted to leave the honor of the grand staircase entrance to me. I had to admit; I had liked the sound of a grand entrance down that staircase. When I was younger, I used to play pretend that I was the belle of the ball, practicing my grand entrance on those stairs, waving to my adoring admirers.

Now that I was grown with actual admirers waiting, the idea had lost a lot of its appeal. More than anything, I felt nervous. I knew this night would set the stage for my future. The longer I waited, the more nervous I became. I knew the signal would come soon and I couldn't stray far, but I couldn't resist the temptation of seeing what I looked like. There was a mirror a little way down the hallway and I knew this might be my only chance to see the full effect of my dress.

I assured the staff I would just be a moment and rushed off around the corner. I came to a dead stop when I saw myself in the mirror. I hardly recognized myself. I easily looked the best I ever had. Funnily enough, despite the amount of effort put into my appearance, what I noticed first was my eyes shining brightly back at me. The blue and green of the necklace and my dress made my eyes pop in a way that took me by surprise. The next thing I noticed was how beautiful my hair looked with some of the loose curls contrasting my pale skin. I had always been self-conscious of how pale my skin was, especially now that the summer had long passed and all the color I had gained over the summer was lost. I worried I would look too pale or even sickly, but the contrast with my dark hair and my deep blue and green necklace and dress was breathtaking. The necklace perfectly mirrored the neckline of the dress. It was like they were made for one another. I hadn't thought it possible, but the necklace looked even better than I had imagined with the dress.

The dress itself was a work of art. The bodice had a sweetheart neckline that hugged my curves perfectly. The necklace hung parallel to the neckline in an alluring way. The dress was a teal blue at the bodice until just below my waist where the skirt started. The skirt was the crowning jewel of the dress. It flared out all around me, ending in a five-foot train that flowed behind me. The skirt was covered in peacock feathers. The feathers were my idea. I had noticed our peacocks shedding their feathers over the summer and had thought them too beautiful to go to waste. I had collected as many as I could, not knowing what I planned to do with them, but knowing I had to have them. When the seamstress had asked what I wanted my look to be, my eyes had fallen on the feathers and I couldn't shake the idea from my mind. It had turned out even more beautiful than I had dreamed. The feathers would ensure I captured every eye in the room.

Much of my earlier nervousness had gone at the sight of my dress. I felt powerful and important in this dress. I would be the most admired and most envied woman in the room. With my newfound confidence, I went back over to my spot in front of the door. I was just in time. A moment after I reclaimed my position, there were two soft knocks on the door. That was the signal. They were ready for me.

I took a deep breath and sent a little last-minute prayer that tonight would be everything I dreamed. I took one more breath, letting myself take in the moment one last time. After all, a girl only debuts once, and I knew this would be a night I wouldn't forget. I wanted to remember the nervous anticipation of this moment. Whether the evening turned good or bad, I could always look back to this moment, to how it felt to be feeling as confident and powerful as I did just then.

I nodded to the butlers to open the doors. They moved in front of me, and each placed their hand on one of the double doors. They looked at and nodded to one another, ensuring synchronicity. At the same moment, they turned their handles and swung the doors inward into the ballroom.

Chapter Thirteen

For a moment, they blocked my view. Then the moment passed and when they parted, I was able to see the ballroom for the first time. Trumpets sounded a fanfare on cue and one of the butlers announced, "Presenting the enchanting and very eligible, Miss Daisy Fay, the sweetheart of Louisville and sole heir to the Fay fortune." Normally, I would have had a difficult time not rolling my eyes at the introduction my mother had clearly written, but I was too in awe to pay much attention.

I took a small step forward, needing a moment to take in everything around me. I had never seen the ballroom looking so crowded or so elegant as it did now. All the chandeliers were lit; the effect was enchanting.

I took another step, and the musicians started playing. I looked around the room again, taking in the crowd. I hadn't known what to expect, but it seemed there were thousands of people there. More likely it was a few hundred, but the crowd felt as daunting and vast as if it had been thousands.

I reached the beginning of the marble staircase and paused. I took a deep breath, knowing I was descending not just into the ballroom, but into the next chapter of my life. I started my descent, praying I looked graceful and that I wouldn't trip or falter.

After a few moments, I nearly stopped dead in my tracks when I recognized the score the musicians were playing. My step faltered for a moment, but I took a deep breath and continued forward. I couldn't believe her. It was the bridal march. As if that introduction hadn't been embarrassing enough! It was just like my mother to pull something like that. Everyone already knew what today symbolized. They didn't need to be classlessly reminded by the cheesy musical accompaniment. I couldn't help thinking maybe it was a mistake giving my mother as much free rein as I had. Although even I had to admit, the ballroom had never looked better.

As the crowd looked up at me, I searched for familiar faces. I was overjoyed to see Jordan's first. She had stationed herself and James a few feet away from the bottom of the stairs on the right, so I would be sure to see her. I felt a wave of relief overcome me at being able to locate a friendly face in the crowd. I met her eye and smiled at her, letting her know how glad I was she was there. I looked around for my parents, worried about what I might find, since I knew my mother would be less than pleased with my dress. When I did find them on the far side of the room, it was worse than I could have imagined. I almost tripped but caught myself in time. The color drained from my face, but I kept moving. My father looked at me with what looked like pride. I was touched, but that was not what gave me pause; it was my mother.

My mother was the only person not watching my descent. She was talking with a man I recognized. He watched me with what I hoped was appreciation, but from the shiver that ran down my spine, I felt the look wasn't that innocent. I held my composure and tried to recover some of the hopes I had for the night, but I couldn't shake my worries. *What is my mother doing talking to him? Why him out of everyone else here?* I looked back to Jordan, who, like most everyone else in the room, was looking at me. Her smile had vanished when she saw the look on my face. I tried to reassure her with a smile, but her expression didn't change. I should have known she would see right through me like she always did.

I wasn't able to shake the sinking feeling I had, but as I reached the bottom of the stairs, I forced a coy smile on my lips. I looked out at the crowd and curtseyed. After a moment, the music changed, cuing our guests to return to dancing, eating, and talking. Most turned away from me. There were a few men that seemed to be summoning the courage to approach me, but Jordan swooped in and grabbed my arm. She ushered me away from the stairs, giving me a moment to breathe and recover before having to engage with the rest of the guests. Even better, she sent James to get her a drink, giving us a few minutes alone.

I could see the curiosity burning in her eyes. I knew we didn't have much time, so I hastened to ask, "Have you seen who's captured my mother's attention?" She shook her head. "Take a look. She's in the back of the room with my father." I indicated where I had seen her. Jordan turned to look while I looked around me, observing some of the men I would likely have to talk with and potentially dance with later. Jordan turned back to me, looking confused.

"Are you sure that's where she was? I don't see her."

I knew I had seen her there. I turned to look for myself but didn't see her either. Confused, I turned back to Jordan, but over her shoulder, I saw my mother. She was making her way across the room, and she wasn't alone. She was being escorted on his arm. I shouldn't have been surprised. They were nearly upon us. I had but a moment to wonder where my father had wandered off to before they converged on us.

I looked at my mother and immediately understood two things; the first being that the gentleman she was bringing to my attention was of great importance and thus must be treated as such, the second being that she was less than pleased about my choice of dress, but that, in her own words 'if I didn't mess up the opportunity with this gentleman, she would be gracious enough to look past my dress.' I had guessed all of this when I saw her on his arm walking over to us, but her face confirmed it beyond a doubt. There was just one problem. This gentleman wasn't a stranger to me, and I knew him to be no gentleman.

Jordan hadn't seen them, so my mother cleared her throat condescendingly. Jordan looked indignant and turned to see who addressed her in that manner. When she saw it was my mother, she swallowed her anger. "Hello, Mrs. Fay. Lovely to see you again."

"Hello, Jordan. It seems I'm always seeing you around my daughter. I must imagine you have somewhere else to be right now."

Her thinly veiled dismissal didn't achieve its objective. Jordan didn't argue, but didn't leave either. My mother wasn't used to being disobeyed. Had he not been there, I'm sure we would have heard her disapproval. Maybe he was good for something after all. She stayed silent, staring pointedly into Jordan's eyes. Jordan didn't shrink away, instead holding her gaze. Neither broke the silence nor looked away.

The moments stretched on before my mother caved. Societal convention dictated she couldn't ignore her guest any longer. She turned to me and said, "Daisy, my dear, I'd like you to meet Marcos Hortense the Third, heir to the Hortense fortune. He's come quite a way to meet you."

He bowed deeply and lightly grasped my hand. He looked up to meet my eye as he planted a soft kiss atop my gloved hand. I met his eye and felt the butterflies in my stomach despite my resolve against him. He was quite handsome … when he wasn't speaking anyway.

"It's a pleasure to meet you, Miss Fay. I have heard such wondrous things about you."

I debated what to say. I knew what was expected. I was supposed to curtsy back and say the pleasure was all mine, but I was not inclined to lie and still keenly felt my anger at his earlier treatment of both myself and Jordan. He stood and released my hand. I felt my mother's eyes on me and knew I should curtsy, but I couldn't bring myself to do it. I refused to lower myself to this man.

Instead, while maintaining eye contact, I nodded in acknowledgment to him and settled for saying, "And how do I fare against your expectations, Mr. Hortense?"

He smiled in surprised delight. That wasn't the reaction I was seeking. I had hoped for him to find me impertinent. Instead, he seemed amused by my lack of warmth. If his reaction was lackluster, my mother's wasn't. I could feel anger radiating from her. I didn't dare turn to look at her.

He chuckled. "Your description does you an injustice. I wasn't prepared in the least for the beauty before me."

Against my wishes, my cheeks colored at the compliment. "I thank you, but I'm curious to know what it is you think of my dear friend Jordan here?" I felt my mother's disbelief and anger as keenly as I felt Jordan's confusion.

He looked confused for a moment until Jordan stepped closer and recognition dawned on his face. "Ah, I do believe we had the pleasure of meeting earlier, but I regret I don't believe I caught your name."

"Jordan Baker," she said in answer to his implied question.

He bowed slightly to her but didn't reach for her hand. "Pleased to make your acquaintance again, Miss Baker, but from the lady's greeting," he looked at me again, "it seems my reputation precedes me."

My face flushed again. I had meant to embarrass him, but it seems he would not be embarrassed. "Yes, it may have been mentioned you had met."

His grin widened at seeing my embarrassment, and chuckled. My mother butted in, saying, "Marcos, I am so sorry. I don't know what has gotten into her. She's usually-"

I was intrigued to hear what I usually was, but he didn't let her finish.

He waved her off. "I hardly mind. I know how ladies love to discuss men. It cannot be helped, nor would I wish it to be." He had the audacity to wink at me. "It's an honor to be discussed by such beauties." His gaze trailed down my face to my lips. "To have my name pass those gorgeous, supple lips is an honor I hope I have the privilege of having repeated."

I knew my face was scarlet now, and by his broad grin, I knew it didn't escape him that he was the cause. "But I must confess," he glanced in Jordan's direction, "although I am sure Jordan has already told you the amusing circumstances of our meeting." He looked back at me with an apologetic smile. "You see, myself and my party had stopped earlier this morning to look upon the grounds in the hopes of catching a glimpse of you. That was when Miss Baker and I first became acquainted. But on first sight, seeing how pretty she was, I thought she had to be you." He turned to Jordan. "Again, I truly am sorry for the confusion. You are quite lovely." He looked back at me. "But now I know how truly unjust your description was. I had been looking for a lovely woman when you are nothing short of divine."

He really was quite skilled with flattery. I couldn't help the butterflies in my stomach or the blush on my face. They grew worse with each passing moment. It felt like he could see right through me. Had I not had the chance of observing him earlier when he thought no one of importance was watching, I might have fallen for his act. He laid it on quite thick. Truthfully, even knowing what I did, I still felt a pull of attraction to him.

"Mr. Hortense, I appreciate flattery, but you will find I value honesty a good deal more."

I suspected my mother likely to either fall into hysterics on the spot or else faint, since, as she would say, 'her poor fragile heart was breaking at seeing her only daughter throw away her one and only chance at happiness'. I knew she felt ill-used, but I couldn't understand why Marcos's favor was so important. With such a large number of gentlemen here, what made him so important? She was acting as if he were the last eligible man in the country.

"Your beauty I had heard numerous tales of; knowledge of your quick wit is not so widespread."

A small smirk came to my face. I cocked an eyebrow at him and asked, "I hope you don't mean to say you would rather your women dim-witted?"

He laughed. "Why, there you go again. I was going to say what a lovely surprise it is that you are so much more than a beautiful woman, but you seem determined to think, or at least to speak ill of me."

My mother jumped in, saying, "I truly don't know what has gotten into her, but she isn't normally like this-"

Again, he didn't let her finish. "I should have rather hoped this was common behavior."

I was shocked. That wasn't at all the reaction I expected. I had expected him to say something about how, in his opinion, 'a woman shouldn't talk quite so much' or 'a woman should show a wealthy, handsome gentleman like himself more respect'. That's what he would have said around his friends and around Pam. I couldn't reconcile the man before me now with the man I had spoken with earlier. So different were his mannerisms that I never would have guessed he was anything except genuine. But I knew firsthand that looks can be deceiving. I silently thanked the universe for having given me that insight into his character. I knew he was a man I would have been very much in danger of falling for. Now, I knew to keep my guard up.

My mother stuttered in confusion, her mouth dropped open. "Y-you what?"

He laughed at her surprise and shrugged his shoulders. "What can I say? I prefer to keep life interesting, and it seems Miss Fay is quite interesting." He looked quickly at me, giving me a subtle smirk before turning back to her and adding, "But if you are quite sure she isn't usually like this, I might have to reconsider-"

My mother rushed in to say, "No! No, no, no, Mr. Hortense, you misunderstand me. I can personally assure you my daughter has always been quite vexing."

At this, I had to laugh. How easily he was able to throw my mother off balance. He might be good for something after all. He smiled brightly at me and added, "Well, I do hope you may consider debasing yourself to honor me with a dance?"

"Yes! She will! She will dance every dance with you if you'll have her."

I wanted to die of embarrassment. My mother was throwing me at the feet of some man we both hardly knew. Furthermore, what I did know of him did little to endear me to him. I wondered if she would be as adamant as she seemed about the match now if she knew he was a scoundrel who had all but propositioned me as a maid but a few short hours earlier. I considered she likely still might. Judging by how she was acting, he must have a substantial fortune. I wondered just how much money he must have had in order to make my normally composed, downright arrogant mother fall at his feet.

He cleared his throat, calling me back to the present. He was staring at me expectantly, waiting for something. Embarrassed at having zoned out, I offered him a small, apologetic smile.

He turned back to my mother and said, "Thank you for offering me your daughter's hand."

He glanced at me with another one of his secret smiles that I knew was intended to make me feel special. He knew his power over women and wielded it well. I felt the iciness in my heart thaw a few degrees. I was still miles away from feeling anything akin to warmth for him, but it was a start. I would have to be more careful.

He looked back at my mother. "It is an honor that I hope will be repeated with higher stakes soon, if I may be so bold." My mother's smile broadened, but he wasn't finished. "However, I would wish to have the lady's opinion on the matter." He turned back to me. My mother's smile deflated, and she shot me a warning look. "Would you care to honor me with a dance?"

I paused a moment. I didn't particularly want this man to have the chance to put his hands on me. I looked at Jordan, who offered me a small smile. I could almost hear her asking what my hesitation was about. Without being in my confidence about his earlier behavior, of course she was confused. After all, even I had to admit he was quite a handsome man with gorgeous dark eyes and a way of making you feel as if you were the only girl in the room. I was in danger. Even knowing he had been a scoundrel, I was having a hard time reminding myself of that in his presence. I was having a hard time thinking at all when I met his eye. I was kicking myself for not having found an opportunity to fill Jordan in earlier today, but it really didn't matter anyway. It wasn't like she could have done anything regardless. Her hands were as tied as mine. I could only wonder what her reaction might have been now if she had known about earlier. On second thought, it was probably better she didn't know. I'm sure if she made any sort of scene, my mother would have thrown her out in a heartbeat and then I would have been truly on my own.

I turned back to him. "I suppose one dance couldn't hurt."

He smiled at me. "That's more like it. I hope you'll allow me more than just a dance, but a dance would be a wonderful start." He took my hand and led me through the crowd toward the dance floor. The crowd parted before us, possibly to show respect, but more likely out of necessity. My dress required a lot of space.

He led me with some force toward the middle of the dance floor. It was hardly necessary. There had been plenty of room for us to not be forced into the middle, but it seemed he needed to be the center of attention. When we reached the middle of the floor, he turned to me with a sly smile. He snaked his arm around my waist, pulling me close. The butterflies were back. I felt my face heat at his proximity. My own body was betraying me.

I tried to breathe. I could do this. Just one dance. I would get through this. He hadn't taken his eyes off me, and his smirk told me what I had feared. My reaction hadn't been missed by him. As he spun me around the dance floor, his arm around my back started to slip lower. He continued lower until he was inches away from impropriety. I tried subtly to move his arm higher, but he was far stronger than me. He wouldn't budge. I was sure the blush wouldn't leave my face anytime soon. I should have expected this. I knew this was a bad idea.

He leaned close and whispered in my ear, "Careful, Miss Fay, you don't want to know the kinds of ideas the blushing of such a beautiful woman would give to a lesser gentleman."

I couldn't help that my blush deepened. He looked ecstatic, chuckling in delight as he whirled me around. "Mr. Hortense, I had no idea you thought so little of yourself, but I can assure you, any ideas you have will be lost on me. Better to turn your attention elsewhere. I have no intention of being an easy target."

My pride at my cleverness vanished when I saw he was unshaken. "You're proving to be even more delightful than I could have imagined. Be careful, Miss Fay. Show me much more of your wit and impertinence and I shall be determined to have you. I do so love a challenge."

I was speechless and needed air. I needed to get away. As if the universe heard my silent prayers, the music ended. He smiled knowingly at me and took my hand. "It seems you're quite lucky. It takes a stubborn woman to resist my charm, but I must be growing on you."

I refused to acknowledge any truth to that, but it seemed my silence was as good as confirmation. He smirked at me, deepening my blush. I was in trouble. He released my hand and bowed. Without thinking, I curtsied in response before rushing away.

Chapter Fourteen

I needed to find Jordan. I needed to talk to her as soon as possible. She would have advice. I needed her levelheadedness, I couldn't think straight myself. I headed in the direction I had left her, thankful that it happened to be away from him. Even more than I wanted to see Jordan, I needed to put more space in between him and myself. In my haste, I wasn't paying attention and collided with another person I would have done better to avoid; my mother.

She clutched my arm, holding me in place. "I have half a mind to drag you back to your room by your hair for what you put me through! I should make you change dresses, too. I knew I should have chosen your dress." She looked me up and down and shuddered. "Had I known it would be this bad, I never would have allowed it! To think, my one and only daughter, who I have been fighting to give some shred of dignity to ever since your indiscretion last year, would disgrace me by showing up to her debut in this," she gestured wildly at my dress, seemingly at a loss for words, "this... monstrosity! Had every gentleman walked out of here when they saw you in this, I wouldn't have blamed them, but for some godforsaken reason, it seems you still have the attention of Mr. Hortense. I don't pretend to know what it is that man is crazy enough to see in you, but he seems to see something in you that he likes. I won't have you ruin this opportunity for yourself! Now, just where do you think you're going? What could possibly be so important to drag you away from what has to be the one man crazy enough to enjoy your antics?"

I hadn't expected to be interrogated and had no answer that I knew would satisfy her. She followed my eye and saw I was looking in Jordan's direction. She saw a gentleman standing there and misunderstood my intentions. I had only wanted to talk to Jordan. She looked at the man appraisingly, but a moment later, shook her head.

"No, no. He won't do. With his light skin mixed with yours, the children would be downright ghostly."

I was upset at her implications and was about to tell her so, but she continued, "Besides, he has chosen to allow himself to be monopolized by Jordan and her beau. Anyone worth your attention would have introduced themselves to me by now. After all, whose good opinion matters more than that of your mother?"

I barely restrained myself from rolling my eyes at that. I could think of many people whose opinions about my husband mattered more to me than my mother's. The most important of whom being Jordan, followed closely by my own.

I knew my own judgment to be more capable of being clouded than Jordan's. I knew her judgment, with everything except her own love interest, was not easily influenced. As I watched, she smiled at the gentleman, which raised my interest even further. It was seldom that Jordan smiled at a man, especially one she didn't know well. She wasn't one to be easily won over, especially by men. The ladies of the town always whispered about how cold she was to men, so to see her smiling at this gentleman was a surprise to say the least.

I resolved to meet the gentleman myself when my mother, reading my intent, scowled. "Never mind that gentleman. He's not worth your attention." Had she wished to dissolve my newfound interest, she couldn't have said worse. I was more intrigued by the gentleman now than I had been before he had raised my mother's scorn. As I moved past her and started in his direction, she raised her voice. "You will march back over there and humbly request another dance with Mr. Hortense before he comes to his senses."

That was the last thing I wanted to do. Marcos seemed to have a big enough ego on his own. The last thing he needed was me rushing back to him mere moments after having taken leave of him to request another dance. I was sure he would think himself irresistible and would become even more intolerable. I could picture the look of triumph on his face and knew I would die of embarrassment. I would sooner strip naked in the middle of the ballroom floor in front of all our guests than walk back over there on my mother's direction to ask for another dance.

My strong feelings on the matter emboldened me to say, "I will do no such thing, and you shouldn't desire it. You have said numerous times that Mr. Hortense likes me for me. I'll have you know that I would, under no circumstances, debase myself to ask a gentleman I had just taken leave of for another dance." Her eyes showed her shock and thinly veiled anger. I expected her to interrupt, but she seemed at a loss for words. "The mother I know would never condone her daughter begging for any gentleman's favor. Tell me just what is it about this Marcos that makes you so adamant I must win his affection?"

She looked at me like I had spontaneously grown two extra heads out of my neck. "Why, his money and reputation, of course! Is that not enough for you? What more could you want?"

I could list more than a few things, but now wasn't the time to rile her up further. "I assumed by his being here that he had money. The trip from New Orleans alone must have cost a small fortune, but his reputation I have heard little of."

"Dear child, you're more daft than I thought. Have you really no notion of how influential the Hortenses of New Orleans are? They may as well be royalty for all their influence and standing, and here you are, ever my ungrateful daughter, shunning the Prince of New Orleans."

I couldn't help rolling my eyes at that. "Mama, he's no Prince. He's just another man from a rich family."

Her eyes nearly bulged out of her head. "Just another rich man? That's like saying the Rockefellers have a little money, like President Wilson is just another politician-"

I couldn't guess how long she would continue, so I hastily interrupted. "Okay, okay, so he's a *very* rich gentleman from a powerful family, but he's no Prince. Whether he is a gentleman is even more debatable still." She looked ready to strangle me in her frustration, so I hastily added, "Worry not, I'll dance with him again." I felt her relax a little before I added, "But not right now."

"But-"

"But nothing. If he likes me for me, I would only gain his disapproval by making myself seem desperate. You can't deny it would seem desperate to re-approach a man I had just taken leave of and ask for his hand for another dance. I have never in my life asked a man to dance, and I do not plan to start tonight. Would you truly wish for others to see me as desperate?" The look on her face told me she was considering my words and could find no cause to argue with them, though I knew she wanted to. "If he likes me well enough, I'm sure he'll find me again and ask me again to dance. I will dance with him again, if, and only if, he asks again."

I could feel her ready to protest, so I added, "If he likes me well enough, I'm sure he'll ask again. If he doesn't like me well enough to ask again, well, then he certainly doesn't like me well enough to ask for my hand. I've told you I'll dance with him again if he asks, but that's all you can ask of me and all I will agree to. If he likes me well enough, he'll ask again, but until then I will be over there meeting that gentleman." She didn't look satisfied, so I added, "Perhaps it will make him jealous enough to ask again sooner." I didn't in truth care if he asked again or not, but I desperately wanted to make sure she wasn't upset enough to follow me or to bring him over to me again.

I could tell she was more satisfied than she had been. She gave me an appraising look and nodded to herself. "Well, it appears I might have raised you right after all. You might not need my help after all."

Not knowing what to say, I smiled and took my leave. As I approached, Jordan looked up and saw me. She smiled widely at me and excused herself from James and the other gentlemen and met me halfway.

"How did it go? You have to tell me what happened!" She frowned slightly, adding, "I hope it wasn't as bad as you thought?"

"He wasn't a complete scoundrel like I had expected, so that was pleasant enough. My mother seems determined we should marry as soon as possible." I laughed and added, "He would have his work cut out for him with me. I've been as cold to him as possible since he introduced himself, and yet he won't take the hint."

"And just what are you hinting? He's certainly handsome. He's not my type, but he seems to really like you, and he admitted on his own to having complimented me. I'm not seeing what there is to not like?"

"*I* like him well enough. He's been charming the entire night and put my mother in her place more than once, which would be enough to endear me to any man. However, *Pam* despises the man and as her and I are essentially attached at the hip, her opinion is not to be lightly ignored." I laughed at my own joke. After a moment, recollection dawned on Jordan and she laughed, too.

"You still haven't told me what happened this morning. Was it that bad?"

"Worse."

"You really will have to update me, but this obviously isn't the time or place."

"Rest assured, the moment the night ends, I'll tell you everything. But until then, if you would do what you could to shield me from his attention, I would be forever indebted to you." I nudged her shoulder while smirking. "After all, he seemed to like you well enough this morning." She laughed along with me. I thought again about this morning and was reminded of how much he liked her and of what he had said about her. My laughter stopped immediately, and I could tell from her face adopting a concerned look that my own face looked more serious. "Actually, on second thought, I don't think you should be any closer to him than necessary, either." I could tell her curiosity was eating at her, but she didn't ask.

She couldn't help herself from trying to lighten the mood, though. She adopted a faux look of concern and said, "Daisy dear, if you're worried I'll steal him from you in this dress," she struck a pose for me with her hand on her hip and wiggled her hips back and forth, "just say the word and I'll disappear." She couldn't hold her straight face and fell into laughter the moment I did.

After a few moments when I caught my breath, I looked at her more seriously this time and told her, "Please, Jord, I need you to trust me. He's bad news. I take back my request. I don't want you anywhere near him, but I have a better idea."

Chapter Fifteen

I took her hand and led her back to James and the gentleman. "Finally, she returns!" James looked at our connected hands in disdain, wrapped his arm around Jordan's waist, effectively pulling our hands apart as he pulled her to his side, and looked at me accusingly. "I thought you would be too busy to be much of a bother-" Jordan abruptly tried to elbow him in the stomach. He dodged just in time, but it seemed he got the message. "I mean, I thought you would be too busy to spend time with us."

Jordan looked at me apologetically, but I waved off her concern and said, "That's really fine. Don't worry about it. You're actually just the man I was looking for."

The pure shock on Jordan's and James's faces was priceless, especially James's. I reveled in his confused, stunned silence for a moment before he jokingly, I hoped, said, "I knew you would come around to wanting me sooner rather than later. There's enough of me to go around."

Jordan and I both started laughing. He turned to Jordan, "What a coincidence. Jordan and I were just talking about inviting you to join-" He stopped abruptly when her elbow landed its target this time. He took a minute to catch his breath. I shot her a confused look, wondering what that was about, but she was too busy glaring at him to meet my eye. He didn't elaborate.

"I never knew you were so funny!" I really wasn't sure if he had been serious or not, but didn't want to ponder the implications that it might not have been a joke. "But, seriously, I need your help."

I wasn't sure whose eyebrows shot up higher, his or Jordan's. They both spoke at the same time.

"He'll do it!"

"Why would I help you?"

They both stared at each other, surprised they disagreed. Jordan spoke first. "We've been over this. You know how important she is to me. I don't care how you feel about her; if she needs your help, you help her. If you don't want to do it for her, then do it for me. I shouldn't have to keep reminding you how important she is to me."

He started to reply, but I cut him off. I knew he would be more than willing to do the task I had in mind and didn't want to continue to see Jordan upset for no reason. "Jordan, it's okay, really. Don't worry about it. I'm sure he'll be begging to help once he hears what I have in mind."

"Okay, okay, you've piqued my interest. What is it you want me to do?"

"Okay so…" I stepped closer to him and turned so I was facing the same direction as he was. "You see that man over there?" I pointed across the ballroom, indicating Marcos.

"You mean the short man with the large mustache?"

"No, on his left."

"Oh, the man with the red hair and the pale face?"

"No, no! On the right of him!"

"The tall okay-looking one in the middle?"

I laughed at the okay-looking comment. I hated the man and even I had to admit he was good looking. I couldn't help but ask, "Is someone a little upset over having some competition? If he is only okay-looking, pray tell me, what does that make you?"

I had been so distracted with recruiting James's help, that I had forgotten the other gentleman was there at all, until I heard him laugh. I smiled in his direction and felt time stop when I met his eye. I couldn't help but be charmed by his smile. His body was the next thing I noticed. I truly couldn't help but admire his physique. He was on the taller side and muscular. I wondered what he did to keep himself so fit.

I was brought out of my wondering by James snapping at him, "You're supposed to be on my side. I did you a favor inviting you here and now you're taking her side?"

He held his hands up placatingly, the smile not leaving his face. "Calm down, James. All I did was laugh. You never said the lady was funny."

"Never mind that. We'll talk about this later." He turned back to me. "So why should I help you?"

"You haven't even heard what I want you to do yet."

"But I'm sure I won't want to."

"How sure are you?"

He had looked confident before I asked, but I sensed his confidence wavering and his curiosity peaking. "Okay, just tell me."

"So that gentleman over there, his name is Marcos Hortense."

His eyes widened in surprise. "Not of the New Orleans Hortenses?"

I was confused but nodded. "The very same. Apparently, they're a big deal?"

He looked at me like I was the crazy one. "Big deal? Even *I've* heard of the Hortense fortune. It's next level. His fortune makes your family money look like chump change."

I was really surprised he had heard of him. "That's good to know, but changes nothing. I need you to befriend him."

"I might be okay with that."

"It gets better. I need you to befriend him and keep him busy for the night, namely, away from me."

He looked at me like this was all the confirmation he needed that I was crazier than he could have imagined. "I might be crazy for asking, and you're right I have no objections to either making friends with a wealthy, powerful man or staying away from you all night, but why wouldn't you want to be near him? I'll loathe myself for trying to help you, but you do know how much he's worth and how influential he is, right?"

"Everyone's been telling me that, but that really doesn't matter to me. I decidedly don't like him. Unfortunately, my mother is convinced he's the most eligible man here and that I should be with him. I don't care to explain why I'm averse to that. I just want you to keep him away from me."

A smile spread slowly across his lips. "And just how badly do you want him kept away from you?"

"Desperately. Say anything you must."

He looked from me to Jordan and back again. "Are you sure?"

"Positive. You can say anything that might spurn his interest."

He turned to Jordan, who was looking at me like I was crazy, but she nodded her assent to him.

He looked at his friend, saying, "I'm sorry to leave you hanging, but this isn't something I can pass up. It's not every day that you're asked to entertain and befriend one of the country's richest men. Never mind that I get to say belittling things about my girlfriend's annoying best friend with my girlfriend's wholehearted support. Do you want to come meet this Marcos with me?" He examined his friend's facial expression before adding, "Or perhaps you'd like to keep the ladies company?"

His friend nodded.

"Okay, suit yourself. I'll see you both later tonight," he said to them before hurrying off in Marcos's direction.

Jordan turned to me, saying, "You're truly mad."

The gentleman shook his head at Jordan's remark. "I can't help but disagree. There's nothing more attractive than a woman who knows what she wants. I only hope you'll tell me what that Marcos did to invite your scorn so I can make sure never to invoke it myself."

We laughed a moment. Then Jordan, who had forgotten I didn't know the gentleman, hastened to introduce us. "I'm sorry. Please forgive my rudeness. Where are my manners? Tom, this is Daisy Fay, but you already know that. Daisy, this is Thomas Buchanan."

He smiled and said to me, "Please call me Tom. It's a pleasure to meet you. My friend," he waved his hand in the direction James had gone, "was not as subtle as I would have liked, but I did ask him for an invitation tonight. I hoped to meet you. I hadn't given much thought to what might happen after. Now, face to face with you, having seen how you react to those who don't have your favor, I'm worried I might not make a good impression. I was foolish to not have worried before."

Again, I blushed. How could he possibly be worried about his reception from me? He was positively charming. Had he only been half as handsome, I still would have preferred him to almost everyone in the room. His worry about impressing me was only further endearing him to me.

I was more glad than ever that I had come over here. I smiled brightly at him. "It's a pleasure, and all you really have to know is I expect to be respected and don't take kindly to anyone who messes with the people I care about. Actually, the most important thing to know is that the person I care most about is my dear Jordan. If someone gets on Jordan's good side, they've already won my good favor."

He chuckled at that, and looked to Jordan with a smile. "Well, it seems I've chosen my companions for the evening well." He turned back to me before saying, "I was going to ask if I was making a favorable impression, but it seems that would be directed at the wrong person." I giggled as I watched him turn back to Jordan and ask, "How do you think I'm doing?"

She looked at me thoughtfully before responding, "Better than I expected when I heard James's friend wanted to attend. I didn't have much hope for you, to be honest. Despite James's assurances, I still thought you would be just another rich friend of his looking to make a move on a rich, attractive friend of mine who I knew to be too good for you." I audibly gasped at her bluntness. She laughed. I shouldn't have been surprised by her bluntness, but I wasn't sure I would ever get used to it. If he was surprised or offended, he held back. After a moment, she added thoughtfully, "Please don't take that personally. I don't believe anyone is good enough for Daisy."

"Of course. You wouldn't be a good friend to her if you did. But tell me, now that you've spent time with me, do you have a better opinion of me? Do I stand a chance?"

I held my breath, but felt my heart soar when I saw the smile she was hiding. She looked him up and down appraisingly, still trying to hide her smile. She failed to hide it from me, but he looked nervous. "Well, I'll tell you I have no current objections to you, which Daisy will tell you is a triumph in itself, as I can be rather blunt and don't give my good opinion often."

"What are some of the opinions you've formed of me?"

I shot her a look of warning that she promptly ignored. "I'll preface my opinion by reminding you both that my opinion is based only on a couple hours' worth of acquaintance." I looked at her, confused. She had introduced me to him. I had assumed she had at least met him before tonight. She turned to me and answered the questioning look on my face. "I knew he was coming and have heard some things about him from James-" She laughed at the worried look on Tom's face and waved off his concern. "Don't worry. I know how James can be, and I take his opinions with a grain of salt."

He visibly relaxed a little, and she turned back to me. "Like I was saying, I've heard things about him, enough to agree that it was acceptable he came, but I hadn't made his acquaintance before tonight." She turned to him. "However, James had vouched for you." She turned back to me. "I know you don't think highly of James." Tom's face showed surprise, and I'm sure mine did, too. I hadn't expected her bluntness, especially in front of one of James's friends. I really hoped she didn't know the extent of my aversion to him. She ignored both of our reactions and continued. "But James has known Tom for a long while. They graduated Yale together a few years back, so I felt he could answer to what sort of person his friend is. Nothing James told me made me think Tom shouldn't come, so I agreed he could invite him. Although I was surprised he wanted to make the trip from Chicago."

I looked at him in surprise. "You came here all the way from Chicago? Why?"

"What can I say? I had heard some pretty compelling reasons, although now I'm questioning how truthful James might have been, for he definitely hadn't accurately described you at all."

I rolled my eyes and laughed a little. "It's not much of a secret that James isn't my biggest fan."

He laughed, too. "I will say he told me more than once I was crazy to make the journey here just to meet you."

Jordan looked annoyed, but I laughed. "Well, I can't really fault him for that. It was quite a long way to come. Tell me, are you enjoying yourself?"

"Very much. Even more so now that I have the pleasure of your acquaintance."

I smiled. "I'm glad to hear it."

"In truth, I had two main reasons for coming, and they are both standing in front of me." James looked at Jordan. "He told me the most wonderful things about you. Any woman who could so fully capture his attention is so rare a breed that I knew I had to meet her. I picked now to come because he told me that your best friend," he then turned back to me, "who I had heard the strangest things about from him, was having a debut. My curiosity got the better of me. I had to see for myself if any of what I had heard was true, and even James couldn't deny your beauty."

"Do you share your friend's opinions of me?"

He laughed and shook his head. "Having met you, I confess myself to have fallen under your charm. I don't understand how he could have possibly formed any sort of negative opinion of you, and I adamantly disagree with his assessment of your beauty." My heart stopped for a cruel moment before he continued, "He vastly under sold your beauty." He turned to Jordan and added, "But it's what's to be expected by a man as afflicted as he is." We must have both looked confused because he laughed a moment before adding to Jordan, "It seems he has fallen quite hard for you. A man as enamored as he cannot be expected to be a reliable judge to the beauty of other women."

I looked to Jordan, wondering how she would respond. I had expected to see some form of joy on her face, but saw only thoughtfulness. We both expected her to say something, but she looked lost in thought.

"Well, I can say from the both of us that we are glad to have made your acquaintance."

"I hope it's a joy that might be repeated." He seemed about to say something else, but stopped and looked toward the musicians, who had just started playing a new score. "This is a favorite of mine." He looked back at me hopefully. "Would you do me the honor of a dance?"

I smiled and nodded, taking his hand as he offered it. He lightly grasped my hand as he led us to the edge of the dance floor. I expected him to continue on like Marcos had, but he stopped. When I looked at him questioningly, he said, "This seemed as good a place as any." He wrapped his arm around my waist and started to lead. "I suspect with you in my arms, the location hardly matters." He looked around before hastily adding, "Not that the ballroom isn't gorgeous, of course."

He was blushing. I felt my butterflies return in full force. He was trying so hard to impress me, and it was working. Normally, when a man tried too hard, I felt there was an ulterior motive, but with Tom, I couldn't possibly doubt his genuineness. He held me with such tenderness, as if I were too precious to be handled too roughly. For the first time, I felt real, tangible hope of happiness. Maybe I could be happy again.

Chapter Sixteen

Jordan

I had thought nothing could be worse than seeing her dance with Marcos. The discomfort had been visible on her face the entire time he held her. I wanted to rip his hands off her. I had had to force myself to act calm and remind myself it was only one dance. It would be over before I knew it and then she would be back with me, and I would make sure he didn't get to dance with her again.

Watching her searching the room for me while they danced had been torture. I had thought that would be the worst I could feel tonight, but this...her and Tom... this might be worse.

I had seen the relief in her entire body when her shoulders slumped the moment the music ended.

I had forced myself to take another deep breath. I should have ripped Marcos's hands off her earlier, her debut and her mother be damned, but I didn't. I wasn't sure that was what she would have wanted. I knew how important tonight was to her and the last thing I wanted was to make a scene and ruin tonight for her. I had held back, but I was worried. I hoped she could handle herself, and that she'd be smart enough to tell me if she couldn't.

I couldn't decide what would have been worse, seeing her start to fall for him or seeing her forced into his arms against her will. I had thought for sure the latter was worse, but I would have been lying to myself if I didn't admit I worried about her falling for him as well.

Even I knew how handsome he was and besides her mysterious aversion to him there seemed to be nothing in her way with him. He was rich and just the sort of man her parents would love her to marry. The thought sparked anxiety.

I hoped her parents wouldn't be terrible enough to try to push her into that arrangement, but one look at her mother's face when Daisy was dancing with Marcos and I knew she had their future planned.

Couldn't she see how unhappy and anxious her daughter was? Daisy wasn't subtle about it. Did she not see it, or did she just not care? Knowing her mother, it was likely the latter.

The moment she had broken away from him, I had watched her rush back to where I was waiting. I had been talking with James and his friend Tom. I was pleasantly surprised at how pleasant Tom was.

When James told me he was bringing a friend, I had been hesitant. I couldn't imagine anything good would come of that. I couldn't imagine he had heard anything good about Daisy from James and worried why he would want to meet her. Whatever the reason, I didn't think it would be a good one.

Contrary to my low expectations, Tom seemed a perfect gentleman. I actually liked him, and it occurred to me that maybe Daisy would, too. I hoped he might be able to deflect Marcos's attention, so when he had asked her to dance, I was happy, until I saw how she looked at him. She hadn't looked at anyone that way since her lieutenant.

I knew I should be happy, but seeing that shocked me. I felt winded, like I had been punched in the gut. I was shocked at my own reaction. More than anything I had wanted her to find happiness, to be happy. So why was I struggling so much with seeing how she looked at Tom? He was certainly kind enough and had made a better first impression on me than most men ever did, but seeing that look on her face. Seeing her unrestrained smile that I was used to only being for me, I felt nauseous.

Now with her out on the dance floor with him, in his arms, smiling at him like she was, I had to fight to keep my composure. I was startled when a man I hadn't even noticed approach cleared his throat.

I looked at him questioningly.

He had the good sense to look apologetic. "I'm sorry, Miss. I had asked if you cared to dance?"

Surprised, I considered it for a moment. Normally, men didn't approach me. Daisy always told me it was because 'if looks could kill none of them would have survived long enough to speak with me.' That was her affectionate way of telling me to loosen up and be more approachable. But this man had been bold enough to ask to dance. He seemed harmless enough, and it would serve James right for how he'd been acting lately to see me on the arm of a stranger, but I wanted to be here when Daisy returned.

I softened my facial expression as much as I could and feigned regret. "I'm sorry. I'm waiting for someone."

He shrugged and said with a smile, "Well if they don't turn up, I'd be happy to fill in."

He took his leave, leaving me alone to contemplate just what had changed to make men more comfortable approaching me and how I could rectify it.

Chapter Seventeen

Daisy

As lost as we were in one another, we had hardly said a word before the music came to a stop. I wasn't ready for this to end, but Tom, the gentlemen that he was, removed his arm from my back the moment the music stopped. I sighed, feeling distinctly the absence of his touch. He bowed in thanks. I reluctantly moved further away and curtsied in return.

"Thank you for indulging me. Having you in my arms was more of a pleasure than I can describe."

"I can assure you the pleasure was all mine."

He smiled. "I know you must have other obligations," he gestured to the rest of the room filled with gentlemen, "but I do hope, if I may be so bold, to have the honor of your hand again tonight?"

I smiled and nodded. Not knowing what to say, not trusting my voice. I was surprised at the profound sadness I felt at our parting.

The last thing I wanted to do was leave him, but he was right. There was no shortage of gentlemen that I was obligated to entertain. Still, it took everything in me to not call out to him as he walked away. I couldn't believe myself. I had only known

Tom for the better part of an hour. I shouldn't have been feeling the sense of loss I did at his walking away.

Lost in thought, I headed in the direction Jordan had been. An approaching gentleman startled me out of my reverie. He asked for a dance and, as there was no reasonable excuse not to, I agreed.

I was then waylaid by gentleman after gentleman introducing themselves and asking for a dance. I danced with a few of them, and it was pleasant enough, but they made no lasting impression. Those dances were nothing compared to the one I shared with Tom. I couldn't get him off my mind.

My mind kept wandering to his charming smile and the adorable way he blushed when he was nervous, the way he had held me as if I were to be treasured, and the way he had been just as lost in my eyes as I was in his. After him, the other gentlemen didn't stand a chance.

A few more introductions and dances later, I was desperate to get back to Jordan. It didn't hurt that she was still talking to Tom, but I would have even welcomed James's company right now if it would have kept me away from further advances of strangers.

I should have known better than to let that thought cross my mind. The moment I thought it, who should walk over but James himself, followed by a most unwelcome presence.

How could I have forgotten?

Marcos.

As they approached, I noticed James looked frustrated, but Marcos was smiling. His smile widened when he saw he had my attention. He looked innocent enough, but there was something about his smile that put me on edge. I shot a questioning look at James, who threw his hands up in the air in exasperation.

When they reached me, Marcos took my hand in his and dipped down to kiss it. He looked into my eyes. "A pleasure we meet again. It seems you're quite popular today."

I gave him as polite a smile as I could muster and said, "Being the woman of the hour, that's hardly surprising."

He laughed. "I was hoping you weren't too in demand to grace me with another dance?"

I internally sighed and hesitated for a moment. The last thing I wanted right now was to dance. Worse still was the idea of dancing with him and giving him another opportunity to put his hands on me. Except, I had told my mother I would agree to another dance. I tried to reason she wouldn't find out, but even I couldn't delude myself about that. She would consider it a most heinous offense and would consider disowning her 'disobedient, ungrateful daughter.' It wasn't worth the risk. I watched as he waited expectantly. It seemed he felt secure in my answer. I wished I could have turned him down. It would have been incredibly satisfying to provide a much-needed blow to his ego.

"I am sure I can spare the time."

He turned back to James and smiled in triumph. "It seems the lady does have time. It was nice speaking with you. I'm sure I will run into you later."

Marcos took my hand and placed it through the crook of his elbow, and led me back onto the dance floor. Once James was out of earshot, he turned to me and said, "I don't know how well you know that man, but he claims intimate knowledge of you. But that can't be true with the crazy things he was saying about you."

I hid my smirk from him. It seemed James was good for something, at least. I was quite curious about what he had said and hoped some of it had negatively colored Marcos's interest in me. James never had failed before in driving away the men I was interested in. I could only hope that he would prove as successful at driving away this man who I held no interest in.

I feigned ignorance. "I'm not sure what it is you're implying, but I've spent a good deal of time with him. He's dating Jordan, whom you met earlier."

He chuckled and said, "Lucky man."

I didn't like the way he said that. I didn't know if he meant to imply that Jordan could be difficult to deal with or that she was pretty enough that any man would be lucky to have her. I knew both to be true, but didn't like how he said it or his implications. It reminded me of how crudely he had talked about her this morning and put me further on edge.

I responded only, "Indeed."

He noticed my mood had changed, but as I noticed he was apt to do, misattributed its cause. "Don't worry; I consider myself even more lucky to have you on my arm tonight."

I was happy to notice that when he snaked his arm around my waist tightly, I felt nothing but annoyance. It was curious. He hadn't changed in the least. He was just as handsome and arrogant as he had been earlier, but something had changed. His appearance didn't hold the same power over me anymore. The butterflies had flown off. The only feeling left was my discomfort.

As I had with every dance since, I couldn't help but compare him to Tom. Like the other gentlemen tonight, the comparison didn't go in his favor. He held me much too tight and paraded me around like I was a trophy he needed to show off, a trophy he was assured he had already won. The longer I spent with him, the more I realized just how possessive his actions were. He held me much too close for my liking, and when I tried to move back to make some space between us, he tightened his hold on me. I was no match for his strength, so I was forced to remain there.

My skin crawled at his touch, but at least the dance would be over soon. Again, his hands started to go lower. I pushed away with all my strength, but he didn't move an inch. He quickened his descent. It was hopeless. I thought about crying out to someone, anyone in the crowd, but I couldn't. What would they think of me? What would they say? The reputation I was struggling to rebuild would be ruined in an instant, so I stayed quiet. I closed my eyes and prayed it would be over soon.

A moment later, the song ended and relief coursed through my body as he was forced to remove his hands from me.

Chapter Eighteen

Tears of relief formed in my eyes. I blinked them back and adopted a polite expression of regret. "Over already? Well, I must be going. As you were saying, I'm in quite high demand tonight. I hope you're able to find another way to entertain yourself. Goodbye."

I went to move past him, but I should have known it wouldn't have been so easy. He grabbed my arm as I passed and gripped it tightly. I stopped short, shocked. "Just where do you think you're going so quickly?" His smirk was back.

I tried to pull away, but when I saw his amusement at my struggle, I stopped.

"I told you, I have somewhere else to be."

He gave an exaggerated eye roll. "I'm sure you can be spared for one more dance."

I tried to keep the panic from my face. I couldn't do that again. I wouldn't. There was no way I would let him touch me again.

I shook my head and said as calmly as I could muster, "I can assure you I can't be." I struggled to come up with a reason, the eagerness on his face disrupting my train of thought.

I blurted out the first thing I could think to say. "I already promised the next dance to someone else."

His expression darkened for a moment before he adopted his trademark smirk. "Well, I'm sure something can be arranged. We'll have to see if this gentleman can spare you for another dance."

I tried to hide the panic in my face. I hadn't expected Marcos to call my bluff. I feigned looking for the gentleman, trying to buy myself a moment to think. I realized I was instinctually looking for Jordan. It had become a habit of mine whenever I was anxious. She always seemed to know just how to make me feel better. In this situation, I don't know what I thought she might be able to do, but I was desperate.

Maybe she could make James dance with me. I would have welcomed dancing with him if it got me away from Marcos.

When my eyes found Jordan, I found a better solution. James was standing with her, but, to my relief, so was Tom. "There he is now!" I moved across the room to him, not looking back to see if Marcos was following. I hoped he might not, but knew it was more likely he would.

As I closed the distance to them, I heard Marcos's laughter from behind me. "You can't mean James?"

I couldn't help but laugh, too. "Of course not. I meant his friend, Mr. Buchanan. I don't believe you have had the pleasure of meeting him yet. I can introduce you."

I was rewarded with a look of displeasure from him, but he continued to follow me. I prayed Tom would play along. Jordan was happy to see me, but looked concerned that Marcos had followed me. James nodded to me, trying to make eye contact with Marcos, but Marcos was glaring intently at Tom. Tom looked both happy and confused. I knew the confusion had to be caused by the hostility from Marcos, but I hoped his happiness was from seeing me again.

I stepped forward, out of Marcos's reach, and threaded my arm through Tom's, saying, "Mr. Buchanan, I hope I didn't keep you waiting too long. I know I promised you the next dance, and I have always been a woman of my word." I looked at him pleadingly, hoping he would play along.

He smiled at me. "I'm honored you remembered. Don't worry another moment about keeping me waiting." I smiled brightly at him, which gave him the courage to add, "Although an additional dance would be more than compensation enough."

I was eternally grateful to him in that moment, but my relief was short-lived. I had thought, seeing I was otherwise engaged, Marcos would have backed off, but he didn't.

He cleared his throat, reminding me of his presence, like I could have forgotten. I turned back with feigned surprise at his still being there and then realized he hadn't been introduced to Tom. "Oh, Mr. Hortense, I hadn't realized you were still there." I looked back to Tom, saying, "Tom…" I paused a moment, startled by the intensity of the jealousy and outrage on Marcos's face that I called Tom by his given name. I gestured to Marcos and said, "This is Mr. Hortense."

He sneered at Tom before turning to me and saying, "My love, I appreciate the urge for propriety, but as you and I are soon to be more intimately tied, you know you can call me Marcos."

I blushed at the implication and my mind reeled with concern about why he sounded so certain it was inevitable. I tried to calm myself by reminding myself he sounded as certain this morning before he had even met me, but this arrogance and certainty seemed, if anything, more assured. I tried to convince myself he was likely putting on a facade to incite jealousy from

Tom. The tension coming from Marcos was tangible, and the silence was deafening.

I realized I hadn't finished the introductions. "Marcos." I decided I didn't like the feel of his given name passing my lips. His look of triumph at hearing it from me increased my anxiety. He looked at me possessively and glared at Tom's arm through which my hand was intertwined. I had to suppress a shudder at the intensity of his glare. "This is Mr. Buchanan."

Marcos's grin widened. I wished I could have called Tom by his given name again, but propriety forbid it when introducing him to a strange man. I was forced to introduce him as Mr. Buchanan, because that was what Tom would want to be addressed by from Marcos, but Marcos's look of triumph made me wish I had shunned propriety altogether.

Marcos extended his left hand to shake Tom's hand, smirking at me while doing it. I was confused for a moment before realizing why he had done it. I was holding on to Tom's left arm. He was my lifeboat harboring me safely from the storm that was Marcos. In reaching out his left hand, even though I suspected him to be right-handed, he was making Tom choose between snubbing him by not shaking his hand or removing my hand from his arm. I knew what he would do before he did it.

He gave me an apologetic smile before gently unwinding my hand from his arm. Marcos's grin widened in triumph at the sight. My control over my emotions slipped for a moment. I knew the displeasure showed on my face, causing Marcos to smirk and Tom to look more regretful. As Tom shook hands with Marcos, I could see Marcos squeezing hard, but Tom didn't flinch. They held onto each other for a few moments too long, neither of them wanting to let go first.

I cleared my throat quietly. Tom acquiesced and pulled his hand away and reached for mine again. "If you'll kindly excuse us, I was promised another dance."

Marcos stepped forward. "About that, the lady had hoped you might excuse her from her obligation so she might have the pleasure of dancing with me again."

Waves of anger crashed over me and my face heated in outrage. I had said no such thing. Tom looked at me with surprise; seeing the look on my face, it seemed he understood. He paused, considering for a moment, before turning back to Marcos and saying, "I would truly hate to disappoint the lady, but I must insist her obligation be honored."

The tension I felt disbursed a little with the relief that not only would I get to dance with Tom again, but he saved me from having to dance with Marcos. He put my hand back into the crook of his arm and led me away.

The moment we were out of earshot, I exclaimed, "Thank you so much! Truly, you're my savior."

He laughed and said, "It was the easiest rescue I could have performed. I'm honored to be used in any capacity you want me." I blushed and giggled at that. He laughed too before adding, "And I am honored to have the pleasure of dancing with you again, even if it is in obligation."

He laughed, and I knew that to have been a joke, but needed to clear the air nonetheless. "On my honor, I never said that."

His eyes lit up as he chuckled. "I guessed as much, but am glad just the same to hear you say it." He adopted a more serious tone before continuing, "But dear sweet Daisy, you have nothing to explain to me. If you had said it, I would still consider myself lucky to have you on my arm for a moment." At his assurances, my smile returned. "There's the smile I was hoping to see. I'm grateful for its return. Also, about earlier, I only asked for a second dance to keep Marcos away from you longer."

"A stroke of brilliance. It hadn't occurred to me to say that, but I'm glad you did."

"I can't imagine what he did to incur such a cold reaction from such a warm, loving person as you. I can't say I blame you, though. There's something off about that man, but even if that weren't the case, I would still be happy to be of service in helping you avoid him. But please don't feel you have to grant me a second dance."

"A second dance would be my pleasure."

"What I've done to be so blessed, I don't know, but best not to question it." With that, he laughed so infectiously, I was compelled to join him.

When he wrapped his arm around my waist, I felt sparks. I felt the heat touch my face. Embarrassed, I looked at him, and was relieved to see he looked flushed as well. Although I knew him to be distracted by my presence, his dancing didn't suffer. He moved precisely, powerfully through the steps. I couldn't stop my eyes from roaming over his muscles. When I looked back at his face and saw he was watching me, we both laughed.

As he spun me around the floor, I knew I was falling. I had dreamed of being swept off my feet by a dashing gentleman, but he was so much more than I had imagined. He was caring, polite, hilarious, and such a gentleman. When he held me, he did so respectfully. Unlike Marcos and most of the other so-called gentlemen tonight, Tom cared about making sure I was comfortable and happy. He showed me respect with both his words and actions. He hadn't once made any improper moves or gave me cause to feel uncomfortable. He was also the first man to ask what I was looking for out of tonight. If the others had asked anything, it had been what my parents wanted for me.

His was a difficult question. In truth, I didn't really know. I had thought my fantasies of being swept off my feet by a handsome stranger were just that, fantasies. But now here I was in his arms, so just what did I want now? I knew in my heart that now that I had met Tom, it would be hard to let him go. I hoped I might not have to. I knew I didn't know much about him, but I knew enough to know I wanted to know more. My heart was set on getting to know him. I didn't want to let him go.

The moment the thought crossed my mind, the music ended, announcing the end of our second dance.

Chapter Nineteen

That profound sense of loss returned as I pulled away from him. I would have loved a third dance, but knew it would hardly be proper. There were still several gentlemen I had not even met, never mind danced with. Still, I hesitated a moment, until I had an overwhelming feeling we were being watched. I turned as casually as I could, unsure of what I was looking for.

Over my shoulder, I saw my mother standing with Marcos and my father. Of all the men they had to take a liking to tonight, of course it would have to be the one I had the strongest objections to. It seemed Marcos and my father were talking and having a great time while my mother was glaring disapprovingly at me. I knew she didn't approve of Tom, but she was being ridiculous. She didn't even know him. For that matter, I barely knew him myself, but I knew I wanted to know more.

However, it didn't seem like I would get more of a chance tonight. I knew the night must have been coming to an end soon, and I was obligated to make some rounds and thank everyone for having come.

I sighed and turned back to Tom. "I'm sorry, but I can't ignore the rest of my duties for the night." He nodded understandingly. "I truly wish we had more time. It was an absolute pleasure to meet you. I hope the pleasure might be one that may soon be repeated."

He wore a sad smile. "Louisville to Chicago is no short trip."

My heart sunk. It hadn't occurred to me I might not see him again. I had rather hoped to spend more time with him and get to know him better, but I knew it wasn't fair to him that I felt disappointed, so I tried as best I could to hide the feeling. "I had let myself forget just how far you had come. I won't say you must come again, but if you do find yourself around here again, I would love for you to come see me."

He smiled again, more warmly this time. "I can promise you that if I do come down again, you will be the first person I come to see."

I smiled more broadly at that. "I do so hope for that to happen soon, but until then, perhaps we could write?"

I knew how forward of a request that was, but I fancied him as someone I would be happy to get to know better. He seemed surprised by my request but assented, saying that James could give me the address if I wished to write.

His response deflated me a little. I had hoped he would have agreed to write himself. However, once again, my disappointment wasn't fair to him. After all, we had only a few hours' worth of acquaintanceship. It was a wonder he agreed at all. I smiled and thanked him again and took my leave.

I made my rounds, introducing myself to those I had not met and thanking them for attending. Some parties were starting to take their leave. I thanked them for coming and assured them it was wonderful to meet them. This obligation took up much of my time and before I knew it, the ballroom had almost emptied entirely. There were some stragglers that I recognized from earlier but hadn't placed any importance on. Among the rest were, of course, my parents and Marcos, who it seemed I wasn't destined to be easily rid of.

His party, whom I had the misfortune of meeting that morning, was waiting by the door for him. At least it was a consolation that his friends appeared as unhappy about his lingering as I did.

I searched the ballroom, looking for Jordan. I was hoping she had stayed. Just then, I saw her stroll in from the garden with James on one arm and Tom on the other. She was smiling and laughing. She looked a picture of beauty and happiness. How everyone in the room wasn't instantly drawn to her presence like I was was quite a mystery to me. I started to cross the room to her, but heard someone clear their throat behind me.

I nearly jumped out of my skin. I turned around quickly, only to see it was just my mother. She gave me a stern look. "Why are you so jumpy?"

"I was startled. I didn't hear you come up behind me."

"Well, proper ladies don't jump or whip themselves around at the slightest of noise."

I knew it wasn't worth arguing, so I just nodded. She looked over her shoulder at my father and Marcos and said excitedly, "I was coming over to tell you just how lucky you are."

I was confused and waited for her to continue, but that seemed to be all she was planning to say. It seemed the longer I stayed silent, the more impatient and angry she became, so I asked, "I'm sorry, but what is it that makes me lucky?"

She glared at me and gestured wildly around the room. "You mean besides having loving parents who spoil you with your own ball? Besides living in a mansion with a full staff at your beck and call? Besides your loving mother doting on your every whim?"

I held in my laugh at her last statement and quickly apologized. "I'm sorry, Mama. Of course, I know I have a lot to be grateful for. I know how lucky I am-"

"I don't think you do."

"I simply meant to ask what you were referring to?"

The reminder seemed to put her back on track, and her excitement returned.

"Why, Mr. Hortense, of course!" I was filled with dread about what that could mean, but tried to reason that I might have been jumping to conclusions. "It seems that despite your," she glared at me while emphasizing her next words, "unlady-like antics, he has taken a liking to you."

I waited for her to say more. I still wasn't sure what she meant by that.

It seemed she expected more of a reaction from me. "Dear girl, why do you look as if I told you you were penniless? Don't you understand? He means to court you! He must be asking your father for his permission now. I just know it!"

The dread multiplied, but I still reasoned that maybe she was wrong. He had barely known me a few hours, and he lived so far away. "But I thought he lived in New Orleans?"

She nodded. "He does, and if things go well and you don't mess anything up, so will you, hopefully soon."

I didn't know what to say. I was at a loss for words and felt the panic rise up in me. I knew what I had agreed to when I asked for a debut, but I had imagined having more of a say in the matter. Had I had my own way, it would have been Tom who was making my father laugh and gaining permission to court me.

I don't know why I had thought things would go any differently. My parents had never consulted me about my life before. I knew after my mother first saw Tom that she wouldn't give him a chance, but I had reasoned that there were plenty of other eligible rich men here. I hoped against hope that they wouldn't try to push Marcos and me together, not that he required pushing. Unlike me, he seemed downright eager.

I reflected on how much of a blessing and a curse it was that I had accidentally met him this morning. I wondered, not for the first time tonight, if I hadn't the knowledge of his true character, if I would have felt a lot differently about him. I wanted to believe I would have disliked him all the same, but I knew deep down that wasn't true. He was charming and disarming. Had I not bumped into him this morning, I would have had no strong objections to his character this evening. I might have thought him a little too forward, but his appearance likely would have tipped the scale in his favor. Had I not known what I did, I might have even been thrilled at the news, but for better or worse, I couldn't forget what I knew.

Chapter Twenty

My mother urged me to follow her over to my father and Marcos. I hesitated a moment, wanting to continue on my way to see Jordan and to see Tom, but she grabbed my arm and dragged me across the ballroom. Knowing resistance was pointless, I picked up the pace and walked beside her over to my father and Marcos. They appeared to still be deep in conversation and were laughing when we approached. My father looked up and smiled when he saw us.

"My girls." He reached for my mother. She dropped my hand and took hold of his. He looked at both me and her, saying, "Just the lovely ladies we were hoping to see." My mother smiled coyly. He laughed and nudged Marcos. "Am I right, Marcos?"

He smirked at me and said, "Why, we had just been talking about-" He stopped himself and looked to my father, hesitating. "Should I tell her, or should it stay between us men for now?"

I was pretty sure I knew what he was going to say, but his hesitation held me in suspense.

My father looked at both me and my mother indulgently before he turned back to Marcos and said, "I don't see why not.

There can hardly be harm in it. I'm sure they want to share in the joy."

He looked at me and said, "Perhaps you would like to take a walk?"

The look in his eye told me all I needed to know about how bad of an idea it would be to take a walk alone with him.

My parents were staring at me expectantly. I panicked for a moment before seeing Jordan over my mother's shoulder on the far side of the room. Seeing her arm in arm with James gave me a brilliant idea. "I would like to, but-" The confusion showed on my father's face, Marcos looked mildly insulted and surprised, and my mother looked downright angry. I finished quickly, adopting an expression of regret

on my face that I didn't feel, "that would hardly be proper." This answer seemed to be satisfactory to both my parents, but not to him.

He urged, "I really must insist on speaking with you, and would rather it not be in the company of your parents."

A moment later, it seemed he realized how what he had said might have been interpreted and turned back to my father to explain himself or apologize, I didn't know which.

My father interrupted with a chuckle. "Don't worry about it, Marcos. I know what you mean. Some things are best said without the presence of a lady's parents."

I was panicking. I had hoped to avoid the encounter altogether, but it seemed that wasn't an option. I had one last hope, one last trick up my sleeve. "It would be lovely to talk without my parents, but it would hardly be proper for me to be wandering about alone with a man I've just met." I looked at my parents. "I'm sure you both want us to have a chaperone. After all, we wouldn't want word getting out that I was seen wandering off alone with a potential suitor." That sealed the deal, and he knew it, too. His face fell, knowing he had lost. My mother looked horrified at the implication and looked wildly around for anyone who could chaperone us. Before she found anyone else, I added, "I just saw Jordan over there somewhere. I am sure she and James wouldn't mind accompanying us on a walk through the gardens."

I hadn't thought it possible for him to look more disappointed than he already had, but his face fell even further into a full-blown scowl.

Before anything else could be said, I caught Jordan's eye and waved her over. To my dismay, Tom came, too. I had hoped he would be spared having to see me interact with Marcos. I worried he wouldn't be able to see through the pleasantries I was forced to engage in with him. I hadn't wanted him to witness this. However, Jordan, James, and Tom all came over. I was determined Marcos not know it bothered me. He had already gone out of his way to stake his claim on me in front of Tom; the last thing I needed was him feeling he had more reason to do so.

I looked at Marcos with a smile that I hoped showed I felt triumphant in how things were going, rather than feeling nauseous and unsettled, like I was. I looked at Jordan, purposefully avoiding Tom's eye. I hoped that if I didn't look at him, he would understand to act distant. I didn't want Marcos to see any further hint that I was interested in Tom. I didn't need anything to happen to cause Marcos to act rashly.

"Jordan, dear, Marcos wanted to go for a walk. I was hoping you and *James*," I placed extra emphasis on James, excluding Tom, hoping she would understand and wildly praying he would also understand, "would join us. I would hate to have anyone saying that Daisy Fay wanders around with strange men at night."

Jordan smirked at me. I could see she was fighting to hold in her laughter at that and at the performance I was putting on for Marcos and my parents. However, Marcos wasn't amused. He moved closer to me and put his arm around my shoulder, pulling me rather suddenly and roughly closer to him. My first instinct was to push him away, but I knew better than to do so in front of my mother.

He chuckled, saying, "My dear, I'm hardly a stranger."

I refused to apologize, but I donned what I hoped was an apologetic look and simply said, "I didn't mean for that to be offensive. I just meant we hardly know each other."

He smiled at me possessively. "I know all I need to."

I smiled politely and turned to Jordan. She jumped in. "Of course we'll join you both."

She turned to Tom, asking if he wanted to go ahead without them or stick around. I prayed he would go ahead without them. He looked thoughtful for a moment, looking at me. Whatever he saw led him to say he would stick around. I tensed under Marcos's arm.

Marcos looked at me with interest. When he smiled more broadly, I realized his mistake. It seemed he had somehow convinced himself I was upset that Tom was coming because I didn't want to be around Tom. Well, if that was what he thought, I certainly didn't need to correct him.

However, Jordan had noticed my reaction, too.

I could only hope Tom hadn't.

We excused ourselves from my parents and the five of us headed out of the ballroom into the gardens.

The gardens were glowing in the moonlight. The hedges, garlands, and multitude of flowers were bathed in moonlight. It was a magical sight, truly romantic. I felt keenly my disappointment and anger that I was here with Marcos and not with Tom. Now that we were out of eyesight of my parents,

I moved Marcos's arm from my shoulder. He took that as a cue to take my hand and held tightly, conveying his strength and power with how tightly he squeezed my hand.

He turned to me, smiling. "Why don't we head down this way?" He pointed to the darkest path leading away from the house. I hesitated a moment but wasn't able to come up with a rational reason or excuse not to, so I let him lead the way.

Chapter Twenty - One

I started at a stroll, but he picked up the pace, dragging me along. Even if I had wanted to hurry along with him, it would have been difficult in the shoes I was wearing. I tried to pull away a couple of times or to slow him, but he wouldn't be deterred. As I was being dragged rather unwillingly, I had to give all my attention to staying upright.

I was confused about where we were headed. There was nothing out this way. It wasn't until we turned another corner on the path that he stopped. I looked around, unsure what I was expecting. My confusion quickly turned to dread when I realized we had lost the others. Despite my best efforts, he had gotten what he wanted. I was alone with him and likely out of earshot of everyone.

He looked at me with a predatory smile that made my skin crawl. Here was the man from this morning. I had almost convinced myself I was unfairly judging him.

As I saw his smile widen, I prayed I would come out of this unscathed, but I was no fool. I looked around wildly for any way out of this. Seeing none, I racked my brain. I tried to think of everything I knew of him from our short acquaintance, anything that could help. I was desperate. I knew if I was going to come out of this unharmed, I would have to play my cards right.

I was hit with a stroke of inspiration. He had been saying all along how much he liked a challenge; maybe if I proved not to be a challenge, he might lose interest. It was an act of desperation, but I felt it was my only hope.

I internally shuddered at what I was about to do. I gave him a sultry smile, feeling ridiculous and nauseated, but hoping it looked genuine. "Finally! I thought we would never be alone."

His eyes widened with confusion and his smile took on a more genuine tone. He cocked an eyebrow at me and said, "We might've been alone much sooner if you hadn't protested so much."

I laughed and looked at him with mock disbelief. "You mean you actually bought that?" I asked, gesturing back in the direction of the house.

He looked even more confused. "I'm not sure what you mean?"

"That good girl act." I laughed while looking at him with disbelief. "The whole 'I couldn't possibly wander around with a man I've just met' act." I rolled my eyes. I wasn't sure he was buying it and shuddered at what might happen if he didn't. I was shaking internally and praying it wasn't showing. "My dear parents want to believe their daughter to be some sort of saint." I rolled my eyes again. "Who am I to deny them that? Personally, I think of it as a rather amusing game." I laughed, and he joined in.

He grinned at me, looking thoroughly impressed.

"I think I might have underestimated you."

I laughed and said in a playfully mocking tone, "But I thought you knew everything you needed to about me."

He laughed. "I thought I did, too. It turns out you're full of surprises."

I heard a noise and prayed it was the others on their way to us. I hastened to distract him in case he noticed and tried to pull me away again. "Speaking of surprises, are you going to continue to keep me in suspense?"

He paused a moment before answering. I was worried he had heard the noise, but he was still grinning and staring at me appraisingly. After a moment, he asked in a teasing tone, "Are you quite sure you don't know?"

I laughed at that and bantered back, adopting the same mock innocent tone I had earlier, looking at him with as wide eyed an innocent look as I could muster. "I can't imagine I do. Perhaps you should enlighten me."

He burst out in laughter. "You really are quite the actress, but now that I know your little secret," he winked at me, "I can assure you I won't fall for the innocent act again." I shuddered internally and worried if I was taking this too far.

I heard louder footsteps. Someone, hopefully Jordan but at this point anyone would be welcome, was approaching quickly. Desperate to distract him, I licked my lips before responding. It had the desired effect. His eyes instantly went to my lips. I knew he was thinking of nothing else. I really hoped I wouldn't regret this, but I knew I had drawn all his attention away from the footsteps if he had heard them.

"Maybe it isn't an act. Maybe I just can't help myself around a big, strong man like you. Maybe I just want to hear you say it."

I was internally cringing at having said that and wondered if I had taken it too far, but one look at his face and I knew I had him enthralled. "I would hate to disappoint such a lovely lady. I asked you here, primarily to get you alone."

My dread intensified, and I prayed whoever was approaching would hurry.

We must have gone further than I thought because if I knew Jordan at all, I knew she was hurrying to my rescue as quickly as she could. "But I did also want to let you know I gained your father's permission to court you." I swallowed my nausea and smiled at him like he was the answer to my prayers. "I had hoped to take you home with me, but it seems your father refused to part with you until something more official had happened." He chuckled. "It seemed he had the same concerns about your reputation as you did." We both laughed at that. He looked me up and down, letting his eyes linger on my curves longer than I would have liked. "It's truly a shame we must part for so long. I will count the days until I'm able to return and stake a stronger claim on you and see more of what Louisville has to offer."

The way he was undressing me with his eyes, I doubted very much if it was Louisville he wanted to see more of. But my heart had leapt with hope onto his comment that we would be long parted.

I hastened to ask, "How long will you be gone?"

He took my haste to be me being upset about his leaving. He grinned and said, "Someone's quite eager for my return. Try not to worry. I won't be gone a minute longer than can be helped." He saw the question on my face and took a more serious tone. "Unfortunately, the holidays, the winter, and some business that absolutely must be taken care of will keep me away a good deal longer than I would like." He thought for a moment before adding, "It would seem impossible for me to return before February, but I will strive for January."

Internally, I was celebrating. I had at least two months to work on my parents and try to convince them to let me out of this before his business would allow him to return. I wondered for a moment what it was he did for business. The thought struck me as funny. I knew so little about this man to whom my parents had all but agreed for me to marry. He watched my reactions and seemed to decide I was still upset at his leaving.

He crossed the small distance between us. Surprised, I took a step back and felt my back hit the hedge behind me. With a predatory smile, he stepped forward, putting his arms to either side of me. He looked around a moment before turning back to me with a grin. "It seems we're quite alone, and I'll be gone for quite a long time. Perhaps you'll give me something to remember you by." He closed the distance between us and his lips crashed onto mine. I tried to move out from under him, but his grip tightened on my arms. I tried to push him off me but I wasn't strong enough.

He felt me struggling and pulled back with a smile that made my skin crawl. "I knew this was too easy. So much for the good girl act being an act."

He chuckled to himself while I continued to struggle to push him away from me, to no avail. I kept struggling. "Wow! Quite a feisty one." He laughed again. "It's a good thing I'm such a big strong man," he said mockingly, emphasizing my earlier words. "I'm more than up to the challenge. I was worried you might make this too easy."

I was shocked at his words and, as focused as I was on trying to escape, I didn't hide my reaction.

He seemed delighted by my response and laughed before saying, "Where's the fun in it if there isn't a little fight? I really have to thank you for turning out to be quite feisty. It's always more fun to break a woman who isn't willing."

Disgusted and shocked, I doubled my efforts to push him away, but he tightened his grip on my arms and pushed me roughly into the hedges. I tried yelling to anyone who might hear, hoping my friends were in earshot, but no one responded to my cries.

He grinned wider. "No one can hear you, my dear. Scream and cry all you want. No one is coming for you."

He laughed to himself and pulled my hands roughly above my head. He grabbed both hands with one of his. I thought that was my moment, that I would be able to get away, but as hard as I fought, he didn't budge. I tried to knee him in the groin, but he sidestepped easily out of the way.

With one of his hands now free, he brought his attention to my dress and began moving my skirts out of the way. I had been fighting until then, but now felt the futility in full force. He was eagerly enjoying my fighting, and I knew there was no way I could overpower him.

I stopped fighting.

I knew it was useless.

A tear slid down my cheek as I felt him touching my thigh. I prayed it would be over quickly.

Chapter Twenty - Two

A moment later, my prayers were answered as he was ripped away from me. It took me a moment to come back to my senses and realize what had happened. When I did, I saw Marcos and Tom wrestling on the ground. Tom had gotten in a few good punches, but Marcos wasn't giving up easily. James and Jordan were standing nearby, but James was too preoccupied restraining Jordan from entering the fray to help Tom. I watched in horror as Marcos landed a couple of punches on Tom.

I ran over to James and yelled, "Do something!" He indicated wildly at Jordan with his eyes. "Never mind Jordan. Go put a stop to this madness!" I took hold of Jordan's shoulders and turned her to face me. I was shocked for a moment by the murder I saw in her eyes. "Jordan, my love, snap out of it. I need you to take a couple of deep breaths and focus on me. I need you."

I worried she would push past me and throw herself into the fight. I was touched she was so worried about me, but the idea of her getting hurt vastly increased my worry. I didn't want to have to worry about her, too. I didn't want anyone getting hurt on my account, except for maybe Marcos.

The thought of his name threatened to bring forth some strong emotions about what had just happened, but I knew now wasn't the time or place. I shook my head to clear my thoughts. I couldn't focus on that right now. I couldn't let myself. I needed to make sure Tom was okay, and that Jordan didn't get herself hurt. I could worry about my own feelings later. I watched as Jordan took a few deep breaths and relaxed her shoulders. She looked at me apologetically.

"Are you okay? Did he hurt you? I swear I will end his miserable life myself if he hurt you."

"Jord, I'm okay. I'm right here and I'm okay, but I need you to calm down."

She took another deep breath. "Are you okay? How are you holding up?"

I was glad to see she had regained her senses. I shrugged my shoulders, not knowing how else to respond. I turned back and watched James grab Marcos by the jacket and yank him off Tom. He then stepped in between them. Tom jumped back up and tried to push past James, but James didn't budge.

As he held Tom back, he looked at Marcos and said curtly, "You had better show yourself out."

Marcos slowly rose to his feet. James was struggling to hold Tom back. All the while, Marcos didn't even flinch. He took his time dusting off his jacket and looked at me and met my eye. He smiled at me and dropped into a bow, not breaking eye contact. "Till next time, my future bride. Farewell, my fair Daisy." He righted himself and turned on his heel, walking back in the direction we came from.

Only once he was around the corner did Tom fall into silence. I turned back to him to see if my fears were warranted or not. I worried he had been badly injured. To my relief, he looked like he would have some bruises, but nothing looked to be serious.

He caught sight of me, and his eyes softened with worry and concern. "Are you quite alright?"

I was so thoroughly moved by his compassion. Here he was with bruises covering him and he was asking about how I was doing. I wasn't prepared for his unexpected kindness. I had been about to apologize to him that he had to get involved and that he had gotten hurt on my account, but *he* wanted to check on *me*. The kindness was too much to handle.

Overwhelmed by emotion, the tears I had been holding back burst out of me. He pulled me into a hug, which was quite unexpected but comforting. He pat my back as I wept. When I pulled away, he said, "I'm so sorry. I had feared the worst when I heard your screams. I am so sorry I didn't make it here in time to have stopped him. Knowing that scoundrel took advantage of you, I won't know a moment of peace until I know he is far from you again."

I thanked him wholeheartedly, but now that I had calmed a little, I felt awkward about having thrown myself weeping into the arms of essentially a stranger. I pulled away sheepishly and turned to face Jordan and James. I was surprised to find Jordan right behind me with her arms waiting for me. I jumped into her arms the moment I saw her, and she held onto me.

"I think we should get you to bed. I'm sure you could use the comfort of your bedroom and some rest."

I nodded. That was exactly what I needed.

I turned to Tom. "You truly are too kind. I hope to see you again soon and hope you don't think worse of me."

He looked indignant. "I would never judge you for the actions of that scoundrel. I know I look in rough shape, but he'll be the one feeling worse tomorrow. I don't blame you in the slightest."

I was relieved, and bid him farewell. I wanted to say more, but as usual, Jordan was right. I was thoroughly exhausted and was feeling uncomfortable and paranoid remaining in the gardens.

She walked me the entire way back through the gardens, through the ballroom, through the series of twisting and turning corridors, all the way to my bedroom.

She didn't stop there. She helped me out of my dress and laid the garment carefully over the armchair in the corner of the room. She helped me into bed and sat on the side of the bed herself.

She looked lovingly at me and started playing with my hair. It helped to calm me. She always knew just what I needed.

"Thank you, Jord, so much."

"For what, darling?"

"For being here... for taking care of me... for being you."

I smiled up at her, wondering what in the world I would ever do without her. I was starting to get sleepy, but I needed to make sure she understood. I needed to make sure I found the words. "Yes, that's it. Thank you for being you."

She smiled sadly at me and continued playing with my hair. "You set the bar so low. I let you down today."

At that, I shot up into a sitting position and whipped my head toward her. "How could you say that? You didn't let me down."

I noticed now that she was blinking back tears. I felt my heart breaking.

"Of course I did. I swore I would protect you and that I would be there for you. I told you I wouldn't let anything happen to you. For God's sake, I told you I would be there for you tonight, and where was I the one time you actually needed me? Nowhere to be found. Tom had to come to your rescue. I can't believe I couldn't protect you."

I took her face in my hands, making her meet my eye. I had to make her understand. "Jord, it's not your job to protect me." She started to protest, but I continued. "If anything had happened to you tonight, I would have never forgiven myself. I wouldn't dream of letting you get hurt for me. It would kill me."

"And how do you think seeing you hurt made me feel? I could have killed him, Dais. I wouldn't have thought twice about ending his life."

"I'm really okay, Jord, I swear."

"I know you are, love. I'm so proud of how strong you are, but you shouldn't have had to be strong. I should've been there to protect you."

"But you have to know you can't always be there to protect me."

"Watch me. I swear I will kill him or any other man who dares to try to touch you against your will again."

I know I should have told her to stop talking like that, to stop thinking like that, but I couldn't bring myself to. It felt nice to be so loved and protected. I knew there was more that needed to be said but I was drifting quickly off to sleep.

"I love you, too, Jord," I muttered sleepily.

Chapter Twenty - Three

The next thing I knew, it was morning. When I first woke, I was certain the night before had been a nightmare. There was no way I was to be engaged to a man I couldn't stand. There was no way that same man tried to attack me in my own gardens. There was no way the only man I met last night that I had the slightest interest in had rescued me by fighting the scoundrel that attacked me. The story was even more wild than my typical dreams. I laughed, thinking I would have to tell Jordan about the crazy story my mind had concocted.

I stretched my arms and flinched back in surprise when my right arm collided with a solid object. Confused and alarmed, I sat up quickly and looked to my right. Jordan was collapsed, still fast asleep, next to me. The sight startled me, and I tried to think past my memories of the vivid dream to what had actually happened last night.

At that moment, a brilliant ray of sunlight came bursting through the window, hitting the armchair.

There was a brilliant explosion of blue and green through the room. I looked to the source and saw that my necklace and dress were laying atop the armchair. It took a moment for the truth to sink in. The moment it did, I let out a horrified gasp. It felt like my world was slipping from beneath my feet. My heart sunk. It wasn't a crazy dream. That had actually happened. Not only had my night been ruined, but I was expected to be courted by and be wed to the very scoundrel of a man who had attacked me. I couldn't believe it.

I felt stirring next to me and looked over apologetic about having woken her. I started to say I was sorry, but she wouldn't hear of my apologizing.

"Don't, darling. You have nothing to apologize for. I'm glad you woke me. I wanted to be awake when you woke up. How are you doing?"

"As well as to be expected. I had truly thought last night to have been a bad dream. I thought it sounded too crazy to have actually happened." I chuckled mirthlessly. "It turns out my life is crazier than my dreams. What happened after I fell asleep? I can't believe you stayed the night. You really didn't have to." I looked down sheepishly, feeling both grateful that she stayed and guilty that she must have felt she had to. I added quickly, "Although I'm quite glad you did. I can imagine this morning would have been much harder on me if I had had to wake up alone."

She turned abruptly to me and took my hands. "How could I have possibly dreamed of leaving you after everything you went through yesterday? You know me better than that." She looked out the window for a moment and said under her breath, more to herself than me, "Unlike some people."

I noticed now, for the first time, how unkempt and upset she looked. I knew her night hadn't been easy either. I was thankful she had left with me when she did. I had been really worried she would have tried to get the upper hand with Marcos. While Jordan was feisty, she would've been no match for him and would've gotten herself hurt for me. I never would've forgiven myself if she had. I knew she hadn't, but all the same,

I inspected her for any signs of physical injuries and was relieved to find none, but she looked upset just the same.

"What happened after I fell asleep, love?" I pressed. "Tell me, are you okay?"

She smiled at me. "Of course you would ask that. You were the one who was assaulted last night, and you're concerned about how *I'm* doing. You're ridiculously kind. Do you want to talk about what happened last night?"

I hesitated, thinking about her question. Did I want to talk about yesterday? I had thought I had so much to tell her. I had wanted to talk to her about Marcos and about my dances with both him and Tom, but it all seemed unimportant now. I knew she wanted to know if I wanted to talk about my feelings about what happened with Marcos, but I didn't think I was ready, so I shook my head.

She nodded. It seemed she expected as much. "But distract me. Please tell me what's bothering you. I'm starting to get worried."

A horrible thought occurred to me, and I looked wildly around the room before blurting out, "Marcos didn't return, did he?!"

She immediately reassured me that he hadn't, and my heart started to beat normally again after a few moments. When she saw I was calmer, she said, "None of us saw another sign of him last night. However, from the staff, we gathered he came back to the house and rather hastily said farewell to your parents with promises to return as soon as possible." I must have looked scared because she added, "But he told them it wouldn't be possible for him to return before January, and that in all likelihood, he would be tied up for all of January as well, but would definitely return by February."

I felt some relief and reassurance that I would have a while to deal with my emotions, but I couldn't see a way out of this. I had no idea what would happen when he returned. I knew he would likely ask for my hand in marriage. I would sooner cut off my hand than promise it to him, but I didn't know if my parents would let me refuse. After how doting my mother had been on Marcos, I worried if I turned him down that my mother might finally follow through on her frequent threats of disowning me.

"What am I going to do?" I quietly asked.

Jordan hugged me. "I truly don't know. I don't know, my dear, but we'll figure something out together. I swear we will. I won't let you end up with a scoundrel like him. It'll be me and you against the world like it's always been."

I laughed, liking the sound of that, but added jokingly, "Yeah, me and you and James. I'm not sure he'll like this turn of events."

I laughed again at the annoyance I knew he would feel at finding out Jordan wanted me around even more than I already had been. But after a moment, I noticed Jordan wasn't laughing along. I looked up at her, confused.

"Well, actually, about that… I meant to tell you, but didn't want you worried about me. I wanted to make sure you were okay, and the last thing I wanted was to make you worry about me this morning."

"I can assure you I'm far more worried not knowing what's wrong."

She sighed. "I know. So much for waiting a couple of days before breaking the news. I normally wouldn't have dreamed of waiting to tell you, but I thought you might need a few days to process your own emotions and didn't want to cloud them with mine. But I don't want you worried over something like this, and you may as well know now. You were going to find out sooner or later, anyway." She paused a moment before saying, "James and I broke up."

I gasped. That was the last thing I had expected. "Oh my..." I trailed off, not knowing what to say. James had been her longest, happiest relationship. I grabbed her hands and took a better look at her. She looked like she might have cried herself to sleep and looked like she hadn't slept a wink. I had thought she was so disheveled from her own feelings about what happened to me last night and potentially from sleeping in a strange bed. It was funny. She had never spent the night until now. I hoped it was something that would be repeated for happier reasons. I looked at her more closely, trying to gauge how she was feeling about things, but her face told me nothing. "What happened, love? Are you okay?"

She looked back at me and sighed. "I'm telling you all this because I know you'll keep poking and prodding at me until it comes out, but I know you might find some way to blame yourself, and that's the last thing I want. Please, do try to hear me out, and know that what happened was my own decision and was in no way your fault, okay?"

Her preface made my heart sink. I knew from how carefully she chose her words, and how much she emphasized that she didn't want me blaming myself, that the breakup was somehow my fault. There was no reason she would have tried to elicit a promise from me to hold myself blameless unless I should hold the blame. I shook my head. I couldn't promise her that. I was already blaming myself and I didn't even know the circumstances yet. She sighed and amended. "Fine, just promise me you won't upset yourself by giving yourself unnecessary blame."

I latched onto the word unnecessary. I could promise not to give myself any more of the blame than necessary, but I was sure there would be blame that fell on my shoulders. I nodded. "I can promise that I won't blame myself more than necessary."

She chuckled humorlessly, saying, "And I suppose that's the best I can get from you promise-wise?"

I nodded. She knew me well enough to know I wouldn't lie to her by promising something I didn't feel I could deliver on.

She sighed before continuing. "Well, I guess that will have to be good enough. So, I suppose I should tell you that James and I had been bickering more than usual lately. I'm sure you noticed he has been a bit ruder than normal to you." I had noticed but didn't want to interrupt, so I gave a slight nod. "Well, I noticed, too, and I wasn't okay with it."

I really hoped there was more to the story than that. I didn't like James, but I had gotten used to him and most of his comments didn't bother me anymore. I learned to ignore him as best I could so that Jordan could be happy.

"I told him over and over again that I wasn't okay with him treating you like that. You're my best friend and him showing you no care or respect after you continued to try to be nice to him was a grave offense to me. I told him he was going to have to be better to you. I told him our future depended on it." I looked at her, horrified. So, it was all my fault.

"Jord, you can't mean that! I'm so, so sorry-"

She cut me off. "Please don't apologize. I'm not done yet. That wasn't the ultimate reason. I had told him he had to be on his best behavior yesterday, and, for the most part, he was. I was happy that he could get along with you and tried to help get Marcos away from you. I hoped he would succeed, but it turns out I must have been wrong about him. I can't believe it took me so long to realize that." She looked at me apologetically. "Especially when the evidence of how he treated you was right in front of my face, but he was always such a gentleman to me, and I really thought he could change."

She sighed. "Anyway, the night was going pretty well, and I had been proud of him for trying to deter Marcos from you. I really thought things were going great. I had a wonderful time with him and with Tom." She looked at me when she said Tom's name. The look she gave me brought color to my cheeks. "Speaking of Tom, I have been dying to ask how things went with him last night." She looked at me suggestively and laughed. I just rolled my eyes and waved my hand at her prompting her to continue. "Okay! Okay. You win, but we will circle back there."

I wasn't surprised. I knew she would do as much. "So, anyway, I was having a wonderful time until the end of the night. You asked us to walk with you and obviously I knew how important it was that we went. I wasn't going to leave you alone with him after knowing how uncomfortable you were around him. I didn't bother asking James if he would come, because I didn't want to give him a chance to say no. I was a little surprised that Tom agreed to come, though." She shot me another suggestive look. "Things must have gone better than I thought if he's already following you around."

I couldn't help laughing. She joined in the laughter and after a few moments when we both caught our breath, I prompted her to continue. She rolled her eyes. "Okay, okay, but we are going to talk about Tom. So, like I was saying, when the five of us all went into the garden, James pulled me aside to talk. He told me I always made you more of a priority than him and how I disrespected him by not asking him if he wanted to come out to walk in the gardens." She rolled her eyes. "It was absurd. I explained to him how worried I was about you and how much Marcos creeps you out and he actually took Marcos's side. He kept telling me that Marcos seems like a real gentleman and that you would be lucky to be with him. It was ridiculous, as if Marcos would be the lucky one. But, anyway, after a few minutes of hashing things out, things were more tense than ever between us and nothing had been resolved but neither of us knew what to say. Then I realized we had lost not only Tom but also you and Marcos. I was really worried and voiced my concern. He had the audacity to ask what I worried might happen to you. Of course, that bothered me fiercely. I told him so and told him I was worried Marcos might hurt you or try to violate you, and James laughed."

I looked at her incredulously. I knew he didn't like me, but I thought her to be exaggerating.

"No. I'm being honest. Honest to goodness, the man laughed when I said I was worried about you." She shuddered, and I could see the leftover anger burning in her eyes. "That wasn't all. I would have killed him if it hadn't been more important to find you. He actually said that Marcos might be the man to put that tease in her place. I asked him what he thought he was saying. It was obvious how angry I was. I thought he might apologize or offer some explanation for what he meant, but he didn't. It got worse." I was about to ask how it could have possibly gotten worse when she continued. "He said that the ice queen could use some thawing and that the floozy of Louisville shouldn't be turning down a gentleman as rich and powerful as Marcos."

She stopped a moment, taking a few deep breaths, trying to calm herself. I was flabbergasted. I couldn't believe James's hatred of me was so strong that he would wish for my pain and suffering. I hadn't done anything to him, besides being friends with Jordan and attempting to form a friendship with him as well. I couldn't help but think I was grateful to Jordan that I wouldn't have to see him again.

She had regained her composure enough to continue. "Well, I ended things on the spot. I told him we were done, and then I headed off in the direction I thought you, Marcos, and

Tom went. I tried to convince myself you would be fine, and that Tom had stuck to you two even if James and I hadn't, but I was still worried.

"I picked up my pace, walking briskly down the path, but I didn't run into you and Marcos, or into Tom. I had almost convinced myself I was imagining things and being overprotective. I had just slowed my pace when I heard you scream. I took off in that direction and made it there faster than I thought I could move. I made it in time to see Tom pull Marcos off you and start hitting him. I was about to join in myself and tried to run forward, only to find myself held back. I thought one of Marcos's friends had showed up to help him, but when I looked as well as I could over my shoulder while being restrained, I saw it was James. He must have followed me. I was incensed at the audacity he had in holding me back."

I went to interject, but she held up her hand.

"I know, I know. Now I understand he was foolishly trying to protect me, but then I was seeing red. I had just ended things with this man and he still dared to touch me. Not only to touch me, but to restrain me from helping you. I felt in that moment, and still do feel now, that I would never forgive him for that offense.

"I know I could have helped Tom. Poor Tom was hurt because James held me back. It was foolish. He should have helped Tom, not restrained me, or, better yet, let me help Tom. Part of me wonders if he was trying to protect Marcos." My eyebrows shot up, and she nodded. "I know. I know it sounds crazy, but I knew he didn't care about your best interest, and I really doubt if he cared about mine, either. I mean, had he cared about me, he wouldn't have stopped me."

"You could have been badly hurt! Jord, you know how highly I think of you, and I know your strength and that you might've been able to hold your own, but it wasn't worth the risk. If you had gotten hurt on my account, I don't know what I would've done. James holding you back is the only thing I don't hold against him."

"I know you feel that way, but imagine if you saw me hurt in front of you and the culprit was attacking another of your friends. I'm sure you would have wanted to help."

"Of course I would have, but I'm glad you didn't all the same, and you know I've never been a big fan of James, but I know how much you cared about him. I'm so sorry for how things ended."

The anger came back into her eyes. "I'm not. I should have done it far sooner. I can't believe it took me as long as it did." The anger subsided after a moment and was replaced with a touch of sadness. "I know it needed to be done. There was no way I would let him near me after what he said about you, but I didn't imagine it would be that hard."

I was the last person to want her and James to work things out, but since it sounded like I had come between Jordan and her happiness, I had to ask, "My dear, are you sure this is what you want? That you want things to be over? You were both upset and angry. Maybe if you talk things over now that you've both had a chance to calm down, maybe things could be different."

She sighed. "Unless he can change the past and take back what he said, there is no mending things. I couldn't forget the things he said about you. There is no forgiveness that I can give a man who would say things like that." I know I looked upset because she added, "It's not just about you. I wouldn't be with a man who said those careless, callous, cruel things about any woman. The fact that it was about you made me jump more swiftly to end things, but regardless of whether it was you or not, I know I would have arrived at the same conclusion. Besides, we did speak after."

I know the surprise showed on my face. I took another look at her. She looked like she had been here all night.

She chuckled at the look on my face and said, "I didn't leave you for long, but something else happened after we came up here and you fell asleep. A little while after you fell asleep, I heard a knock on your door. I thought it would be one of the staff, or maybe even one of your parents inquiring after you with everything that happened."

I outright laughed at that.

"I know. I should have known better. But, anyway, I wasn't prepared to see James on the other side of the door."

"So, what happened?" I blurted out.

"Well, I went out into the hall with him and we talked. He apologized for saying the things he did and asked me to let him walk me home. I refused. He didn't take it well, which was ridiculous. It wasn't even me turning him down. I might have let him walk me home, I don't really know. But I didn't even consider it since I knew I wasn't going home. I explained to him that I wasn't going to leave you alone, and he rolled his eyes. I mean, I know he thinks we spend too much time together, but there was no chance I was leaving you alone yesterday after everything that happened. He didn't get it and it's obvious he never will. If I had been considering forgiving him, which I wasn't, his attitude affirmed everything I already knew."

I knew her well enough to see past her tough exterior. Plus, anyone with eyes could tell she had been crying. I knew she was having a harder time with their breakup than she was willing to admit to. I wrapped her in my arms and hugged her for a long while.

After a while, she asked what I meant to do about Marcos and my parents. I sighed. I hadn't the slightest clue what to do. I told her as much, and we spent most of the day shut up in my room, talking about what to do about the future.

I didn't know how, but I knew I needed to end any attachments with Marcos. There was no way I could ever allow that man near me again. I was relieved that he wasn't returning until February. A couple of months was more than enough time to come up with a plan.

Chapter Twenty - Four

It turns out now that Jordan was single, she had a lot more time on her hands. I knew she was healing from her breakup and tried to be sensitive and lend an ear to her when she needed to talk, but it was hard to be truly sad about the outcome. I never did like James and knew she would be better off without him.

I was overjoyed at being able to spend so much more time with Jordan. I had missed her dearly and was grateful to see her as often as I did. She hadn't changed a bit with *me*, but I did notice a change in her. She had always been assertive and guarded. She was never guarded with me, but she certainly was with the rest of the world. James had broken her out of her shell a bit more, but now that they were over, her walls were back up and higher than ever. While I enjoyed that her time was now exclusively mine and her own, it hurt me that she was hurting. I knew it was hard for her to open up to people, and she had opened up to James and things hadn't worked out. I had guessed she would become a bit more cynical, but wasn't prepared for how guarded she became with the world. I knew how much she was hurting and tried to help as much as I could.

It seemed all she wanted to do was spend time with me, which I couldn't have been happier about. We spent all her free time together. As a result, the weeks flew by. We talked now and again about what was to be done about Marcos, but we kept coming up blank. We assured ourselves there was time to think it over and come up with a plan.

Except, before we knew it, the Christmas season was upon us and there was ample to be done to prepare. The Fays always threw a big holiday feast. My parents had expected Marcos to come in for the occasion and were sorely disappointed.

They didn't want their darling daughter without a date at the first event after her debut. They begged and pleaded with me to beg Marcos to attend. Needless to say, I never agreed. They then switched the question, asking if there was any man I would invite to be my date. The question had taken me by surprise, and my thoughts jumped to Tom. I wondered if I could write to him and ask him to come. I hadn't written to him these past weeks, because I didn't know what I would say and had hoped he might write to me, but he didn't.

If I did write, would he even come? I tried a few times to write out the words, but I couldn't figure out what to say. Jordan encouraged me, saying she knew he must be smitten and would come running, but I didn't know whether to believe her. He hadn't written. If he cared, why wouldn't he have written?

We were only a couple weeks out from Christmas, and I knew I was running out of time. Jordan was lying on my bed while I was sitting at my vanity trying to write. The floor was littered with several unfinished letters I had deemed not right and crumpled. I was deep in thought, trying to figure out what to say next, when there was a knock on the door.

I turned around quickly, surprised. The staff normally didn't interrupt when Jordan was here.

She raised an eyebrow at me. I knew she was as curious as I was. I shrugged in response since I didn't have any more answer than she did and opened the door.

It was one of the maids with what looked to be a thick stack of envelopes. She looked over her shoulder before thrusting them into my hands and leaving in a hurry. I stood there trying to understand what had happened. Jordan, sick of waiting, came to my side. She closed the door and looked at what I was holding.

"Letters?"

Her voice brought me back to reality. I looked down at the parcel in my hands. "Looks like it."

"Do you think they could be from him?"

I couldn't imagine Tom would have nearly that much to stay in the few weeks we had been parted, so I shook my head. "I wish, but with my luck, it's probably Marcos."

I eyed the letters warily. This couldn't be anything good. Jordan led me back to my bed, and we sat down, both looking at the letters. The return address didn't give a name, just an address from France. Well, that ruled out Marcos. I couldn't imagine who the letters would be from. I had never been far from Louisville, never mind to France. The letters themselves looked rather beaten up. Unlike the letters I sometimes received from admirers, these hadn't been sealed with a family crest. They hadn't been well sealed at all.

Jordan piped up. "It really doesn't look like these are from Marcos."

I carefully took the first one off the pile and examined the handwriting. I don't know what I thought I was looking for, but I didn't recognize the writing.

"Well, here goes nothing." I carefully opened the envelope and looked inside. I pulled out and unfolded the letter, scanning the words for a signature. The moment I saw the name, the letter fell from my hand. It couldn't be.

Jordan looked at me, curious and concerned.

"Well?"

I was too stunned to answer.

"Who is it from?"

Still, I wasn't able to form a reply. Impatient, she picked up the letter off the ground and looked for herself.

"Jay? Who's Jay?"

"It can't be." This couldn't be real. I only knew one Jay and it couldn't possibly be him. There was no way it was him, but the evidence of the letter was undeniable.

"Can't be? Why? Who's Jay?"

"Jay... Jay Gatsby... the lieutenant."

Finally, her face mirrored my own shock.

Jordan examined the rest of the letters. "They're all from him."

The memories came rushing back. I was back in my car with him all those months ago, laughing and talking about life. I felt I had my whole life figured out and that if I could just be with him forever, I would be happy for as long. I tried to stop myself from thinking of our last night together and his leaving, but the thoughts couldn't be stopped. I was pleasantly surprised that the raw pain had dulled to more of an ache now. I hadn't thought about him in so long. I had been so sure he wouldn't make it out alive. Did he? When were the letters from?

I looked down at the first letter and saw it was from April. Eight months ago. I quickly asked, "When are the others from?"

She looked at me, confused by my urgency, but after seeing the anxiety on my face, she began ripping the envelopes open and checking the dates.

"April, May, May."

He kept writing. I hadn't received a single one of his letters, but he had kept writing.

"Three from June."

Six months ago. He was still writing to me six months ago. I was trying to mend my broken heart with man after man, and he had been thinking about me the whole time.

"Three more from July. And one from August."

That had to be the last. He had to have given up then. It had taken me a long time to get over him, but by the end of the summer, I had pretty much worked through my grief.

I started to ask to see the one from August when she added, "And one from November."

"November? You mean last November?"

She shook her head.

"You can't mean from November a few weeks ago?"

She nodded.

My heart dropped.

He had written a few weeks ago. Could he really have survived the war? Was he still holding on to his feelings? Had he really cared as much as I thought? Why was he still writing? Why hadn't I received any of these letters? I held my hand out for the letter.

She didn't seem to want to hand it over. She looked at me carefully and asked, " Dais, are you sure this is a good idea?"

"Not at all, but we both know I have to know what it says."

"I could read it if you'd like?"

I considered that for a moment, before remembering how things had ended between Jay and me. I blushed at the thought of what he might have written about our night together and shook my head. "It has to be me."

She sighed and reluctantly parted with the letter. I took a deep breath and started from the beginning.

My Dearest Daisy,

From the long months of silence, I can only draw one of two conclusions; the first being that my letters have not been reaching you, whether because of the war or some familial interference, I can't be sure. The other conclusion would be that you have moved on. I can't allow myself to think the latter to be possible, so I must believe the former. In which case, now that the war is over, I hope you receive this.

Please know I wrote to you often and thought of you more still. I thought especially often of our last night together. It is those thoughts that assure me you can't possibly have moved on. The thoughts of you alone, of our future life together, pushed me to survive what might otherwise have taken my life.

I am assured of your faithfulness to me, but I would be lying if I didn't mention I worry about your parents' influence on you. Since we parted, I have been doing all I can to better my station in life to make myself more deserving of your parents' approval. For I have held onto the fact that you are mine in all but name alone. You have been since our last night together.

If only you had made it to New York before I was shipped out, we would not have to worry about the world conspiring to separate what God had joined together. But, alas, my dear, I waited in vain, for you didn't come. You failed me and left me waiting, but I forgave you as I always generously have.

Rest assured, my love for you has only grown and my love will bring me back to you. I hope to be coming home soon to whisk you away and make up for lost time. I count the days.

...Forever yours,

Jay

He was coming home. He had survived the war and was coming home. I couldn't believe it. From all the stories we had heard about the horrors and bloodbath of the war, I had assumed the worst. I had thought that if he were alive, I would have heard from him. Since I hadn't heard a single word from him, I believed him to be dead and had mourned him. Now I had proof that he was not only alive, but that he had been thinking about me the whole time. I didn't know how to feel. The letters were undeniable proof of how he felt. Jay Gatsby was back from the dead, so why wasn't I happier?

I knew why. There was a very tall, handsome reason. Besides that, I had given up on Jay. I had mourned him and grieved and resigned myself to having to move on. I had been heartbroken over losing him, but as time had gone on, I opened myself up to new possibilities. I opened myself up, and Tom fought his way through my defenses and gained my admiration. I knew my heart hadn't fully healed from the grievous wound, but he helped me to recover.

But now Jay was alive. Jay was alive. I had to keep repeating it to myself because it felt so unbelievable. I couldn't think. I didn't know how to feel or what to do. Jay was alive, and he still wanted me. I didn't know how to take that. Had his letters reached me when they were supposed to, things would have been a lot different, but I had spent a year thinking he had left me. I spent a year knowing after the night we spent together, he just walked away. A year thinking he was dead. A year ago, I would have been overjoyed at his words, but now, things were different.

I had thought he left me.

I mean, he did leave me. I still don't know why he didn't come back to say goodbye. He could have come back or even written to me. I couldn't understand why he hadn't written if he had meant for things between us to continue. Now I had proof he'd written, but not until April. Why hadn't he written before? A goodbye from him or a letter right after he left would have killed all my doubts, but he left me doubting.

He had even brought up New York.

I can't believe he had the audacity to be disappointed I hadn't shown up. I can't believe he had the nerve to say how he waited for me and I never came. *He* was the one who left without a goodbye. *He* left me waiting. *He* was the one who left before we could make any solid plans. He can't have seriously thought I would run away to New York to meet him? I hadn't heard a single word from him after our last night together. He hadn't bothered to come say goodbye or to pick up a pen. What in the world could have made him think I would go to New York? Even I knew my impulsive plan to run off to New York had been foolish. I hadn't the slightest idea where to look for Jay or even if he would have been there.

If I'm being honest with myself, even then, I knew our talk of eloping was a daydream with no hope of becoming a reality. I knew he could harbor no real hope as to elopement either with his being in the army. We both knew it couldn't happen. After all, neither of us had the means to support ourselves or each other if we ran from our expectations. I felt stifled by my parents' expectations, and it seemed he felt stifled by those of the army. Our talk of a better life and of elopement was just that, talk. It was an escape to me, a daydream.

He talked of becoming a hero in the war and making a name for himself and coming back home to sweep me off my feet, but we both knew that was nothing more than a dream. At least that was what I had thought, especially after he left without so much as a goodbye.

Even after he left, I had held on to some delusional hope that he might write, but I received no letters. I convinced myself that there were three possibilities; that he was dead, that he had stopped caring for me, or that he had given up holding on to the false hope of our daydream.

With all the bloody stories we heard from the war, as much as I did not want to admit it to myself, I knew the former was more likely. I tried not to think about the possibilities. I reasoned that even if he were alive, he still had made no move to contact me, so he must not have wanted to. Whether it was because he had lost feelings for me, or cut contact knowing things would go nowhere, hardly mattered. The result was the same; he was lost to me forever.

I was heartbroken over losing him, but as time had gone on, I opened myself up to new possibilities.

Now Jay wanted to just waltz back into my life as if he never left? Did he expect me to come running like he never abandoned me to my doubts and suffering? And he had the audacity to offer his forgiveness! How dare he! How dare he offer his own forgiveness when he should have been seeking mine!

I had thought he was dead. Even if I was able to move past everything that had happened, now I was somewhat committed to Marcos. I hoped to remedy that, but it was undeniable that things were different now. I was in quite a mess. Here I was sitting in my room, trying to figure out what to write to Tom when Jay returns from the dead. Honestly, how was anyone supposed to cope with that?

Jordan's voice shook me out of my thoughts.

"Well?"

All I managed to say was, "He's coming home."

Her jaw dropped. "What?"

"He's coming home."

"You said that already." She took the letter from my hand, looking at me for permission to read it. I nodded. She quickly read the letter to herself and a few moments later, met my eye again. "Oh."

"Yeah."

"Well?"

"I don't know."

"You don't know?"

I sighed. "I don't know. I should be happy, right? I mean, a few months ago, I would have been ecstatic. He's alive! He's actually alive, and he wants me still... so why aren't I happier? I don't really know what to feel. I just can't believe it. He seems to think I was just waiting around for him. He left without a goodbye and yet he thinks I'm still just waiting for him. And the audacity! After what he put me through to say he forgives me...I just, I don't know. This is supposed to be good news. I mean, he's coming back safe and sound and still wants me. A few months ago, this would have been everything I wanted to hear. I would have been ecstatic."

"What changed?"

I shrugged my shoulders. "I don't really know. I mean, I guess *I* changed. I might have loved him, but now he feels like more of a stranger. I mean, I knew him for hardly a month before he left. How well did I really know him, anyway? And now he's coming home for me... I don't know what to think. Things might have been different if I had gotten the rest of the letters before, but maybe I wasn't meant to? Maybe I was supposed to move on? I can't help thinking that this can't be all there is for me."

She smirked at me. "You mean it wasn't a mistake to not run off with him?"

I playfully shoved her, but couldn't help laughing. "Now is so not the time for 'I told you so'."

She laughed. "In your opinion, there would never be a good time for it."

"On the contrary, there is ample time for it when it comes from me." We both laughed for a moment before I turned back to the letter. "I don't know what to do."

"Well, what do you want to do?"

"I don't know."

She sighed. "Maybe I can help. Close your eyes."

I looked at her skeptically. "Why?"

She rolled her eyes. "Just do it. Trust me."

I made a show of slowly closing my eyes. "Okay, now what?"

"Take a deep breath." I did. "Now picture yourself in ten years. You're older, wiser, and, most importantly, happier."

"And prettier, too, right?" I joked. I couldn't help myself.

She laughed, and I heard her say under her breath, "As if that were possible." Louder, she said to me, "Stop joking around. I'm being serious."

I put up my hands in surrender. "Okay! Okay, I'll be serious."

"So, this older, wiser, happier version of you, what do you see around her?"

I tried to picture it. I saw myself laughing, talking to someone. It was a little girl. I examined my thoughts more closely and couldn't help but see the resemblance. "I have a daughter!" I couldn't believe it. "She's beautiful!" I gushed.

Jordan laughed. "Of course she is. She's *your* daughter."

I laughed, too. "She's telling me about her day and talking about her Aunt Jordan, the pro golfer." I beamed at that. "She sounds so proud of you."

I opened my eyes and saw Jordan's smile. "Well, I can't wait to meet her."

"That was wonderful, but how does that help me now?"

"Well, I'll admit I hadn't expected things to go that way. I thought thinking of your happiness would bring to mind one man or another, but it seems you're full of surprises. I hadn't known you wanted to be a mother."

I hadn't really known it myself, but I couldn't shake the image of my daughter and how happy I was with her. "I just learned that myself."

She smiled. "So, we are making progress." She thought for a moment before saying, "I have one more idea we can try."

"Okay! I'll try anything. What do you need me to do?"

"It's simple, really. Just answer my questions as quickly as you can with the first thought that pops into your mind."

"Okay. Sounds easy enough."

"What's your favorite flower?"

"Daisies."

"Who do you get along with better, your mother or father?"

"Father."

"What color hair did your daughter have?"

"Brown."

"What are you going to name your daughter?"

"Pamela."

"Jay or Tom?"

"Tom."

It took a moment of her staring at me for me to register what I had said. Tom. What was it about him that made me so sure I wanted him? I hardly knew him, so why did I feel so strongly about him? I only spent a single night with him. Yes, he was charming, handsome, hilarious, respectful, and kind. And, yes, he had saved me from being taken advantage of and defended my honor. Okay, maybe I had fallen for him, *hard*.

What was wrong with me? For months, all I could think about was Jay. All I wanted was for him to come back and sweep me off my feet. Now here he was, back from the dead and writing that he was coming home to do just that, and now that he was returning, it wasn't what I wanted anymore? That was the truth of the matter. He wasn't what I wanted anymore. It wasn't about Tom. It was about Jay. Okay; maybe it was about Tom a little bit. He did speed up my moving on, but he wasn't to blame for my feelings for Jay going away.

Jay did that all on his own. He slept with me and left me alone to deal with the aftermath of that decision. Yes; he had to leave. He was in the army and didn't have a choice, but he had a choice that night. I had a choice as well and I know I made the wrong one, but so did he. He could have stayed, but he didn't. He had a choice that morning, as well. He could have returned to say goodbye, but he didn't. He could have proposed to me. He didn't. He left me, and whether I knew it or not then, the part of me that wanted to be with him started to die that day.

Now that I better understood my feelings, I couldn't begin to guess what I was supposed to do. I looked to Jordan for guidance. She nudged me with her shoulder. "So, it's Tom, huh?"

I couldn't help but laugh. "It looks like it, but I think I came on too strong. I haven't heard from him since the ball."

She looked incredulous. "The man took a beating for you and your honor. Do you really think he doesn't feel strongly about you?"

I had to concede that she had a point. "You have me there, but if he felt so strongly, why hasn't he written?"

She looked at a loss as well. "I can't imagine what's stopping him. I know if someone as beautiful, caring, and sweet as you took a liking to me, I would be sure to write."

I laughed at that. "I promise you'll find a man worthy of your attention one of these days." Her eyes darkened and her expression changed. I hastened to add, "I'm really sorry it wasn't James, but I promise you'll find someone better."

She seemed lost in thought and only nodded. After a few minutes of silence, I couldn't hold back voicing my worries. "So, Jay's coming home and expects me to be waiting for him. What am I going to do? Even if I wanted to marry him, now that Marcos is in the picture, my parents would never allow it."

She looked thoughtful and asked, "When is he planning to return?"

I took another look at the letter. "He doesn't say."

"It might be worth writing to him and letting him know about your soon-to-be engagement." I looked at her questioningly before she continued, "Well, one of two things will happen then. He might change his plan and not come, which would free you from feeling guilty about him coming all this way just to get turned down."

"You're right. I owe it to him to tell him. Yes, he never said goodbye, but I owe it to the man he was."

"I'm glad you agree, but you haven't even heard scenario two yet, and that's the better reason. In scenario two, he gets your letter and is consumed with jealousy." She clutched the letter to her chest and dramatically threw her hand to her forehead in a look of mock anguish. I grabbed the nearest pillow and lobbed it at her. She fell into a fit of giggles at that. I couldn't help but follow suit. When she composed herself again, she continued, "As I was saying, before I was so rudely interrupted..." She looked at me with feigned annoyance. I rolled my eyes. "In scenario two, he comes here anyway and fights for your hand. It would be a losing battle, of course, but it might be enough to get Marcos to leave."

I couldn't imagine it was possible to scare Marcos off, but a part of me hoped Jay would try. I didn't want to give him the wrong idea. I knew it wouldn't be fair to him, but I reasoned that I would be telling him the truth. I was in quite a predicament and was to soon be engaged. It wouldn't be a lie to say that.

"You're right. I should tell him, anyway. If he does come, that isn't my fault. I'll write to him."

I crossed the room and took up my abandoned station. I crumpled up the latest draft to Tom and began to write.

Dear Jay,

You were correct in assuming I hadn't received your letters.

That wasn't right. It sounded too cold and emotionless. I crumpled up the paper and started over.

Dear Jay,

It pains me to think of you waiting for my letters.

No. I couldn't lie to him and wouldn't exaggerate my feelings. I started again.

Dear Jay,

I just now received your letters. I hadn't thought I would hear from you again. I worried the worst had happened to you. I am pleased to hear you are doing well. It took me by great surprise to receive all these months of correspondence at once. I can't imagine how it must have bothered you at my lack of response. I am truly sorry you had to endure that. Please forgive my silence and know I would have written much sooner had I known.

There isn't an easy way to tell you this, but things have changed since you left. You've been gone so long. I'm not the same girl you left behind. It won't surprise you to hear my parents have their hopes set on me marrying rich and soon.

I had my debut last month. My parents have all but signed my fate with a gentleman who is anything but. I make no exaggeration in saying I detest the man and the idea of marrying him would never have crossed my mind if he were the last man on Earth. I wish I had more of a say in my own future, but this isn't a woman's world we live in. I know my position and don't expect to be consulted about my future. I know my parents will sign my life away to the highest bidder.

Please know that if it were up to me, things would be different. You must know I care for you, and a part of me thinks we would have been really happy together, but I know that's not our reality. I hope you find happiness. If I can't be happy, I hope fate is kinder to you.

With Love,

Daisy

Finished, I reread the letter. I didn't have time to overthink this. It needed to be sent as soon as possible if I had any hope of reaching him before he arrived. I hoped he might understand. I glanced at it once more before folding it closed. It was as good as it was going to get. I knew Jordan was curious, but I knew the longer I looked at it, the more I would overthink it.

"If you wouldn't mind, could you please take this to a maid or butler to be sent out? If I spend much longer looking at it, I worry I might lose my nerve."

She nodded. "Do you want me to take a look at it?"

I shrugged. "It's as good as it's going to get. I was truthful and tried to spare his feelings as much as I could. I won't change anything, but I don't mind you reading it. I know you must be curious, and you know I don't keep anything from you."

She took the letter from my hand, saying, "I'll be back in just a moment," before rushing out with the letter, leaving me alone.

With that settled, I turned back to address the problem at hand. I went to go back to my vanity, but I couldn't ignore the state my room was in. There was crumpled paper everywhere. Some were from my failed letters to Tom and some were from Jay, but I had no desire to look at either much longer. I grabbed my trash bin and started throwing out the papers. When Jordan returned a few minutes later, she looked impressed.

She just stared at me until I finally asked, "What?"

She closed the distance between us and wrapped me in a hug. "I'm so proud of you, love. I know that can't have been nearly as easy as you're acting like it was, and I want you to know how proud I am of you. It's difficult figuring out what you want, and even harder finding the courage to act on it. Even I don't have the courage to act on the things I want. I'm just so proud of you. To be honest, I half expected you to chase me down and take the letter back. I thought you might change your mind. I remember how hard it was on you when he left. I'm just amazed at how quickly you've grown and matured."

I started to tear up, but had to laugh at her last comment. "Hey!" I said playfully. "*I'm* the adult here."

We both laughed at that. When she let go, she saw what I was doing and asked, "Are you sure you don't want to look at the other letters?"

"I'm sure. I have the closure I needed, and I hope the letter I sent will give him the closure he needs."

She looked even more impressed and helped me pick up the rest of the mess. We talked about me writing to Tom, but I couldn't bring myself to do it. I decided I would write to him at some point soon, but it didn't feel right to ask him to a dinner in which he would be the fill-in for Marcos. As much as I would have loved his company, it didn't feel right, and in all honesty, a part of me worried he might not come. After all, I hadn't heard from him. Maybe he didn't care as much as I did. If that were the case, I knew I wasn't ready to find out.

In the end, I invited Jordan. She was more than happy to be there for me, but less than thrilled to deal with my parents.

They were horrified when I turned up with Jordan on my arm and the town was awash with the scandalous rumors of how Miss Daisy Fay couldn't get a single gentleman to escort her. They said no one would have me and my tarnished reputation. They had meant to hurt me, but they didn't know their words were the very things I needed to hear. They gave me an idea.

Shortly after Christmas, I wrote to Marcos. I prayed it would reach him in time. I prayed it would change his mind. I prayed someone was listening and would answer my prayers.

As the days passed by and we neared the middle of January, I started to feel hopeless. I worried the letter wouldn't change his mind. I worried he would have come before receiving the letter. I worried about every horrible thing I could think of that might happen, but it turned out my worry was unfounded. The universe must have been listening after all, for in the last week of January, my prayers were answered in the form of a letter.

The letter was full of some of the most degrading things I have ever read, but it only filled me with joy. Marcos wasn't coming! He didn't want me anymore! I was free! I couldn't even muster up annoyance with his words. I was just so elated to be free, and to think all I had to do was tell the truth.

In my letter, I had written that I felt I needed to come clean in the hopes that he would still have me for my family's sake. From the little I knew of his heart, I knew if I made it clear I didn't want him, that he would be all the more determined to have me. I made sure to pen the letter with as much affection as I could muster. I shuddered through my apologies to him for my behavior of denying him my body. I told him that I had been thinking about that moment and that I regretted having used him so poorly. That was quite possibly the biggest lie I would ever tell, but I needed him to believe me.

I told him I was too embarrassed to let him have his way with me, because it wasn't fair to him since he didn't know. I told him I had to come clean that he wouldn't have been the first man I was with. I told him that with that now off my chest and no further secrets between us, I sincerely hoped we could move forward and continue our courtship. In the long weeks that I waited for his reply, I second guessed myself. I worried I understood him wrong and that my letter would encourage him, but I worried for nothing.

His reply told me that he would never sully his family name by continuing to court a floozy like me. He said far worse things, but that was the gist of his reply.

I went to my parents straight away to tell them. I left out that I had sent a letter and said he must have heard some of the rumors. They were devastated. My mother blamed me, saying I would bring ruin and misfortune on us all. She said they would never live down the embarrassment.

I tried to convince them it wasn't such a bad thing after all, but they wouldn't listen. It turns out they had reason to be embarrassed. In anticipation of my engagement to Marcos, that they had arranged with him to happen at the beginning of February, they had invited all their friends and more than half the town to a celebration in our honor.

My mother made it known she blamed me for his refusal to marry me. I was sorry I had caused them any suffering, but that was where my sympathy ended. I couldn't muster up any false sadness at the ending of what was without a doubt the worst relationship I could have possibly imagined. My parents started contacting the guests that had been invited and making whatever excuses they could think of. But I doubted their damage control would be nearly as effective as they hoped.

Chapter Twenty - Five

I was more right than I could have imagined. It turns out their invitations had gone as far and wide as the invitations for the ball. Had I had the ability to feel any regret or embarrassment, I would have, but I was too relieved to be free. It turned out they weren't able to get word to everyone in time to stop them from coming. As a consequence, throughout the first week of February, friends and invited guests began arriving from out of town, only to hear the news that there was to be no celebration.

Evidently, the celebration had caught the attention of more than just those invited. The town was awhirl in rumors about my engagement and what might have happened. It seemed my parents were telling people the celebration had to be postponed since the future groom couldn't yet make it up from New Orleans. I wondered with some renewed interest what they meant to happen. They had to know they couldn't keep up the ruse forever. I had half a mind to set the record straight myself, but after giving it more than a few moments' thought, I decided it wasn't worth the effort. The town would believe what they wanted to believe, anyway.

It turns out rumors of my engagement had gone even further than I supposed. They must have made their way all the way to Chicago, for, a day before the celebration was planned, I received a most welcome gentleman caller.

When one of the maids told me there was a man at the door requesting to see me, I felt a sudden wave of anxiety overcome me. I knew it was likely someone from out of town that was either coming to congratulate me about my engagement or that had heard the celebration was cancelled and wanted to inquire about what was going on. Even knowing that, I couldn't push away the dread. I was worried it might be Marcos.

I knew from his letter that he hoped to never see me again, but I worried he might have heard word of the celebration and became angry enough to come here. I worried I would have to see him again and potentially deal with his anger. I almost didn't go to the door, but rationally, I knew it wasn't him. It couldn't be, but the anxiety continued. I summoned all the nerve I had and headed to the door, resolved to my fate.

As I approached the door, I was sure the entire house could hear the loud, frantic beating of my heart. I felt my stomach drop as I opened the door, anticipating the worst. When I saw who was outside, I was as relieved as I was shocked. My jaw nearly dropped to the floor. I couldn't believe my eyes.

"Tom?! Am I seeing things? Can you really be here?"

He laughed as I took in the sight of him. His smile widened when I recovered from my surprise enough to smile. "I hope it is not an unwelcome intrusion."

"Of course not! I hadn't dreamed of seeing you again, but you're most welcome!"

I wondered what he was doing here. From our last conversation, I hadn't thought I would see him again. It had sounded as if he couldn't afford to repeat his trip from Chicago.

He seemed hesitant. "You're truly happy to see me? I worried on my trip here that I might've been overly optimistic in coming, that I might have exaggerated what passed between us."

My heart soared at his words. "I felt the same. I cautioned myself against writing because I didn't want to be too forward. I had hoped you would write, but you never did."

My face must have fallen a little with that last statement because he rushed to say, "I had the same worries. I didn't feel I had made your acquaintance enough to write, but when I heard the announcement of your engagement, I knew I had to come."

So, he hadn't yet heard. "About my engagement-"

He interrupted before I could explain. "I will do everything I can to put a stop to it. The idea of such a precious flower as you being legally bound to the likes of him, a brute and a scoundrel." He shuddered in revulsion. "I couldn't bear knowing anyone had come to that fate, but that fate for you who, if I'm not too forward in saying, I've come to have feelings for, is entirely unbearable. Especially when it might be in my power to stop it."

I was only able to stare at him, awestruck. He had come all this way for me? He had come to rescue me from my fate. I was elated to hear he had feelings for me. I needed to tell him that things had changed, and I wasn't engaged, but I was too stunned to speak. I could only stare at him.

As I watched him, he smiled a moment more before his countenance became more serious. "Do I have grounds in hoping those feelings are returned?"

A grin spread across my face. In answer, I threw my arms around him, wrapping him in an embrace that he was quick to return. I whispered to him, "I dreamt so many times of you showing up and sweeping me off my feet, but I never imagined it would happen."

"I was worried you might not want me."

"How could you think such a thing?"

"You never wrote."

"Neither did you."

He chuckled. "True enough, but you said you'd write."

"I did, but I realized afterward how forward it was of me to ask and worried it wouldn't be well received by you if I had. Plus, with the looming engagement, I was a bit preoccupied."

"It would have been eagerly received by me. The postman can attest to that since I questioned him daily about any letters for me from Louisville." He chuckled before saying, "And about the engagement, I can only hope I'm not too late to change things."

I was momentarily thrown into confusion at his proclamation.

If I was engaged to Marcos, what could he hope to do to change that? What had he meant earlier when he said he might have the power to stop it? What did he mean by remarking he hoped he wasn't too late? I wasn't sure what he was getting at.

My silence seemed to confirm his fears. "Well, no matter. We can still fix this, but we must act quickly. Is there a maid or a butler around?" My confusion had only grown, but he seemed in quite a hurry, so without thinking, I looked back into the hallway for anyone who could be of assistance.

I saw a maid on the far side of the hallway and beckoned her to come over. She came at once and asked what she could help me with. I was at a loss. When Tom saw her standing there, he told her to find my parents at once and to bid them to meet us in the ballroom. I couldn't imagine what business he had with my parents.

"Tom, are you sure that's a good idea? I'm not sure my parents will be as happy about your presence as I am."

He frowned a moment, considering my words. His frown smoothed out into a smile that didn't quite touch his eyes. "I'm sure everything will be fine once I talk to them. I've received the assurances I needed from you, and once I speak with them, I'm sure everything can be fixed."

He took my hand and requested I lead him to the ballroom. I did, but while we hurried, I continued to try to get an explanation from him. "Tom, you really must tell me what is going on, and you really should know that Marcos-"

"You don't have to explain anything to me, my sweet. You don't have to remind me what happened with Marcos. I was there and it would be cruel indeed to make you relive it."

"You're quite a gentleman, but it's not about that. It's about the engagement-"

"My dear, you don't have to trouble yourself with that anymore. Please don't worry about it further. I promise I'll fix things."

"But that's the thing. There's nothing to be fixed."

"That's the spirit! There'll be nothing left to be fixed once I talk to your parents."

"Tom, please, can we talk a moment?"

"My sweet flower, I promise there'll be plenty of time for talking the moment my business with your parents is taken care of."

"But you don't understand-"

I stopped cold when we entered the ballroom and I saw my mother glaring at me. She looked quite disheveled. I guessed it was mainly due to still having to inform quite a few people that the celebration was off, but I knew the interruption hadn't improved her mood. My father looked confused and overwhelmed. I couldn't decide if that was more likely attributed to still trying to cancel the celebration or to being around my mother. My parents both looked at me for an explanation, but I was as clueless as they were.

I instinctively went to drop his hand that I had been holding, but he tightened his grip on my hand. He gave my hand a reassuring squeeze and led me across the room. When he was in front of my parents, he extended his other hand to my father. "How do you do, sir?"

My father, still in the daze of confusion, took Tom's proffered hand and shook it. He looked at me as if to ask who this man was and why he was here. I shrugged in answer. Tom turned to my mother. I braced myself for the worst.

He bowed to her. "Mrs. Fay, you are looking quite lovely this morning. It is such a pleasure to make your acquaintance."

She seemed momentarily placated by the flattery, which was a much better outcome than I could have hoped for. She looked at him, now more confused than angry, and asked, "And you would be…?"

He chuckled as if she had made a joke and said, "Of course, how could I forget? I'm Thomas Buchanan. I travelled all the way from Chicago to see your lovely daughter again." I blushed at that. "When I heard news of her engagement, I couldn't believe my ears. Your dear, innocent, flower of a daughter shouldn't be with a brute like Marcos. I know having just made your acquaintance that means little to nothing, but I'm well enough acquainted with his character to know he has no right to be with your daughter."

My parents looked between him and me in confusion. I was praying with all my might that he wouldn't bring up what happened with Marcos the night of my debut. The last thing I needed was for my parents to hear that. I knew my mother would find some way to make his actions my fault. Somehow or another, the failed engagement would be my fault for refusing him. That was the last thing I needed. Thankfully, he didn't continue.

He turned to me and said, "Daisy, my sweet flower, I know you could never be happy with the likes of him. I know you know how much of a scoundrel he is and how undeserving he is of any woman, never mind someone as sweet and perfect as you. He could never make you happy. Since the day I met you, I've known what a kind, loving, innocent, perfect flower of a woman you are, not to mention breathtakingly beautiful. You deserve happiness and if I may be so bold, I think you would be happy with me."

I didn't have a chance to register the meaning of his last words before he knelt down on one knee in front of me and pulled out something from behind his back. "Daisy Fay, will you allow me to spend my life trying to make you happy? Will you do me the honor of giving me your hand in marriage?"

I was stunned. I had thought it was a surprise that he came at all. I hadn't held much hope of seeing him again and here he was proposing I stay by his side for our entire lives. I knew he would make me happy, but was I ready for marriage? I was silent for a moment as my thoughts caught up to me. The happiness on his face started to fade. I knew in that moment that I would say yes. He had come rushing down to Louisville to be my knight in shining armor. What more could I ask of him? He was such a genuinely sweet, caring man and incredibly handsome. I knew he would make me happy and that I would be lucky to have him.

"Yes!"

He was elated. He stood up quickly and pulled me into an embrace. He held onto me for a moment before my father cleared his throat. I pulled away and looked at them. I'm not sure what he was going to say because he never got the chance before my mother butted in.

"And just who do you think you are? Sweeping in here like that trying to steal our daughter without our permission? What makes you think you're worthy of her?"

I flushed at that. To an outsider, it would sound like she was looking to protect me and ask him how he was going to treat me, but I knew better. She was asking how he would support me and if he had money or a family name.

"Why, I'm her future husband, of course, but I *am* sorry I got a little carried away. I had planned to ask your permission. That's why I called you both here, but it seemed a little hasty to seek out your permission before I was assured that this was what Daisy wanted. I only want her happiness and will do everything in my power to make sure she is happy."

"And just what exactly is in your power?" she asked snidely.

I couldn't believe how curt and direct she was being. Although, I really shouldn't have been surprised. He looked at me, confused. I leaned in and whispered, blushing even more, "I'm so sorry. She wants to know about your money and your family. You don't have to answer that."

To my surprise, he broke into a grin and chuckled, saying to me, "Oh, is that all?" He turned to them. "I hadn't made this known to Daisy before now, but now is as good a time as any. My mother's maiden name was McCormick, of the Chicago McCormicks."

Both my parents looked stunned, but their amazement was nothing compared to my own. Even *I* had heard of the vast fortune of the McCormicks. I had no idea that Tom had money at all, never mind that he was a McCormick! I hadn't hoped to see him again because I didn't think it likely he would be able to justify the expense of travelling from Chicago to Louisville and back again. I couldn't believe it.

"You can't be serious?"

He grinned. "You really didn't know?"

"Of course I didn't!"

"How else would I have been able to afford this ring?"

He took my hand and slipped it on my finger. It was the first time I actually took the time to look at it. The weight alone of the diamonds was shocking enough, but the ring itself was breathtaking. The largest diamond was circular with a yellow tint. It was surrounded on all sides by nine smaller white diamonds. It looked like a flower. After a moment, I understood the meaning of the yellow tint on the diamond. It was a daisy.

"Tom! You shouldn't have gone to all this trouble! It's perfect! I love it!"

His grin widened further. My mother had moved closer to see the ring and when she did, her amazement quickly turned to warmth toward Tom. She actually smiled at him. "Well, it seems I'm going to have a new son after all."

He laughed at that and whispered to me, "A real shame I stole that honor right from under Marcos's nose." I giggled at that. I would have to tell him later what had happened with Marcos, but it didn't seem important enough to mention now.

He smiled at my mother and thanked her.

My father stepped forward, extending his hand. "Well, my dear boy, welcome to the family!"

He thanked my father, and then my father and mother excused themselves. I suspected it was as much to give us space as it was to start writing to their friends and telling anyone who would listen about my, and their, good fortune. One moment, their daughter had a broken engagement and was destined to bring shame to the family and die alone; the next moment, she was engaged to a son of one of the wealthiest families in the country. I was willing to bet they couldn't believe their luck and that my mother especially wouldn't wait long before making it known all over town that I was to be married to a McCormick. I assumed she would leave out that his surname was actually Buchanan.

When we had the space to ourselves, he pulled me close and put his hands on my waist and picked me up, spinning me around the room. His joy made me sure I had made the right decision. I had never thought I would find someone I cared for again after how abruptly things ended with Jay. I had worried I wouldn't be able to move on, but now I was so happy I had.

After a moment, he placed me lightly back on the floor and brushed my hair off my face gently with his fingertips. As he did, our eyes locked, and he leaned closer. I met him halfway and our lips met. It was gentle and tender. It felt nice, comforting. I couldn't help thinking it wasn't the heat I had felt with Jay, but his joy was contagious and I was happy. When I pulled away, he smiled at me.

"In my wildest dreams, I hadn't thought it would be this easy. After how you received me, I hoped this would be welcomed from you, but I thought it would take a lot longer to win over your parents. If I had known their approval would come so easy after knowing my story, I would have mentioned my family far sooner."

I laughed at that. "I'm sorry about my parents. I truly am. They want only the best for me, and to them the best means..." I rolled my eyes before finishing my sentence. "...rich. But why didn't you tell me sooner?"

"I thought it was obvious."

"You thought I knew?"

"Well, at first I did. You have to understand that I've lived most of my life in Chicago and am used to not being able to go anywhere without someone knowing my name. It's a feeling I would enjoy if I had done something to earn it, but since my only merit to them is my name, I feel awkward under their scrutiny. Women were always throwing themselves at me before they even bothered to get to know me. I had seen it happen so many times. A woman would all but ignore me until

I would see her friend whisper to her and then, all of a sudden, she would be fawning all over me.

"I was so used to people being fake with me that once I realized you really didn't know who I was, I was hesitant to tell you. I didn't want anything to change. I liked being just Tom to you. I liked that even though you thought I was essentially a nobody that you chose to spend time with me, that you chose me over everyone. I was worried you might change your mind about me if you found out who I was, or worse, I worried you would treat me differently and stop being as genuine with me. I knew how strongly you disliked Marcos and worried that it might be partly due to his wealth and arrogance. I worried if I told you my name, you might think I was as proud and arrogant as he was. I couldn't stand the idea of you, the kind, beautiful woman who had shown genuine interest in me, thinking that of me, so I didn't say anything.

"Even when you asked if you could write," he chuckled, "you might have noticed I hesitated. I wasn't sure how to give you my address without you realizing who I was. I didn't write myself because I worried you would see my address and know. I hoped you would write or that you would put me out of my misery by having figured it out on your own, but I was kept waiting. I assumed you had changed your mind and didn't care to speak with me anymore. I tried to force myself to be okay with that, but when I heard word of your engagement to Marcos, I couldn't stay silent anymore.

"The thought of you being forced to spend your life with such a cruel man as him made me as outraged and angry as I was jealous. Before I fully realized it, I had formed a plan. I was delayed a day or two after I commissioned that beauty," he gestured to my ring, "from the jeweler, but I know now it was worth it, seeing how happy it made you. I resolved to rush down here as soon as possible, to do everything I could to free you from him and, if you would happily have me, to connect you to myself. I resolved I would save you from a doomed marriage to him and that I would offer you my own hand in marriage.

"My entire journey, I cursed myself for not having mentioned my name and situation sooner. I worried I would be too late. I worried you would have already been forced to accept him, or worse, that something might have happened in my absence that might have moved you to willingly accept the likes of him. I hoped I would be welcomed by you, but I never guessed your parents would welcome me as easily as they did, and that they would so quickly allow you to choose me over Marcos, who your mother determined you to be destined for. I figured it would involve more deliberation than it did."

"Well, it's not like it was their choice."

He chuckled and nodded. "Well, of course not. The moment you said yes, they knew their choice to be lost."

I laughed at that. "You overestimate the importance they place on my decisions. You had won me over, but without their blessing, I'm not sure things would have gone nearly as smoothly as they did."

He looked confused and asked, "Well, of course, but I thought you just said you wouldn't have let it be their choice?"

"Well, of course I would have done everything I could to sway them, and I know they would have been persuaded once they knew who you are. Had it still been a contest between you and Marcos, with them knowing who you are and that I fancied you, they would have allowed me to make the choice I wanted and choose you. I just meant Marcos didn't force them to make that decision."

His confusion intensified. "I'm not sure I understand you."

I smiled at him. "I've been trying to tell you since you arrived that the celebration was cancelled. Let's just say Marcos and I arrived at an agreement to call off the engagement."

His jaw dropped. He was stunned into silence for a moment. "But I heard you were engaged…"

I laughed before explaining. "You know how my mother can be. She probably started those rumors herself. She started the planning and invitations for our engagement celebration before anything had been finalized. You know how much I detested Marcos. At the last minute, I came up with a plan to sway him against me. You must know how relieved I was that it worked! My parents have been scrambling all week to get some sort of word out that the celebration was not happening. They'd been so overwhelmed and had convinced themselves I was unmarriable." I laughed at that. "To tell you the truth, I think they couldn't quite believe their luck that an eligible gentleman," I nudged him while laughing at the term I knew my mother would have used, "had dropped out of nowhere with an offer to marry their daughter."

He still remained silent. I had expected him to laugh along with me, or be happier for me, that I had been able to end things with Marcos on my own. The silence was becoming a little uncomfortable, and I was relieved when he finally spoke again. "You mean you didn't need my rescuing after all…?"

I shrugged my shoulders. "You didn't rescue me from Marcos, per se, but my heart was in sore need of saving." I laughed. "It truly was a miracle that brought you here."

"But what you're saying is you didn't need a marriage proposal to save you from the terrible fate of marrying Marcos?"

My heart sank. Had he only proposed because he thought himself to be my only choice? "No; I didn't need a proposal," I said slowly. "Are you saying that's the only reason you proposed?" My right hand moved to my left and grasped the ring on my finger. "Because if you only proposed out of pity or to save me, you should have saved yourself the effort." I started to pull the ring off my finger.

It seemed that finally freed his tongue. His face became apologetic, and he reached for my hands. I didn't move mine. Worry appeared on his face, and he hastened to say, "My darling Daisy, my flower, you misunderstand me. That was the reason I came running as quickly as I did and the reason I proposed as soon as I did, but even if I had known, I wouldn't have been able to stay away from you for long."

My smile slowly started to return. "You truly mean it? I don't want this if your heart isn't in it."

"I do truly mean it. I'm sorry, my dear. It just took me a few moments to process my surprise. I should have let you tell me earlier, and I should have known something was up when your parents were so quick to be won over."

I slowly started to move my hand away from the ring. I had still been holding on to it, worried he might take it and his proposal back. I had been picturing how broken I would feel, how empty, without the ring and him in my life. I was instantly reminded of how long it took me to recover from my last heartbreak. It was an easier task than I would have liked to admit, recalling just how deeply I was wounded and how empty I felt.

I imagined this would feel the same. I imagined my parents to be right, that I would be alone forever with no one to love me. His reassurances started to put my fears out of my mind, and the beginnings of a smile appeared on my face. He again reached for my hands, and this time I let him take them.

"Tell me what I can do to make this up to you. I want you to know I know I'm truly the luckiest man on Earth to be blessed with your hand."

I blushed at that and told him my only request was to spend more time with him. He seemed to sense I was holding something back. "Are you quite sure there's nothing else? You can ask me for anything, my dear. Anything at all. If it's in my power, you will have it."

I still hesitated a moment before saying, "I want a quick wedding."

He looked at me, surprised. That clearly wasn't what he was expecting, but it was what I wanted. I wanted to be swept off my feet and whisked away with him. I wanted to be rescued from my life. I didn't know how much longer I could continue to share a roof with my mother.

Seeing his continued surprise, I rushed to explain, "I've always thought long engagements to be silly. Why waste time drawing things out? I don't want to be separated from you longer than I have to." I chuckled and added, "Plus, the longer the engagement, the more time my mother has to plan a monstrosity of an over-the-top wedding. You saw what she did in a few weeks with my debut."

"A few weeks?" he exclaimed in disbelief.

I laughed at that and nodded. "Can you imagine what she would do with a few months? Or even a year?" The horror in his eyes as he imagined the prospect. I laughed again, taking his face for agreement. "Exactly. It's too much for words."

He laughed at that.

"Okay, so no long engagements."

"This town isn't ready for the wedding my mother would plan if given a long engagement to do it."

He laughed and added, "Neither are we."

I chuckled at that. We talked a bit longer, and he told me he had arranged to stay for a few days. I negotiated him up to a week, but he pointed out if it were to be a brief engagement, he couldn't stay much longer than a week before he would be required to leave and make arrangements back home. Apparently, there was much to be done and no time to waste.

The next few days flew by.

We told Jordan the news at the very first opportunity. She was incredibly surprised to see Tom, but that was nothing compared to her shock at our happy news. It took her a few minutes to recover from the shock and congratulate us. I had been, and still was, a little worried about what she might have been thinking. Luckily, Tom understood and made an excuse to leave so her and I could have some time alone. I was grateful to him for his understanding.

We talked for a while. It turns out I was right; she was worried about me. She was worried I might have been rushing into things and worried that I really didn't know Tom all that well. She cautioned me to wait longer, to have a longer engagement, but I worried he might change his mind. I worried he might leave like Jay did. I worried I might lose my last chance at happiness.

The further advantage of leaving my parents' home and leaving their care was another big reason I wished to hurry things along. I wanted freedom. Tom was my quickest and best chance at freedom and happiness and I was scared the chance would pass through my fingers if I waited. I told her as much and said I was sorry I couldn't take her advice. I told her I didn't feel I had the liberty of time. She told me she was still worried but hoped I was right, and that this decision would bring me happiness. I was worried she might not want to be involved, but I needed her there with me. I knew I couldn't get married without her by my side.

When I asked her to be a bridesmaid, I anxiously awaited her answer. She didn't pause more than a moment before saying, "Yes, of course!" I let out a sigh of relief, and she continued, "Daisy, my dear, I'm not always going to agree with your choices, but I do truly hope you're right and that this brings you the utmost happiness. I can't promise to always agree with you, but I will always be there to love and support you."

I had never felt more loved than I did at that moment. I wrapped her in a long hug and when we parted, I felt a renewed happiness.

Chapter Twenty - Six

Jordan

I would have never said it out loud or admitted it to anyone besides myself, but I missed Daisy. There was nothing inherently wrong with missing her, just that I felt ridiculous since it had only been a couple days that I hadn't seen her.

I suspected her parents were forcing her to help explain her lack of engagement and knew that couldn't be pleasant.

I had given her some space, but it had been a long time since we'd gone a few days without being together. I had been waiting for her to come here. I knew she was stressed with her parents and the last thing I wanted to do was cause her more anxiety, so I had waited, but today I would go to her. I missed her and she might need me, so I would go.

The moment I was ready, I rushed to the door, only to stop dead in my tracks.

She was here, but she wasn't alone.

Tom had returned.

I couldn't believe it! She had told me numerous times that it would likely be a long while until he was able to return, if he did return at all.

I racked my brain, but couldn't think of a single explanation for his being here. Had she finally wrote to him? I dismissed that thought quickly; she would have told me the moment she did.

Then I noticed she was holding his hand.

I knew Daisy didn't take things like that lightly. Yes, she had dated around quite frequently, but never on any of those occasions had I seen her let any of them hold her hand for long. She hadn't let any of them touch her for longer than could be avoided. Even with the gentlemen she seemed interested in, she was wary about being seen touching them.

When I had asked her about it once, she had laughed it off and said she didn't need more of a reputation and didn't need the men getting ideas. She acted as if she were joking, but I saw the truth in her words.

She worried about her reputation far more than I had ever guessed. It was surprising, but her comment about not wanting to give the men ideas was the one that really pained me. It should have been innocent enough of her to hold a man's hand. What was she holding on to? What part of her past made her think she had to fear touching a man? Had to fear the man getting ideas and trying to push her?

More than anything, I wanted to ask, but the look in her eyes made me hold back. There was a pain there that I knew she didn't want to talk about. If she ever did tell me, I would make damn sure that whoever caused that look would regret it.

Seeing her hand in his and seeing the happiness on her face, my heart sunk. I knew this was serious. I shouldn't have been surprised. It wasn't too long ago that she had turned down her lieutenant because of him.

She had made it clear it wasn't about Tom, but that Tom had shown her how different she was now. She was a different girl from the one who had fallen for her lieutenant. I had been so proud of her, reading her response to him. She was honest and caring, but told him in no uncertain terms that things were over. With how much of a mess she had been when he left, I had worried when I saw those letters that she would run right back to him. Worried that she would give him another chance to hurt her, but she hadn't.

At the time, I had thanked my lucky stars for Tom having come around, if only because he saved her from running back to her lieutenant. I should have known then how serious things were. I shouldn't have been surprised to see him here, but she was so sure Tom didn't share her feelings. I should have known better.

Tom was nice enough and certainly not a dumb guy. He would have had to have been stupid to turn down a shot with Daisy.

This shouldn't be a surprise, but I was still blindsided. Seeing her smiling helped, but I couldn't help the jealousy I was feeling. Judging by the dopey grin on both of their faces, and her holding his hand, I guessed what she was going to tell me.

He must have gotten her father's permission to court her. How he managed that after the whole Marcos debacle I couldn't imagine, but I was sure she would tell me everything soon.

Daisy took me out of my thoughts by exclaiming, "Jordan! I've missed you!"

She let go of his hand and bounced over, embracing me in a hug.

I couldn't help but laugh. "Dais, it's only been a couple days."

She laughed, her cheeks warming at that. "I know, I know, but I missed you."

I had missed her, too, but she knew that and knew she wouldn't get me to admit it.

"It's nice to see you, too, dear." I held her for another moment before letting go. The moment I let go, she drifted back to Tom and didn't hesitate to take his hand again, like it was second nature. That hurt a little more than I expected.

They barely knew each other, so the fact that she already felt that comfortable with him was as baffling as it was hard to watch. I forced a smile before turning to him.

"And, Tom, you're back. What a wonderful surprise! To what do we owe the pleasure?"

His smile broadened. "Wonderful to see you in good health and spirits!" He smiled at Daisy before saying, "Daisy dragged me here the moment we could get away." Daisy's laughter told me he wasn't joking. "She said she couldn't wait a minute longer than necessary to tell you."

I smiled. I knew it. He was officially courting her. But I wouldn't ruin their fun of telling me. I would act surprised and delighted. I was happy for them, I really was. Daisy deserved every bit of the happiness I saw on her face, but a small part of me was screaming that *I* wanted to be the reason she smiled like that. I pushed it away as best I could.

"Tell me what?"

Daisy was practically bouncing with delight. "We have the most wonderful news! Don't we, Tom?"

He smiled at her indulgently and turned to me. "Yes, yes we do. Daisy has made me the happiest man in the world today. We're-"

She didn't let him finish. She blurted out, "We're engaged to be married!"

My jaw dropped. I couldn't have heard her right. Married?! They had spent all of three days together and they were going to be married?! I knew the shock showed on my face, but I couldn't help it.

Daisy's own smile dimmed, and she tentatively took her hand out of his and stepped closer to me. Then I saw what I can't believe I had missed earlier.

The ring. An engagement ring.

She shyly held her hand out to me. The middle diamond alone had to weigh a ton. I don't know how she could bare the weight of it.

I couldn't believe it. Daisy, *my* Daisy, was engaged to be married. She would become his wife. *His* Daisy. I would lose her. I knew it would happen eventually, I wasn't a fool, but this was crazy! They barely knew each other! How could she have said yes?

I knew she was expecting me to say something, but I couldn't tear my eyes from that ring. That ring he had put on her finger. He had no right to even touch her and now he was going to be her husband?

I tore my eyes away from the ring and met Daisy's. She looked worried but even her worry didn't hide her excitement and happiness.

I was such a lousy friend. She was ecstatic about her future and wanted to share her excitement and happiness with me. More than anything, I wanted to share in her happiness. She deserved to be happy.

I would have to learn to ignore my more spiteful thoughts about how he didn't deserve her and couldn't make her as happy as she should be.

I was struggling even then to admit my true thoughts to myself; he wouldn't make her as happy as *I* could. But I knew what she wanted to hear and I wasn't in the habit of denying her what she wanted. I schooled my expression into a smile.

"I can't believe it! What happy news! Congratulations," I glanced in his direction adding, "to you both. What a lucky man!"

Her smile brightened and he smiled at me as well before looking at her lovingly. "I couldn't quite believe my own luck."

At least he knew what was no secret to me; he wasn't nearly good enough for her. To his credit, though, I didn't know a single person I would have deemed good enough for her. It was a small consolation that he understood he was the lucky one.

She blushed before saying, "Nonsense. We all know I'm the lucky one. After Marcos, I didn't dare dream of such a happy marital match."

She smiled at him without looking at me. The pain in my gut told me that she may not have even remembered I was there at all. "I didn't dare dream I would be so lucky. I still can't believe my own luck."

His eyes lit up at that. For a moment, I was glad neither of them remembered I was there. I don't know I could have hid my pain and disapproval from my face. He glanced at me quicker than I expected. A small part of me hoped he had seen my disapproval, but rationally I knew that would only spell trouble. I fixed my features back into a smile in time for Daisy to see. But I was left wondering what Tom might have seen on my face, especially when he spoke up again.

"Daisy insisted I come and share in the delight of telling you our most happy news, but, unfortunately, I can't stay. I have a few pressing matters that require my attention. There are many letters to be written and plans to be made if the wedding is to happen as soon as we wish it to. I beg both your pardons, but I should be going."

Daisy looked surprised, but she wasn't upset, which I was grateful for.

"Don't worry yourself about it. It was wonderful seeing you, and I'm sure I'll be seeing much more of you now. Dais, are you staying?" I prayed she would.

"Yes, of course! We have so much to talk about." She giggled.

After a moment, I excused myself into the house to give them some privacy to say goodbye.

I couldn't help myself from lingering by the window. I watched as he pulled her in close, saw her giggle, and saw him lean in closer. I looked away, not wanting to see whatever came next. I didn't think I would be able to stomach it.

When she wandered in a few minutes later, she was practically floating. It was a delight seeing her happy, but I was worried and not just about him not deserving her. I didn't like how quickly things were going. Maybe it was my jealousy talking, but I didn't think so. I wasn't sure whether I should tell her, but I didn't like holding things back from her.

She turned to me and said, "I can't believe how lucky I am."

I knew I needed to be careful. I didn't want to upset her. "I'm really glad you're happy."

She turned to me, a whisper of her earlier concern on her face. "Are you happy for me?"

"Of course, my dear. I would support anything that makes you this happy."

She crossed the room to the window. She sighed, looking out, watching him retreat. "Tom's gone now. You can tell me what you're actually thinking."

I sighed and crossed the room to meet her. I paused, not sure whether to bridge the rest of the gap to her. Not sure if I should touch her.

"I'm glad you're happy, I really am. It's just," I struggled with how to word my thoughts, "don't you think this might be a little soon?"

"I'll admit it was a little sudden, but I feel good about it."

"I'm really glad to hear that, Dais. You know your happiness is my own. I just worry about you."

She sighed again and finally turned to face me. "You know you worry too much."

I couldn't help but laugh a little at that. "I can't help it, especially when it comes to you. I care too much about you. You know how much I want you to be happy; it just seems a little soon."

She sighed and looked away. "I thought you might say that. And I haven't even told you the part that I thought might worry you."

I wasn't sure what to think about that. She didn't ever hold things back from me. She must have been really nervous. I took her hands in mine and she again met my gaze. "What is it, love? You can tell me."

"We're to be married in June."

I was speechless. "You mean next June?" I asked, already nearly sure of the answer.

She took a long breath before responding, "No."

"Oh wow." She looked down at her feet. I hastened to say, "I mean, that's wonderful news."

After a moment, she turned back to me and stared incredulously. "Don't lie to me, Jord. I know you. I know how you think, and I know you think this is much too soon. Tell me I'm being stupid and crazy. I don't care, just don't lie to me."

My voice wobbled over the thickness in my throat. "I'm sorry, love. I really am. I want to be happy for you. I really do. It's just... what do you really know about him? What makes you sure he can make you happy?"

"I won't lie to you and say I'm assured of my own happiness, but I will say that I know Tom is my best chance at happiness."

My knees felt weak. "What do you mean, your best chance at happiness?"

She started to pace the room. "You know exactly what I mean. I'm damaged goods. I ruined my reputation, and as much as I hate to admit it, my mother is right. Especially after Marcos. If word got out that he had left me, as thrilled as I am that I made that happen, I would be even worse off. You know me, I wouldn't have considered for a moment saying yes to Tom if I didn't think I would be happy. I don't pretend him and I know each other as well as I would like, but I know he's a good man. He's funny, kind, charming..." She laughed before adding, "And it doesn't hurt that he's rich and handsome. I don't pretend to love him yet, but he's the sort of man I know it will be easy to fall for. I have high hopes that my affection for him will grow into love. I think that's the best I can hope for."

She stopped in front of the window, again looking out at the drive, not meeting my eye. My heart ached for her, and there was a numbness spreading in my body. I hadn't had any idea she felt like that. When had she gotten so practical? When had the world wiped away her optimism? "You aren't damaged. Far from it. I know you're worried about the future, and I hope you're right that you'll be happy with Tom, but what's the rush? Why get married so soon? Why not have a longer engagement?"

"And give him time to change his mind?"

I couldn't understand her worries. Anyone would be lucky to have her. There was no way he would change his mind. "He wouldn't. He'd have to be crazy to change his mind."

"Jay did."

My heart broke for her. I wished, not for the first time, that I could get my hands on him, give him a piece of my mind. He deserved to suffer for how broken he left her. I clenched my fists. She deserved so much better. I wished I could whisk her away from here, from her troubles. I wished she didn't have to make such hard decisions so young. I wished women were given more choices, that there was anything I could do for her, but I knew there wasn't. "He never deserved you."

She finally turned around and I saw the tears on her face. It was a struggle to not collapse then and there. My knees had turned to jelly, but I somehow made it across the room to her. I gently touched my hand to her face and brushed the tears away.

"I'm so sorry that he hurt you, but I promise it won't happen again. I won't let it happen again."

"I know. It can't happen again. That's why I said yes to Tom. He's so kind and gentle. I know he would never hurt me."

I couldn't argue with her there. While I barely knew him, he was a perfect gentleman so far.

"I love you, Jord, you know I do, and you might be right. Maybe it would be wiser to wait, but I can't risk it. He's my best chance at happiness and I have to take it."

I clenched and unclenched my fists. Anger coursed through my veins at the unfairness of the situation. Anger at the world for not letting women support themselves. Anger at her parents for being so forceful about her needing to be married when they have plenty of money to continue to support her. Anger at her for not fighting harder for what she wanted, not standing up for herself. Anger at her lieutenant for having stolen her innocence and by consequence her freedom to make her own choices about her future. Anger at Tom for being the best option available to her. And, most of all, anger at myself for not being able to support her, not being able to save her from this.

But I knew none of this was fair to her. She had been so happy and excited before I opened my mouth. She had decided, and I knew there would be no changing her mind. The best thing I could do for her now was to bring the smile back to her face.

I unclenched my fists again and took a few deep breaths and said all I could think to say. "I wish you all the happiness in the world, and if you say he's your best shot, then I believe you. I wish you both all the happiness."

She smiled tentatively before saying hesitantly, "There's one more thing."

Something else? I didn't think my heart could handle anything else. "Oh?"

She smiled a little more. "Yes, the most important thing."

"Well? Don't keep me in suspense." I hoped it would be something I could handle.

"Will you be my bridesmaid? I need you up there with me."

I was so relieved I nearly collapsed. I had been terrified about what she might say. I took a couple seconds to calm my racing heart and to hold in the relieved hysterical laughter I felt bubbling up. When I looked at her and saw the anxiety, I blurted out, "Yes, of course!" She let out a sigh of relief. "Daisy, my dear, I'm not always going to agree with your choices, but I do truly hope you are right and that this brings you the utmost happiness. I can't promise to always agree with you, but I will always be there to love and support you."

I caught a quick glimpse of the grin on her face before she launched herself into my arms. I held tight, not wanting her to see the couple tears that trailed down my face. When, after a long while, she pulled away, I was relieved to see her smiling. I made myself a promise I would do whatever it took to make sure that smile stayed on her face. For her happiness, no price was too high.

Daisy

The majority of what I had hoped to be my week alone with Tom to spend getting to know him better was taken up by my mother. She monopolized more of our time than I would have liked, but the moment she found out we wanted a quick wedding, she was determined to pack an entire year's worth of planning into however long she had. Much to her dismay, we arranged for it to be a spring wedding, giving my mother less than three months for the planning.

Tom planned to hire private cars to bring down his closest, and, per my mother's tactless request, richest friends and family. I would have been happy to have the festivities in our ballroom where we met, and where he proposed, but, according to my mother, that was quite unacceptable. The only place we all agreed on was the Muhlbach. It was the grandest hotel I had ever seen. It had been there most of my life, but my mother said it was a newer addition to Louisville. Having never been to Europe myself, I couldn't attest to the accuracy of the comparison, but most people said the hotel looked like something that would be found in Paris or Vienna. My mother said it was built in the French Renaissance style.

All I knew was that it was unlike anything I had seen before. If that was a taste of France, I knew I would like to see more. We agreed on the Grand Ballroom of the Muhlbach, which was quite unlike the other venues the city had to offer, being on the roof of the hotel. Even *I* had to agree the spectacular views gave it a leg up over our own ballroom. It was decided, and Tom made arrangements to rent a whole floor of the hotel.

We had hardly spent more than an hour alone the entire week before Tom regretfully had to return to Chicago to make the necessary preparations for his absence and our honeymoon. I knew it had to be done, but it didn't make the goodbye any easier. I would see him in three long months. It hadn't sounded long when we fixed the date, but now, facing the separation, it felt like far too long.

Chapter Twenty - Seven

For the next couple months, Jordan and I were attached at the hip. The winter gave her more time than ever to spend with me since golf was put on hold until the Spring. Not to mention with her being single and my fiancé being in Chicago, we were free from male distractions. That's not to say there wasn't plenty of male attention given to us both, but it was well known I was soon to be off the market, and Jordan, it seemed, was still healing from things ending with James and didn't entertain any of the attention she received. Again, the heartless gossip-mongers of the town whispered about how she was cold to men and unmarriable. They said she would die a spinster since no man would have her. I worried about her myself, but I hoped with more time, she would continue to heal. I knew anyone would be lucky to be with her and hoped that she might begin to open her heart up to another soon. I hoped she might find someone worthy of her. It wouldn't be an easy task, but she deserved all the happiness in the world, and I wanted that for her.

With June creeping closer, it started to dawn on me just how much I might have been giving up by marrying. I had been thinking of marriage as my liberation, my freedom from being under my parents' control and in their home, but now I thought about how much I would miss them. I didn't always get along with them, but they always wanted what was best, or at least what they *thought* was best, for me. I worried I might be trading one set of shackles for another.

Yes, I would be considered an adult, no longer a young woman under her parents' control, but I would be married. I would be a married woman beheld to my husband's wishes. I worried that type of control might have been worse than what I was enduring now. I quickly pushed the thought out of my mind. Marriage to Marcos would have indeed been worse than staying under my parents' control, but Tom was not Marcos. He was kindhearted and cared about what I wanted, and what I thought, and cared for me.

I knew how lucky I was to be blessed enough to be engaged to a kind, rich man. According to my mother, unmarried rich men were scarce in themselves. When I told her I meant to wait for a kind man that I loved, she had laughed, saying a kind rich man would be an impossibility for there could not be more than a handful and those handful weren't likely to be unmarried. I knew I would prove her wrong, or else I would find a kind man and learn to adapt to a less affluent lifestyle. I wouldn't trade happiness for comfort. I knew I couldn't be truly comfortable without being happy.

Tom was a truly good man, but I was still worried about the implications of marriage and of the freedoms I might have been giving up instead of gaining. I wouldn't be able to see my family or Jordan whenever I wanted. I assumed we would likely settle in Chicago, but I couldn't say that with any certainty. I couldn't believe in our week together, I hadn't once thought to ask him where we were meant to live. It would be a terrible sacrifice to not be able to see Jordan as frequently as I wished, but I hoped that Tom's money and Jordan's money would mean frequent visits. I didn't know where he meant to settle, but knew it wouldn't be in Louisville.

Was I really ready to give up the only home I had ever known? I fought through my doubts and reminded myself it would be worth it to be free of my parents and married to Tom.

As the days crept closer, Jordan and I spent even more time together. She supported me through my doubts and fears and helped me think things through. She helped keep me sane, but I was even more grateful that she understood how important it was to me to squeeze in every second I could with her until Tom came and whisked me away to who-knows-where. It helped me to know that Tom liked Jordan well enough and that she would be a welcome visitor wherever we went, but saying goodbye wasn't going to be easy.

The rest of May flew by and before she and I knew it, there were only two days left until the wedding. Thanks to my mother's rigorous planning, I didn't have much to do besides relax and, as she told me many times, 'get some beauty rest.'

She was less than happy to find out Jordan was staying over with me tonight as well as tomorrow night. She lived close enough that it wasn't a necessity, but ever since the night of my debut, it had become normal for her to sleep in my room with me. I knew I would need her support more than ever to get through the next couple of days.

A million little worries crossed my mind, the biggest of which was the realization that I would be meeting my new family for the first time tomorrow. I worried what they might think of me and hoped to make a good impression. My family was wealthy, but our wealth was far from comparable to the wealth and influence of his family. I worried they might think I was only marrying him for his money. I knew I shouldn't worry. He knew the truth and that should be good enough for me and for them, but I was still worried.

The worries took hold throughout the day, and before I knew it, the day was over. Jordan and I talked well into the night. She reassured me it was normal to be worried about the wedding. She reassured me that once I saw Tom again tomorrow and talked to him that everything else would work itself out. She said she knew how much I cared about him and how much I wanted to be with him. I can't remember when we finally fell asleep, but I know I must have drifted off at some point.

The first thing I noticed was that my dress was all wrong. Where I had wanted the dress loose, it was tight and in the spots that were supposed to be tight, it was far too loose. I tried on the veil, hoping it would help pull the dress together and distract from its shortcomings, but I noticed a large rip running through the lace of the veil. I held back my tears as I looked around for any other options. I blinked and was all of a sudden in the dress at the back of the church, waiting for the doors to be opened for me to walk down the aisle.

My father was supposed to be standing with me. He was supposed to walk me down the aisle. I was panicking. Where was he? The music played my cue before I found him and the doors burst open.

I felt myself shoved into the room. I tripped a little before recovering my balance. All eyes were on me. I felt exposed, laid bare in front of all these people. I glided as gracefully as I could down the aisle, but couldn't ignore the snickers and giggles at the state of my dress.

My sense of dread deepened the closer I got to the aisle. When I was able to see Tom, I met his eye. He grinned at me. It helped calm some of my nerves, but I still felt a lingering sense of something being wrong. When I reached the altar, Tom took my hand and placed it in the crook of his elbow and we both faced the minister. Before I could blink, the minister and Tom and all our guests were staring at me. I didn't know why. Had the minister said something?

I blushed. "I'm sorry. What did you say?"

I couldn't believe I had zoned out at my own wedding. The minister smiled awkwardly and said, "I asked, do you take this man to be your lawfully wedded husband?"

"Oh, of course!" I giggled. "Yes, absolutely!"

Tom laughed and so did the rest of our guests.

The minister smiled and looked at me apologetically. "I'm sorry, Miss Fay, but I need an 'I do'."

I blushed profusely. How could I have forgotten? "Of course. I'm so sorry. I do, of course I do."

It was then that my sense of dread returned in full force. I felt a paralyzing fear emanating from the tips of my fingers, the part of me touching Tom. With dread in my heart, I slowly looked over at him. Confusion swept over me. There was something wrong with Tom's face. His body had not changed. It was still his own, but there was something off about his face. I couldn't believe my eyes as his face changed under my gaze. His hair darkened from his light honey color to a dark brown, so dark it was almost black. His lips twisted from his smile into a cruel-looking smirk. My heart froze in fear. I knew those features. I looked up to meet his eyes, but they too had turned dark. There was a cruel triumph in them.

Somehow, Tom's face had transformed into the likeness of Marcos. I was terrified and tried to pull my hand away, but he put his hand over my own and held me there against my will. I struggled against him, but no one seemed to notice.

The minister beamed brightly at us and said, "Well then, I now pronounce you Mr. and Mrs. Thomas Hortense the Third."

I tried harder to pull away.

He laughed outright at me. "My beautiful flower, I told you you would be mine."

I screamed and fought him as hard as I could, but no one seemed to notice. The guests and the minister watched expectantly, waiting for our first kiss. I kept screaming and trying to pull away, but he pulled me closer.

Just as his lips crashed onto mine, my eyes popped open.

Chapter Twenty - Eight

Jordan was leaning over me, shaking me. When she saw my eyes open, she looked relieved and concerned. "Daisy! You're awake! Thank goodness! Are you okay?"

It took me a minute to regain my senses and slow my racing heart. I nodded and took a few deep breaths. "I think so." I looked around and saw we were in my room. I saw my veil neatly folded on my vanity table. There was no rip. I looked outside. The sun was starting to peak through the windows. I let out a sigh of relief. "It was just a dream."

"What happened? You were screaming in your sleep. I was really worried. I'm surprised you didn't wake half the house." I looked to my door, worried, but it seemed secure and no one was knocking or asking questions. I took another deep breath.

"Thank goodness. It must have been a dream. But it felt so real... Tell me, is it Sunday?" I hoped it wasn't.

She looked at me with increasing concern. "No, my dear, it's only Saturday. Are you sure you're quite alright?"

I nodded, relieved. "Yes. Yes; I'm sure I'm fine. Just a little shaken up. That's all."

She looked curious, but mostly concerned. "Are you sure you don't want to talk about it?"

"Yes, quite sure. It was just a silly dream, not worth discussing."

I prayed she would accept that and not question me further. I wasn't ready to talk about it. I didn't even want to think about it. I knew it was just my stress building up, but I felt like having a nightmare about your wedding right before said wedding was not a good omen. I was more worried than ever and knew that I might break down if I talked about it. I silently pleaded for her to understand.

She still looked unsure but nodded before sinking back into her pillow. I turned away from her, hiding my face. A single tear ran down my cheek. The day could only get better from there.

Jordan and I were quick to rise and get ready that morning. I knew she was worried and wanted to help, but she seemed to know I needed her silence. I had other worries on my mind.

Tom, his family, and their close friends were all arriving today. One hundred strangers who were all important to Tom and who all wanted to meet me. One hundred strangers with whom I was expected to make a good impression. I didn't have time to worry about my feelings; I needed today and tomorrow to go perfectly. My future happiness was riding on it. I had never felt so stressed and overwhelmed in my life. I couldn't afford for anything to go wrong. I knew Tom and I would be happy together. He was my best shot at happiness, and I had to take it.

Before I knew it, we received a call from the Muhlbach that the McCormick parties had arrived. I hoped everything had gone smoothly with their trip. I wanted to rush over and meet Tom. I wanted to see him again and to reassure myself that everything was fine, but I wasn't ready to face all the newcomers. I wasn't ready for the introductions, so I waited for him to stop by like we had planned.

When he finally arrived, to my relief, he came alone. I saw him appear in the gardens while I was pacing the halls and ran to meet him. I threw myself into his arms.

He caught me with a laugh. "My dear Daisy, my flower, it is so good to see you!" He chuckled as he hugged me tighter. "To think it's only been a couple of months." He started to pull away, but I held tight. He laughed again and tightened his grip on me. "I missed you, too, my dear sweet Daisy." After a moment, he looked down at my face. I hesitated to meet his eye. "Is everything okay, my flower?"

I nodded, but he kept staring at me. After a moment of not knowing what to say, I added, "Of course! I just missed you. It's been far too long."

"My thoughts exactly. But once we marry, we won't ever have to be apart again."

I didn't know how to respond and couldn't decide the meaning of the butterflies in my stomach. Were they nerves because I was making a big scary decision, or was it my gut being terrified because I was making the wrong decision? I didn't know what to say, so I just nodded and pulled him closer.

When he stepped back, I noticed for the first time he held a wrapped box in his hand. He seemed to remember it at the same moment I noticed it. He laughed and handed it to me. "Just a little something for you, my sweet flower. I hoped it would be the perfect compliment to your dress for tomorrow."

I smiled. I was incredibly touched he had brought me a gift. He really didn't have to do that, but I hesitated. Here he was, incredibly handsome and caring and kind. He was incredibly happy to see me and excited about tomorrow, as was I, but he was relaxed and seemed so sure of everything. I didn't feel like I deserved his gift. Besides, I already knew exactly what I was wearing with my dress tomorrow.

I was wearing my favorite pearls. The string I wore everywhere. The thought that I wouldn't be able to wear them was almost enough to make me burst into tears right then and there. I held back my emotions and thanked him.

He laughed at my hesitation. "I know, I know. I'm not supposed to have any input on your dress or your jewelry, but just open it. If you hate it, you don't have to wear it."

I couldn't help but laugh. "Was I that obvious?"

"Your face doesn't exactly keep your emotions secret."

I laughed at that, feeling some relief at his assurances that I wouldn't have to wear it. I carefully and hesitantly unwrapped the box. I slowly opened it and gasped. I couldn't believe my eyes. It was a delicate strand of pearls with the most beautiful, subtle pink tint. They were even more stunning than my favorite pearls and looked all the more expensive. I had been so worried he expected me to break away from wearing pearls. I was worried he would have gotten me an expensive, flashy diamond or jeweled necklace. It would have been excusable since I wore an incredibly flashy necklace to my debut, but he truly knew me.

I felt my worries drift away. I had nothing to worry about, after all. He knew me well enough to know I wouldn't want anything that flashy on my wedding day. He knew how much I loved pearls. I was so grateful to him and felt so loved. I pulled him into a passionate kiss. After a moment, I pulled away, needing to catch my breath.

He laughed. "So, I'm guessing you like them?"

"I love them! They're perfect!" I said, beaming at him.

He smiled. "I'm so glad to hear it. I really hoped you would like them. I wish I had more time, but I really have to be getting back to the hotel. Our guests are expecting me back any minute." My face fell at the realization he was leaving again so soon. He chuckled and said, "I'll see you at dinner in a few hours. No need to be upset." He hugged me quickly and then left me alone with my thoughts.

I would have liked to stay in the gardens a bit longer but knew Jordan was waiting for me.

Chapter Twenty - Nine

I headed back to my room, and when I got there, I was surprised to see Jordan and a maid talking in hushed tones. The maid was handing something, an envelope, to Jordan, who was shaking her head and trying to give it back to her. I stepped closer and made my presence known.

The color drained from Jordan's face when she saw me. My confusion multiplied, and I started to worry. What was wrong? Jordan didn't keep things from me, so why did she look guilty now? The maid capitalized on Jordan's distraction, shoving the envelope into her hands and disappearing around the bend in the hall before Jordan or I could say anything.

I looked at Jordan for an explanation. She sighed and pulled me into my room. She shut and latched the door behind us, saying, "I'm sure this is a bad idea."

"What is it, Jord? You're scaring me."

She tried to lighten her serious expression, but couldn't seem to change her mood. "I just have a bad feeling about this, that's all." She turned the envelope over in her hands. With anyone else, I would have been furious, but with Jordan, it was different. I was incapable of believing she had anything but my best interest at heart. So, I sighed and reached for the envelope.

"Well, now I'm here and have seen it, so let me have a look at it."

She sighed and handed it over. "Okay, but for the record, I don't think it's a good idea. This letter arriving the day before your wedding can't mean anything good...probably best to get rid of it, like I was telling the maid to."

I tried to ignore the creeping feeling that she might be right, but I couldn't shake it. "You really don't think I should open it?"

She looked hopeful for a moment before her face fell again. "I really don't, but I know you're far too curious to leave it unopened."

I laughed at that and tried to adopt an air of ease I didn't feel. I could tell Jordan wasn't convinced either. "Well, if you really think I shouldn't, I don't see the harm in taking your advice and ignoring the letter."

She chuckled. "I really wish you would, but I don't see it happening."

Internally, I agreed with her. I felt the letter would weigh on my mind until I inevitably opened it, but I wanted her to be wrong. I would prove her wrong. I would listen to my gut telling me she was right and the letter wouldn't bring me any happiness. I wouldn't open it.

Her eyes widened in shock when I set the letter face down on my vanity without hesitation. I resisted flipping it over to see the address. "I won't open it. I trust you, and besides, I don't have a good feeling about it either."

She smiled, but it didn't touch the worry in her eyes. I changed the subject, and we talked about the bridal dinner and about the wedding, but I suspected she was as distracted by the letter as I was. It hung like an unwelcome presence in the room, haunting my thoughts. I reasoned that one little peek wouldn't hurt. Even if I just flipped the envelope over to closer inspect the writing.

I had a creeping suspicion I knew who it was from. But I was finished with him. I was over him, so why was I so worried about whether it was his handwriting and what it might say?

I paced the room while we talked and as I thought. Each pass of the room bringing me within reach of the letter. Out of the corner of my eye, I noticed Jordan tense when I was within reach of the letter and visibly relax when I passed without grasping it. After noticing her distress, I stopped pacing and sat down with her on my bed. I pushed the letter out of my mind and the rest of the morning and early afternoon passed smoothly until Jordan had to leave.

She hadn't planned to get ready for the bridal dinner here, so she had to leave early to get ready at her own house. Before she left, she asked if I was going to be okay. She knew how nervous I was about the dinner and the wedding. I laughed it off and assured her I could get ready on my own and would see her soon. The dinner was in a few hours. She said she would be back in two hour's time and then we would head to the hotel together.

That startled me out of my thoughts. I only had a couple hours to get ready. I had lost track of time. She smiled at me reassuringly and called the maids to help as she left.

One of them brought in a bottle of what looked to be expensive wine. It had a yellowy hue to it. When I asked about it, they said it was a present sent from one of my future relatives. That was quite nice of them. I took the bottle from the maid and thanked her for bringing it and discarded it on the vanity table next to the letter. I didn't drink, but it was a nice gesture all the same.

Another of the maids had brought in my dress for dinner. It was a pale pink flowery dress that made me think of spring and accentuated my curves in the best way. After they helped me into the dress, one of the maids had me sit at my vanity and went to work on my hair.

The letter lay tantalizingly in front of me while she worked on my hair. After a few minutes, I noticed my fingers had inched toward the letter. I reasoned I could just flip it over and peek at the handwriting. That wouldn't do any harm and I wouldn't have misled Jordan. I wouldn't open it. I just needed to know if it was from him.

I reached for the letter and was about to flip it over when I heard the door open. I withdrew my hand quickly, feeling guilty, but when I looked in the mirror behind me, it was only another maid.

She had brought some jewelry for me to pick from for dinner. I was struggling with whether to wear Tom's pearls tonight in addition to tomorrow, or if I should save them for tomorrow. I told her to leave the jewelry, since I needed more time to decide.

I felt like I couldn't think straight about anything. My mind was too focused on the letter. I felt like I wouldn't be able to decide on anything until I had just glanced at the handwriting.

With only slight hesitation, I reached out and turned the letter over. I paused at the handwriting. I don't know why I thought I would be able to tell from the handwriting alone if the letter was from him. I had only seen his penmanship once in the one letter I read from him. The handwriting itself gave me no clues.

I paused at the address, though. It was addressed to Daisy, not Miss Daisy Fay or Miss Fay or even Daisy Fay, just Daisy. Only someone who was well known to me would be so bold as to address me in such a way. My curiosity peaked. I sighed. I should have listened to Jordan and gotten rid of the letter when I had the chance. I knew now that I had seen the handwriting, which looked to be that of a man's, I was going to open it. I had narrowed down the likely suspects to Jay or Marcos. I knew I shouldn't open it. Nothing good would come of it, but I knew I would open it.

For a brief, hopeful moment, I thought the letter might be from Tom, but quickly dismissed the thought. He had been with me when the letter arrived and had given me the pearls. If he had a letter or something else to give me, he would have given it to me then.

I reasoned I had to just quickly open it, glimpse at the signature and then I would know whether to read it. I reassured myself that finding out who it was from would sate my curiosity and clear my mind to focus on today and tomorrow's festivities.

I had seen a couple of curious glances from the maids and decided it would be better to have some privacy. The moment my hair was finished, I ushered them out. I told them I needed to be alone and would call them when I needed further assistance. After they left, I sat back down in front of the vanity and looked at the letter. I tried to tell myself how silly my anxiety and dread were. It was just a letter, after all. I reasoned all I would do was open it and look at who sent it. I didn't even have to read it afterward. I just needed to know who sent it.

I broke the seal and opened the envelope. The paper was thick, but I could tell through what was visible that the front was covered in writing. I slowly unfolded the letter and tried to focus my eyes on looking for the signature. I couldn't help that a few words seemed to grab my attention before my eyes made it to the bottom. 'Jealousy. Anger. Betrayal. Future.' My dread and curiosity both peaked. Even if I wanted to, it would have been impossible to tear myself away now without finding out who wrote such a mysterious, ominous sounding letter.

When my eyes made it to the bottom of the page, my fears were confirmed. It was Jay. I should have known, but there was no turning back now. I needed to know what he had to say.

My Dearest Daisy,

I know it's been a long while since I last wrote. You can't imagine everything I went through when I finally received your letter. I knew you couldn't have been receiving my letters. I knew if you had, you would have written sooner. There are no words to express how much I longed for and missed you. It was the thought of you and our future together that got me through the war, and the memories of our last night that sustained me through the long, lonely nights.

So, you can imagine my shock when your long-awaited letter arrived only for me to find out you were being forced into marriage with another. I couldn't contain the anger and betrayal I felt.

Rest assured, I knew you weren't entirely to blame. It is hardly your fault that you weren't strong enough to stand up to your parents, to stand up for our love. As sheltered and coddled as you have been your whole life, I could have hardly expected less. I hoped you might come around sooner or later. I waited for another letter that it had been called off and that you were waiting for me, but that letter never came.

I had half a mind to come home anyway. I would have, had there been any way to do so, but as fate would have it, I've been stuck in England studying at Oxford. I have been spending my time doing everything I can to be worthy of your parents' approval, but I doubt whether I will ever be enough for them. But still I try, because I know it isn't you I need to impress. I know without their approval, your adoration means nothing. But they don't know about us. How could they be selling you to some rich man if they knew you were already mine? I had half a mind to write to them and tell them of our last night together, but I held my tongue and pen because I expected you would find your own way out of the situation.

I can't be the only one fighting for our love. I waited and waited, just like I did in New York. I waited for you and yet again you disappointed me.

I kept waiting, kept expecting the happy news that you were again unbetrothed, so you can imagine how I felt seeing the announcement...your name next to his...as if you belonged to him and no longer to me...I cannot describe the anger and jealousy and betrayal I felt.

I hold on to the fact that I know you to be entering into the union most unwillingly. I know your feelings and know nothing less than your parents' forceful hands could pry you away from me. I hold on to the fact that you are mine in all but name alone, but that does little good if you legally become another man's property.

If only you had made it to New York before I was shipped out, we would not have to worry about the world conspiring to separate what God had joined together. Alas, my dear, you failed me and left me waiting. But I generously forgave you, as I always have.

I want you to know my feelings remain unchanged. Even the anger I feel at your engagement is something that I know can be overcome if you simply leave him now. I know I will be able to find forgiveness in my heart. Just don't say 'I do' and all will be forgiven. I am the only one who can promise you happiness and love.

Daisy, my dear, don't marry him... If you say 'I do', I know you will regret it... I will make sure of it... for you are mine as surely as I am...

...Forever yours
~Jay

Well, Jordan was certainly going to say she told me so. We both knew opening the letter was a bad idea. She was right. I should have thrown out the letter without opening it. Little good that did me now, though.

I couldn't believe he spoke of betrayal and anger. He had always been so kind to me; I hadn't expected him to be so forceful. I couldn't believe *he* was upset with *me*. *He* was the one who broke *my* heart and yet he made himself the victim. He stole my innocence and now he had the audacity to use that to claim me as his. I couldn't believe him. I hadn't seen him in a year and a half and he simply expected me to be waiting for him?

For months I had thought him dead, and long before that, he had left without a goodbye. He ran away with my innocence. What was I supposed to think? I waited for him. *I* was the one left waiting, and *I* was the one left disappointed.

Yes, I was also the one who didn't go to New York, but how could I have? Did he expect me to travel half the country on my own without a plan of where to meet him? Without an idea of where he would be? Why would I have come running after he left me?

He left me broken and alone with a wound I thought would never heal. I was heartbroken over losing him, and knew I would never be happy again. Until I met Tom. He swept me off my feet and thawed my heart. He saved me both figuratively and literally. He saved me from loneliness and sadness and from Marcos's torment. He proposed to me to save me from a loveless marriage. He was incredibly selfless, and I was happy with him. Now Jay wanted to just waltz back into my life as if he never left? He wanted to saunter back and ruin my happiness? Did he really expect me to come running like he never abandoned me to my doubts and suffering? And again, he had the audacity to offer his forgiveness! How dare he!

How dare he do this to me the day before my wedding! I couldn't believe he was trying to ruin my happiness. Tomorrow should be the happiest day of my life. I should have been incredibly happy and excited. I was going to marry Tom tomorrow, and he made me incredibly happy. I was happy with Tom, wasn't I? Yes, I had been having my doubts, but that was normal, wasn't it?

I couldn't think. I didn't know how to feel or what to do. I looked up and my eyes landed on the bottle. I had never been a drinker before, but I figured now was as good a time as any to start. I poured myself a glass and held it to my lips. I paused, having seen something out of the corner of my eye. I looked, but it was only my reflection in the mirror. The sight of myself holding a drink to my lips made me giggle. I raised my glass in a toast to the girl in the mirror before swallowing half the glass.

The taste was indescribable. It was heavenly sweet and tasted of peaches and honey. I took another long sip and noticed my glass was empty. That made me giggle more. I looked down and saw the letter where I had dropped it. If I ever needed a drink, now would be the time. I poured myself another glass and turned back to the letter.

So, Jay still wanted me. I had done everything I could to turn him away, and he still wanted me. I didn't know what to think. *He* was the one who left *me*, so why was he making me out to be the coldhearted one? He could have come to say goodbye or written, but he didn't. When he received my last letter, he could have come back and tried to win me back, but he didn't. He could have written to me sooner, but he didn't.

I took another long sip of my drink. I didn't know what to think. I was happy and now along came Jay the day before my wedding with a letter about six months too late. Had he written back in December before things had taken off with Tom, he might have had a chance at my forgiveness. He might have had a chance with me, but now I was too far gone. I had fallen too far for Tom to put him out of my mind. I couldn't picture a future without Tom. I couldn't be happy without him, could I? I gulped down more of my wine.

How dare Jay come along and make me question everything! Yes, I was feeling uneasy before his letter, but that was normal. My eyes went back to the letter and lingered on the more offensive passages. He called me weak for not standing up to my parents. As if he knew how much he was asking. To marry a penniless man without their approval would be a death sentence. We couldn't dream of supporting ourselves without their money. I had loved him, but I wasn't stupid. I knew how the world worked. I knew if my parents promised my hand to someone, I had little hope of undoing it. I wasn't weak; I just didn't hold his sense of unwavering optimism. I mean, even when I tried to reject him, it hadn't shaken his faith. He still was sure we would be together, still sure that was what I wanted.

Part of his hope was my own fault. I had written to him that I was being betrothed against my will, which, at the time, was true. I couldn't remember if I had ever named Marcos as my soon-to-be husband, but I doubted I had. He must have assumed that it was Tom I had been referring to, which couldn't have been further from the truth. I had been overjoyed when Tom proposed. I couldn't believe my luck. The kindest, most selfless man I knew, who also happened to be incredibly handsome, wanted to marry me. I was elated.

Now Jay had the audacity to say he would make sure I regretted my marriage. Even if he thought me to be entering it unwillingly, how dare he make threats like that! I couldn't begin to understand what he could mean by that, but I was outraged nonetheless. Had he come to me asking for forgiveness, I might have been more tempted.

I shook my head, trying to clear those thoughts from my head. I was marrying Tom tomorrow. I couldn't be entertaining fantasies. I couldn't be thinking of Jay. I put the letter down and picked my drink back up to take another sip, but was surprised to find it empty.

I reached for the bottle to pour myself more. If all wine tasted like this, I had really been missing out. I had lost track a long while ago how much I had drank but when I reached for the bottle to refill my glass, I was surprised to find it much lighter. I poured myself more and stood.

I was confused to feel the room wobble and shake under my feet. Feeling unsteady, I sat back down.

I should have walked away and put more distance between the letter and myself. The longer I looked at it, the more conflicted I became. My anger started to fade, and I found myself more drawn to the beginning of the letter. With my anger receding, I had trouble not feeling sentimental. I felt my heart moved at the idea that he had been working all this time to be more deserving of me and that he had not forgotten me, but why in Heaven's name did he wait this long to write?

He wrote to me a day before my wedding expecting it would change things. It didn't change a thing. It couldn't change anything. I was to be married tomorrow. I loved Tom. Well, I cared for Tom, and he had been there for me and cared for me.

But Jay and I had a history I couldn't easily ignore.

And how well did I really know Tom? I had only met him six short months ago. Was that really long enough to get to know someone, especially after only having spent a handful of days with him? How well did I really know him? I tried to convince myself I knew him well enough, but the assurances fell flat. It seemed the only thing I was sure about was that Tom cared for me and that he was a good man, but what did I really know of him? Was I really agreeing to sign myself and my life over to a man I knew so little about? A man I had just met six months ago?

I was overwhelmed, and the room was spinning. I collapsed on my bed. Could I really do this? I didn't know.

I came to my senses at a loud knock on the door. I didn't know how long I had stayed like that. I must have dozed off. It took me a few moments to regain my bearings. I was in my bed, holding a bottle of wine and a letter.

The wine. It must have been the wine. If drinking made you feel like this, I hadn't been missing out on much. Sitting next to me on the bed was a wastebasket. Why was there a wastebasket on my bed? My attention was drawn to the door when I heard it open.

I saw a fuzzy outline of a woman enter. I tried to sit up more and felt my stomach lurch. That explained the wastebasket. Had I vomited? I didn't think so, but looked in the basket to be sure. No; it was empty except for a string of the most beautiful pearls. I searched my brain for where they had come from and why they were in the wastebasket, but came up blank.

The female figure moved toward me. As I squinted, the figure changed shape and became clearer. After a moment, the figure took the shape of Jordan, except there were...two? Did Jordan have a twin? Why didn't she tell me?

I gestured toward her twin to ask when I noticed again the bottle of wine in my hand. I squinted again at Jordan and the two merged back into one. It was just Jordan. I couldn't believe the things a little wine could do to you.

I tried to say congratulate me, but what tumbled out of my mouth sounded more like, "'Gratulate me." Even through the haze in my mind, I could see she was incredibly concerned. In explanation, I gestured to the wine. "Never had a drink before, but oh how I do enjoy it."

When I looked back, her twin had returned. Both Jordans leaned forward, asking, "What's the matter, Dais?"

I tried to think, what was the matter? I looked around again and my eyes landed on the letter. I had a vague memory of being upset by the letter. I pulled the wastebasket to me, intending to throw out the letter, but when I glanced at it again, I saw the signature.

Jay Gatsby.

The name meant something to me, if I could only remember. The name made me feel giddy, but I couldn't explain the feeling. That was when I noticed the pearls again. They were far too nice to be in a wastebasket. I couldn't remember why they were there or where they came from.

After a moment, I was hit with a recollection of a young man giving me the pearls. A man, I thought with a start, that I was supposed to marry tomorrow. Marriage. I wasn't ready for that. I was still a child.

I looked up and saw both Jordans staring at me. I gestured for them to come closer. Neither Jordan moved. "Here, dearies." I grabbed for the offensive, commitment-binding pearls. I missed a few times before my hands felt the smooth pearls and pulled them out of the trash. I looked up at both Jordans and thrust the pearls to them, not caring which one took the pearls. "Take 'em downstairs and give 'em back to whoever they belong to."

I couldn't think of the young man's name. I was supposed to marry that man tomorrow and I couldn't think of his name. I couldn't do this.

The room felt hot and stifling. I was having trouble breathing. I couldn't do it. "Tell 'em all Daisy's change' her mine." I was having a hard time focusing my eyes on either of the Jordans. Neither responded. I needed them to understand how important this was, but my words came out slurred, "Say: 'Daisy's change' her mine!'"

I started to cry. I couldn't stop myself.

Jordan, I saw through my tears there was only one again, came closer and hugged me tightly. I cried harder. She hugged me tighter and then started to let go. That made me cry even harder. She pet my head and smoothed down my hair, telling me she would be right back.

After a few moments, she returned with a maid and before I knew it, I was in a freezing bath. The cold water made it a little easier to think. I looked down with surprise and saw the letter was still in my hand. I squeezed it, trying to wring out the water, but it started to come apart in my hands. Jordan held out her hand and took it from me.

I started to sober up, soaking in the cold water. I started to come back to my senses and was too embarrassed to say anything else to Jordan. The maid made me smell something and put ice on my forehead. As if the ice-cold bath wasn't cold enough, but it seemed the maid was right because not long after, I regained the rest of my senses.

Everything came back to me after that. Tom and the pearls and Jay and the letter. That cursed letter. Jordan was right. I never should have opened it in the first place.

I cared for Tom, and he had been there for me and shown how much he cared since the day he met me. He saved me from my fate, and I would not abandon him now that Jay had decided to turn back up. Good riddance. He was too late. It would have been far less cruel for him to never reach back out at all.

I tried to regain some of my excitement for the festivities today and my wedding tomorrow, but couldn't muster the same excitement I had before. It seemed to have been another life altogether, in which I was worried about the impression I would make on Tom's relatives. Now, I couldn't bring myself to care.

Chapter Thirty

The moment I was ready again, Jordan and I hurried to the bridal dinner. Luckily, the dinner went off without a hitch. I tried to hide my worries from Tom, but couldn't shake the lingering doubts I was having. I worried he had noticed. It turned out he had. He pulled me aside the first chance he had after dinner. We went out and took a stroll for some privacy.

"Are you okay? You hardly seem yourself. Are you feeling quite alright?"

Internally, I sighed, but I forced a smile. "Of course I am, dear!"

He looked at me, unconvinced. I laughed a little before saying, "Okay, okay. I suppose it won't hurt to admit it. I got into a little wine earlier today."

He chuckled. "Wine? I thought you didn't drink."

I laughed, too. "I don't. That was a big part of the problem."

We laughed some more before he returned to looking more serious. "Are you sure that's all that's wrong? I was worried you might be having doubts."

I rushed to say, "No, no. Of course not!"

"Are you sure, darling? I would understand if you were."

He looked intently at me and, as much as I wanted to hold back, I didn't feel I could keep anything from such a kind, caring man. I nodded sheepishly. "Okay, maybe a little, but not about you. I care a lot about you. I just worry this might be a little soon."

He chuckled. "You mean I should have waited another month to propose?" I laughed at that, glad he knew how to improve my mood. "I can hardly blame you for having doubts. You are still quite young, and we haven't known each other for too long. Besides, I only proposed to save you from marriage to another man."

My face fell. He froze for a moment, seeming to realize what he had said. He rushed to explain, "Well, I mean initially that's why I proposed when I did, but I wouldn't have proposed to you if I hadn't known how happy I would be with you. The idea of you having to marry that scoundrel just sped up the process. Well, that and someone," he drew out the someone and nudged me, "wanted a quick wedding."

I laughed. "Who would want that? What a crazy thing to propose."

"Almost as crazy as proposing after having only known someone a few months."

We both laughed. I was more grateful than I could say to him for lightening the mood and being as supportive as he was. "But really, my flower, if you don't want to go through with this, just say the word. We can have a longer engagement if that's what you want, or," his face fell a little, but he finished, "we don't have to get married at all."

Seeing the hurt in his eyes, I knew I couldn't let him feel that way. Besides, he had eased almost all my concerns. "It's not that. I do want to be with you. I'm just worried; worried that

I'm young and that we don't know each other all that well." I sighed and added, "I'm worried you might eventually find out something about me you won't like." I was worried he would run away when he got to know me more. I worried he would get what he wanted and then leave, like Jay had.

It was a hard thing to admit, even to myself, that that was what Jay had done. He had ran when things had gotten difficult. He hadn't even stayed until the morning to say goodbye. He took my innocence and ran. I worried Tom too might leave if things got tough. Sure, things seemed like they would be easy. After all, our families approved of each other and we knew money would never be an issue with his family's money and my own. But I still couldn't shake the doubt.

"What could I ever possibly learn about you that would make me like you any less than I do now?"

Still having Jay on my mind, I blurted out my biggest fear without thinking. "I'm worried you'll leave the minute you find out I'm not a virgin."

It wasn't a big secret around town, but I hadn't wanted Tom to find out. I was worried it would change the way he looked at me. I really should have told him more tactfully, but now I had blurted it out, there was no going back.

I watched as his face went from confusion, to shock, and back to calm again before he spoke. "My dear, I'm so sorry."

Here it comes. He's sorry, but he can't be with me. He's sorry, but he won't marry me. The silence stretched on until I eventually said, "You're so sorry but…?"

"But nothing. I'm just really sorry. I mean, of course I knew something had happened. I just didn't think things had progressed that far." I wasn't sure what he meant by that or what to think. I went to ask, but he kept going, "I hope you know it doesn't matter to me. You're still my sweet, innocent flower, and I don't want you to worry. You couldn't ever say anything that would change my mind about that."

I was stunned. I had just told him what I thought to be the biggest secret I had from him and things turned out okay. They were more than okay. He was still here. He hadn't wanted to run from me.

Relief coursed through me, and I nuzzled myself into his arms. He embraced me tightly. I met his eye, and he leaned in close. He kissed me and everything felt right with the world again. The day had been overwhelming to say the least, but I was sure about one thing now. I was sure I was making the right choice. Tom stood by me when a lesser man would have left. He cared about me more than any man ever had. I was going to marry him tomorrow, and I would be the luckiest girl in the world to be Mrs. Thomas Buchanan.

Chapter Thirty - One

Jordan

A few more hours and the torture would end. A few more hours and Daisy would be more out of reach than she had ever been. All week she had been having doubts. All week I wondered whether she was right to have those doubts. I fought with myself about whether I should say anything. I knew now beyond a shadow of a doubt how I felt about her, but it didn't change a thing. She wouldn't feel the same. She couldn't possibly. Telling her would only ruin our friendship and confuse her.

This was Daisy we were talking about; incurably straight, innocent, uncorruptible Daisy. She didn't feel the same. I had been reminding myself all week that my own feelings didn't matter. They couldn't matter. This week was about Daisy and her happiness. Her taking her best shot at happiness.

The last thing she needed was me confusing her feelings. She had told me herself he's her best shot at happiness, and she was going to take it. I had to let her take it. I couldn't interfere. I would grin and bear it. I would be happy for her. Well, maybe that wasn't realistic, but I would certainly *try* to be happy for her. She needed me. She needed her best friend to care for and support her through her doubts. The last thing she needed was to hear my feelings.

I had gone all week with a pasted-on smile, hiding my feelings from her. I was determined she never know I was hurting. If I couldn't be the one to make her happy, I could at least do what little I could to help assure she would be happy.

Tom wasn't a bad guy. I knew he cared about her, and I hoped he would treat her like she deserved to be treated. Before any of this had happened, I had liked Tom. He was a good guy, the kind of guy I had wanted her to end up with, but everything changed when I heard they were going to be married. I couldn't believe my ears when she told me.

I had been stabbed in the heart and left to bleed in secret. I told her I was worried about her and that it seemed too soon, which was true, but that wasn't my biggest objection. How could she possibly be happy with him? How could he make her as happy as she deserved to be? He didn't even know her! And he still didn't.

A few days ago, when he first got into town, he came to me. He brought with him a present for Daisy, a necklace for her to wear for the wedding. He wanted to make sure she would like it. When he showed me the necklace he had picked out, I knew immediately it was all wrong. It was a bold, heavy necklace comprised of thousands of dollars worth of diamonds. It was blinding, and she would hate it. Her taste was louder than my own, but even she wouldn't be caught dead in that, never mind want to wear it on her wedding day.

I knew she felt like her wedding was going to be one of the best days of her life, and I saw all that changing in the reflection of those diamonds. I knew what I had to do. There really was no other choice. I knew she would wear whatever he gave her, despite how she felt about it. Despite how much it would bother her and how much she would hate the necklace, she would wear it to make him happy. She was always doing everything for everyone else. Always trying to please everyone else, but this was her day. This was her wedding, and I would be damned if I didn't make sure the day would be perfect for her.

"There's no easy way to say this, but I won't water down the truth. I don't know what you were thinking, but she would never wear that," I'd told him.

He looked crushed. I felt a little guilty, but mostly I felt smug and angry. I couldn't believe she was marrying a man who didn't know the first thing about her. Anyone who had seen her more than a couple times would know she almost always wore pearls. Anyone would know she almost never parted with her pearls and that any other necklace wouldn't do for her wedding day. How could she marry a man who didn't know the first thing about her? I took a calming breath. None of this was Tom's fault, and it wasn't fair of me to take my feelings out on him.

He looked heartbroken. "What am I going to do? I picked this out special for her. I thought she would love it! I can't show up empty-handed after not having seen her for a couple months."

He was right, and he was lucky. He was lucky that I cared so much about her happiness. Lucky I wasn't choosing to be selfish when my heart was screaming at me to be selfish. I ignored it as best I could. Nothing mattered except Daisy's happiness, and if I couldn't be the one to make her happy, I would make damn sure he was making her happy.

"It's a very thoughtful gift, just misguided. But I have just the thing. Wait here."

I left him and went to get my own present for her. I had been saving every cent of my golf winnings for this. It would kill me to part with it. The idea of him giving it to her and taking the credit for it... But the idea of her loving it and being happy was enough to make me grab the box.

In the box was a delicate strand of beautiful pearls. They had a pale pink tint to them that I knew she would love. They rivaled her own favorite pearls. I had dared to think they would be her new favorite. They were going to be my wedding present to her. I had pictured her face lighting up when I gave them to her. Her wrapping her arms around me. Her thanking me and telling me how much they meant to her, especially because they came from me. I felt all of that slipping away as I walked the box out to where Tom was waiting. I sighed. It would be worth it for her to be happy. I tried to tell myself it didn't matter *who* made her happy.

I had believed it in that moment, but when she was gushing over the pearls to me and talking about how well he knew her and how much they meant to her, I wanted to die. I knew the truth. He didn't know her, not really. How could he? They had only spent a handful of days together. She and I were inseparable. I knew everything about her. If anyone knew how to make her happy, it was me. I already spent every waking hour thinking about her and making sure she was happy. What had Tom ever done for her?

I knew I wasn't being fair, but this hardly felt fair. I was in love with her. It was killing me to finally admit, but I loved Daisy. I was madly, desperately in love with my hopelessly straight best friend. I was asking for heartbreak. I couldn't be mad that the inevitable was happening. I couldn't be mad at Daisy for loving the pearls. I couldn't be mad at Tom for taking them and giving them to her. I couldn't even be mad at myself for giving him the pearls. It was the right thing to do, and I would have done it again. I would have done anything to assure her happiness. That wasn't why I was mad at myself. I was mad at myself for having let myself indulge in my fantasies for too long. She didn't feel the same. She didn't even know how I felt, and it was best for the both of us if it stayed that way.

As I walked on cue down the aisle to my place at the head of the church, I hoped no one could see through my pasted-on grin. I prayed it would be enough to get me through the rest of the day.

Only a few more hours of this torment before I could go home and let myself feel miserable. In a few short hours, I would be free to once again feel how I was feeling, but she would be gone. She would be his wife and she would share his bed.

Try as I might, I couldn't push the thoughts from my mind, but I'd be damned if I let anyone see how much I was hurting, especially Daisy. She couldn't know.

I took a deep breath and told myself I would be more in control.

Then the bridal march began, and everyone in the room turned to look at her. I took another deep breath and turned to see her myself.

She took my breath away. She always did. I heard Tom gasp beside me. It was a small consolation to know he appreciated her.

As I watched her start her glide down the aisle, the moment she looked up and into the crowd, she locked eyes with me. I smiled through the pain. She had looked for *me*. She was marrying Tom today and she still looked at *me* before looking at him.

Her smile took the breath from my lungs.

My tears started to fall. I couldn't help myself. I smiled through my pain and through the tears. She smiled at me, with tears in her eyes. I had never felt further from her than I did in that moment with her crying tears of joy and me trying to stop the ones gushing from my broken heart.

When her eyes moved to him, all I could think was he was the luckiest man in the world and had better be the best damn husband the world had ever known. My beautiful, sweet, loving Daisy deserved the world and there would be hell to pay if he didn't give it to her.

Chapter Thirty - Two

Daisy

I *was* the luckiest girl in the world... for a while. The wedding went perfectly. Louisville had never seen a more extravagant event. I felt like royalty. My dress was stunning, and the ballroom was gorgeous. It was the wedding I had always imagined, even better because it was Tom waiting for me at the end of the aisle. I felt incredibly lucky to be marrying him. It was truly a dream come true.

After the wedding, he whisked me away on a three-month long trip to the South Seas. I had never even left the country before. Everything was new and exciting to me. We spent the first few weeks in marital bliss.

My only complaint about the otherwise perfect getaway was how much I missed Jordan. I had been used to seeing her every day for the past few months and was missing her dearly now. But I knew she was happy for me and that she would come visit the moment we were back in the country, so I pushed aside my feelings and focused my time and energy on enjoying my time with Tom.

We explored the islands together, spending every moment together. It was truly the adventure of a lifetime. He was the perfect loving husband, doting on me and giving me all the attention I could want. He was truly the most chivalrous man I had ever met. He spared me any unhappiness or inconvenience within his power. He even carried me back to our hotel when the ground was still wet from the rain. I was quite fond of the shoes I was wearing and knew the mud would ruin them. I had sighed and told him so, resigned to their fate and resolving to buy a new pair when we returned to the States.

He grinned at me and said, "Nonsense," before scooping me up into his arms.

I giggled and put my arms around his neck and kissed him. He truly treated me like royalty. He carried me the entire mile back to our hotel without a single complaint and without the smile disappearing from his lips. I had never loved him more than in that moment.

My feelings for him had grown stronger by the day and I knew them now for what they were. He had spoken of love before, but I had held back. I hadn't known if love was quite what I was feeling. It was different than what I had felt for Jay. With Jay, there was intensity and passion. With Tom, there was a gentler respect and adoration. I hadn't known if it was love, but had hoped it could grow to be. In that moment, I knew it had.

I whispered into his ear, "I love you, Tom." I knew I was blushing.

His smile widened. "I love you, too, my dear. I always have. Since the moment I laid eyes on you, I knew I would have to make you mine. You were, and still are, the most beautiful woman I have ever seen and only the best would do."

I giggled at that. I had been giggling a lot lately, but that was to be expected. It was a most welcome symptom of my affliction.

This was the most time we had ever spent together, and I was determined to get to know my husband better. We talked about our childhoods and our hopes for the future. We talked about our relationships with our families. I tried as best I could to explain the dynamic with my mother. When I finished, he said he would make sure to arrange it so we didn't visit often. He truly was perfect.

He talked of his parents and their high expectations for him. We both felt a lot of pressure to adhere to the expectations of our parents. We talked about how we both tried as hard as we could to please others, but felt like we always fell short of everyone's expectations.

I felt like I could talk to him about anything. Nothing was off limits.

I was happier than I had been in a long time. It was starting to sink in that not only was I a happily married woman, but now I had gained independence from my parents. For the first time, I had some control over my life. I would be able to do as I pleased without having to consult anyone. I mean, of course I cared what Tom thought, but I was truly lucky that Tom wasn't the type to try to restrict me. He and I would take the world by storm.

Well, him and I and Jordan, of course. He knew well enough now that when we married, he was also agreeing to spend a lot of time around Jordan.

He knew I missed her terribly and asked me a lot about her and our relationship. I was more than happy to talk about her, but I was ecstatic that he showed genuine interest in learning more about me and about her. I talked about how much we had been through together and how much she meant to me.

Eventually, the conversation turned to James, and I didn't stop myself from asking, "Are you and James still well acquainted?"

He laughed. "For better or worse, yes, I still make his acquaintance now and again. Why?"

I was a little disappointed to hear that. I hadn't thought well of him while he and Jordan were together, and the ending of their relationship did nothing to improve my opinion of him. "Just curious. Him and I have never been the best of friends. Now I'm sure his dislike for me has increased. If I know him at all, I would guess he blames me for Jordan ending their relationship, so I can't imagine his opinion of me has improved."

He chuckled. "He really doesn't like you, does he?" I shook my head. "You really should have heard the stories he told about you. Really, the craziest things. It was a big reason I knew I wanted to meet you." He laughed. "I was dying to see what it was about this crazy Daisy that had my friend so wound up." I laughed a little, but he must have noticed the laughter didn't touch my eyes, because he rushed to reassure me. "You really have nothing to worry about. I know enough of James to know he can be overly opinionated and not to trust what he says. You really should have heard some of the things he said about you. He would go on and on about Jordan's friend Daisy, who simply wouldn't leave him alone. He told me he thought you must have fancied him with how much you insisted on being around them."

How dare he!

"I did not!"

Tom laughed. "I know, I know. He really has the worst habit of exaggerating things. He used to say that this Daisy, the Daisy of his own invention, mind you, because she really bears only a slight resemblance to you, was known as the floozy of Louisville."

I blushed at that. It had been quite a while since anyone had brought up those old rumors. I had thought it would be less embarrassing with the passing of time, but hearing my husband talk of it brought back some of the old shame I had felt.

Tom saw my embarrassment and said, "Don't worry, love, I never believed him for a minute. He tends to let his imagination run away with him. He even used to say you would be out with a different man every day of the week."

My embarrassment multiplied. I had thought Tom would understand about my past. After all, he knew I hadn't been a virgin before I met him. I thought he would have assumed I had dated plenty of men before him, but it seemed he didn't. I blanched at the thought that I was going to have to correct him and tell him more about my past than I cared to.

He laughed. "My sweet innocent flower, I promise you I don't believe any of that nonsense. James just likes to hear himself talk. You should know that, having spent as much time with him as you did. He even told me he made a sport of chasing away the men you seemed interested in and encouraging the ones that didn't interest you."

I was angry for a moment. I knew he had been discouraging some of the men I was interested in, but I hadn't imagined he would brag about it. I also hadn't known he was the reason some of the men I had no wish to talk to again had kept calling long past the time they should have given up. It was just like James to stoop so low.

What had I ever done to him? All I did was try to be kind to him and try to make him like me, but he was set against me from the first moment he met me. Just what was so threatening about Jordan having a friend?

After a moment, I remembered myself and tried to calm down. That was the past and didn't matter. What mattered now was that I was going to have to tell Tom more about my past. I hadn't thought to worry. I had told him what I thought to be the worst of my past and he had told me it was okay, that nothing I said would change his perception of me. I hadn't felt any cause to worry, until now. I struggled with where to start, with what to say, but he spoke before I had the chance.

"Don't worry, my dear. I know you. You don't have to worry about me thinking ill of you because of some crazy things your best friend's ex-boyfriend told me. Speaking of which, he never did tell me what happened between them. He just kept insisting that it was your fault. I know that isn't true, but I'm really curious about what actually happened."

The night was seared into my mind, but it wasn't something I liked to talk about. I shrugged my shoulders. "Honestly, it sort of was my fault." He looked confused. "Well, I mean not directly, but eventually, the rift between me and James was too much for her. He kept pushing her to choose, which was a rather ill-thought-out plan. I never would've dreamed of asking her to do anything of the sort. Her happiness mattered too much to me to ever think of pushing her like that. I thought him and I had come to the same conclusion, but apparently not. He finally said a few things to Jordan that don't bear repeating about me and that was the last straw for her."

He looked concerned and upset. "What was it he said?"

I shook my head. "It really doesn't matter. It was quite a while ago, anyhow. I can hardly recall."

He didn't look convinced. "Try to recall."

Surprised at his shortness, I answered without thinking, "He told her I would be lucky to have Marcos and that he was hoping Marcos would be the one to put me in my place."

He looked livid. "I can't believe he said that about you! Especially about that lowlife who raped you. I can't believe he would say that!" I was so focused on my surprise at his remark about Marcos that I almost missed his quieter, much calmer, but much more threatening remark. "He better hope to never see me again." I felt a shiver pass through my body at his tone. It took a few moments before I regained my ability to speak again.

"Tom, it's really okay. I'm quite over his remarks. It wasn't a surprise to me that he didn't like me. It was a little upsetting to hear, but it was so long ago. I've moved past it. Although I wouldn't object to not having to see him again. And about Marcos-"

Some of his anger was replaced with concern. "You don't have to talk about him. I didn't mean to bring up such a painful memory."

I was touched by his concern, but I wanted to set the record straight. "I really appreciate the concern. It was a rather unpleasant way to end an otherwise wonderful night, but he didn't violate me in that way. I was petrified he might, but you came along and saved me before he could do me any harm. You can't imagine how grateful I was to see you-"

"Wait..."

I paused and looked at him. He looked confused. "I thought you said I wasn't your first."

Realization struck, sucking the breath from my lungs. He thought Marcos took my virginity. Our conversation came back to me in flashes. No wonder he had said he was sorry and that it didn't change anything. He thought I had been taken by force. The color drained from my face.

My voice came out barely louder than a whisper. "I did."

He looked confused for another moment before his face changed. I watched for a moment as his face flashed through several emotions too quickly for me to process before smoothing over into an emotionless mask.

When he did speak, it was in a low, slow voice, drawing out each word. "But it wasn't Marcos?"

I shook my head.

"Say it," he demanded quietly.

"It wasn't Marcos."

"Were you ever going to tell me, or were you hoping to keep me thinking you were sweet and innocent? Were you going to keep me in the dark and make me look like a fool?"

I was stunned. I felt tears well up in my eyes, but tried to hold them back. I couldn't believe this was happening. This was my sweet, caring, loving Tom. My husband who had been there for me in ways no other man had and showed he cared for me time and time again. This couldn't be happening.

"Tom, I'm so sorry-"

"No! Tell me the truth for once! Were you ever going to tell me?"

"Tom, you don't get it. I tried-"

"You tried? Tried what? Tried to keep me looking stupid?"

Now I was starting to get angry. "Tom, listen to me for a moment-"

"Listen to more of your lies?"

I was so hurt and angry. This wasn't the man I married. This wasn't my sweet, caring Tom. "Tom, listen to me! I didn't lie to you once. I told you I wasn't a virgin! You went into this knowing that. I don't understand why you're being so boorish about it now."

"You know damn well why! You let me think Marcos raped you! God, I'm so stupid. Did you even need rescuing that night, or were you upset to be interrupted?"

"How dare you! You saw how upset and shaken up I was! You were the one who rescued me, for God's sake! How could you say that? I told you how much I didn't like Marcos and didn't want to be near him! Are you really doubting that?"

"I'm doubting a lot of things. Maybe I should have listened to James. Maybe he was just trying to warn me away from you. I bet he was telling the truth. Just how many men have you dated, anyway?" I had no answer to that. He didn't take my silence well. "I should have known. How could I have been so stupid? I heard those rumors about you having slept with half the town, but still I fell for the innocent act."

"It's not an act. I never put on any act with you."

"Well, you sure as hell aren't innocent. And now I'm the one paying for it. I'm the one who walked Louisville's biggest floozy down the aisle."

I felt my heart breaking into a million pieces. This couldn't be happening. I tried to speak but couldn't find my voice. When I eventually was able to say something, it came out almost inaudible. "Please don't say that."

"You don't get to tell me what to do or how to react. You made me look like a fool and now I'm stuck with you as a wife."

He stormed out of our hotel room.

I burst into gut wrenching sobs the moment the door closed. I couldn't believe this. I thought I did everything right. I had told Tom the truth. I loved him. He helped put my heart back together after Jay shattered it. I never thought Tom, of all people, would make me feel that way again.

I cried for what felt like hours and woke up the next morning still alone.

After an hour or so of lying in bed, feeling sorry for myself, I resolved to go look for him. We had a major fight the night before, but he was my husband and I needed to make things right. I hoped he would feel the same.

I had my hand on the door when it turned. It was Tom.

When he entered, I was shocked to find he stank of alcohol. He had never been a big drinker, either. It was one of the things we had in common, but after the night we had, it didn't surprise me he drank more than usual. I was just relieved to see him; I was worried I wouldn't be able to find him or that he wouldn't want to see me.

I smiled at him. I didn't ask where he spent the night. I was just happy to see he was back.

He offered a small smile and said, "Well, that sure was a night. I hope we never have another fight like that again." I nodded, feeling hopeful for the first time since our fight. "After all, we're married and we're going to have to work through this. I'll have to find a way to forgive you and to accept the reality that you're not the girl I thought I married." I frowned a little at that, but thought better than to interrupt. "But I'm sure I can move past it. I mean, even if I had known, there's still a good chance I would have married you just for your body alone."

I was torn about how to feel. I was happy he was willing to try to put things behind us and move on, but I was less than thrilled with how he was talking to me. "I'm really happy to hear you say we can start fresh. I really care about you, and I want to make this marriage work."

"It will work. McCormicks don't divorce."

Well, that wasn't the ideal response, but at least he wanted to make it work, too.

We tried, or at least I tried, to put things back to normal for the rest of our trip. I spent all my time with him and tried to be as positive and loving as possible. Whenever I felt scared or angry or lonely, I pushed my feelings away and told myself I was lucky he still wanted to be with me.

He started drinking much more heavily. He would be happy for a while when he was drinking. I hadn't indulged since my ill-fated encounter the day before the wedding, but I was supportive of anything that made him happier. It was a tough balance, and I learned slower than I would have liked how much was too much for him. One drink wasn't enough to change his mood. Two or three drinks, and he was elated and loving.

It was easy to pretend things were back to normal again. He was kind to me again. I lived for those moments.

But then … four or five drinks in and he got mean. I would try to stop him at three drinks before he drank more, but often that would only bring about his temper quicker.

I tried to keep him happy, but that wasn't an easy task. I hadn't noticed before, but Tom had a jealous streak. Anytime I even glanced at another man, he would tense up and get angry. I don't mean I was lusting after other men. I mean when I would look at men nearby or when I would thank a male staff member at the hotel, he would become scarily jealous. I made the mistake of smiling in the direction of another man and he yanked my arm so hard I thought it might break.

He pulled me in that manner to him and said in a hushed tone, "Do you mean to sleep with him, too?"

I hadn't even noticed the man before he said that.

His behavior scared me. I was afraid to so much as look away from him in public. I didn't want to risk upsetting him. I wasn't normally this meek creature that cowered when confronted with the anger of a man, but this wasn't any man. This was Tom. I cared for him and desperately wanted to fix things between us. I wanted the man that I had married back. I still hoped it was possible.

I convinced myself if I simply didn't look at other men and did whatever he asked, that things between us would get better. I needed them to. I couldn't be married to the man he was becoming. I needed my gentle, loving Tom back.

For weeks, I tiptoed around him, trying not to make him angry or jealous. I made sure to give him every morsel of my attention, both in public and in private. I told him endlessly how much I cared about him and how he was the only man for me.

When he continued to berate me and degrade me, I held both my tongue and my tears. I prayed it would be enough to bring back the man I married. I held on to hope, clinging to it like a life raft in the storm that was now my marriage.

Chapter Thirty - Three

Our honeymoon was coming to an end, but we had long since left the honeymoon stage of our marriage. We ended our tour of the South Sea and landed in Santa Barbara. I thought we were headed to Chicago, but Tom had arranged to stay in Santa Barbara as a surprise. He knew I had never been to the West coast and thought I might have an interest in exploring.

I was incredibly touched and hoped beyond hope that the gesture meant he was making progress with forgiving me. That hope was crushed when he went out of his way to inform me that the detour had been arranged before we had even left.

I felt even more sharply what I had lost when Jordan arrived at his direction. He had arranged for her to meet us in Santa Barbara the moment we arrived. He had told her he knew how much I would miss her and that it would bring both him and me pleasure to be able to enjoy her company upon our return to the country.

I resolved to try even harder to please him. I knew how much he had cared about me. It was evident in the care he took planning the surprise detour for me. He had cared for me well above and beyond any other man in my life ever had. I had to get that back. He couldn't have just stopped caring that quickly.

I could still fix this.

I had to.

I did my best to hide my worries from Jordan, but she was always so observant that I wasn't sure I would succeed. It was hard to enjoy the time with her like I normally would have. I was so worried about trying not to upset Tom and about trying not to let her see how bad things had gotten.

Any time he left us alone together, I would be worried about where he was going or what he was doing, I could hardly focus on anything else. I was scared that he was upset again, or that I had done something wrong. I just wanted him to be happy. *I* wanted to be happy. I wanted what we had back.

There was no way Jordan didn't notice the tension. Anytime he left the room, I was uneasy while waiting for him to come back. Whenever we were out in public, I doted on him, giving him all my attention. It was exhausting, but I told myself it would be worth it if I could change things back to how they were before. I tried everything I could, but I still worried it wouldn't be enough. If anything, his jealousy and anger seemed to be getting worse.

When Jordan left a week later, I was incredibly sad to see her go, but felt some relief that I wouldn't have to keep working so hard to hide my feelings from her. I knew she probably noticed something was off, but hoped she hadn't guessed the extent of things. I didn't want her to worry about me. I felt ashamed and didn't want anyone to know about what happened. I had never felt worse about myself in my entire life. The one man who was supposed to always be there for me, the man I married, didn't trust me and didn't seem to want anything to do with me.

When Jordan left, he would leave me alone for long periods. He would take off, saying he needed space and needed time to think. I felt devastated. I cried myself to sleep a few nights in a row. I worried and wondered where he was and why he didn't come back at night. Every night, I wondered if that would be the last time I saw him. If that was the night he would decide to call it quits and leave me.

It wasn't until I happened to see a newspaper later that week that I found out where he'd been sleeping, or not sleeping.

He was in the papers with one of the hotel maids. They were in a car accident together. I hadn't even known he had been in a car accident. He hadn't bothered to tell me. It was a little ironic that he had been so paranoid about me with any other man, but especially the hotel staff. I had thought that was because the hotel staff were the only men I couldn't avoid talking to in his presence, but now it seemed it might have been his guilty conscience. Although I wondered if he felt any guilt at all.

I had been trying so hard to put the pieces of our marriage back together and bring back what we had. I had been trying so hard and all that time he had already checked out. He didn't want to be with me. My own husband didn't want me.

What was left of my heart shattered. I didn't know what to do now. We were married. He agreed to marry me, and I thought he had known what he was getting into. I had been honest and open with him about who I was and thought he accepted me for me. I had given him everything.

It was obvious now that what I was giving him wasn't enough. I had been giving him all my time, energy, and love exclusively and it still wasn't enough.

I would never be enough for him.

Chapter Thirty - Four

I had never felt worse in my life. I wasn't enough for my own husband. He continued to say I was going to cheat. He continued to tell me I was still trying to act innocent. He continued to berate me for trying to deceive him.

In one of my darker moments alone at night, with Tom who knows where, I had finally had enough. My feelings were too much to handle. The thoughts wouldn't go away. Thoughts that I wasn't in control of anything in my life. Thoughts that I would never be enough for anyone. Thoughts that I didn't deserve to be happy. I couldn't take it anymore. I went to the bathroom and grabbed a sharp pair of scissors.

All my life, everyone had told me how beautiful I was, how lucky I was. I didn't feel beautiful, and I felt far from lucky. I was sick of acting like everything was fine. Sick of pretending to be perfect. Sick of everyone not being able to see past my looks.

Before I could think more about it, I gathered my hair in one hand and the scissors in the other. I brought the scissors to my hair and … *SNIP.*

With the swift motion, I felt some relief, like a weight had been lifted. I watched as my beautiful locks fell to the ground.

SNIP. More hair fell to the ground.

SNIP. SNIP. SNIP.

When I finally stopped and looked at myself in the mirror, what was left of my beautiful hair fell just above my shoulder. The curls were still there, but I defied anyone to call me innocent anymore. Now maybe Tom's anger would be stilled. Let men look at me now. I was not the innocent beauty I used to be. I was not the girl I used to be, and I was done pretending.

When Tom finally returned, reeking of alcohol after having been gone for a couple days straight, he was too far gone to even notice the change. When he woke up hungover the next morning and saw me, he laughed.

"Thank you. I needed that."

"Needed what?"

"A good laugh. What've you done to yourself? At least I won't have to worry about you with other men now."

"There aren't other men. It's always only been you. You're the only man in my life."

He looked me up and down before saying, "Well, you certainly didn't do this for me."

"I did it for me."

He looked annoyed. "Of course you did. You've always been selfish. I shouldn't be surprised you didn't bother asking my opinion. I hope you don't expect me to find you attractive. How anyone could now is beyond me."

He left shortly after that, and the moment the door shut, the tears came. I was proud of myself for having held them as long as I did. I couldn't believe this was my life now. I couldn't keep going on like this.

Now more than ever I needed Jordan. I needed my best friend. I knew I should've been more honest with her when she was here. I just thought that things could still get better. I thought maybe if I kept trying and showed him how much I cared, we could get back what we had.

I knew Jordan wouldn't have understood. She would have told me he wasn't worth it and would have wanted me to leave. I was powerless, and I knew it. I couldn't leave. I had no money of my own and if I left my husband, I would likely have no place I could run to.

I doubted my parents would take me in. It was likely my mother would drag me back to my husband herself.

I wondered if Tom would even let me go. I didn't have a mind for legal matters, but I knew as his wife, everything I had was his. Even my own body was essentially his property.

I felt trapped and hopeless. I felt I had nothing to lose anymore, so I wrote to Jordan and begged her to come back. I could only wait and hope my letter found her soon.

Chapter Thirty - Five

Jordan

My visit ended much too soon. I hadn't wanted to leave her. I had missed her terribly, but I felt this was something more than that. When I said goodbye to Daisy, I hadn't been able to shake the feeling that something wasn't right. I hadn't been able to understand or explain my reaction, but I couldn't shake it. I tried to tell myself I just didn't want to leave her. I tried to write off my feelings as lingering jealousy about her being married, but even that didn't account for the sinking feeling in my gut. I had learned over the years to trust my instincts, and I wasn't about to start doubting myself.

I postponed my return trip indefinitely and took up lodging at a hotel a few blocks away. I felt crazy, but I didn't know what else was to be done. I didn't even know what it was I was worried about or what I planned to do. I decided if nothing happened in the span of a week, I would go home.

I spent my days exploring the city, making sure to stay far away from where I knew Daisy to frequent. It pained me to not see her, but I didn't know how to explain my worries and didn't know what I would tell her if she saw me.

It turns out I wasn't the only one hiding from Daisy.

The day had started off like every other, with me wandering around the city. Contrary to my worries, nothing out of the ordinary had happened and I was feeling ridiculous. I resolved I would leave the next day. I must have been wrong.

I was thinking about how tedious the trip home would be when I looked up and saw Tom. He was sitting in a cafe at a table for two, alone. I quickly ducked around a corner, not wanting to be seen. I figured Daisy had to be nearby. Although I couldn't imagine what they would be doing here.

Daisy had never talked about straying this far into the city. Normally, she liked to spend her time closer to the ocean. It was unusual she would want to come out this far, but stranger things had happened. I went to take my leave, but something stopped me. Another gut feeling told me to stay a little longer.

This whole week I was pretty sure I was going crazy, wandering around the city in secret. Now as I hunched behind the corner watching Tom sitting in a cafe, I knew for certain I'd gone crazy. But I still couldn't bring myself to turn away. I resolved to leave after another minute. I was lucky I hadn't been noticed yet, but with my luck, Daisy would come up behind me and I would be forced to come up with some sort of explanation. I was pushing my luck and I knew it. I stood up, turning to leave, when I heard his voice.

"There you are! If you kept me waiting any longer, you would have been dining alone."

I whipped around. That didn't sound like the Tom I knew. He wouldn't speak to Daisy like that. He would never had said a word about having to wait for her, which was for the better since she was more often than not late. But what I saw when I turned was even more startling than having heard him talk to her like that. There was a brunette walking toward him, but it wasn't Daisy.

My eyes widened. I couldn't believe it. But maybe there was an explanation. Maybe she was a friend, maybe Daisy would be joining them later. Maybe this wasn't what it looked like. I watched as she continued toward him. He held out his arms to her. I held my breath.

He was a good guy; he wouldn't do this to Daisy. I inhaled sharply and watched as he leaned closer and closer. I couldn't look away. I couldn't believe it, but the sight was undeniable. As I watched, his lips met hers. My heart broke for her. I was seeing red and knew I had to get out of there. Inflicting the pain on him that I wanted to wouldn't solve anything. My heart was screaming out for Daisy. I couldn't believe that no good cad would two time her like that! I couldn't believe it! Tom had been a good man. What the hell happened?

Not knowing where else to go or what else to do, I found myself heading back to my hotel. I knew I was thinking rashly and that I needed to calm down before doing anything.

The whole walk there I replayed the scene in my mind and became more and more angry for her, more and more worried about her. By the time I reached the hotel, I was no more calm than I had been when I had started back.

I was astonished to find a letter from Daisy waiting for me. After what I had just seen, I shouldn't have been surprised. I was beyond grateful that I had the forethought to have the postmaster send any outgoing mail to me here. My hands were trembling as I ripped open the envelope. There were only two thoughts racing through my mind: was she okay and how much did she know? I couldn't open the letter fast enough.

I skimmed through the letter. It was brief and there was so much I could tell she still held back. She said things were bad and that she could use a friend. She needed me if there was any way for me to return. The moment I saw her asking me to return, I dropped the letter. I grabbed my coat and bolted out the door. I hurried over to her hotel, not quite knowing what to expect when I got there but knowing it wouldn't be good.

I swung the door open, not bothering to knock. She tensed, but when she saw it was me, all the tension eased from her body. I held my arms up just in time for her to fall into them.

Daisy

I was shocked when not even an hour after I sent the letter, Jordan came bursting through the door. I couldn't believe it! I didn't know what to say. I didn't even know how it was possible, never mind how I could possibly express my gratitude for her being here. She opened her arms to me, and I launched myself into them. At last, I felt I was home.

After a few minutes of her comforting me, I started to get nervous that Tom would show up. I wasn't sure how to explain Jordan's renewed presence without him knowing I had written for her to come. I worried he would be angry. I doubted very much he wanted anyone to know how he had been acting and how he had been treating me. She sensed my unease and asked if I would be missed if we went to her hotel. I quickly assured her I wouldn't be missed.

I prayed that was true. If he did return while I was gone and didn't find me patiently waiting for him like the repentant good wife he expected me to be, I worried about what might happen.

Based on how he had been thinking and acting lately, my absence alone might have been enough to confirm to him that I was cheating on him. After all, simply looking at another man was enough to arouse his suspicion. I couldn't imagine the anger he would have if I weren't waiting for him to return. The thought both scared me and fueled some anger of my own.

To think, I was afraid that my cheating husband would think me a cheater. I was worried he would treat me worse than he had been, but that couldn't be possible. Things couldn't be worse than they had been. It simply wasn't possible.

Jordan and I had been walking in silence while I thought things through. She gave me the time to think that she somehow knew I needed. I knew she had to be incredibly worried. I tried not to look at her face. I knew the worry I would see there and knew her kindness and concern would bring me to tears. I knew the tears were inevitable, but I hoped to make it to her room before breaking.

We made it through the hotel and to her room in a matter of minutes. I crossed the room and shut the curtains. I had never been this paranoid before. Then again, I had never had a reason. I didn't want anyone that might recognize me to see me in a strange hotel. Tom might already think I was cheating, but hearing I was at another hotel would be as good as confirming it in his mind.

I took a seat on the edge of the bed and waited for Jordan. She had shut the door and was fastening the locks. She must have understood from my closing the curtains that discretion and security were of the utmost importance.

She crossed the room and, as I knew I would when I met her eye, I couldn't hold back the tears anymore. She let me cry my eyes out, holding me and comforting me the entire time. After my tears had stopped and my breathing was more rhythmic, she asked, "Sweetie, I've been so patient, but I must insist. You're scaring me. You have to tell me what's the matter."

"I'm so sorry. I didn't want you to worry. I almost didn't send word because I couldn't bear the thought of worrying you, but as you can see, I ended up being selfish."

"You are quite possibly the least selfish person I know. I hope you know you can ask me for anything at any time. Nothing is too big of a request from you. I would have come running in a heartbeat even if I had been back in Louisville."

"I don't know what I did to get so lucky with you. Why are you still here, anyway? I'm grateful, but also curious."

"I can't really explain it, but something seemed off. I really hoped I was wrong, but-" She looked me up and down again. "It seems like I wasn't. There was something about the way you were with him. I've seen you in relationships before and seen how you are with the people you care about, and something didn't feel right. If I had to put words to it, you were doting on him too much." I looked at her, confused. She laughed. "I know it sounds crazy, but I felt like you were being too careful with him and paying him too much attention."

She was right. I had been walking on eggshells with him and tiptoeing around him, hoping to not make him angry, hoping to get back what I had lost. I couldn't believe she had gleaned so much from my behavior. Anyone else would have thought I was madly in love. She knew me well enough to know there was nothing secure or healthy about the way I was acting.

"I tried all week to shake the feeling, but I couldn't. The idea of parting ways under those conditions was too much to bear. I hoped I was wrong, but I decided to stick around longer just in case. I needed to make sure you were okay. I couldn't leave you without knowing you would be okay."

I was overwhelmed with gratitude and love for her. She was the only person in my entire life who had ever treated me with as much care and kindness as she did.

She sat with me and listened while I explained what happened with Tom. I told her about our talk before the wedding and his assumptions. I told her about the good times we had on the honeymoon, and finally, I told her about the fight we had.

I watched her go through all the same emotions I had. I saw the disbelief and shock, and then watched her eyes darken with anger. It was just like Jordan to be angry, to find a way to blame anyone besides me. Of course, she would be angry with him and ignore my own wrongdoings.

I tried to explain things to her. "I know how much you care about me, but you have to see that I'm the one in the wrong here."

Her eyes widened with shock and disbelief.

I hurried to continue, "I thought I was being honest with him. I thought he understood and was choosing to accept me as I was. It was foolish of me to hope that was the case. I should have been more honest with him." I felt my eyes start to well up again. "No wonder he doesn't trust me." The tears fell.

She stared at me a moment before cupping my face in her hands and looking into my eyes. "My dear sweet Daisy, you truly are crazy." I hadn't expected her to say that, and it caught me off guard. I was so surprised that my tears stopped. She brushed away a tear from my face. "You must be crazy to be able to make this at all your fault."

I didn't understand what she could mean by that. Of course it was my fault.

I was the one who didn't wait until marriage. I was the one who wasn't completely honest with him. I started to say something to that affect, but she stopped me. "You were honest with him. You didn't feel right about marrying him unless he knew the truth. You have such a pure heart and are truly the most beautiful, loving, kind, and caring person I know. His own assumptions are not your fault. You had no obligation to even tell him about your past." I could see she was starting to get angry again. She took a couple of deep breaths before continuing. "His anger and inability to deal with the fact that you had a life before him are his own shortcomings. He has no right to be upset or to complain. Do you really think he was celibate until he met you?"

That hadn't occurred to me. Tom was seven years my senior. It was doubtful that at twenty-six years of age, when we met, that he had never been with a woman. I wasn't naive enough to think he had been a virgin, and I hadn't cared. Why was it that it was okay for him, but not for me?

I had never even thought to ask him about his past. I didn't care to know and didn't think it was my place to ask unless he wanted to tell me. Why was it that he couldn't grant me the same courtesy?

Furthermore, why did society tell me I was worthless once I was no longer a virgin when men were given the ability to lay with multiple women before settling down? Why was I held to a higher standard than my husband? If I had any doubts about his past, how quickly he ended up in bed with another woman gave me all the proof I needed. A man who had only been with one woman would not so quickly abandon his faithfulness to her. That man would not have been as reckless.

Jordan closely watched my change of emotions before continuing. "He had no right to your loyalty before you had even met him. You are your own person and had as much of a right as he did to have slept with whomever you wanted. While I understand he might be jealous of your past, he has no right to treat you the way he has been! He's driving you away with his jealousy. He's been treating you terribly when he should have been working hard to ensure he had your love and loyalty instead of terrorizing you.

"I can't believe he's acting like this over simply hearing that you had a past with another man. As if *he* knows anything about jealousy! *He* didn't have to watch you try to mend your broken heart in the arms of boy after boy who couldn't have possibly cared about you. They didn't even know you! How could they have given you what you wanted? *He* didn't have to suffer through watching you put yourself out there again and again to the wrong people."

I was taken aback by the rawness in her tone and words. I hadn't realized my actions might have had any effect on anyone besides myself. I hadn't realized how blinded by youth I was. I hadn't imagined anyone would be caused pain by my actions. I couldn't debate the truth of her words, but I was confused by the emotion in them. I wondered if I had caused her some sort of pain. As my best friend, it must not have been easy to see me try unsuccessfully again and again to find love and affection in the arms of boy after boy.

I went to say something, but she was too caught in her own thoughts to notice and continued, "*He* wasn't overlooked day after day while you ran from boy to boy, chasing love they couldn't give. *He* didn't have to suffer any of that, and he still has the audacity to talk of jealousy and to treat you this terribly after your only crime was being honest with him. You were honest with him and only slept with one man. You were far from reckless. Who knows how many women he's slept with! I can't believe he thinks this sort of behavior is in any way even remotely acceptable! No wonder he and James are friends! I never understood it. James was so temperamental, jealous, and hotheaded."

I tried to hold back my, "I told you so" look, but she must have noticed because she laughed. "I know, I know. I should have seen that sooner than I did, but I was young, blind, and just plain stupid. I saw how popular you were with boys, and I started to get jealous. Most of the boys that approached me did so to get to you or because they thought they couldn't get you. I wanted a taste of what it was like to be the girl everyone wanted. I don't know if you remember, but you were there the first time I met him. He came up to me and I was expecting him to ask about you, but he asked about me. He told me I was the most gorgeous woman in the room, if not the world, and he would have been stupid to leave without trying to talk to me. I fell for it and I fell for him, *hard*. I wanted someone to look past you and see me. For some reason, even with you there with me, he saw me."

I was shocked. I had no idea she had felt that way. If I was being honest with myself, I knew there must have been a chance she did, but she never seemed to want the attention. She never seemed excited when she was approached by boys. I had no idea it was because she always felt like a second choice. It was crazy of her. I couldn't believe anyone had overlooked her for me. Maybe it was because of her age? She had still been young at the time, although she hadn't looked it. I looked at her now and had to stifle a laugh at the thought that she had ever felt jealous of me.

She had grown even taller and had grown into her incredibly long legs. She no longer looked tall and lanky like she had in her youth, but a tall, statuesque goddess. She had the body of an athlete from her rigorous training. Her sharp grey eyes contrasted beautifully with her short, blonde hair. She had always worn it short. She said it was a matter of convenience, that she wanted it out of her way for golf. I suspected it had more to do with her aversion to her hair. She had always resented being blonde, resented the assumptions made by others about blonde women. She was incredibly intelligent and wanted to be viewed as such.

For most women, it was enough to have the admiration of men, but Jordan was different. She wanted their respect. She wanted and would settle for nothing less than being viewed as an equal. I envied her ability to pull begrudging respect from men. I had always caught their eyes, but she demanded their respect.

Her short hair gave her a more serious air, but did nothing to detract from her beauty. I had been holding my tongue, not wanting to interrupt her, but I couldn't stay silent any longer. "I don't know how it's possible you don't see what I see when you view yourself."

She tilted her head to the side and looked at me with interest. "What do you see?"

She was staring at me so intently I could hardly think. I shrugged, at a loss for words. I gestured wildly at her with my hands. "I see what everyone but you sees!"

"Which is?"

I didn't know how to better explain, so I dragged her over to the mirror. I held her in place in front of me and met her eyes in the mirror. I looked the vision in the mirror up and down before meeting her eye again. I didn't even know where to begin to describe how I, and everyone else, saw her, but I reminded myself this was for Jordan. I would do anything for her, and this was a simple enough task, or it should have been.

"I see an amazing friend who has an incredibly big heart. A caring, kind, loving-" She rolled her eyes, so I stopped. "If you're not going to listen, I don't have to go on."

At that, she laughed and tried to look contrite, but her eyes were sparkling too much with amusement for her purpose. "It's just that, of course *you* would describe my personality. You're my closest friend. You've grown to love me, but that couldn't have possibly been what you meant that everyone would see."

I blushed a little under her intense gaze, but couldn't look away. "Okay, okay. You're right. Well, anyone with eyes couldn't help but notice your height and your long legs."

She laughed. "Just what every girl aspires to be, tall."

"Okay, fine. You're right. Tall isn't the right word. You look like a statuesque goddess who lesser men cower from and greater men beg to worship. You could have the world in the palm of your hand if you didn't push people away. If you would only open up and let someone in. Any man would be lucky to have you!"

She looked more serious now and looked at me appraisingly before saying, "Well, that's a problem."

"How is any of that possibly a problem?! How is having any man you want at all a problem?"

She paused a moment before saying, "What if I don't want a man?"

I rolled my eyes at that. She and I had had this discussion enough before that I knew what she was going to say and didn't give her the chance. "I know, I know. You want your independence and think a man would get in the way, but it doesn't have to be like that."

She caught me off guard when she whirled around to face me. She looked more frustrated than I had ever seen her. Her eyes burned, with what I didn't know. "You don't get it! It's not about men! It's never been about men!" I didn't know what I had done to get this reaction, but she seemed angry. She stared at me intently. I tried to look away from the intensity. She seemed to realize that she was alarming me. She reached out and put her hands gently on either side of my face, keeping my gaze on her. I saw the fire in her eyes dim and when she spoke, it was softly and slowly. She seemed to be willing me to understand. "What if it's not a man I want?"

She paused. I continued to stare at her, waiting for her to continue or to explain. After a few moments, the truth came crashing down over me. It wasn't about men. She didn't want to be alone. I had thought she would never find the right man. I had worried she would never find love. All this time, it hadn't been that she was waiting for the right man. There was no right man. I had no idea she had felt that way, but now that she had said it, everything started to make sense.

She continued to look at me. I could see some worry on her face. I searched for the right thing to say, knowing it didn't matter what I said as long as I didn't make her sad. I smiled at her.

"Well, what I was saying still applies. Man, woman, or whoever, it doesn't matter. Anyone would be lucky to have you."

She still looked hesitant. "You really mean it?"

"Absolutely!" She smiled more brightly and wrapped me in a hug. She held me for a few moments before I went to pull away. When I moved back, she took my hands in her own and looked intently at me. I needed her to understand this didn't change anything. As I looked into her eyes, I added, "Anyone would be crazy to not want you-"

I was abruptly cut off by her lips crashing on mine. I didn't have time to register shock. My mind was clouded by the explosion of sparks I felt. Heat rushed through my body. I had never felt anything like this. Not with Jay, and certainly not with Tom.

I melted into her arms. All I could think about was how soft her lips were and how good they felt on mine. She tasted of something sweet I couldn't place. I was too stunned to kiss her back. She pulled away far too quickly for my liking.

She looked at me guiltily and rushed to say, "I'm so sorry! I don't know what came over me. The last thing I want to do is ruin our friendship. I promise I'll never do that again."

Never again? The words echoed in my mind. She waited impatiently for me to speak. How did I feel about it? I had never given thought to women before. I knew I liked men. Was it possible to like both? Did it even matter? I would do anything for Jordan and loved her more fiercely than I thought possible, but was I attracted to her? Was it possible?

I looked at her again. I saw the tall, statuesque blonde in front of me and thought about how her lips made me feel. Then I thought about her words, that she would never do that again. I thought about what that would mean. Never feeling her lips on mine again. Would she find another woman? Could I bear to watch her kiss another?

Before I could lose my courage or change my mind, I blurted out, "Never again?"

She nodded fiercely. "I promise."

"You should really be more careful not to make promises you can't keep."

She looked dumbfounded. "What do you mean? Of course I-"

I didn't let her finish. I closed the distance between us and kissed her hard. As my lips moved against hers, I felt her shock. It took her a moment to regain her senses, and then I felt her lips move against mine. For a moment, we battled for dominance, but as I felt her tongue press against my lips, I knew I had lost. I had never felt anything like this. This was Jordan, my best friend, the one person who knew everything about me. It turned out she knew better than anyone else how to bring me to my knees. I felt weak in her arms as I gave in to the sensations.

She gently guided us to the bed and laid me down. She was straddling me. She tried to break our kiss, but I pulled her mouth back to mine, not wanting the feeling to end. I felt the vibrations of her laughter against my mouth. After a few more moments, she pulled away. I was too breathless to stop her, but she didn't miss the disappointment on my face.

She pulled back, still straddling me, but out of reach of my hands that were yearning to pull her face back to mine. She raked her eyes over my body, every nerve in my body was on edge. Her eyes were full of joy and mischief.

"I was worried I was pushing you too far."

I tried to reach back up and pull her close. She chuckled at that and deftly took both my hands and stretched them above my head. In the blink of an eye, she had both my hands trapped under one of hers. I tried in vain to move them, but she was quite the athlete and was much stronger than me. I whimpered in frustration and pouted. She laughed more and looked at me with the same burning in her eyes that I now recognized for what it was: passion. Her free hand slowly trailed down my arm. My body was on fire. I needed her touch. I needed her lips on mine.

I strained again to reach her, but it was no use. She chuckled as I squirmed. Her fingers lightly traced up my arm until she reached my face. She lightly touched my lips with her finger. This woman was maddening. From my lips, she moved to my chin and made her way down to my neck. She slowed her fingers and stroked the base of my neck. She knew as well as I did how ticklish I was. I tried to pull back but couldn't move. I burst into a fit of giggles.

"Jord, stop! Please stop. You know how ticklish I am!"
She didn't stop.
"Jord! Stop, please! I'm begging you!"
Her fingers slowed.

"Please…"

"Begging sounds good coming from you. I've never heard anything quite so sweet."

She redoubled her efforts.

I was out of breath and desperate. "Please, please. I can't breathe." I interrupted myself with more giggles. "Please, I'll do anything!"

She smiled more seductively than I had ever seen her do and pulled her hand back up to my chin. "We'll see about that." She finally pressed her lips back to mine.

Chapter Thirty - Six

A few hours later, I was back in my hotel room, still trying to wrap my head around what had happened. Jordan and me. Looking back on my friendship with her, there had always been little moments that didn't quite make sense. Moments of tension between us I couldn't understand. Little things she said, things that now made sense, but that I couldn't understand at the time.

Things with me were more complicated. I had never considered I might not be straight. It wasn't a secret to anyone that I was attracted to men. Could I be attracted to women, too? What did this mean for me? Did it even matter? I knew I was attracted to Jordan. I knew I loved Jordan in every possible way. I hadn't known it to be romantic love, but now that I knew how this felt, I knew it must have been.

If this was how love felt, I knew without question I had never been in love. With Jay, it had been an infatuation of youth. With the numerous men after, they were merely flings. Even with Tom, I had liked him and been hopeful we could be happy together, but even at his best, I hadn't loved him the way I knew I loved Jordan. I had thought I had, but my feelings for him didn't come anywhere close to the extent of my feelings for

Jordan. Even at our best, I hadn't felt a fraction of what I felt for Jordan for him.

I had hoped I would grow to love him the more I got to know him, but I knew now I didn't love Tom.

Tom. His name in my mind brought my thoughts to a crashing halt. Tom, my husband. I had cheated on my husband. I hadn't been faithful to him. I couldn't believe I hadn't thought of that before, but once Jordan's lips touched mine, I would have been hard-pressed to think of his name never mind the fact that something that felt so right could be considered wrong.

I had always been flighty when it came to men, but I had never been unfaithful or dishonest. I couldn't believe I had cheated on the man I had married, but was Tom still the man I married? Had he still been as kind and caring as he had been when I married him, I highly doubt I would have entertained the idea of cheating on him. And he was hardly a stranger to infidelity. He had just been caught with a hotel maid. He was the first one to break our marriage vows.

I shook my head, trying to clear my thoughts. This was Jordan I was talking about. I wouldn't sully what happened between us by making my actions out to be revenge for his cheating. I had loved her long before I had known the truth myself. Even if Tom had still been the kind, caring man he was when I had married him, it wouldn't have changed my feelings for Jordan. I could have tried to bury them, but they still would have been there.

Had Tom still been the gentleman I married, I would have planned to sit down and talk to him about what happened and how I was feeling. I didn't delude myself into thinking that I would still handle things like that with the person Tom was now. He was already violently jealous. I would like to think he would never hurt me, but I had every reason to be fearful of how he would react. He had manhandled me in his jealousy before, when he didn't even have cause to be jealous. I couldn't imagine how he would react if he knew.

I couldn't let him find out. Not only for me, but for Jordan. I would do anything to protect her and would rather die than see her harmed.

She and I had arranged to meet again tomorrow to figure out what to do. I had hid from her just how worried I was. I didn't want to worry her. It hadn't seemed like Tom had been back to notice my absence, but I still worried. She and I would need to come up with a plan. I had worried for a few brief moments that she might not be thinking the same things I was, but this was Jordan I was talking about. I knew her feelings and thoughts better than my own. I knew her love for me to be as strong, if not stronger, than my love for her. I hadn't recognized it to be a passionate love before, but I knew it to be love nonetheless.

What remained to be figured out was what to do. I was in love with my best friend, but I didn't have the liberty to act on my feelings. I was married. My husband had become a cruel, bitter man, but I was still married to him. I didn't love him and would have gladly thrown my marriage vows away to be with Jordan, but that wasn't possible.

If Jordan had been a rich man, I would have run away with them in an instant, marriage vows be damned. Tom wasn't faithful to me. I didn't owe him my loyalty, but, more importantly, it was clear neither of us was happy in our union.

I might have even considered running away with female Jordan if I thought there was any way we could support ourselves in relative comfort, but I knew that wouldn't be the case. My only money came from my husband and my parents. I was almost certain that my parents would be so scandalized by my actions that they would let me starve before I saw any money from them. It would be scandalizing enough to leave my marriage to, as my mother would say, 'the only rich man who was dumb enough to have me', but to do so for a woman no less would be the ultimate scandal. I would be disowned.

I could live with being disowned, but I had no money of my own that we could live off of. Jordan was far from broke herself, but her money, too, was conditional. She was beheld to the whims of her elderly aunt. Time and time again she had complained of how her aunt kept threatening to withhold money if Jordan didn't settle down with a nice young man. I could imagine her aunt would have a heart attack on the spot if Jordan told her she was going to settle down with a nice young woman instead.

Jordan's golf career was blooming, but I knew she couldn't afford to support us both. I didn't know what we would do. How could I possibly go back to my life as it was? How could I continue to live the way I had been, knowing there was something better, someone better, out there waiting for me? There had to be something we could do.

To my relief, when Tom returned, again reeking of alcohol, he didn't notice anything was amiss. I tried to act how I had been acting before, but couldn't quite muster the same doting energy I had before. I still tiptoed around him and tried my best to stay out of his way, but I was sure he must have noticed I had changed. My world had changed so monumentally, I felt certain there must be some external sign of that change. How was it possible my very existence itself had been altered and yet my husband didn't notice? I was thankful he hadn't. I didn't have any safe explanation, but his lack of attention to any details regarding me further hardened my heart against him.

The rest of the evening was uneventful, and Tom left first thing in the morning. A mere day ago, the thought of his finding comfort in the arms of another woman and leaving me alone without so much as a word of excuse would have been enough to put me to tears. But not today. Today was different. Today felt more hopeful.

I wandered around town full of nervous energy. It was ridiculous to be this nervous about seeing my best friend. Jordan had been my rock for what felt like forever, the only one I could depend on. Why was I nervous to see her? It dawned on me that I was worried she would have changed her mind, that yesterday might have been a fluke, that she might not feel the same. I had all but planned out our life together over the past night. Maybe I was thinking prematurely.

By the time we had set to meet, I was positively shaking with nerves. I let myself into the hotel and found her room. I stood in the hallway for a couple of moments, trying to drum up the courage to knock. After a couple of false starts, I finally put my hand to the door to knock.

Before I could make a noise, the door swung open and I was pulled inside. I was startled and started to cry out, but saw it was Jordan. She was grinning and spun me around the room. We both started laughing. She spun me close and pulled me into a deep kiss. I had thought the feeling would take me less by surprise than it had the first time, but I was wrong. I knew I would never get used to that.

When she pulled away, I had to catch my breath. She laughed and pulled me into a hug. Her energy was contagious, and I felt all my nerves melt away. I stayed there for hours as we talked about the future. With anyone else, it would have seemed hasty and crazy, but this was Jordan. I had loved her long before I had ever realized I might be attracted to her. Loving her was as easy as breathing. I couldn't remember a time I hadn't loved her. Loving her was the easy part. Figuring out how to be together was far harder.

I used to think love was all you needed. I had always thought that if you truly loved someone, everything else would fall into place. The universe would push them your way and help the two of you stay together. I wanted to believe in something. I needed to believe there was some plan for us. It would be far too cruel for me and Jordan to have finally realized our feelings, only to be torn apart now.

I couldn't help but think I was partly responsible. I had let my mother's worries cloud my judgment and had married young. I had partly believed her that no other man would want me because of the rumors going around about me. I thought Tom's offer, the offer of marriage to a nice, caring, rich gentleman that I cared about, sounded too good to be true and was too good to pass up. I had never been both more right and more wrong; it was too good to be true and I should have passed up on the offer. But there was no use going over things I wish I could have changed. Jordan and I were on the same page. Now that we had one another, we wouldn't let go for the world, but there was one big problem that wasn't easy to ignore—Tom. I was a married woman, after all.

Naturally, my solution was more impulsive than Jordan's. I wanted to run.

It felt like I was a young woman again, talking of running away with her lover. I laughed at how starkly different my life had become over the past two years. If you had told me back at eighteen-years-old that in two years' time I would be unhappily married and aiming to run away with my female lover, I would have called you mad.

I understood now how Jay must have felt when I wasn't willing to take the risk to run. I kept trying to press Jordan into agreeing, but she thought the plan was too risky. She was my junior but had grown much wiser in her years than I had in mine. She brought up that, legally, if I ran, Tom could report me missing and have me brought back to him. He could report me a thief if I took anything with me, for legally everything I owned was his property. It was legally debatable whether my own person was his property.

A select few women had some luck with divorces, but that was hardly reliable. A few of the less than lucky women had been ruled incompetent and locked in asylums. Of the women that had succeeded, the men had almost always had numerous public affairs and signs of abuse.

My situation wasn't nearly as dire as theirs had been.

Jordan urged me numerous times to wait. She kept saying that she wished there was something more that could be done right now, but that it was too soon. She asked if I felt at all in danger with Tom. I gave a lot of thought to it and decided that I didn't. Most of his violent energy had faded with his recent infidelity. I wondered if that was how our lives together would be, us both hiding our infidelities from the other and pretending to the world to be a happy couple. There had to be another way.

Jordan's solution was much more practical, but far less appealing. She needed me to stay with him longer. I knew the situation was dire for her, of all people, to be asking that of me. She explained we needed more money and, ideally, I needed a divorce. I didn't like the thought of waiting, but she was right. It was by far the best plan. Her plan was to play in even more tournaments and save all the money she could until she could afford to support us both and finance my divorce.

I felt helpless. I had no skills or way to contribute. Even if I could find some way to contribute, none of my assets were my own. They all belonged to Tom. It was incredibly frustrating that I couldn't do anything to help. I was more grateful than I could express that Jordan was willing to tackle such a monumental task for me, but I was less than enthusiastic about the prospect of having to wait. She estimated it would be a few years before she had the money we would need. It felt like a death sentence. I was to stay trapped in a loveless marriage for a few more years. Even worse, I was in love, but powerless to be with her.

She brought up her worries about him possibly finding out. She explained the best way to execute her plan was for him to stay in the dark until she was able to finance the divorce. I agreed. I couldn't imagine living with him, with him knowing I wanted to leave. She was worried he might try to have me committed or some other heinous act.

She also cautioned against me coming to see her often, but that was where I drew the line. I couldn't help myself. I was drawn to her. With everything else in my world crumbling, I needed her now more than ever. Now that we were finally together, I didn't intend to be separated for longer than could be helped.

The next few weeks passed in the same manner with me visiting her and us talking about the future between kisses. She urged me not to come back the next day, saying he would get suspicious. She threatened to leave for home, but every day, I returned and every day, she was there to meet me.

Chapter Thirty - Seven

Tom and I continued to stay out of each other's way. I didn't speak to him when it could be avoided, and it seemed he had given up on me.

I was curious what our plan was and when we were going to leave town. I knew we had stayed long past intended. I wondered absentmindedly if it was still the hotel maid I could attribute our extended stay to or if there might already have been another woman.

It was a relief to me to not be under his scrutiny anymore. I became more relaxed about my liaisons with Jordan. I didn't worry nearly as much about being seen as I had.

Jordan stopped telling me not to come visit. We both knew I would anyway, and with each passing day, she worried less. I did wonder when we would leave and what would happen after, but Jordan hoped to follow us back to Chicago. It was selfish of me to agree, but I couldn't imagine going without her, so I didn't protest.

The weeks passed with September fading into October and still we stayed in Santa Barbara. Tom must have found another woman, or he must have truly been infatuated with the maid. I didn't ask. It didn't matter to me. I spent every day with

Jordan, returning home before the evening. Most nights he wouldn't bother returning, which was fine by me.

With each passing day, we became more and more comfortable. I was feeling on top of the world. Yes, things weren't ideal, but for the first time in my life, I was happy and in love. My feelings weren't complicated. I knew beyond a shadow of a doubt that I loved her and wanted the whole world to know how happy I was. She deserved nothing but the best, and it wasn't fair to her that we had to hide. I wanted to go out and enjoy ourselves. I wanted to go on a real date with her.

She reacted as if I had said I wanted to go streaking. "Are you crazy? We can't do that!"

I laughed and asked, "And why not?"

"What if someone sees us?"

"So what if they do?"

"They might tell Tom!"

"Tell him what? That I'm having the time of my life with you? That I'm happy? Let them tell him. I'm sick of hiding. I'm sick of making you feel like we have to hide. You don't deserve this! I want you to know how special you are to me. I'm sick of hiding."

She looked doubtful. "I'm not sure it's a good idea, but," a small smile started to form on her lips, "I can't say I hate the idea. What do you have in mind?"

"Nothing crazy, I promise. Let's go dancing!"

"Dancing?" She looked at me incredulously.

I laughed. "Yes! Dancing! It's so romantic and intimate. I would love to take you out dancing."

"Are you sure? I can think of some far more intimate things we could do without leaving the comfort of this room."

I laughed at that. "Tempting, but there's plenty of time for that. I want to take you dancing." She looked like she was considering it. "Please, Jord? It would mean the world to me."

She laughed and playfully shoved my shoulder. "That's cheating and you know it!"

I tried to act innocent. "What did I do?"

She laughed. "You know exactly what you did. You know I can't say no to you."

I batted my eyelashes at her. "Well then, don't say no."

She sighed and grabbed me, pulling me close to her, kissing my neck. "Are you sure you can't be convinced to stay in?"

I lost myself in the feeling for a few moments. I felt if she kept going, I would agree to anything she asked. I pulled away quickly and turned back to her. "And who's cheating now?"

She put her hands up in surrender. "Okay, okay. You can't blame a girl for trying."

I laughed. She must have known I was a minute or two away from surrendering myself, but this was important to me. I had danced with more men than I could count, but I had never danced with her. I loved dancing and wanted to share that with her. "Okay, so it's settled. We'll meet back here in a couple of hours and hit the town!"

She blanched at that. I laughed and quickly said, "Okay, okay, not the whole town, but we will go dancing somewhere."

"I suppose there's no way to talk you out of it?"

I smiled. "Absolutely not."

"And I suppose you have the perfect dress for dancing?"

My smile widened into a grin. "Of course! I can't wait for you to see it on me!"

She grinned. "I can't wait to see it off of you."

I laughed and kissed her hard before pulling quickly away. "It's settled then. We're going dancing."

I left her room quickly, before she could change her mind. I rushed back to my hotel and got ready as quickly as I could. I didn't want to be away from Jordan for longer than I had to, and I worried Tom might come back and see me getting ready. If he did, I would have hell to pay, but he was hardly ever around and I was feeling rebellious and couldn't bring myself to care like I knew I should. It turned out my worries were for nothing, since I was in and out without any sign of him.

When I got to the hotel lobby and saw her, my heart skipped a beat. She was gorgeous enough already, but now she took my breath away. I ran up to her and wrapped her in a hug. She laughed and hugged me back, but I could tell she was a bit on edge.

The hotel's band was playing, so I took her hand and led her to the dance floor. In her arms, I was the happiest I had ever been. As she spun me around the dance floor, I couldn't help but think how lucky I was. In her arms, I felt like I was finally home.

She was as graceful on the dance floor as she was on the golf course. She moved purposefully and powerfully, leading better than anyone I had ever danced with. It felt natural to follow her lead. I would have followed her anywhere.

I noticed a few times that she was looking around the room and seemed nervous. I tried to push her to relax, and she seemed to be enjoying herself, but I could tell she was still worried. She tried to hide it, since she knew how badly I wanted this, but I could tell she was worried. I guessed she was worried Tom might turn up. The last thing I wanted was to prolong her being uncomfortable. I had danced to my heart's content and felt happier than I ever had.

After one more dance, I let her lead me back to her room, where, once again, she took the lead...

We didn't repeat our little adventure again, but every day I continued to go see Jordan. I would always wake up eager to see her.

Until one morning in early October, I woke up with a bad feeling in my gut. What was wrong with me? Tom was nowhere to be found, and I was going to see Jordan. I had no reason to be feeling uneasy. I slowly sat up in bed and my stomach lurched. I ran to the bathroom just in time for the contents of my stomach to make it into the toilet.

After my stomach was empty, the real dread set in. What was wrong with me? Was I going to be okay? Could it be the dreaded flu? I didn't think so. The rest of my body felt fine and from what I had heard, I didn't think that would be the case if I had succumbed to illness. I couldn't imagine what might have been wrong. I worried that the trip to Jordan's might make me feel worse. I dreaded the idea of not seeing her, but it didn't seem smart to go. I placated myself with the idea that it was only one day. Tomorrow, I would go see her.

The day passed slowly. Without anything else to do, I drifted in and out of sleep. I was startled awake when Tom reentered. He was laughing and talking with someone over his shoulder. I didn't know who it was, but it wasn't hard to guess.

He stopped dead when he saw me. He whispered something to his companion, and they stopped outside. I didn't think he could still surprise me with anything he did, but I admit I was a little surprised he had the nerve to take her to our room.

He was surprised to see me. He looked almost offended I had the nerve to be in our room. I supposed that meant he had noticed my absence. I would have been worried about that if I hadn't quite obviously caught him sneaking his mistress into our room.

After a moment of staring at me, he asked curtly what I was doing here. I told him I was feeling under the weather. At that, he looked anxious and inched further away from me. Without another word, he turned on his heel and left. I heard him make excuses to his companion and heard them retreat down the hall. He didn't return that night.

The next morning, I wasn't feeling any better. I repeated the same rushed trip to the bathroom from the previous morning.

But I resolved to try to get up and go see Jordan anyway. I couldn't bring myself to go another day without seeing her. I thought she was probably worried and didn't want to make her wait longer. I had resolved to go when I felt the now familiar turning of my stomach. I had to admit defeat. I didn't want to vomit in the street on my way there, and I didn't want to be sick in front of Jordan.

I must have drifted back off to sleep because I was woken by the sound of a bang, followed by two short knocks. I knew that knock anywhere. Of course she had come. I told her to come in, but she was already turning the doorknob. When she burst in, I could see the worry written all over her face. I started to reassure her I was fine, but she didn't wait. She ran to me and threw her arms around me. I was grateful she had come.

After a few minutes, she pulled away, and I was able to see she had been crying. I was terrified. Jordan never cried.

"What happened? My love, are you okay? What's wrong?"

She looked at me, confused. "I was so worried. You didn't come yesterday. I spent most of the day waiting and the rest of the day imagining what could have happened to you. I was so worried about you." She took a better look at me and the worry returned. She felt my forehead, relaxing a little after that. "You're not warm, but you look exhausted. Have you been ill?"

"I mean, not exactly." I didn't really want to talk of vomiting with her, but she just stared at me, waiting for me to elaborate. I sighed. "I didn't want to worry you, but I did vomit a couple times this morning." She looked at me with more concern. I didn't want to continue, but I had never hidden things from her before and certainly wasn't going to start now. "It was the same as yesterday. I woke up feeling nauseous and when I went to get out of bed, I had to immediately rush to the bathroom to avoid vomiting on the floor."

She put her hand back to my forehead to reassure herself. We both knew well enough that vomiting and a fever could be deadly. From my forehead, she ran her fingers through my hair soothingly.

"Well, no fever. Do you think it might've been something you ate?"

I shook my head. "I doubt it. I can't remember what I ate the day before last, but yesterday I hardly touched a thing. I was so tired and worried I slept most of the day."

She looked pained. "I'm so sorry. I knew I should have come sooner. I was so worried that he had found out. I was worried you needed me to stay away. I would have come in a minute if I had known. Where is he, anyway?" She looked around, as if expecting him to appear from thin air. "Did he really not return at all in the last two days?"

"He probably won't be back for some time. He showed up yesterday a little while after I normally leave, and he had someone with him." Her eyes widened. "I didn't get a good look, but it had to have been her. I mean, who else would he be sneaking into the room?"

She looked even more surprised. "You can't mean you caught him in the act? He was really dumb enough to bring her here? To the room you share with him?"

I could only nod. "Like I said, I didn't really see her, but it had to have been her."

She gasped as she came to another realization. "You can't mean he knew you were feeling ill and still left?"

I shrugged. "I wouldn't have wanted him to stay, anyway." I wasn't sure if she even heard me. She looked livid. I reached for her head and gently turned her face to look at me. "Jord, please, I'm okay. There's no reason to be upset."

She took a couple deep breaths, trying to calm herself down before saying, "I can't believe you're defending him. That lowlife saw you like this with his own two eyes and still left you alone. He must have truly lost all chivalry, all decency, all the love in his heart. I can't believe someone that undeserving, selfish, and cruel gets to call you his wife." She took a few more deep breaths before turning her attention back to me. "And you're not fine. Something is clearly wrong. Someone who's fine doesn't sleep the entire day or vomit in the morning."

I shrugged. "I don't feel sick. I just feel tired." The nausea had subsided. She looked at me in a funny manner that I couldn't explain. She paused for a few moments before asking, "You don't happen to know when the last time you bled was?"

I was confused about why that mattered. I had bled plenty of times without feeling nauseous. I tried to think about when the last time had been. Things had been so crazy with the honeymoon I hadn't given it much thought. Now that I was thinking about it, I remembered having one on our honeymoon.

"On the honeymoon."

She chuckled a moment before saying, "My love, you're technically still on your honeymoon, so you're going to have to be a little more specific. Do you remember a month?"

"Well, now that I think about it, I can't remember having one since we've been in Santa Barbara."

How was that possible? We had been in Santa Barbara for over two months, long past when I should have bled. I looked at Jordan, but she just watched me closely. I wasn't sure what to think. After a moment, it dawned on me what it all meant. The missed bleeding, the exhaustion, and the vomiting; it really could only mean one thing.

Chapter Thirty - Eight

I couldn't believe I was going to be a mother.

I was going to be sick again.

I couldn't even begin to know how to feel. I knew I should have been happy. Most women would be. But I was in a loveless marriage to a cheating husband with a temper. Here I was, in love with my best friend, engaging in infidelity while my husband was lying in the bed of another.

How could I bring a child into our lives now? I knew the laws and knew what a child would mean. My plans for escape vanished into thin air. Jordan would have had a difficult time supporting me and herself, never mind a child that she didn't ask for and probably didn't want.

Not to mention Tom. I couldn't imagine he would let me divorce him and take our child from him. The full weight of the situation hit me all at once; I couldn't run anymore. He would have me and our child brought right back to him and no one would bat an eye. It would be his right. I worried about his newly developed temper. How would he treat a child?

How was he even going to react to the news that he was going to be a father? He couldn't possibly be happy about it. Would he blame me? Would he think I did this on purpose somehow to improve our marriage? Would he even care? I couldn't imagine how things would go.

Jordan watched me go through a million different emotions. Unable to contain myself longer, I burst into tears. She hugged me tight and let me cry. It took a long while for my tears to stop and my breathing to slow. When it did, she pulled back a little to meet my eye and said, "Dais, my love, I can't imagine how you're feeling."

I sighed. "Scared and trapped. I feel like all my choices have been taken from me. Tell me, how could I possibly run now? How could I divorce him with a child involved? How could I possibly risk leaving our child with him if he wanted custody? I feel like my world is crumbling around me." I felt more tears run down my cheeks. She pulled me back in tight and stroked my head.

"I'm so sorry. This happiest of news couldn't have come at a worse time, but you're going to be a mother. That's truly wonderful."

I couldn't quite see past my grievances to the wonder of the situation. I tried to picture myself with a child. All I could see was a little girl who was a mirror image of me. I saw her being broken and beaten by the world like I had. I saw myself powerless to protect her. I couldn't imagine that for my child. That was what it meant to be a woman in this world. You were always inferior, beaten down to the liking of the men of the world.

"I hope it will be a boy."

I could try to teach him the chivalry and caring I had first seen in his father. The values that made me say yes to marrying Tom in the first place, before he changed.

Jordan looked confused for a moment before nodding. She had always envied men for their position in the world. The ease with which things came to them. The power and respect they commanded without having to earn it. I had watched time and time again as she tried to fight her way to the top in a man's sport. She had to be twice as good as the men she was competing against to have any chance of recognition or respect. Even then, a lot of the time she was met with anger. Many men that she bested accused her of cheating. They couldn't wrap their minds around the fact that she had beaten them fair and square.

At her very first golf tournament, one of her competitors, who she had beaten badly, started a rumor that she had cheated by moving her ball from a bad position. She hadn't, but the truth hardly mattered when it was her word against that of a man. Eventually, the man's conscious must have asserted itself because he did retract his statement. However, the story followed her and whenever she did win, there were whispers of her having cheated. She was presumed guilty until proven innocent. Even when her innocence was proven, people still supposed her to have been guilty.

Of course she understood why I would want to have a boy, why I would want for my child the full advantages of the world and none of the disadvantages attached to being a woman.

She sat with me and comforted me as best she could, but most of my grief was in coming to terms with the new reality of our situation. I knew Jordan would back away from me. She would still be my best friend and support me as best she could, but she couldn't possibly want to still be with me. Not now that I was pregnant with Tom's child.

Even if she did still want the same things, she would push her own wants aside for the benefit of my child. She told me I needed to tell Tom and that we would figure things out from there. She told me the news that he was going to be a father might bring about some change in him. I prayed it would soften him to the Tom I married, but I didn't hold any real hope. I sincerely doubted whether she did either, but her comments were enough to let me know my suspicions were right.

She thought if the marriage could still be fixed for the sake of our child, that it ought to be. I wallowed over the fact that I had fallen in love with such a selfless woman. I wanted to be selfish. I wanted to say, "Tom's feelings be damned, it's still my life and I want you," but I didn't. I didn't know how she would have reacted, but I worried she would think me selfish. I was ashamed of myself for longing to be selfish.

I knew she was right. I couldn't put my own selfish wants ahead of the wellbeing of my child. Even *I* couldn't deny that a child raised as a Buchanan, in essence a McCormick, would fare much better than a child of divorce being raised by two women who could barely afford to support themselves. The Buchanan child would have the world at its feet. How could I possibly take those advantages away from my child for the simple sake of my own happiness? I knew I couldn't, and I knew even if I tried that Jordan wouldn't support it. As long as I was safe with Tom, as long as his violence improved, both she and I knew I should stay with him for the sake of my child.

The tears likely would have continued, but we heard a commotion in the hall before the door burst open. I stayed where I was in Jordan's arms. I was too upset and overwhelmed to care. I trusted Jordan to deal with whomever it was and now that we both knew what we had was ending, being caught didn't worry me like it had before.

There was a silence before I heard Tom's voice. "Thank goodness! Jordan, I don't know what you're doing here, but I'm so glad you're here. I've been running around the city all night trying to find a doctor."

My eyes rolled. He had ignored me for days and had left when he found me ill. I didn't buy his act for a moment and doubted very much whether Jordan would either. It was almost funny that now that Jordan was here, he needed to put on the facade of a loving husband. Neither she nor I responded.

He continued, "Those damn doctors wouldn't agree to come out when they heard of the vomiting. I offered more money than I ought to have, quite a small fortune, but none of them would come. They all asked if I had checked for a fever. I hadn't known it would matter! The moment I saw how ill you were, I didn't waste a minute running out for help."

In my mind, I corrected him. He didn't waste a minute whisking his mistress away from his wife. He didn't waste a minute getting as far from my potentially ill body as he could. His actions hadn't surprised me, but I was surprised he was so elaborately trying to cover them now.

"Those damn doctors kept going on about how they wouldn't see you without knowing if there was a fever. I told them to come check themselves, but no one would. They said a fever was a death sentence and not worth my money." I could hear the panic in his voice. "She doesn't have a fever, does she?" I felt Jordan shake her head. I couldn't believe how far he was taking this. "Thank goodness!" He addressed me directly now. "Daisy, I really hope you're feeling better, but just in case, I did bring help." Surprised and wanting to verify the truth of that for myself, I pulled away from Jordan and saw for the first time that he wasn't alone. "Those damn doctors wouldn't come, but I was able to find a nurse who didn't turn me down."

She was an older woman, likely in her forties, with graying hair. Had it been a younger woman, I might have doubted him. I might have thought that again he had been caught trying to sneak another woman into our room, but the woman standing with him was clearly a nurse.

She cleared her throat and asked if I was the patient. I nodded, and she set forward and began asking me a series of questions about my symptoms. I answered them as best I could, but was struggling to focus. I was too shocked. Tom had actually brought a nurse. That must mean the rest of his story was true as well, or at least that some of it must have been. He didn't fully abandon me. Not only did he come back, he spent time and effort looking for help for me and offered to pay them handsomely to come. Maybe the Tom I cared about was still there after all. I couldn't delude myself into thinking that I could ever have with him what I knew I could have had with Jordan, but maybe there was still some potential there.

She tested my heart, my lungs, and checked me for a fever. As Jordan had suspected, I was in perfect health. Then the nurse asked about when the last time I bled was. I told her and she smiled at me and Tom. She told us she had good news; I wasn't ill. She told us we were going to be parents.

I may not have been ill, but I certainly felt ill at her confirmation. I looked at him and saw his face whiten. He thanked her for coming and bid her leave. He was too stunned to shut the door behind her.

Jordan looked at me questioningly. She seemed to be asking if I would be okay, asking if she should leave. I hesitated a moment. Of course I wanted her to stay, but my fairytale had shattered, and I knew now she couldn't always be around. I was going to have to deal with my own problems without her. It seemed as good a time as any to start. I ever so slightly nodded to her. She stepped out and shut the door behind her.

Tom turned to me and asked, "How are you feeling?"

"I'm feeling alright. A little nervous. A little scared."

"Of course. Of course."

He looked awkwardly at me before crossing the room. "May I?" he asked, indicating my hands. I nodded, and he took them into his own. "There really is no delicate way to ask, but is it mine?"

I was shocked. I stared openmouthed at him for a moment. "The baby? Of course it is! Just who else's would it be?"

He nodded. "I thought so, but I couldn't be sure. I had heard from the hotel clerks that you often left around the same time every morning and returned just before I did. I had built it up in my head that you were sleeping with yet another man." I started to say something, but he chimed in, "I'm truly sorry for how I've been treating you. You must understand, I thought you were cheating on me. Now I see it must have been Jordan you were meeting."

I blushed at that. He was right in a way about his suspicions, but the result was the same. There was no possible way the baby could be anyone's but his.

"Although, why you kept it a secret she was still in town is beyond me. Anyway, I took some time and did some thinking..."

It took all my willpower to not roll my eyes. He had been doing his thinking all over town with God knows who. He might have even done some thinking in our bed. I only knew he wasn't doing his thinking with me.

"...and I decided I haven't been treating you fairly. We're going to be parents. As long as your indiscretions are quite behind you, we can make this work."

I was upset by his tone and implication. He was the one running around with strange women and he was accusing me of having cheated on him with any man who looked my way. His accusations were way off base, but I couldn't deny I had been cheating on him, just not with a man. The guilt made me hold my tongue. I considered for a brief moment whether I should tell him, but I couldn't. I couldn't risk how he might take it, especially with us bringing a baby into the world together. I hoped Jordan would stay in my life, and I knew if I told him, he likely wouldn't allow her to continue to visit. I couldn't risk that.

It occurred to me that Jordan and I hadn't talked this through. I had no idea what our friendship would look like going forward. Would she even still want to be my friend? Could she be in my life and not be with me? Could I have her in my life and not be with her? I knew it would be painful, but the alternative was worse.

Chapter Thirty - Nine

Jordan

I had to fight the urge to turn around when I let myself out of her room. I softly closed the door behind me, but the sound echoed in my mind and I knew it would be one that haunted me for a long time.

I couldn't believe how much had changed in a single day. Here I was back on the outside and there he was, at her side again. As if he were fit to even hold her hand. After his cheating and how abysmally he had been treating her, I couldn't believe she wanted to hear him out. But Daisy was always too forgiving, always too kind, always getting herself hurt. She was too open. I suppose if she hadn't been, she never would have been so accepting of my own feelings, but I couldn't help but worry about her. My whole body was tense and I felt my muscles clench. I wasn't angry with her, but I was definitely angry. In that moment, when she nodded to me to leave, I knew I had lost her. She was going back with him, and the worst part was that I couldn't even blame her.

She was going to be a mother now; she had more to worry about than just herself and her own happiness. At least I knew she wouldn't be as happy with him as she could have been with me.

A moment later, I came to my senses and realized just how selfish I was being. I loved her with everything in me. I was hurting, but I understood the choices I knew she would make, and I couldn't blame her. It was just so hard to believe we were in this situation.

I should have known from the moment she kissed me that something this perfect, this heart wrenchingly beautiful, couldn't last. I had thought myself blessed. I couldn't imagine what I had done right in my life to be given her love. I should have known it was too good to be true, but I didn't want to believe it. I was happy and for once in my life, I let myself hope. I let myself dream about our future, about the possibilities. I let myself imagine we could be happy together, that I could be the one to make her happy, to protect her. I had been so naive.

I couldn't help thinking I might've been better off never having said anything to her at all about my feelings.

I almost hadn't said anything that day. She had been so upset it hadn't even crossed my mind to say anything, until I heard how unhappy she was. But even in my wildest dreams, I had never thought she might feel the same.

I had sat there listening to her blaming herself for everything, for his crazy actions, for his tantrums and I couldn't stand it. How could she not see how selfish and manipulative he was being? She even blamed herself for his cheating.

I couldn't stand seeing her so torn apart over someone so unworthy of her time. I tried to explain to her how mixed up her thinking was, but she continued to blame herself, and continued to find reason in his crazy. She felt that she had driven him to this, that he cared too much.

I couldn't help my own anger at that. I knew I was letting too much of my own feelings out, but she had to understand.

This wasn't even remotely her fault. She excused his behavior because he was 'jealous'. It was ridiculous! What did he even know of jealousy? *I* was the one who had to watch her try again and again with boy after boy who didn't deserve her, who didn't know a thing about her! I had been out of my mind with jealousy, but I had fought it. Never once did I let my own jealousy affect how I treated her, how I talked to her. I told her a censored version of my thoughts.

I was relieved when she started to come around a little from despair more toward indignation and anger. She *should* be angry! He was treating her terribly just for the sin of having had a life before him. It was insanity. I couldn't help but think about how similar Tom was acting to how James had acted about me and Daisy.

I knew she would hate the comparison, but it would show her just how undeniably crazy he was being, so I told her. I told her more than I intended to about James and why I started dating him. I didn't hold things back from her generally, but I hadn't expected myself to get as real as I did.

I didn't want to make this about me, but noticing how distracted she was listening to me, I couldn't help it. Anything that would momentarily take the pain from her eyes was worth saying or doing. I accidentally let it slip that I had felt I was in Daisy's shadow. It shouldn't have surprised her, no one could possibly hold a candle to her, but she had been surprised anyway.

Her surprise quickly turned to disbelief. I wondered if I had said something wrong before she made it clear she thought I was the crazy one to not see my own beauty. She told me she wished I could see what she did. My heart had quickened at that, but I tried to tamper down my hope as best I could. She was my best friend and of course she was trying to make me feel better.

I knew Daisy; there wasn't much she wouldn't say to make me happy, true or not. But I couldn't resist asking her what she saw.

I fought back a smile at the adorable frustration written all over her face. Her nose wrinkled as she tried to give her thoughts a voice. After gesturing at me wildly and not actually answering my question, she dragged me in front of the mirror. When I noticed the way she was looking at me, my heart started racing. But she couldn't be looking at me like that. It couldn't mean the same to her as it did to me when I looked at her that way. I knew I must have been seeing things. It must have been wishful thinking.

I knew I was right when she started to describe my personality instead of my looks. I couldn't help rolling my eyes and laughing at the adorably indignant look on her face. I reminded her that describing my personality, and a rather skewed flowery version of my personality at that, wasn't what we were talking about. I desperately needed to know what she had meant earlier. I needed to know what she saw when she looked at me.

I tried to convince myself I was only asking in order to continue to distract her from her own emotions, but even I couldn't make myself believe that. My motivations were purely selfish, but I needed to know once and for all what she thought. If there was even a small chance she felt at all how I did, I needed to know. When I turned my attention back to her after having told her essentially that she was dodging my question, I noticed she was blushing. I felt my pulse quicken, but I tried not to let my hopes get up too high. Daisy was easily embarrassed. While her blushing was irritatingly adorable and made it hard for me to think, she did blush quite frequently. When she spoke again and mentioned my height, I couldn't help my laughter. I knew then I was reading too much into how she was acting. If Daisy, my sweet caring Daisy, could only think of my height to compliment, then I had no cause to hope she might be looking at me the way I looked at her.

I couldn't help giving her a hard time about it. It was funny really, how much I had let my hopes soar and to her I was just tall. She tensed at my laughter, her lips pinched together as she exhaled loudly through her nose. I waited for her to continue.

A moment later, her words came racing out. "Okay, fine. You're right. Tall isn't the right word. You look like a statuesque goddess who lesser men cower from and greater men beg to worship. You could have the world in the palm of your hand if you didn't push people away. If you would only open up and let someone in. Any man would be lucky to have you!"

I couldn't believe it. Did she really think of me in that way? Or was she just being kind like usual? I had seconds to decide how to respond. I knew if I took this chance, I could be ruining everything, but if I didn't, I knew I would never stop regretting it. I decided, for worse or for better, I had to know. I had to put all the cards on the table.

Before I could lose my nerve, I responded, "Well, that's a problem."

She threw her hands up in the air. She was so cute when she was frustrated. Well, that's misleading. She was cute all of the time. "How is any of that possibly a problem?! How is having any man you want at all a problem?"

I paused a moment. Was I really going to do this? How far could I push her? How much was I willing to risk? I knew I was playing with fire, flying too close to the sun, but I couldn't help it. Even being burned by her would have been a privilege.

I mustered all the courage I could find before saying, "What if I don't want a man?"

She rolled her eyes. I was shocked. I had just revealed the only truth I had ever hid from her and she wasn't at all surprised? Had she known all along? And she had rolled her eyes at me as if I was being dramatic by telling her. I felt indignant. I had expected her compassion, this wasn't at all what I expected. I was about to tell her so when she continued, "I know, I know. You want your independence and think a man would get in the way, but it doesn't have to be like that."

She didn't get it. Of course she didn't. She wasn't listening. I whirled around to face her, barely able to contain my frustration. "You don't get it! It's not about men! It's never been about men!" I stopped and just stared, waiting for the truth to catch up with her, but she wouldn't meet my eye. Half a second later, I noticed she was leaning away from me and trying to make herself as small as possible. The sight stopped my frustration dead in it's tracks. My heart broke for her. I vowed then and there that I would never make her feel like that again and would never let anyone else make her cower like that again. Instantly more calm, I knew I needed to fix this. I gently reached for her face and when I spoke again, it was more softly and slowly. Maybe it was a lost cause, but I was in too deep now. For better or worse, I needed to know what she was thinking. "What if it's not a man I want?"

I paused again, giving her time to understand, willing her to understand. I didn't know how else I could possibly say it if she didn't understand. I didn't know how I would find the nerve to tell her again. She just looked at me. She was still looking at me when I saw the understanding dawn on her. She didn't say anything right away. I tried to wait patiently for her to form her thoughts. I knew this had to be a shock for her. I nervously waited for her to say something, expecting her to pull away from me, worried she wouldn't want to be near me. She was still silent. She still hadn't said anything. I was becoming restless and could feel a tightness in my chest. This couldn't be good. But then she smiled.

I held my breath, waiting, praying her smile meant what I hoped it meant. "Well, what I was saying still applies. Man, woman, or whoever, it doesn't matter. Anyone would be lucky to have you."

It was a better response than I could have ever hoped for, but it seemed she still didn't fully understand. I didn't want just *anyone*, I wanted *her*. But if she really felt like anyone would be lucky to have me, maybe, just maybe, there was a small chance she felt that way herself.

I looked at her hesitantly and quietly asked, "You really mean it?"

She didn't pause before saying, "Absolutely!"

I didn't dare to dream she meant that, but maybe there was a small chance. If I could find the words to better explain how I felt, but I was tongue tied. I wrapped her in a hug, wanting to hide my face from her scrutiny as I weighed out my options. If I didn't say or do something now, I knew I never would. I would lose my nerve and wouldn't ever tell her. I thought I could live with that, but with her in my arms, my resolve hardened. I needed to know for better or worse. I would tell her. I would find a way to explain. But when she pulled away, the words died on my lips.

I took her hands in my own, not wanting to part from her, but not having the words to say so. She was looking at me tentatively, but that wasn't what caught my attention. She was biting her lip and I couldn't tear my eyes from it. I felt her eyes on me, and knew I should look up, but my universe was reduced to her lips. They started to move, and I knew I should have been listening, but I couldn't help myself. I couldn't tell her how I felt, but I could show her.

I closed the space between us, wrapped my arms around her and brought my lips to hers. At the feel of her soft lips, sparks exploded in my mind. I felt weightless, euphoric. Until, after a moment, I noticed she hadn't moved. I quickly pulled away, realization dawning on me about just how severely I had ruined things. She didn't feel the same. Of course she didn't! I couldn't believe I let myself think for a moment she might. I had taken advantage of her trust. I couldn't believe I had kissed her. She hadn't kissed me back.

I couldn't believe I had done that, but I couldn't bring myself to regret it. I would suffer through the consequences of my actions. I deserved it. I deserved her scorn, her distrust, her anger … whatever she was feeling, I deserved it, but selfishly even if I could, I would never have taken back that kiss. I knew it would replay in my mind for the rest of my days as the happiest I had ever been. Even as the guilt overwhelmed me, I wouldn't have changed a thing. I rushed to apologize, needing her to know how sorry I was.

"I'm so sorry! I don't know what came over me. The last thing I want to do is ruin our friendship. I promise I'll never do that again."

She didn't respond. I waited impatiently. She had to understand I meant every word. She had to know how much I cared about her, know that I would never do anything to upset her and that I would never do that again, but would that be enough for her to be willing to salvage what was left of our friendship? I didn't know if it would. I knew I deserved every agonizing moment of her silence. But I couldn't take much more suspense. I was relieved when she finally spoke again.

"Never again?"

Thank goodness! I didn't know how I got so lucky, but I wouldn't take our friendship for granted another moment. I was lucky just to be her friend and I wouldn't ever let myself forget that. I nodded fiercely, "I promise."

She cocked her head and looked at me appraisingly. My mouth went dry and I felt dread form in the pit of my stomach at the look on her face. She finally responded, "You should really be more careful not to make promises you can't keep."

I was dumbfounded. My blood ran cold. She didn't believe me. I was going to lose her. I started to panic. "What do you mean? Of course I-"

It took me a full minute to realize her lips were on mine. She was kissing me! Daisy, my sweet, sweet Daisy was kissing me. I had been too shocked to kiss her back, but I came to my senses quickly. I deepened the kiss, kissing her with all the passion I had been building up over the years for her. Every stolen glance, every smile, every ounce of love I had for her, I was determined she feel it in that kiss. Her own enthusiasm almost had me on my knees. She was enjoying this nearly as much as I was. I couldn't believe it. I pressed my luck further, pressing my tongue against her lips.

A few moments later, I felt her start to go weak. How I was still on my feet myself, I didn't know. I moved us to the bed and slowly laid her down. I meant to break the kiss and lay next to her, but she pulled me down with her. She was full of surprises. From my position above her, I started to pull away, but she pulled me back, not willing to let me go. I couldn't help laughing at that. I couldn't believe my sweet Daisy had this in her. This was better than my wildest dreams. After a few more moments, I pulled away. The disappointment on her face was exquisite. I was in paradise. I hadn't moved from my position on top of her, but I made sure my face was out of her reach. I was enjoying the view too much to be pulled back quite yet. I let my eyes roam over her body freely.

"I was worried I was pushing you too far."

She was too out of breath to answer, and just reached for me. I laughed and took both her hands in my own and stretched them above her head, grasping them both in my hand. With my free hand, I slowly traced my fingers down her arm. She pulled against me, trying to reach for me again, but I wasn't done quite yet. When she realized I wasn't letting her go yet, she started to pout. I couldn't help but laugh at that. She was extremely adorable when she was frustrated. I moved my fingers to her face and traced her beautiful, soft lips. I had dreamed of this for so long. I was going to take my time exploring her. She watched me intently, desire in her eyes. I moved my fingers slowly from her lips, down her chin, and couldn't help myself. I slowly stroked the base of her neck where I knew she was ticklish. Not a moment later, her musical laugh filled the room. She begged me to stop.

I couldn't help myself from saying, "Begging sounds good coming from you. I've never heard anything quite so sweet." I slowed my assault, but didn't stop entirely.

Her voice came out rushed and breathy, "Please, please. I can't breathe." I almost stopped but I saw the look in her eye. She laughed again and rushed to say, "Please, I'll do anything."

Anything? I'd have to see about that. I smiled at her and moved my fingers up to her chin, tilting her head to meet my eye. I wanted to see every inch of her reaction. "We'll see about that." The look of lust in her eyes was enough that I immediately stopped teasing her and moved my lips back to hers.

Those moments and the following weeks of bliss I spent with her would forever be branded in my mind, would forever be the happiest I had ever and would ever be.

Would I change a thing now, knowing how things ended? Knowing that things had to end? I knew I wouldn't. I would have gone through any amount of hell to have just kissed her once. She had made me the happiest woman alive, and I wouldn't trade a minute of it, even now, even knowing it had been destined to end badly.

I had realized it sooner than she had. The moment I figured out she didn't have any other symptoms besides morning nausea and tiredness, I had known. I had asked her when the last time she bled was, but even then I knew. I knew what it meant, and I knew how she would react. I knew she would be devastated.

It was crazy. I knew how badly she wanted to be a mother, but it couldn't have been a worse time or with a worse man. The way he was acting who knows if Tom would be the father he should be. I was worried for her. I held her while she cried and cried. Not knowing what to do or say to make things any better.

My heart was breaking, too. I knew she wouldn't run now. She might not ever leave him now. All our plans were out the window. My future happiness had been ripped away from me. But now wasn't about me. There would be time for me to mourn my own loss later. At that moment, she needed me. I hugged her tightly, savoring the feel of her in my arms. I knew this would be the last time. I knew there wasn't any chance she would put her happiness and my own above the happiness and comfort of her child.

I knew she would fix things with Tom, and I couldn't even really blame her. That was the worst part, that I couldn't even be mad at her because I understood her decision. Every piece of my heart was fracturing into tiny pieces, but she was doing the right thing. I couldn't have even supported her alone right now, never mind her and her child. I would happily take on the task, but I knew she wouldn't let me. She wouldn't want to burden me with that, and she would want the best possible for her child. She would want to give her child all the advantages that would come with being a Buchanan, and by extension a McCormick. How could I compete with that? How could anyone?

Before she even finished crying, I knew what she was going to say. I resolved to make it as easy on her as possible. It was the least I could do for her. She looked at me through her tears. "I hope it will be a boy." That surprised me. When we were younger, she had imagined she would have a little girl. She had been so excited about the idea, that felt like ages ago.

Now we were older, and even she had become much more cynical about things. I only nodded. I couldn't find the words to convey how heartbreaking that statement was coming from her. She used to be so optimistic, a brilliant ray of hope in a cruel, calculating world. To see her so beaten down by the world, to see *her*, of all people, turn cynical was too much for me. I felt destroyed.

I didn't know what to say, but I knew I needed to make this easier on her. The only way I could think to do that was to let her know I knew what she was thinking and that I was okay with it.

I wasn't.

My whole world was crumbling down around me, but that didn't matter.

I told her she needed to talk to Tom and that things could be figured out from there. And for the first time in a long time, I lied to her. I told her that I believed that Tom finding out he was going to be a father might bring about a change in him. I didn't believe it, but for her, I hoped it might be true. I knew how badly she needed to hear it and how badly she needed it to be true. I don't know what pained me more; that she mostly looked unconvinced or that there was a small spark of hope in her eyes at my words.

I wanted to grab her and hold her tight. I wanted to kiss her hard and tell her I loved her more than anything and would do anything for her and for the baby. I wanted to tell her we should run away together. That me, her, and the baby could be a happy family. But I didn't. I couldn't. She and the baby would have a much better life if I stepped out of the picture. As much as it killed me to admit it, I knew it was the truth. She knew it herself, otherwise she would have protested. Had she told me she didn't care about Tom or what the future might hold and still wanted to be together, I don't think I would have had the willpower to keep resisting. I would have given in the second she asked, I would have given her anything she asked. I was selfish enough I would have happily taken her and her child away from their life of comfort to make her and myself happy, but I knew I couldn't do that. I couldn't be selfish with her. She deserved better.

She was still crying a while later when Tom barged in. He looked a mad man, disheveled and panicked. I tensed, worried, until I noticed him visibly relax when he saw Daisy in my arms. He ushered in a woman who looked to be a nurse of some sort. At least he had done that much right. That man had better count his lucky stars each night to have so kind and forgiving a wife. She was too good for him.

After Daisy calmed down a little more and the nurse confirmed what I already knew, I was unsure what to do. I looked to her, asking with my eyes if she wanted me to stay. I held my breath, knowing her answer was bigger than today. Her answer would tell me everything I needed to know about our future, about whether we might still have a future in her mind. She looked and saw me standing by the door. I hadn't wanted to intrude longer if I wasn't wanted. She took in the sight of me standing by the door and nodded slightly, telling me she would be okay on her own, that she didn't need me.

I felt devastated and heartbroken. How cruel the universe was indeed to give me a taste of pure happiness just to snatch it away. I continued to wonder about whether knowing how things ended if I would change a thing, but I knew I wouldn't have. I wouldn't trade my time with her for the world. I was lucky to have been burned by her, blessed to have been given the chance to be with her at all, even if it was just for a short time. When I made it back to my hotel room and shut the door behind me, I stopped fighting altogether and let the tears fall.

Chapter Forty

Daisy

After Jordan left, Tom and I spent most of the night and the next day talking about our plans. He never brought up or apologized for his own infidelity and continued to allude to my indiscretions, but things were looking up. He and I spent the day together for the first time in months, and he was mostly civil with me. We talked about the future of our child, and he listened to my thoughts.

We were unsure about where to raise our child. He asked if I wanted our child raised around my parents. Although I liked Louisville enough, I didn't want my child around my parents that frequently. *I* didn't even want to be around them that frequently. It was a quick decision that Louisville was out. I assumed he would want us to settle in Chicago, but he wasn't sure about that. I wondered why. Before the honeymoon, we had planned to live in Chicago on our return. I wondered what had changed. It occurred to me that maybe he didn't want to be around his family either, or maybe he just didn't want *me* around his family. I didn't know his family well enough to know which might be the case.

Either way, it was settled we wouldn't settle down in either of our hometowns.

When he suggested France, I was both scared and delighted. Before our honeymoon, I had never been far outside of Louisville. The idea of living and raising our child in a foreign country was a terrifying but exciting one. I wasn't sure I could handle that amount of adventure, but I had always wanted to go to France. I was touched he remembered.

When he saw my pause, he explained we could go for a year or two and then come back here to settle down. He said it could be like a honeymoon for us and the baby. I was delighted. We could use a fresh start. As much as I dreaded being away from Jordan, I thought this might be best. Now that I was pregnant, I knew there was no way we could be together, but I felt too strongly about her. I knew if I was around her too often, I wouldn't be able to stop myself.

Tom was offering me a fresh start. He didn't know the truth of my sins, but he was offering a fresh start and, as the mother of his child, I needed to take it.

When I went to see Jordan the next day at our normal time, she wasn't there. I waited for about an hour before giving up. I felt like a fool. Of course she wouldn't be there. Everything had changed. She wasn't mine anymore, and I should have known she wouldn't be waiting for me. Feeling dejected, I went to leave the hotel. I stopped dead in my tracks when I saw Jordan sitting in the hotel lobby with a woman I didn't recognize. She was laughing, and the woman was smiling. I felt my heart miss a beat and my eyes stung. I had come at our usual time, but she was too busy enjoying this other woman's company to remember. I felt more hurt than I had a right to, considering her and I had essentially ended what we had a couple of days ago.

I went to turn away, but Jordan saw me. She looked surprised but smiled at me and held up her hand, asking me to wait a moment. She said a few more things to her companion before leaning toward her.

I held my breath.

She pulled her into a hug.

I looked at my feet, not wanting to witness another woman in her arms for longer than I already had. When I looked back up, Jordan was making her way over to me. She smiled and asked if I wanted to go back to her room. I shook my head. It was probably best for the both of us to stay in public. I suggested we go for a walk. I didn't ask about the other woman. I wanted to. It was all I could think about, but I was a pregnant, married woman and it wasn't my place anymore. It wasn't my right to know if Jordan didn't want to tell me.

As we walked, I told her about France. I told her that Tom and I thought a fresh start would be best. I had never had to fight harder to keep in tears. What killed me the most was that she genuinely looked happy for me. My heart was breaking with every word, but she was somehow able to smile. She agreed a fresh start sounded brilliant. I asked what it would mean for our friendship. I wanted to know how she felt about going back to being my friend. Could she do it? I worried she might not want to.

Her answer didn't give much away. All she told me was that France was quite far, but that she would try to write or possibly come visit. It was both more and less than I had hoped for. I had hoped for a more concrete answer and to know where I stood with her, but this was hopeful. Her saying she might write or visit was more than I deserved. I hoped she meant it.

When we parted that day, we both knew without saying that it would be the last time we met for a while. I went in to hug her, and she took a hesitant step back. I paused at that, again fighting the tears that I felt threatened to spill over. I felt a tightness in my throat that made it hard to breathe. She had moved away from me. I hadn't thought this could hurt any more than it already did, but that action shattered the few pieces of my broken heart I had been managing to hold together. After a moment, she relented and stepped forward to meet me.

When I wrapped my arms around her, I didn't want to let go. I knew this would be a moment I replayed in my mind for the rest of my life. I knew the moment I turned away, I would break down. I knew this was a heartbreak I might never recover from. I knew this might possibly be the last time I held her, so I didn't focus on that. I focused on how it felt to hold her in my arms one last time.

When I did eventually walk away, I stopped fighting and let the tears fall.

"True love will triumph in the end - which may or may not be a lie, but if it is a lie, it's the most beautiful lie we have."
— **John Green**, *Looking for Alaska*

Will Daisy and Jordan continue to go their separate ways and find happiness on their own, or will they find their way back together?
Will Tom stay reformed and become a good father and a good husband, or will he slip back into his old ways?
Will anyone get a happy ending…?

The answers to these questions and more…
Stay Tuned…

Coming soon…

An Illusion Shattered

So, what did you think?

I would love to hear any and all of your thoughts! If you would be so kind as to leave any review it would be greatly appreciated. Any review, good or bad, short or long, is always welcome. I would die for positive reviews and would love to hear your critiques on how I can improve.

For updates on my next book or to tell me what you thought about this one, you can find me:
Visit my website: Thelibraryofsarahzane.com
Or follow me on TikTok or Instagram: Libraryofsarahzane
Like my Facebook page: Sarah Zane (libraryofsarahzane)

My TikTok is hilarious if I do say so myself.

Please come find me on any of those platforms, I would love to hear what you thought about my book!

ABOUT THE AUTHOR

Sarah is a bisexual feminist and a licensed therapist. Her books (just the one now, but she has big plans) often deal with themes of feminism, trauma, sexuality, and mental health. Before this book, she was still in the closet (SURPRISE Mom and Dad! Just Kidding, I promise I told them a few months before the book released), but when this book pushed itself out of her mind onto paper, it pushed her out of the closet. Borrowing some courage from the strong women in her book, she finally spoke and is now living her truth.

She lives in New England with her husband and 2 black cats named Gatsby and Mr. Darcy. When she isn't writing, she can be found perusing a book in her home library that features over 400 books, making chaotic book themed videos for TikTok (aka Booktok), or cuddled up with one of her cats crying over fictional characters or yelling at them about how badly they need therapy.

Hmm…what else can I tell you that you don't already know? If you take Daisy, bring her into the 2000s, move her to New England, and give her less money and better parents, you have me. Optimistic to the point of delusion, very in tune with the emotions of others but somehow is still able to miss the bigger picture, hopeless romantic, chaotic bisexual, obsessed with wanting to go to France, loves dresses, pearls, and dancing… she is in every way a depiction of how I was at her age. I can only thank my lucky stars I was born with the privileges I have and the luxury to not have to make the difficult choices she did.

ACKNOWLEDGEMENTS

First and foremost, I have to thank my husband without whom this book wouldn't have happened. Diego, my love, I'm sure you didn't know the chaos you were signing up for when after I told you about one of my more vivid dreams, you told me I should write a book. I appreciate more than you know how much you have supported me throughout the whole endeavor by listening to my complaints about my characters going off script and my plot issues. I know you didn't imagine how much of my time this project would take up or how far my aspirations would rise, so thank you so much for your support. It means the world to me.

To Bookclub Sean, my best friend and book club partner in crime, Thank you for not laughing when I said I was going to write and self-publish a book. Thank you for being there for me and supporting my dream. Thank you for hyping me up when I felt low.

To my friends, thank you all so much for your support, your love, and your understanding that it now takes me forever to respond to texts. To all my friends who have stuck by me through me my anxiety, depression, and now the disassociating that turned into this book, I love and appreciate you more than you could know.

To my family, specifically my parents, thank you for listening. Thank you for being nothing like Daisy's parents and for supporting me in everything I do.

To my grandma who let me mooch off her Microsoft Office Family plan, who always talks to me about books and liked to remind me to publish this quickly so she would "still be around to read it." I love you so much and hope you and your friends that I know you'll try to share this book with will love it, too.

To my Booktok community, the wonderful authors, readers, and new friends who have been so supportive from the start. I love you all.

To Zelda Fitzgerald, I wholeheartedly thank you for writing the Beautiful Little Fool quote that had a chokehold on my thoughts long after I first read it. I knew that couldn't have possibly been written by a man. For years, I wondered what the Great Gatsby could have been if it had been written by a woman. I hope I have done your memory justice.

To Daisy and Jordan, my dear sweet girls, thank you for coming along on this journey with me. Thank you for being so opinionated about how the story should go and for practically writing it yourselves. Thank you for being strong women that others can look up and thank you for lending me the courage to finally come out of the closet and start living my truth.

Thank you to everyone who has been supportive of me and my journey. I have love for each and every one of you.

www.ingramcontent.com/pod-product-compliance
Lightning Source LLC
Chambersburg PA
CBHW030113310726
48970CB00004B/1266